CW00602271

Dedalus Europe
General Editor: Timothy Lane

THE RIDICULOUS AGE

Margherita Giacobino

THE
RIDICULOUS
AGE

translated by
Graham Anderson

Dedalus

This work has been translated with the contribution of the Centre for Books and Reading of the Italian Ministry of Culture.

CENTRO
PER IL LIBRO
E LA LETTURA

Published in the UK by Dedalus Limited
24-26, St Judith's Lane, Sawtry, Cambs, PE28 5XE
info@dedalusbooks.com
www.dedalusbooks.com

ISBN printed book 978 1 915568 28 1
ISBN ebook 978 1 915568 52 6

Dedalus is distributed in the USA & Canada by SCB Distributors
15608 South New Century Drive, Gardena, CA 90248
info@scbdistributors.com   www.scbdistributors.com

Dedalus is distributed in Australia by Peribo Pty Ltd
58, Beaumont Road, Mount Kuring-gai, N.S.W. 2080
info@peribo.com.au   www.peribo.com.au

First published by Dedalus in 2024
L'età ridicola copyright © Margherita Giacobino 2018
Translation The Ridiculous Age copyright © Graham Anderson 2024
This translation has been made possible thanks to the mediation of r. vivian literary agency-padova-Italy

The right of Margherita Giacobino to be identified as the author & Graham Anderson as the translator of this work has been asserted by them in accordance with the Copyright, Designs and Patents Act, 1988.

Printed and bound in the UK by Clays Elcograf S.p.A.
Typeset by Marie Lane

The Author

Margherita Giacobino was born in 1952 and lives in Turin. She is a writer, journalist and translator. Dedalus has published three books by her: *Portrait of a Family with a Fat Daughter* (2017), *The Price of Dreams* (2020) which is a fictionalised account of the life of Patricia Highsmith and *The Ridiculous Age* (2024).

The film rights of *The Ridiculous Age* have been sold and filming began in October 2023.

The Translator

Graham Anderson was born in London. After reading French and Italian at Cambridge, he worked on the book pages of *City Limits* and reviewed fiction for *The Independent* and *The Sunday Telegraph.*

His translations for Dedalus from Italian are Grazia Deledda's short story collections *The Queen of Darkness* and *The Christmas Present,* and her novel *Marianna Sirca.* Forthcoming in 2024 is Diego Marani's *The Celestial City.*

His own short fiction has won or been shortlisted for three literary prizes. He is married and lives in Oxfordshire.

Author's Acknowledgements

Thank you to the indispensable Rita Vivian, my agent, who has believed in me for many years and supported my work with great sensitivity, competence and energy. Thank you to Marilena Rossi, who despite being busy with those precious little creatures of her own has found time to take care of my elderly creature as well. Thank you to Barbara Gatti who has kept all the threads of this work together and to Alessandra Maffiolini who has brought a breath of youthful lightness and humour to the doings of my nonagenarian.

Translator's Note

Three songs which are quoted from or referred to in the novel can all be enjoyed on YouTube:

Page 156: The Pretty Washerwoman is *La Bella Lavanderina*.

Page 237: What shall we do? is *Babbo non vuole*.

Page 319: "A song by Vecchioni" is Roberto Vecchioni's 1977 song, *Samarcanda*.

Contents

Contents

I

Global terror and other senile inconveniences

Seven thirty-two in the morning. I am awake because Venom the cat and pains in the arms have woken me, I am tired of grinding through life and being ground down by it, as tired as an elderly earthworm who lives in a cemetery. I have made myself a coffee and returned to bed. I am reading, or trying to. The telephone rings. I always keep it next to me because it might be Malvina and indeed it is her. But she is not ill, she is just excited. She asks if I have heard the news. What news, I say, and she tells me to turn on the radio.

I say that the radio in the bedroom which I turned on a while ago is tuned to Rai 5 which only plays classical music.

Not that one! The one in the kitchen!

Yes, but I'm in bed. Why would I be in the kitchen at this hour of the day? It's cold. Malvina tells me that Germana has been killed in a terrorist attack. In Birmingham.

In Birmingham? What was she doing there? Don't her people live in Liverpool?

No, Birmingham! Don't you remember anything at all?

9

Well, but Germana's son-in-law comes from Liverpool, that's where her daughter went to live, I say, rummaging through my memory in search of old telephone conversations in which Germana spoke of her extremely tedious visits to her daughter's family. I don't remember how many grandchildren she has, the last time I asked her she just said: too many.

Malvina ploughs on unstoppably, like a Panzer tank, about the attack, and what if she is right? She says that Germana is not answering her mobile, it's very strange, she always answers, and this is the morning she was due to arrive in Birmingham, at the airport, where two bombs exploded, maybe three, there's no clear news yet but Malvina is convinced of the worst, a voice inside is telling her so. My mind's eye sees Germana lying on a bloodstained floor, strewn with remnants of humanity and its appurtenances, newspapers, plastic cups, a hand still clutching a boarding card. A large, male hand, covered in pale hairs, and finger tips so square and stubby they seem to have been chopped off. Here ends the man, with those stubby fingers that reach for no human skin, or leaves, or animal fur but are self-contained digits that say I, I, I, god, god, god, and I realise that the man I am thinking of is Germana's son-in-law, an abusive member of the God-squad who has planted himself in her daughter's life and sold her the ten commandments to the accompaniment of love and domestic violence. It would be highly appropriate if a man like him were reduced to pieces in a collision with the coercive powers of other terrorists. No, I see Germana quite composed, all in one piece, her iron-grey hair barely touched by faint traces of blood, certainly not sprawled on the floor all soiled and sullied. At the most she may have lost a shoe, those awful narrow ladies' shoes she favours, with fringes on the toes.

I am about to ask Malvina how she has become so intimate with Germana that she knows when she answers her mobile and when she doesn't, but now that I have loosened my memory, another detail comes to mind.

The radio is filling my bedroom: the Vienna Philharmonic is playing Mahler. Symphony No.6, the 'Tragic'. The pathos of it overwhelms me. At this time of day they should be broadcasting only Mozart, or maybe the Beatles. Instilling a bit of insensate joy into the dawn of our dusks.

But the coffee is getting cold. I stretch a hand towards the cup on the bedside table, I sip at it listening to Malvina.

At the first break in her agitated outpourings I say: Malvina, listen, Germana wasn't in Birmingham, even if that should have been Liverpool, because she died three years ago and they held the service for her in the chapel at the cemetery. I didn't go, but you did.

Malvina takes a moment to reflect. She is wondering whether she should deny it, accuse me of having a wandering mind or change the subject.

Instead she takes another direction, an unexpected one. All right, she says, she won't have been killed but it could have happened. Think about it, if she was in Birmingham this morning she would definitely have died.

Is there a flash of nonsensical truth in this assertion, or is Malvina moving ever further along the lonely but crowded pathways of dementia? What did Germana die of? I don't remember, but she had reached the age where family and friends no longer feel the need to justify her passing.

Listen, I say, thank you for the news. If the voice inside

you warns you next time *beforehand* that some disaster is happening, let me know so that maybe I can get there in time. If you'd told me yesterday I'd have taken the aeroplane to Birmingham, and that way you'd now have a valid reason to be upset.

I would be there, stretched out on the lino floor sticky with beer and chips, not composed and in one piece like Germana but flung down like a wet rag, a piece here, a piece there, stick hurled against a wall and hopefully in its trajectory exterminating a wife-beater who would otherwise have got away unhurt, and it wouldn't matter if I was missing a leg or a few bones no longer needed, with a little luck dying instantly or at least very quickly, before starting to feel any pain or think about health insurance, and it would be not a bad death at all.

At ten to eight, punctual as ever in her early arrival, Gabriela arrives.

Neat, fresh, smiling, tightly encased in her tomato-coloured padded jacket. Little Red Riding Hood who has only this morning escaped from the wolf.

In the old woman who cautiously opens the door, Gabriela inspires, as always, a profound sense of marvel.

It is something to carry on living for, the sense of marvel. Even if it is mixed with diffidence. And between them, those two things form a barrier to love, an arabesque of railings like iron flowers, sharp as blades, beyond which stretch the green and deceptive pastures of the future. They are a mirage, the old woman is aware of it. She never even dreams of opening the barrier, she restricts herself to peering through it, her arthritic hands clutching the cold metallic spirals of wrought iron.

But why do they set off bombs? Gabriela suddenly asks the old woman, who does not wish to be called *signora* because she has never felt herself to be a *signora*, and who is listening with one ear to the radio news whilst simultaneously scrolling, with a grimace on her face, through the literary pages of an online daily paper.

There is nothing more stupid and repetitive than bad news.

Now, with Gabriela in the house — that industrious bundle of youthfulness — she is able to bear it, even to laugh it off. Gabriela, a shoulder-shrugging innocent, protects her from the world, the girl is her bastion, the fortified citadel behind which her threadbare good humour can dance again, lifting its multi-coloured and outmoded skirts.

No reply to Gabriela's question. The old woman reads the literary pages and snorts.

But are we still parroting that same old thing about happy people having no story to tell? she says snappily. It's a man writing, obviously. Some spoilt husband cossetted in Tolstoy-esque fashion by an oppressed wife, who sets the smoking samovar in front of his nose while he, the god of the house, comes up with big ideas to launch on the literary marketplace.

The girl, mindless of her green rubber gloves foaming with detergent, wrings her hands. What drives them to kill people? she asks in her stubborn little voice, preoccupied.

You know what Tolstoy said? That every happy family is happy in the same way, while every unhappy family is unhappy in its own particular way.

That's wonderful! Gabriela brightens, holding the gloves to her chest.

It isn't wonderful at all, it's a pile of rubbish! Exactly the opposite is true. Happiness comes in many forms, it's diverse, unaccountable, it can't be defined or grasped. It is art. It is dangerous, and for that reason little is said about it. It is unhappiness that is always the same (misery death envy hate depression silence and blood) the same ingredients cooked up into sauces that only differ from each other according to fashion.

She interrupts herself because she realises she is talking about evil — that idiotic conviction, as ever, that evil and unhappiness are the same thing, whereas it has been proved that there are people who do evil with pleasure, with joy, with deep satisfaction.

I don't know anything, she mutters in the end, remembering that the girl is waiting for an answer. It's no good asking me, I've never understood the first thing about this world.

The girl can't have heard because after a minute she persists. Do they hate us? she asks.

The old woman raises her head, looks at her over the top of her spectacles. Certainly, she grumbles, irritated and at the same time relieved to be diverted from thoughts that have nowhere to go. All of them. They even hate you, with your pretty little well-scrubbed face.

But they die as well. Why do they want to die? They're young.

The old woman is annoyed. She mumbles something about hard drugs, crack, heroin, prayer. The violence triggered by addiction, poverty, ignorance. She ends by telling her to ask one of them, if she ever comes across one.

After some minutes of laborious silence, Gabriela informs

her, while continuing to rinse the dishes, that in fact she does know one, one of these foreign fighters, he's a certain Dorin who has recently announced to her his conversion to Islam and his intention to go to the Middle East.

Gabriela is tiny but strong, with a great capacity for work, like all the women from her country. She has a round face permanently expressing surprise, enormous eyes, Bambi-like. But when her eyelashes flutter over that innocent look of hers, it is not out of malice, it is to signal retreat. At the least sign of danger Gabriela withdraws into herself and erects her defences, the way a porcupine rolls into a ball or a hermit crab retreats into its shell, and in the meantime she might spill tears or wring her hands or offer lavish apologies, but they are only the many ways in which she covers her retreat.

Once she has gained the safety of her own internal space, nothing can reach her any more.

She is just soap and water, even if recently she has taken to painting her lips with geranium-pink lipstick.

She puts it on for herself, for Gabriela. It is for herself that she combs her hair so carefully, and files the little almond-shaped nails at the ends of her tireless little fingers. Gabriela has never had a mother, and so acts as her own mother. She does not have a lover and who knows if she ever will, and so she blushes at the expression in her eyes when she sees herself in the mirror. She is twenty-six and a virgin.

To his improbable revelations about himself, Dorin has seemingly appended an offer of marriage. But she, Gabriela, won't even consider it. Put a veil over her head, no, thank you.

And marry someone who wants to kill people.

The old woman stares at her, frowning. Then: Where did he spring from, this Dorin? she asks, just to make conversation.

I've known him for ages, says the girl evasively. He wasn't always like this.

Like what?

Horrible! she informs her. He bites his nails, he's too thin. He never laughs. And then men with beards revolt me, she adds, with a shudder which is very pretty to see.

Quite right, the old woman approves. Tell him that if he doesn't shave it off you won't even think about it.

The girl appears to ponder this suggestion. The glasses emerge gleaming from the tea towel she is using to dry them. A ray of sunshine falls on her face, an apple newly plucked from the tree, vibrant with freshness.

He is not yet born, the man who will suit Gabriela. A woman perhaps? No, that person has already come and gone, was born and died some time ago. Gabriela arrived in the world as one of twins and lost the other half of herself when she was only six. How it happened depends on the vagaries of her partial and fantastical assertions: a car accident in which her sister was thrown through the windscreen; the drunken father struck her with a bottle; she died of a sudden and unexpected fever. The mother — more an absence than a presence — went away immediately afterwards, removing herself to another of those regions devastated by alcohol and real socialism where she later died from unknown but almost certainly not natural causes. Apart from the fact that there is nothing more natural than violent death, thinks the old woman. The little girl who was left was entrusted to the care of her maternal grandma and somehow, protected by the grandmother or thanks to her own resilience or the whims of chance, she survived cohabitation with an alcoholic father, in a fire-hazard of a house with no running water. Fortune, in the form of a rapidly progressing brain tumour, left her an orphan in her adolescence, before the father could have other ideas. Ten years ago she emigrated to Italy along with her half-sister, daughter of her father's first marriage.

Perhaps Gabriela would like to pursue the broken conversation, but the old woman is no longer listening, raises a hand to command silence, the radio is discussing the drought, a hundred and forty-two days now since it last rained. The temperature remains mild and incomprehensible, the plants on the windowsill are unwittingly turning green and producing buds notwithstanding the calendar indicating the depths of winter.

I know that Gabriela is a compulsive storyteller, naturally. Or, simply, a liar.

She is intelligent and has been to school, she almost achieved a diploma in something, I have forgotten what, she used to study at night while working by day but she had to stop to act as babysitter to some small niece or other, she is able to work out in her head a simple addition of two numbers and can even do multiplication if provided with pen and paper. She is deliciously old-fashioned, although equipped with the innate know-how of the younger digital generation, she can do anything and everything on her mobile, but hardly ever uses it as a telephone, nor does one ever see her tapping out messages. She has a ramshackle family — a sort of half-sister, a certain number of nephews, nieces and other relatives — but has been living alone for some time, a decision to which I can only give hearty approval.

But what is true in the things that she tells me or hides from me, or in the spiteful gossip purveyed by Ana? Her contradictions, her expression that looks the more dubious the more she intends to appear sincere. Her mysteries, her switches of mood, the sudden transitions between light and dark. Gabriela is not one of those helpers who skim off some of the shopping money for themselves, no, she skims off some of reality. Probably her life would be unliveable if she didn't make things up.

From time to time I allow my mind to wander in futile speculation about the girl. It happens in the night, maybe, when sleep dries up like rivers after months of burning heat, and I remain stranded, my arms behind my head, with the catarrhal breathing of Venom that accompanies my own creating the maddening soundtrack of insomnia. Then I imagine Gabriela's home, a spick and span two-room apartment facing a strip of parched parkland and a river the colour of waste matter, the realm of voracious seagulls and big brown rats that look alarmingly like otters. But Gabriela's home sparkles, her small, reddened knuckles are tireless and the gaze of those hazel eyes is sharp beneath a brow creased with the constant preoccupations of daily life. Soaps, detergents, brushes, Gabriela is a fetishist for cleanliness. Dear absurd little child.

In those moments I am happy to be as old as I am, and not to feel anything for her except perhaps an abstract benevolence, yes, the old-fashioned word is exactly right, a well-wishing that is airy and wide like an ancient window blown open by the wind, I wish you every possible good my child, so run my thoughts, I who have never had children. But even benevolence needs to be maintained at arm's length, the wind blows and passes and I remain, I close the window which no longer, or barely, serves to shield me these days. I do not wish to know too much about your life, which in any case you keep closely guarded like an old love letter that has never been opened. I would not know how, nor would I want, to protect you, and I do not even know — ah blessed ignorance — whether you hate me, tolerate me, feel sorry for me or are fond of me, whether you rob me as well like those who preceded you, whether you study my movements, whether you are planning to betray me... it doesn't matter, it doesn't matter.

I have already made a will stating that on my death a certain sum, not too large — I am not rich — goes to the girl. The rest to a charity for the protection of cats, recommended by that muddle-headed Malvina. I hope that Gabriela will not reveal herself to be a little snake, which would oblige me to change my will. Stay strong, Gabriela. I did not even wish to know very much about the charity, I like to imagine it as a sort of free-range haven, a retreat for crazy old cat ladies a little like tramps, and I have no intention of finding out if I am deluded.

What did the old woman do before becoming old?

Does it matter? And anyway, when a person has abandoned it decades ago, a profession tends to fade into oblivion.

But Gabriela is young and curious and gathers pieces of evidence. She is a slow and cautious investigator, but determined. More a secret agent than a Sherlock Holmes. One of those obscure agents who operate alone, to a plan whose reach they do not understand, receiving orders from faceless messengers and not knowing the names of those who come either before or after them.

A sepia photograph hanging in the hallway particularly fascinates her: a lady dressed as a page kneels before another lady in flowing white robes and proffers her a long-stemmed lily.

Do you like it? the old woman asks coming out of the bathroom and finding her lost in contemplation of the photo. She points to the kneeling page and stands in profile to demonstrate the resemblance, which might or might not be there to see.

I was an actress once.

Really? When? exclaims the girl, enthusiastic.

But the old woman makes a gesture as if to say: so many years ago you couldn't even imagine, and looks at her with those eyes that confuse. The old woman rarely answers direct questions. She seems to be amusing herself at her expense, at times Gabriela has to ask herself if she has misused a word or said something foolish, and blushes. The old woman and her house filled with books prompt in her a certain respect, and also a measure of pride. Sometimes her employer shouts at her, or is impatient; but usually she is kind. She is not malevolent like number two, or wayward like number one, who was always changing her mind and did it on purpose to put her in difficulties.

Gabriela knows she is very lucky: not only does she have a steady job, regularly paid and with her social security contributions included, but in addition she works for a single and self-sufficient lady. Who gets dressed by herself and smells nice. The last one, number three, she had to change four, five times a day, and in the evening she could still smell her pee and poo on her own person, she contracted an allergy from having to wash so often and disinfect her clothes and linen. And the family members were never satisfied, always there hovering over her work, suspecting her of petty theft. When the incontinent old woman died she cried, from sadness and relief.

The girl is constantly walking past the photograph. To her it seems incredibly old, but it is impossible to give it a precise age. The years that came before her own birth all mingle in a nebulous past, a history that does not concern her and which in any case she has never been taught, except in brief outline, in a language almost incomprehensible to her, even though she has been speaking it for years.

Her relationship with the world is for Gabriela an enormous effort of interpretation. What do they mean, the signals that are constantly offered, thrust, whispered or flung in her direction? The things are there, the words are said — it is up to her to interpret them. This is her personal no-man's-land. Interpretation.

Gabriela is brilliant and diligent. In the places where she has lived, in the schools she has attended, she has studied Russian, English and a bit of German. Italian she has learned in the field, like virtually all the immigrants from her country. The women that is, because language seems to matter less to the men — can that be because they work as bricklayers or lorry drivers or in trades where there is less need to speak, or because they know they can make themselves understood one way or another, obtain whatever it is they want?

As a complete stranger to the languages she uses, and so to the worlds she lives in, painfully uncertain how to take the most obvious things, the girl has the constant feeling that the sense of words escapes her. Their real, deep sense. What they really mean, for other people, in real life, in the world of things that have angles and edges and that can hurt you.

She makes her way gropingly. She forces herself to be calm, to speak slowly. She knows that if she becomes agitated, if she becomes frightened, the words will desert her, or turn on her.

It is her personal handicap, which she must hide if she wants to survive.

This is another reason for those preoccupied creases that pucker her forehead. She is perennially on the alert. Things are not as they seem, it would be nice to be trusting but it is too dangerous.

Months ago the old woman told her that she once had a restaurant of her own and was a celebrated chef. Gabriela believed her, two or three times she has seen the *signora* cooking refined little dishes, on the occasions when her friend Malvina was invited to dinner.

Then she realised she was joking. Not from malice but just anyway, for the pleasure of inventing things. The trouble is that she is always straight-faced and serious and it is impossible to tell when she is joking and when she isn't.

At other moments the *signora* — this is what Gabriela calls her, she would not dream of calling her the old woman, not even in her private thoughts when no one is listening — has declared herself to be a captain of industry, an opera singer, a ballet teacher, a forest ranger, a street girl and other things besides.

A street girl?

Not one normal occupation, teacher, clerk, nurse, shop assistant.

Gabriela keeps to herself. She is watchful, she is on her guard. As always, as everywhere. She tries to ingratiate herself with the old woman, in ways that are not too obvious, because she knows that flattery would produce the opposite effect. She makes every effort. In any case she has understood that here, in the old woman's house, the range of horrors that could befall her is much narrower than in the world outside. At certain moments she even relaxes. She forgets to be preoccupied.

From time to time, especially when she is ironing, the three small creases fade away and Gabriela's forehead becomes as smooth as a new-born baby's. She smiles secretly, an internal smile just for herself.

The old woman watches her and reflects on how opaque human beings are, indecipherable and unpredictable, every human being on earth, but this one in particular. Gabriela. What lies deep in that bunker inside her, where words play no part?

What will become of her, in the rest of her life, which the old woman will not see?

Will she have an honest and limited life, a little ant, holding back from all excesses, including happiness — or will she suddenly throw herself into some foolish love affair or undertaking? Will she follow a guru, devote herself to other people's children or produce some herself, though they will never completely be her own? Will she be expunged from the scene by chance or by history, or will she survive to a ripe old age? Will she ever learn to know herself and the world?

(If there still is a world, in thirty, fifty years' time.)

Questions which the old woman has no way of answering.

Gabriela is an enigma, and it could not be otherwise: she is young, she is on her own. She is a woman, she is a foreigner. She is as uncertain as the future.

She has never asked her if she has been married, if she has had children. Initially because she did not dare — the old woman is somewhat formidable, in her responses as in her silences — but then because she realised on reflection that these are exactly the questions that are asked of her, and which irritate her. When I was your age, they tell her, I was married, I had two small children. Not even engaged? What are you waiting for?

Quite, what is she waiting for?

Is it because she doesn't enjoy going dancing, like her younger but much more lively nieces, and doesn't spend hours trying on make-up and listening to music and talking about boys or men?

If only these occupations had held any interest for her — but that has never been the case — now Gabriela is too old for that kind of thing. And she was too old even last year, and the one before, and the one before that. That is the way it has always been. From her early childhood Gabriela has been older than her age — perhaps because she was born a few minutes before the other, her twin? Or because when she lost her she aged several years in a single moment, and time has never been the same again?

THE RIDICULOUS AGE

According to his theory of relativity, Einstein predicted, and his scientific colleagues subsequently confirmed, that time passes more quickly at high altitudes than at low, and that a twin living at sea level will find the twin living in the mountains a little older than himself. In the case of Gabriela, the difference between the twin on high ground swept by the winds of fate and the one who dwells in the bowels of memory is not a matter of a few seconds but of centuries. Living side by side in the girl are a little old lady, wise, diffident, cautious and even miserly — and hidden away in the subsoil and the half-light, a naïve little girl who believes in fairy stories. This is the most precious part of her, the treasure to be protected. Perhaps Gabriela is a privileged person in this respect, for it has been revealed to her from an early age that the truest core of each of us is what we have lost for ever.

It must be thanks to this 'little old lady' side of her that Gabriela gets on well with her employer. When — judiciously, prudently — she escorts her in the street, adjusting her pace to the old woman's as if born to do exactly this, one would think, looking at them from a distance, that they were almost contemporaries.

One might even think, seeing them cross the road together, that there is a resemblance between them — or at least something that unites them despite their being so very different, maybe their distance from the rest of humanity.

Lulled by the hypnotic movement of the iron which slides back and forth over the white blouses, Gabriela allows herself to dream. In her dreams there is no Prince Charming, there is no male, however strong and gallant, there are no girlfriends to laugh with and confide in, there is a house, simple — her dreams are not grandiose — clean, filled with plants and flowers. Around the house is a small meadow, a vegetable garden, behind which one can maybe glimpse a field of corn and rows of tomatoes, but she is not sure about those, there is too much light to make things out properly, a wall of light separates the house from the rest of the world and protects the shady depth of the earth floor over which her feet move, noiselessly. The only other presence besides her in this house is an old woman — her grandmother perhaps, but she resembles more closely her employer, she smells of orange blossom rather than stinks of sweat and alcohol and chicken dung and she speaks without shouting, it is to this old woman that the girl relates, in her fantasies, the trivial events of her day, it is to her that she turns with her questions. The old woman listens patiently, replies, reveals secrets and mysteries. Gabriela listens, tries hard to understand, to remember… and the dream breaks off.

The first day, when the *signora* interviewed her for the job, she offered her coffee and that was a stroke of luck because they naturally went into the kitchen, which is much lighter than the formal and rather dark sitting room, and since it was May Gabriela saw the window framed by jasmine in full flower. A cry of wonder caught in her throat, she was careful not to let it escape but her attention wandered and the *signora*, noticing where her eyes were turned, repeated her question.

The jasmine was the *coup de foudre*. All the rest suddenly made sense, sprang to life, coalescing around the jasmine: the iron grille at the window with its spiral bars, the old and solid furniture, the carpets, the white and wrinkled hands. Her

26

desire was so strong it left a bitter taste in her mouth. A little life consummated in an instant: to live and die here, in this house. Never to leave it.

The *signora* told her she was very young, really very young to be doing this kind of work. Of course she meant very stupid, Gabriela thought, dropping her gaze to her pink canvas shoes.

But at the end, when she got up to go, the *signora* said to her: Fine, so come tomorrow morning at eight, and Gabriela nodded yes, without even daring to smile.

The old woman is thinking about death. It is normal, at her age. Life is like a tight-rope on which we dance, very proud when young of our gifts of agility and balance, some are so sure of themselves they manage to exchange the rope for a wide and solid road, but there comes a moment when everyone realises that the other end of the rope is near, one seems to catch a glimpse of it, the foot wobbles. Then naturally one's steps become hesitant. Turning back is impossible, the rope dissolves bit by bit behind our back as we make our way along it, how did we never notice it before? Of what has been, of what we have been, only memory and dreams remain, and neither of these two rivals and lovers can explain to us how we have advanced along a high-wire that does not exist, or only for an instant and is attached to nothing at either end.

The old woman is well aware that the end of her personal rope is coming near, soon her feet will plunge into the great nothingness, her hand will have no hold to hang on to, she knows this, she feels it in her bones and in her thoughts, both of which are thoroughly exhausted. She wonders how it will be, when, at what precise moment. What her final sensations will be.

She thinks of the woman she loved more than her own self, she was called Nora. She died more than ten years ago. She thinks about how it was, what she experienced, Nora, in her final moments.

She ought to know, but she doesn't. She was there, a few metres away, but asleep. Like the Apostles in the garden of Gethsemane, thinks the old woman, who does not believe in god but believes in stories.

When death entered her house — of all arrivals the greatest, the ultimate visitation — she was sleeping. Which is why, now, she knows nothing about actual death: when, how, where.

It is this total lack of control, the inability to exercise her willpower, that is wearing her out.

Consciousness, consciousness as I know it, she thinks, crumbling the seconds of the night between her withered fingers, is an artificial product, a flower produced in the age-old greenhouse of human thought. Decorative, frequently and deliberately poisonous. Almost always useless, and above all fragile.

Pure and simple nature, blind nature, terrifies it. And rightly so, for nature has the capacity to reduce it to dust in a puff of air.

To save their hides and ward off this terror, the so-called philosophers have for centuries denied that nature exists. Only human thought exists, or the mind, or culture, history, science and its advances — this is what they cry, burying their heads in the sand. And then they croak, exactly like all the others.

But give me a story at least, a meaning, something to manufacture. An illusion. How long has it been since I had any such thing?

If I had one, even death would be bearable.

Perhaps, if I believed in god, she thinks, turning over on her side, the one that hurts less (the arthritis gnaws at her bones, these windy nights).

But god has no appeal for her. The only things she has ever believed in, in her life, were love and work. Too many years have passed since she lost them both.

Nora, says the old woman out loud.

And Nora appears. No, not in the darkness of the room, but in the lightning flashes that criss-cross her mind, Nora reveals herself for a split-second, an obscure disturbance, warm, breathing, terrible, a seismic tremor of love. And instantly disappears. The old woman groans, covers her face with her hands, sucked down, tumbling, into the undertow of loss, of missing someone. Grief has the gift of making you feel things vividly. It rips away the cobwebs of habit. It shatters the worm-eaten beams of survival.

If Nora appears, it is solely to force her to acknowledge that she isn't here, she isn't here any more and never will be again. Obedient to the summons — I have evoked you and you have come! — what a wretched triumph of the will, what a risible feat of memory, in reality assisted by technology, for there is not a day goes past when the old woman does not look at some photograph of Nora on the computer. More rarely she allows herself a video or voice recording, when she is seized with panic about forgetting her voice she listens again to a poem, a song, a soliloquy, how fortunate that she compiled that archive for which Nora used to mock her so roundly, or what would she do now?

What would she do, hearing again the voice without which her life is no longer her life, but a dried-up sea? Usually she listens for a few minutes, then suddenly starts to whimper, turns the machine off, makes herself a tisane or, if it is nearly evening, a strong drink. She forces herself to breathe in a regular rhythm. To fix her mind on some object apart, the flight of a fly, the sleeping of Venom.

Grief is a great thing, but it cannot be borne for long. So she drinks something strong, breathes, life resumes. Life, or what is left of it.

If only grief were capable of finishing her off! The old woman curses her sturdy heart. There is something not right about a heart so wretchedly clinging to life.

Cynical, critical, more intelligent than empathic. More rational than emotional. Always that tendency to doubt everything, to argue about everything. That look that came to be regarded as pitiless. She loved only Nora and her work. Hard-hearted. Mean. Serves you right.

She has read somewhere (a best-selling paperback?) the story of an oriental sage who died when he made the decision to. He stretched out comfortably on his bed, slowed his breathing down until he made it cease altogether and *paf!* he was dead.

Sublime bullshit. You can't die to order.

She has tried.

Slow down the breathing. Empty the head of thoughts (this is the hardest, the mind abhors a vacuum, if it's not thinking it plays silly games, or worse still falls prey to the werewolves of the daily horror-story, becomes a sounding-box for the evils of the world). Feel oneself floating off into nothingness. Breathe more slowly still, faintly only, very faintly. A mild sense of cloudiness, probably due to the diminished supply of oxygen to the brain, memories of joints smoked in youth, which never did much for her, no affinity with drugs. Breathe in less air, ever less…

Then, without knowing how, she is distracted by something, has begun to breathe normally, and no, she is not dead.

Death does not come when you summon it. At least not here in the West. Summoned by an incorrigible unbeliever, death turns a deaf ear.

Or is it her voice, does it carry insufficient firmness and conviction?

She still has some duties to perform on this earth, she thinks in the extreme weariness of early morning.

Her old cat and her old friend, two scatter-brained creatures who without her would be lost.

As if he had heard, Venom gets up from the corner of the bed where he has been curled up fast asleep — the old woman seems to hear his rheumatic little cat bones creaking — and comes to settle beside her face, his feral breath just under her nose, his whiskers tickling her.

This is what remains to me of love, the old woman thinks, pushing the cat's nose away from her face. The first tram of the morning passes in the street.

The old woman spends a lot of time observing things, after the second cataract operation and with the expensive new glasses her distance vision is quite good, whereas her close-up vision is more of an effort, which is why in recent times she has been reading less and observing more. She has got into the habit of watching from her windows, now from one, now from another, the apartment is big and has so many of them.

Observing other beings — when there are any, naturally. What is visible of them, what is not hidden by walls and the misty corners of the old woman's eyes. It may happen that for a whole afternoon there is nothing to observe except the social life of the pigeons on the open gallery of the building opposite. She recognises each of them individually, the one with the feet eaten away as if by leprosy, the domineering male who chases the females away from the food and tries to mount them, the desperate mother calling out, the terrified chick cheeping from a ledge, the winners and losers in the battle for survival. At night she throws them breadcrumbs and grains of rice, some of which land on the neighbours' balconies, provoking angry comments.

Until a few years ago Venom would also eye them from behind the iron grille at the window, leaning forward and quivering, uttering little trills of anxiety and desire, the call of the wild or in his case more modestly the call of the windowsill, the moans of a frustrated hunting urge. But now he doesn't bother. It seems he no longer needs distraction, no longer needs to find a remedy from the endless tedium of the hours. He is content to sleep, to eat, to share with her the bed, the armchair, the room, to warm one another's bones.

Who knows if he too thinks about death, in his own way, the old woman wonders, slowly passing her wrinkled and spotted hand over the mangy fur of the cat, which snores lightly, eyes closed.

In this way, little by little, the moments pass until it is time to go out.

Outside, beneath a section of the porch, a homeless person has recently taken up residence, the umpteenth one, a man who reads all day long with apparent intensity. A good marketing policy: establish a point of difference, don't just be one of the crowd. The old woman, however, stopped giving him money when she saw what he reads: rubbish. And anyway it is not all that original, other readers are soon springing up everywhere, each armed with a dog-eared bestseller, one of those volumes you can buy for a euro on market stalls, it's clear this is some kind of franchised begging system, maybe organised by a second-hand bookseller.

Further on is the woman with the dog. She is still young, barely forty, Italian, articulate and correctly dressed; the dog is a white mongrel with a black patch over its left eye, and the old woman felt a small, warm surge of joy when she saw it jump up and snap at the hand she put out. A proper dog, alive. But other customers do not seem to attract its interest and now the animal, quiet, dozes all day long on a blanket, its eyes dull.

Sometimes the old woman has fantasies of buying it. How much do you want for the dog? she would ask the blonde woman smoking a cigarette and examining her nails. Obviously she will not do so, she no longer has the energy to live with a dog. There must be a distribution centre for dogs on the fringes of the city, the applicants queue up in the morning at the counter where the animals are allocated and everyone is assigned a dog in better or worse condition, either on the random principle or maybe according to its colour and whether it tones in with their clothing. The dog, sedated, will lie for hours on a mat or in a padded holdall. From time to time the beggar will scratch its head absent-mindedly or get it to rest its nose on his lap, passers-by like seeing that, the love between man and dog, the responsibility, the dog inspires pity but it is a pity they manage to bear, and at the same time it ennobles the owner, restores to him that humanity from which his profession of beggar tends to detract, in the eyes of the customers. The coins drop into the tin. What happens when the dogs get sick or become unruly? Are they eliminated? (How?) And probably dumped at some illegal rubbish tip outside the city...

And the beggars? When they give up the whole racket because it's unproductive, where do they end up? On one of those sliding drawers in the morgue that you see at the cinema? With a white cardboard label tied to their big toe, on which no one will ever write a name?

Every time she passes that way, the old woman observes the piebald mongrel and sends it a subliminal message: Rebel! Bite! Kill!

The dog doesn't blink, doesn't twitch an ear.

Will he be there today or won't he, the old Moroccan, under the arcade in the market square? Impossible to say. Sitting with his legs drawn up to his chest, he is most often dozing against a pillar like a Bedouin against his dromedary, until his head drops and bumps on the layers of ragged old coats that cover his knees. Then he suddenly jerks upright, opening his eyes towards the passers-by in a gaze of age-old sadness, and returns to his slumbers. Summer and winter he is bundled up in threadbare jackets, shawls and coats, when it is cold he wraps his head in a cloth as well.

They have known each other for forty years, one could say they have grown old together, the old woman thinks, passing before him and dropping a euro on to his greatcoat. At one time, though, he did not sleep so much. And anyway she too needed fewer naps at one time. And she used to walk faster, without a stick. What she likes about this man, about whom she knows nothing, not even his name, is the slow dignity with which he sells his wares, his eyes staring into infinity, and especially his sadness. It is rare, these days, to find an authentic, disinterested sadness. There are moments when she would like to sit down next to him and join him in staring into the void.

Every now and again she wonders what he does when he is not there, in those periods, sometimes for months, when he vanishes: does he go back to Morocco, where perhaps he has a family? With the money from donations and selling cigarette lighters, has he perhaps bought himself a child bride who is even now waiting for him in a village at the edge of the desert? There is no way of knowing. Not a word between them in forty years, apart from some restrained greeting (Good morning, she says, with measured cordiality, *Signora*, he says with a respectful inclination of the head, years ago he used to call her friend, but with age, the detachment from human intercourse widens, the sadness in the eyes of the Bedouin deepens, it is over-familiar to say 'friend' to a passing shadow).

In the square, Malvina is already slumped on the usual bench, assailed by the windy verbosity of her female bodyguard. This is where they see each other, every day if it is not raining, for her hour of taking the air.

Ana is thirty-five, vast backside forcibly crammed into elasticated jeans, broad and hard face, blouse decorated with hearts picked out in rhinestones, cobalt-coloured nails. The old woman loathes her and has no hesitation in holding her responsible for the rapid and progressive regression into childhood of her friend. Malvina, the gentle, confused Malvina half-closes her eyes against the winter sun and turns on the world a vague smile, absorbed ever more frequently in something remote and far away, perhaps the great nothingness which is knocking at her door. In those moments of absence she looks like a blind person, her eyes filmed by an opaque amniotic sack of light, turned in on themselves. At her friend's approach, however, she wakes up, her face animated by flickers of emotion, relief, joy, even mischief.

She has very few lines and wrinkles, Malvina. Every now and then the old woman thinks she glimpses the girl she has been, sees her emerge beneath the tired and drooping skin, like an actress who has been aged before her time by an expert make-up artist and is waiting patiently to be released from the layers of age to return to her true self.

They walk slowly, arm in arm, the two old women, while the two young ones speed off across the square in the direction of the supermarkets and the stalls, Gabriela almost running to shake Ana off and Ana struggling to follow at her heels, deep into some ghastly feminine saga that she insists on pouring into the other's reluctant ears.

They say this is a world of old people. They say it to make us feel we are to blame. We are old and we are too many. We ought to turn up spontaneously for a programme of voluntary extermination and die with a smile on our lips.

In fact the means are already provided, but they are not enough. Potholes, uneven surfaces and the thousand pitfalls set there to trip us: inadequate, sufficient only for a fracture of the femur. More effective are cars and motorbikes or worst of all, cyclists who flash past aggressively with earbuds in their ears and who are always in the right, how I dream of stretching a steel wire across the pavements invaded by their arrogant alternative high-mindedness and see them go flying over the old wrecks that are their technological inferiors and smash into a wall! Like a visual gag in a silent film, but seriously, with blood and broken teeth.

This constant feeling of being too slow, too vulnerable, too myopic, of having reflexes not rapid enough, like a decrepit tortoise that has lost its shell and drags its soft and quivering pulp on to a six-lane motorway.

If a cyclist did knock me over however it would be unlikely to kill me. My crumbling bones would be put back together after a fashion in a hospital bed at the expense of the public health service, which is increasingly less healthy and less public. I would not die but my remaining life would be shorter and more painful. Much better a car, but here in the city centre they go so slowly!

The most sneaky and lethal weapon, though, is not aimed at my withered and wavering body, but at my head. My thoughts are slow, fragile and they too are prey to all manner of fears, because in growing older I have lost the illusion of being able to tame the world with the brilliant ideas produced by my lucid and agile brain. In any case, who cares what I think? Who has any desire to listen to an old woman?

An old woman can only have old ideas. Outdated, inadequate and ridiculous. If she claims to have thoughts she is swiftly told, in no uncertain terms, that she is too old to have any. That she is no longer capable of understanding today's world.

But on my side, who is there that I still want to talk to?

Is there anyone I don't feel estranged from, anyone who doesn't get on my nerves or doesn't utterly weary me?

Certainly not the young women like the one coming towards me at this moment, with a mass of hair tied on top of her head like a great bunch of curly chicory, it's funny, as if big hair had come back into fashion, but not elaborate and artificial as in the days of Marie Antoinette or even the tortuous hair-dos of the Sixties which reduced the head to a balloon of spun sugar sticky with lacquer, no these are impromptu arrangements, full of bold confidence, held on top of their heads by aggressive look-at-me elasticated bands, once again women are placing all their pride in their hair, they hoist it high in defiance, they smack you in the face with it, I am sex, that's what these hair-dos say, of course they are right, the zealots of all faiths, hair equals sex, and the more a woman is her hair the more she is reduced to her sexual identity, which is why the first man to walk by is cordially invited to seize her and drag her off by her crowning glory, and now look, just as I thought, this young woman doesn't step aside by so much as a centimetre to give Malvina room, even though she can see she is unsteady on her feet, that stepping off the pavement costs her some effort, that she even risks falling, but what am I saying, she can see? She can't see us, for her we don't exist, we are usurpers of air and space, we should already be dead, is that what you really think, girl? In that case I, for my part, will make sure you see we are the undead, we are dangerous bitches!

The old woman jabs her stick at the ankles of this girl, who deftly jumps aside and turns round to stare at her, and only then, perhaps, does she see her. And as she moves away she mutters something that could be 'watch where you're going' or even 'mad old woman'.

Malvina, who has not noticed a thing, leans heavily on her arm. She ought to lose some weight, the old woman thinks, her legs can hardly support her any more.

Suddenly exhausted, the old woman questions the real reason for her rage. I am a wreck with neither desires nor curiosity any more, she thinks. It is not the world's fault at all, the fault is mine. It is pointless to take it out on other people, the thing I lack nobody can give me. The willpower to get up in the morning, to face the day ahead.

If only Malvina was at least listening. Then she could find relief in telling her about her fantasy of zoological apocalypse: just think, what if we discovered that right here, in the city, in the Royal Gardens, closed down and abandoned years ago, invaded by undergrowth and nettles, whole new species of hybrid animals have been proliferating, wolves with boars' tusks, tigers with hyenas' mocking laughter, and one day they escape from the park and devour us. What do you say, eh, wouldn't that be entertaining?

Malvina smiles, absent, her eyes far away.

You've always been hard of hearing, but now you're as deaf as a stone! the old woman yells, tugging at her. You bought yourself some hearing aids! Why don't you use them? I bet you don't even know where you put them.

I can't bear those things, says Malvina, guilty but obstinate. They make a humming in my head. And she pulls her towards the window of a clothes shop that has been attracting her attention for a few minutes.

But what are you always complaining about? the old woman asks her own reflection in the window, with a snort of disgust. You're reasonably healthy, you can still walk; the doctor told you, talking to you as if you were an imbecile: Clever you, well done, you have the heart of a young girl. A touch of breathlessness but that's nothing, if you take the pill it'll pump away for another twenty years. Great news, thanks! You have your own home, enough money to pay your own personal bodyguard. What more could you want? Do you think you're smarter than twenty and thirty-year-olds because you've stepped back from the world? Because you've scraped together the risible amount of knowledge a human being might lay her hands on over the course of ninety years? And why does everything make you sick and annoy you?

What? says Malvina. The old woman has not realised she is talking out loud. Loud, but not loud enough to be heard by Malvina. Who is now pulling her towards the shop doorway, she would like to try on that air-force blue blouse she likes so much. Incredulous, the old woman eyes the object of her friend's lust: a garment of minute size, designed for a body of unreal slenderness, high at the bosom and tight at the waist, in which Malvina might perhaps once have been able to squeeze herself, holding her breath, at the age of twenty.

But what do you want with another blouse? You've got

40

wardrobes full of them, she tells her, clamping her arm beneath her own, and giving her a light slap on her soft and puffy hand. And anyway, she adds with authority, you can see it's not your sort of thing at all, a dull colour like that is going to murder your complexion, and it's a bit tacky too.

Obediently, Malvina allows herself to be convinced, and after a few steps she has already forgotten.

Gabriela pushes the trolley ahead of her. Ana talks to her back, a wall of muscle hunched against the cataract of waters that swirl round her, that threaten to submerge her every day.

Have you seen your fiancé again? she asks.

He is not my fiancé, Gabriela says, eyes aimed like laser guns on the tinned peas. He is my half-cousin.

And while Ana explains what she already knows perfectly well, that he is not really her cousin because he is the son of Gogu's previous marriage, Gogu being the husband of her half-sister Petra, and therefore they are not even related, implying that there is nothing to prevent a possible marriage, Gabriela concentrates ferociously on the music she heard on the radio this morning while she was having coffee with the *signora*, was it Beethoven or Brahms? Why doesn't she remember the names of the musicians? She must be more attentive. Listen more, read more. Or she will end up like Ana, she thinks with a shiver.

Gabriela selects products from the shelves, rapidly and precisely, it is clear she is mentally ticking off a specific list. Ana by contrast reaches for things on impulse and piles them all on top of each other, family packs for preference, her trolley is already full.

Why do you need six beers? The *signora* doesn't drink beer! observes Gabriela.

What do you know about it? She certainly does drink beer. She doesn't tell the other one, but she drinks it all right.

What about those brioches, she doesn't eat those, for sure.

They're for me, says Ana. And while they are standing at the cold meats counter and Gabriela is waiting her turn for a quarter of *prosciutto crudo*, Ana returns to the ultimate topic of conversation, men. The men who please her and those who don't (not many), those she has known and the ones she is yet to know, the handsome and the ugly, the young and the old, the real and the imaginary. Her ideas are confused but ambitious, they grow like magic tendrils as she speaks, come to life in the gleaming of her eyes, she interrupts herself only to have slices of *taleggio* and *castelmagno* cut for her. Men are her drug, Gabriela thinks, fascinated in spite of herself, she's lost all sense of reason, not that she has much to lose, and now Ana is telling her that these days almost all the men are wearing beards, it's the fashion, not that she personally dislikes it, as far as she is concerned everything that is hairy gets her going.

Gabriela hides — not completely — a grimace of disgust.

But you realise that this man, Ana persists, in Italian as if she wants to involve in their conversation the assistant who is handing her the cheeses, this man is ab-so-lute-ly madly in love with you!

Gabriela flushes. Not with virginal modesty, as Ana imagines, hugely amused, but with fury. No one, no one has the right to be in love with her. As for *madly*!

No one has the right, she thinks, clenching her little fists on the handle of the trolley, to make her feel guilty or to subject her to questioning on a sentiment she does not share, does not want, does not believe in and which she finds insulting, but she will never be able to say so because she will not be understood. Just as she has not confided in a living soul what Dorin has told her about his conversion and his shady terrorist intentions. Which are perhaps just fantasies. Dorin is mad, has always been, maybe not exactly mad but different, disturbed, and even dangerous. She knows this, but seems to be the only one who knows it and anyway there is nothing she can do about it. Why, why has he turned up again at this particular moment? He has been in prison, and Gabriela can't help thinking that they should have kept him in for longer, because if he were in prison now he would not be here, claiming to be in love with her and tormenting her.

She has not told anyone, except the *signora*. That was a mistake, she realised it straightaway, these things are of no interest to the *signora*, it was a false step, she doesn't know how to behave, she must be more careful. She hopes she has not given a negative impression of herself. It would be too cruel if the *signora* thought badly of her. She promises herself yet again not to mention him any more.

I walk arm in arm with my friend Malvina, whom I have known from when she was a slender young woman who danced, shaking her curly head, on the floor of a nightclub called *Fire*, and everyone used to stare at her, men and women, the men liked her because she looked like a little boy, the women because she wasn't.

I walk arm in arm with Malvina and I tell her I can't stand living in such a viciously stupid world any longer. The morning news ruins the taste of my coffee, I envy Venom because he doesn't understand and doesn't become enraged.

Obviously I am talking to myself.

From time to time I give Malvina a nudge, she is getting deafer and more absent-minded every day, and she smiles at me and says yes, yes, yes, whatever it is I am saying. I can't even get cross with her, the truth is she's doing her best. She spends her life agreeing with me, even when I'm wrong. Except when she digs her heels in, as in the case of Germana and Birmingham.

A spurt of desperation rises from my stomach like an acid reflux.

Talk to me, I plead. Tell me something.

Do you know I saw Germana this morning? Malvina says, very happy.

For heaven's sake, not that fixation again?

Then she tells me that coming away from the ATM this morning she ran into Germana, whom she has always fancied, if from a respectful distance — an older woman, authoritative, surrounded by an aura of intellectualism, and it is of no consequence that she was married and firmly hetero, Malvina was a little infatuated with her. And this morning there she was, in a grey overcoat outside the automatic doors to the ATM booth, it seemed as if she was waiting for her. Germana! Malvina exclaimed, don't you remember me? I'm Malvina Pesenti! And Germana's face broke into a wide smile, she greeted her warmly, they even embraced.

Which, if it were not for the even more convincing fact that Germana died three years ago, would be enough to prove it was not her. Germana was a woman who looked at you as if she had a nasty smell under her nose, warm she was not.

Sorry, but in this case you're being unjust, she counters. With me she has always been very kind, you remember, that time she mentioned me in one of her articles.

Enough of that old story! Let's have no more of this abject gratitude because the great Germana Starnazza, She-Who-Squawks, once mentioned you in one of her articles! You were the best film editor in the country, whereas the Starnazza-Squawker woman was only a critic full of her own importance.

But she wasn't called Starnazza, I don't think, says Malvina doubtfully.

No, but she should have been. You're making me cross, look, I'm getting agitated and I can feel palpitations coming on.

Malvina apologises, but it doesn't stop her from telling me about her encounter with the dead woman, who wanted to accompany her all the way back to her doorstep, and said she would come and see her soon. How old was this Good Samaritan? I ask. As beautiful as ever, Malvina replies, and I point out that Germana, just supposing it had been her come back to life, would now be going on for a hundred, and anyway beautiful was one thing she had never been.

And what was that bright spark Ana doing while you were spending time with ghosts? Doesn't she know you shouldn't trust strangers?

Malvina is paying no attention however, now she wants a coffee with whipped cream on top, and so here we are at a minuscule table in an overheated bar full of tourists, waiting for our coffee.

I watch Malvina greedily spooning up her whipped cream

and think that she already has a foot in that place, in that wonderful and terrible immensity where there are no limits or marked roads, where one is finally free from the tyranny of reason and the constraints of common discourse, from the fictitious barriers that separate yesterday from today, dream from waking, the living from the dead. Maybe that world is more true and more humane than the one I stubbornly persist in considering the only real one.

And therefore (to give the creature her real name) it is probably true that she has met Germana Strazza this morning at the ATM. In a certain sense.

Why, says Gabriela.

Then she frowns, looks anxiously around and concentrates on the button she is sewing on a pair of smoke-grey velvet trousers.

In the room can be heard: the ticking of the alarm clock, which is one of the old type, not digital, with big numbers; the announcer on *RaiTre* who — from the kitchen — is talking about stabbings and shootings in the streets of cities, bombings, shipwrecks and nuclear threats; the notes of Chopin from the bedroom; the shrieks of the neighbours opposite who are quarrelling on the other side of the condominium's narrow courtyard; a sneeze from Venom, who has caught a cold.

After a number of attempts, engaging forward and reverse gear, and after some false starts, Gabriela finally succeeds, like a novice parker, in extricating herself from her verbal awkwardness and rejoins the highway of speech.

Why is he called Venom?

The old woman, who has been observing her over the top

of her lowered spectacles, spends a long minute in reflection.

Just as the girl is about to apologise for her indiscretion, get up and go into the kitchen to check the potatoes are cooking all right, she answers.

Because he once swallowed something that was poisoned.

Oh! Gabriela says, drawing in her breath, opening her eyes wide and bringing a hand up to her mouth. It does not escape the old woman's notice that these delightful and silly manifestations of girlish sensibility are reserved for the trivia of conversation, they do not touch her closely, whereas when she speaks of the domestic killings of her past, true or imaginary, Gabriela is cold and cynical like Marlene Dietrich in the role of Shanghai Lily.

Who was it?

I have no idea. Someone who hates cats. There is always someone who hates cats. Or some other categories of persons or creatures. Amongst whom, incidentally, each of us might well be numbered.

But don't cats notice, if their food has been poisoned?

Maybe they do. There are times when one feels like deciding whether to die of hunger or poisoning. Gabriela lowers her eyes to her button. Is she pondering? Or is she simply thinking the old woman is a bit touched?

I wasn't the one to see it. Or perhaps I decided not to see it, a barely perceptible movement out of the corner of my eye and promptly censored, something out of keeping with this magnificent day, something that smells of pain and the irremediable. And I turned my head aside.

The cat was writhing weakly at the side of the road, on a

layer of refuse blown together by the wind, litter, dry leaves.

It was a late afternoon at the end of the summer, we had been sunbathing, I remember the rustling of the sea breeze through the eucalyptus trees, this was before it all happened, in the happy former times.

For a moment more I pretended not to see, to know, car keys in my hand. But Nora had crouched beside the dirty, convulsing little mass. And I thought: Oh no!

Why is life confronting us with this minor drama, why is it obliging us to do something, or nothing? Even doing nothing, not wishing to see, is a decision. Why today, why us?

Nora has always been stronger than me, more decisive. She had already gathered up this parcel of dirty fur, was pressing me, quick, quick, open the door, give me a towel. As I drove I turned from time to time to see her golden arms speckled with brown freckles, her grey hair tousled and stiff with salt, she had wrapped the cat in the beach towel, was holding it in her arms and speaking to it, I thought the cat would die and Nora would be sad for the rest of the holiday.

But the cat did not die. We had arrived in time, the vet returned it to us after injecting it with a serum and recommended we keep it warm. Smuggled into the hotel in our beach bag, the cat slept between us while we continually woke up to check it was still there, dazed but alive.

The next morning we found it hiding under the bed, its pupils dilated with terror, Nora talked to it for a long time, lying stretched out on the carpet and then slowly pulled it out, clasped it to her chest. Enfolded in her embrace, after ten minutes the cat was purring loudly, pressing itself to her like butter spread on bread. They happen, these instant and total alliances between animals and humans, and who was I to oppose it? We would have a cat, and its name would be Venom. Like a warrior, Nora had said, who takes the name of his defeated enemy and thereby celebrates his victory over death.

It was a young male of about six months, undernourished, with enormous eyes. Striped, as so many are, grey, shading into the tawny colouring of a forest floor in the soft fur close to its skin, the down that keeps it warm in winter, which clogs brushes and floats about the house in summer.

Venom, my friend. We are brothers in mourning, ours is a bond of blood and absence, like the suture that joins the edges of an amputated stump.

They had had to leave the hotel, losing two days already paid for because animals were not allowed. They had argued with the manager, happy and belligerent. Venom was an adventure. They bought him tins of tuna and in the restaurant ordered fish to take back to him. Smuggled on to the ferry as well, the cat had left the island and returned to dry land wrapped in a woollen jumper, showing a quite disarming faith and without a single meow.

In the past there had been other animals, they had died, their natural cycle accomplished, unless an illness had overtaken them. They had decided not to have any more, they wanted to be able to travel in peace, without having to think about it.

And instead death had been waiting for them at the side of the road and they had defied it, they felt strong. They did not know that death does not allow itself to be defeated with impunity, that it always takes its revenge.

How young they still were, although over sixty.

Tonight she dreamed of Nora. No, that is inexact: she did not dream of her. Nora came to find her.

It was not a dream, but a visit, the one thing most passionately desired in the exhausted semi-sleep of old age, when you no longer even have the strength to desire, but nevertheless, all at once and for an instant, passion overflows like a wave, drags you with it, submerges you, and throws you back half dead and gasping for breath between the covers.

It was one of those dreams in which you see yourself as you are and where you are, and the old woman was in her bed, in her room, and was sleeping lying on her left side. Exactly as she was in reality.

It was one of those moments in which two worlds meet, a door, huge and hidden, half-opens for an instant.

Something was moving, lightly brushing the sleeping woman's skin. She thought: it's Venom.

And then suddenly she knew it was not the cat touching her. Those were hands that were reaching for her under the blanket.

They were her hands, it was Nora. It was all very natural, and very surprising.

It's you, the old woman says, or thinks, but it is as if she were saying it, and anyway who can testify as to whether, in the silence of the dark, a voice is present, who knows what the difference is between a word spoken and a word thought?

In the darkness the presence of her love becomes denser, resonates, it is a living being with its warmth, odour, breath, that bends over her as she lies asleep.

How many times has she tried to bring her image into focus with that most deceptive of all the senses, sight? To see Nora as she was in reality, or maybe now only in her memory, her face no longer young but still very beautiful, not the shrunken face of those last, terrible times. But the image that takes shape in her mind is only the ghost of Nora, transient and precarious, created by her cowardly desire. Even in a dream sight is a talentless artist, a bird without wings, it tries to compose the portrait of a beloved spectre and only succeeds in making a mess like a child whose pencil slips from its fingers.

But tonight, the hands.

It is her, Nora. Hands do not lie, touch, warmth do not lie.

The sense of touch recognises with absolute certainty the fingers of Nora on her own. They stroke their tips, they encircle her wrists as if to draw her closer. Skin speaks to skin, in an ancient language, passed on by numbers of mothers and lovers beyond counting, their first embrace contained the tremor of a primordial connection.

Tonight they are two astronauts of memory floating in the black and infinite space of the bedroom joined together hand to hand.

Hold me! Hold me! the old woman cries out in her sleep.

Which means: keep me with you, take me where you are!

And at the same time a violent joy pierces her heart and takes her breath away. She wakes gasping for air, her heart hammering, her whole body permeated with a heat as keen as a blade of incandescent ice, an absence of weight, as if she really had floated into the void of nothingness.

In the kitchen Gabriela comes out with another of those questions slowly gestated and formulated in her thoughtful little head.

But you and *signora* Malvina, she says, have you never thought of living together?

The old woman, still under the softening influence of last night's enchanting dream, smiles.

You get along so well, you are such friends, the girl insists.

We are too different, the old woman says, at our age it is hard enough to bear ourselves, never mind other people, and then we each have a home of our own.

But there is so much space here, the girl says indicating the apartment, with its generous measurements, five rooms, kitchen and two bathrooms, not counting the balconies, *signora* Malvina could sleep in the corner bedroom, and use the other bathroom! She could let her apartment, and she wouldn't need Ana any more. I could easily manage here, no? What is there to do? Not that much at all. Think of the saving!

For a moment the old woman allows herself the pleasure of imagining it. Not so much for the suggestion as for the honest solicitude that inspires it.

It is so rare, pleasure, at her age. And even if she does so with due caution — she knows it is an illusion and will not last — why should she not indulge it? The girl's face is radiant, and to the old woman's mind comes something a writer (Margaret Atwood?) has one of her characters say, an old woman like herself: how beautiful the young are, even the plain ones, and they don't even know it!

Gabriela — who is not plain — is she conscious of being beautiful?

(How genuine is beauty? Does beauty still exist, now that there is no Nora?)

But you would have too much work, says the old woman slyly. You would have to give up your day off.

That doesn't matter! I never know what to do on my day off.

And suddenly she blushes at having let slip this confession. To which the old woman is wary of attaching much credence.

The old woman smiles, she relishes the sight of her carer (she really ought to start calling her that, even if for the present she is merely a home help) setting herself up for a territorial battle, creating the conditions for an increase in salary and a more binding engagement, in effect asserting her desire to become even more indispensable, to get a hold on her, on her life, and Malvina's too as her friend. And all of this not just for personal gain, but also with the altruistic intention of supplanting and defeating her rival Ana, whom she detests with all the impure young heart of an orphan who has survived every kind of family carnage.

For Gabriela, Ana represents perdition, an abyss she is perhaps frightened of falling into. Ana is foul-mouthed, fun-loving and tragic. She is gloriously ignorant, constantly on the look-out for men, she finds one, gets herself pregnant by him, he rejects her and heaps insults on her, she has an abortion, but after a few months she is out hunting again, because what on earth is a woman without a man?

That is what she declared one day while she was basking in the look of disdainful lust simmering in the eyes of an Arab selling mint in the market. Gabriela did not deign to respond, her little face hard and mute, she packed the remark away like an incriminating exhibit and pulls it out, from time to time, to shock herself with, not without relish.

And this is how we free ourselves from 'what-on-earth-is-a-woman-without-a-man', the old woman now says, casting her the bait.

Gabriela seizes it dexterously, lights up all over. How can she have so little respect for herself? And now she's with a new man again, an Italian. He's fifty! He still lives with his mamma! He's as ugly as sin! And the way he treats her! I want to see if he marries her.

But you have your suitors as well, don't you? the old woman interrupts, wearying of all this. What was that fellow called, the terrorist?

Gabriela's expression hardens, she shakes her head, no. That man! I don't even want to talk about him. Luckily he's disappeared. No one has seen him for two weeks, not even his family.

The old woman wonders, fleetingly, if the girl really is, as she sometimes appears, a delicate moth that any fat spider could help himself to, sucking her up bit by bit. Or if instead she isn't the one spinning her webs, a novice's webs but on the right lines...

But it does not interest her very much, in the end. She does not see a future together. She does not see a future, full stop.

And today what she sees, no, what she feels, are the hands of Nora, gripping her own and guiding her into the vast and weightless dark.

Malvina lives on the third floor of a grand nineteenth century *palazzo*, in a large bourgeois apartment which has remained as it was when it was the home of her parents, who went on their way more years ago than anyone can remember, being already almost elderly when she was born. The sister and brother, quite a lot older than her, vanished years ago after relieving her of the legacy of the past by selling a good part of the furniture, china and pictures bequeathed to the three of them, including the youngest, without even consulting her. Malvina has always lived in two rooms and a kitchen, the remaining rooms transformed into a museum, or a repository of junk, depending on the kindness of whoever is looking.

What's happened? the old woman asks, banging her stick on the floor, impatient to be outside again, in the light. That something has happened is undeniable, there are blankets strewn on the floor, newspapers, a black rubbish bag, open and overflowing, that looks as if someone has been rummaging through its contents.

Malvina is dishevelled and confused. She is hunched, shoulders curved, ever more bent, the old woman thinks. Thousands of years of evolutionary effort to achieve an upright posture, and after eighty wretched years nature takes its revenge on the single individual.

We are the first generation of women to wear trousers not just as youngsters but when we are old as well, she thinks incongruously, her glance descending from the once immature and barely lifted breasts of Malvina, now shapeless beneath her blouse, to the thickened hips and legs squeezed into jogging bottoms. And the gym shoes, not because we do gymnastics, but because they are the only form of footwear we can still get our corns and bunions into. Malvina has swollen ankles, two blueish sausages that bulge from her trousers and over her shoes. She ought to do something, massages, pills, creams, something. Walk more, drink more water. Go on a diet. Become young again.

She, the old woman, still has slender ankles, but there is no escape, she too is reduced to sports shoes. In her cupboards dozens of pairs of shoes in every colour are fading like leather roses, soft and wrinkled, enveloped in the musty and sickly-sweet smell of the past.

Ana is upset, sweating — the stink rising from her causes the delicate nostrils of Gabriela to wrinkle — and as she speaks she waves her arms about, stoops to pick something up, lets it drop again, searches in her pocket, mops her face with a tissue. She is scared of being accused, there has been an incident involving Malvina and she knows they are going to blame her. Who is going to tell *signor* Osvaldo?

Never mind *signor* Osvaldo! the old woman declares. What has he got to do with it?

He has to do with it because it was Osvaldo, Malvina's nephew, who interviewed Ana for the job. It is he who pays her wages and sends in her social security contributions, even if the money is Malvina's, drawn from her bank account.

It's more convenient that way, Malvina says in justification, these things I... then I forget them...

And now what will Osvaldo say when he knows that thieves have been in here? But how could it have happened?

About an hour ago, a man knocked at the door. Middle-aged, well turned-out, very polite. A good-looking man, Ana specifies, determined to leave no important detail out. Tall, grey-haired but young.

He showed an ID card from the Gas Company. He said

there was a gas leak in the apartment, it needed to be checked urgently.

And you let him in! the old woman yelps.

Ana and Malvina cling to each other, a sight that enrages her even more.

See, this is what we've come to, we're becoming laughing-stocks, they sneak up on us, they rob us and we don't even notice, we say thank you, we offer them coffee. That is what the two unlucky wretches did, while the thief pulled the wool over their eyes with his ID cards and his fine words, telling them idiotic tales about how to preserve money and valuables from the harmful effects of gas, no problem, you just need to put them in a black rubbish sack and stow them under the bed. Malvina, conscientious, followed the inspector (as he called himself, in Gogol fashion) and his instructions, went from room to room gathering together money, watches, a few rings. Meanwhile Ana was dutifully in the kitchen, standing by the gas rings, keeping an eagle eye on the flame, aware of the importance of her mission.

Then the inspector took his leave with smiles and assurances and jokes on the sad state of the times, so few decent people left these days — a real street-performer's trick — and only by chance, after his exit from the scene, does it occur to Ana to check whether the sack stowed under the bed for safety is properly closed, and what does she see? Nothing!

Under the bed, no black plastic sack. Just a few balls of fluff.

The chaos, then, they have created themselves, looking for the treasure which has now disappeared along pathways not marked on any map. They have been tipping drawers out on to the floor, throwing open cupboard doors, sifting through the rubbish — as if the sack, of its own volition, had decided to play hide and seek.

This character wasn't alone, the old woman says, thoughtfully. There was someone else with him, an accomplice who entered the apartment and you never noticed. Heaven knows how they did it, how they got to know they'd find two half-wits here. Has anyone been following you, these last few days? Have you met any strangers who took an interest in you? People who asked questions, tried to get inside the house?

Ana says no, putting a hand over her heart, or rather her overflowing boobs.

That lady… says Gabriela. The one who was outside the ATM yesterday…

But of course, the one who accompanied you home! I bet you told her your whole life story! The old woman is choking with anger, and would like to give Ana a good kicking here and now. She tries to calm down. Ana admits that yes, the *signora* from yesterday stood talking to them for a good while, such a nice woman, amusing, a young forty, ankle boots, very fashionable, she would love a pair herself, so considerate, she saw that *signora* Malvina was a little tired and gave her her arm to lean on, she wanted to go up with her in the lift and right to the door of the apartment…

And you let her! Gabriela accuses, pointing a finger.

She was a friend, they knew each other, says Ana, who is beginning to understand, her eyes shining with tears. She turns to Malvina who has been standing there listening, bewildered, and senses, in a confused way, that she has been found guilty of something.

They exchange looks, the old woman and Gabriela. Their looks say: there are only two of us doing any thinking here. And the old woman is suddenly very tired, her legs won't support her, she has to sit down. She is eager to get away, but how can she leave Malvina alone in that house, with the genius from Moldova?

Something must be done. Quickly.

Go to the police? Malvina sitting for hours in a waiting room, ever more lost and unhappy. With her backache and her anxiety. And for what? She can imagine it, the uniformed man sitting at his computer, his expression as her friend stutters and hesitates. But why isn't this person in an old people's home? *Signora*, she opened her door to a stranger. One more to add to the dreary statistics of thefts and scams on the elderly.

Prospects of recovering the stolen goods: nil.

And if Ana was... Gabriela insinuates.

No, I don't want to hear anything of that sort, the old woman commands. Ana is an idiot, but if she wanted to steal from her employer why would she have waited so long? She could have done so herself, at any time, without getting in accomplices who give every sign of being veterans in the business.

The Moldovan genius is not a thief, she's sure. It is an instinct, inside her, that rarely makes mistakes.

Malvina on the other hand has always been a bit too decent and credulous, her family brought her up that way. Gentle, meek Malvina, who let herself be fleeced by brother and sister, why not by a so-called inspector-general of the Gas Company and his partner, the opportunist who latched on to the chance to impersonate Germana-the-Squawker (not that it took much)? Once a fool, always a fool.

Dear Malvina. Her heart contracts, her breath falters, to hell with Malvina, she finds she is crying.

And laughing at her at the same time. What's fifteen hundred euros, a couple of rings and watches, forget it! At our age! Have a good laugh at yourself and don't think about it anymore, she told her this evening on the telephone.

And then: Are you all right? Do you think you'll sleep? Do you want to come and sleep here? Have you locked your door properly?

Thank you, thank you, Malvina whispers, I've put the chain on, I'm staying here. But do you really think Germana…

It wasn't Germana, how can I get it across to you? Germana is dead!

There follows a long silence, possibly an offended one. After which: Good night, then.

A small and undignified drama. Germana. That inspector, such a fine-looking man. Each of us sees only her own silly dreams.

But Ana, and here Gabriela is right, cannot get out of it so easily. A carer is someone who cares for another person, and Ana doesn't know how to care for anyone, not even herself. At thirty-five, she has been through everything, borders illegally crossed, night marches through the forests, abortions, encounters on the internet with strangers who could have hacked her to pieces, living a life off grid, popping up here, and what good has it done her? None, daft as a brush.

With the fantasy swirling in her head of Prince Charming, of the Italian family. Let me in by the tradesman's entrance, please! Ana is a woman for arranged marriages, and seeing that she doesn't have a family to arrange one for her, she tries to arrange it for herself. She turns herself into a piece of merchandise, sells herself in exchange for a bit of normality, to be like other people, never mind what the other people are like.

Ana, she tells her, undressing and lying on the bed which will not see her get any sleep, not tonight, Ana, I can't entrust Malvina to your safe-keeping any more. She is the last person I have left, without her I am only an old woman who no longer has any past or any name, in the hands of people like you. Malvina needs someone who will keep an eye on her, give her her medicines at the right time, take her out every day, someone who does the thinking for her, and even loves her a little. She needs a mother, do you understand that or not? You who want to have little children, babies with an Italian father who will legitimise you in the world, you are not capable of caring for an elderly child, more defenceless than any infant, my Malvina. How can you think of looking after a child if you're not a mother?

Indeed, so far you have aborted them all. No, Gabriela is right, Ana cannot stay. I need to find someone else.

But the old woman cannot manage it alone, she can't even count on the support of Malvina herself, who would resist any change and say, as she has consistently said up to now: what are you trying to do, it might as well be her as anyone else, what difference does it make? They're all like that. You have to put up with it.

The old woman turns over in bed, kicks out her legs. She is sick of putting up with things. Where has putting up with things got us? Or to express it better: Where has it got us, this fear of change, of giving life a good shake-up? Nowhere, Malvina. You see, here we are, two old hags waiting to die. Why don't we do what we want? Why, when any desire timidly surfaces, does it always get choked off by a thousand fears?

She, the old woman, decades before, when she met her love, was ready to give the whole thing up after a week. So as not to leave the well-marked path, not to feel different, not trusting in fate. It's not going to be a normal thing to do, to fall in love so completely, to feel such an overwhelming desire for someone, a woman what's more, it's frightening, the ground disappears from under your feet, what will happen now? Better to retreat to safe ground, to the world of conventionality and emotions kept in check. If it had not been for Nora, who was more courageous and bold, everything would have ended after a few days, and she would have remained what she was before, the woman who only half lived and wondered what the meaning was of all this anxious rushing around that we call life.

But Nora is not here anymore. In the end she betrayed her with that other, that most dreaded of rivals, the one that always wins.

Would it have been better to have given up then and there, all those years ago, rather than go through the suffering and the emptiness of the last few years?

The old woman tries to imagine her life without Nora. In the flat she used to live in when she was thirty, in another part of town, in a single bed, with no cat. As if he has sensed the thought that expunges him from the record, Venom moans in his sleep, a long shiver passes through his body, he wakes up.

The old woman puts out an arm, draws him towards her, consoles him. Venom, a human-friendly cat if ever there was one, who needs only to be touched to be happy, promptly begins to emit loud purrs.

No, she can't imagine a life without Nora. She would have died from emptiness, from boredom, even while continuing to breathe. To be the first to go, that is what should have happened.

Now, in this bed, with the cat breathing its loving and noxious breath in her face, it should be Nora. She, quick to work things out and make decisions, unafraid to face the consequences, she would know what to do. Probably Nora would consider Gabriela's idea, get rid of Ana and share the apartment with Malvina...

The night is long, and just as lengthy her thoughts.

There comes the point when she cannot stand night-time any more. The cat, who has had enough — he may be human-friendly but he is still just a cat — moves to the armchair while she thrashes about and battles insomnia with her legs, her arms, with every part of her overheated body which feels too heavy and is afflicted by sharp rheumatic pains, a battle destined for perennial and ever more definitive defeat on the desolate field that is her bed in the depths of night, when merciful dawn is still far away.

And then finally, after a brief and deep sleep, it is morning, and the first thing the old woman sets herself to, before even having her coffee, is a telephone call.

With a mixture of annoyance and contempt for herself she is conscious of how her voice is forcing itself to sound reasonable and firm, the voice of a person still in command of her mental faculties, but also suitably respectful in order to ingratiate herself with the adversary. Osvaldo, the nephew, must hear what has happened, and take the sensible steps (her sensible steps, the old woman's). She explains to him that Ana must be dismissed, she is an overgrown child, Malvina is not safe with her, she needs an energetic woman, responsible and above all endowed with common sense. To convince him she uses all the powers of persuasion she has left, all the patience and tolerance that old age allows, because the hand that signs the cheques is the hand that rules Malvina's destiny.

The old woman sits beside the radio, the newspaper on her lap. She is waiting for the latest instalment of the day's crimes. No sense in denying the immense potential for entertainment that common crimes have.

Even if it's a case of just the usual. The usual collection of husbands and boyfriends who kill their women which has wearied her by this time. She follows them distractedly with one ear, and only in cases that have unusual details or which are unusually macabre, like the woman who was put in a rubbish bag while she was still breathing and was nearly gathered up in the wheelie bin and tipped straight on to the municipal rubbish dump. Shudder! So she managed to escape, then? Huh. It hardly needs saying the public prefers death, a clearly defined thing, final. And anyway, what is the point of a homicide victim who comes back to life? What has that got to tell us, that we shouldn't be scared of things anymore? Perhaps life is improved by having already died once? We all suspect it is not improved, it can only be made worse, leave scars, probably leave us with a permanent disability, nightmares, and our neighbours no less bastards, taxes no less unfair and diseases no less infectious just because we have returned to life again. No, give us a tragedy that really is a tragedy, we are conservative in these matters: in the end they all die, and that is a consolation to us, even from our uncomfortable seats in the ranks of spectators.

Crime is the art form of the brutish. People who cannot sing, paint, write poetry, they can always kill. It is the only truly democratic way to transcend the limits, feel oneself empowered, stand out from the herd, make daring experiments. For a few instants. But even in this form of popular and primitive art, true artists are rare.

And the victims? Little girls, they always interest everyone. But for the duration of a gust of wind. Adolescence is short, even more so innocence (a word which from time to time enjoys modest though unfounded revivals), short, too, the attention span of the listening ear. How many virgins of similarly young age has the world lost on the streets, from Minos to today, from Iphigenia to the schoolgirl disappearing on the way home from school, there is in the very idea of young virgins something sacrificial, like the sulphur on the head of a wax match, except that though wax matches are not made any more, young virgins continue to be born and also to die.

Then there are the mothers who kill their children, which makes much more news than when it's fathers. Apparently fathers butcher their offspring for two reasons: 1) to spite the woman who brought them into the world (and yet in our somewhat musty arsenal of myths and legends there is a Medea but no *Medeo*); 2) to adorn their tombs with suicides, in the way that barbarian kings used to cram them with slaves, horses and funeral goods. The king dies, so along with him die his most treasured possessions, it is a humanitarian impulse that drives this, if they were to survive him they might fall into the hands of another ruler, less magnanimous than him. And perhaps because it is rooted in ancient traditions, this sort of crime scandalises people less, it touches ancestral chords in the depths of our not very civilised breasts.

But mothers, the old woman thinks, why do mothers kill, if not out of self-hatred, exterminating themselves in their children? It has to be admitted however that beyond the tragic follies there are those given to the sudden whims of depression, the ones who, having brought another being into the world, are not satisfied, like housewives who have bought a defective product, and not being able to give it back or exchange it for another one adopt extreme measures, often more simple and within hand's reach, which do not involve the troublesome process of making personal changes. Some of these have been seen in recent years, these little women — quite different from the flame-eyed virago, the all-devouring mother — who are in fact the true and proper starlets of infanticide. They too are merely wearisome to her now.

As for crimes between neighbours, they are the miserable offspring of the union of Italian comedies from the fifties and sixties and B-movie horror films, two genres which have never attracted her interest. The old woman reads about them with one eye only, she prefers the weather forecasts.

It is rare that a good story crops up, worthy of the pen of a Balzac, a Dickens or a Highsmith. The last was that of the woman a few years ago, a teacher. A middle-aged virgin, homely and credulous, and a cheapskate Lucifer ready to seduce her, strip her of her savings and throw her down a well way out in the countryside. And all those fine characters around her, families, associates, the provincial authorities, fertile ground for anachronistic passions; and boasting, manipulation, fraud and naivety; and above all there were the eternal elements of our wonder: Eros who sets the breast trembling as the wind shakes the mountain oaks, evil which surges from the gushing wellspring of the human soul, the stupidity of the victim and of the murderer, no less authentic for having been recited millions of times with minimal variations.

She has ceased to feel guilty for indulging in the cheap poetry of the crime reports. What do these killings amount to after all compared to the other chronicling — that of numbers, for example: today 84 victims in Nigeria, 47 in Syria, 18 in Istanbul, 33 in Afghanistan, 39 in the Mediterranean, not to mention those who die without even being counted or recorded — which is the background noise of every day? Small stuff, the DIY of death.

The old woman dozes off. It happens, especially when she has had a bad night.

In her armchair, while Gabriela moves silently from one room to the other, the old woman sleeps and dreams of killing Ana and Malvina's nephew, Osvaldo. Or rather, she is trying to kill them, to liberate Malvina from their poisonous presence, but it is more difficult than expected. She sets on them with her fists, with her octogenarian's arms, arthritic hands, insults them, uttering Samurai war-cries which come out as feeble whispers. She is furious. But they smile, unperturbed.

Even in dreams, human desire is subject to severe limitations.

Malvina, I've told you, it's a perfectly sensible idea. You move in with me, I'll arrange the corner room for you, there's the folding divan, you've slept on it loads of times when you came to stay with us, we'll put on a new mattress that's right for your back. We'll even put in a bedside table, it's easily done.

Malvina's face comes to life with a feeble glow, a lamp that flickers before going out.

At our age we don't need so much space, don't you find? I persist.

She nods her head. And where does Ana sleep? she asks.

Ana is going away, no more Ana, *finis*! We don't need her any more.

But then, what if in the night... Malvina sighs and breaks off. Perhaps she doesn't want to tell me, perhaps she has forgotten in the meantime what she wanted to say.

What if in the night she has a leak? If she wakes up and doesn't know where she is, if she gets out of bed and falls? If she takes it into her head to leave the house at four in the morning, in her slippers, as it seems she tried to do last week, and would have succeeded if a kind neighbour, a night owl, had not brought her home?

But Ana doesn't sleep at your place every night.

Not every night... Malvina repeats, whose responses are becoming with increasing frequency echoes of others' words, speech balloons that escape and float in a dreamy sky, her unfocused gaze following them with confused wonder.

We remain in silence, sitting on the bench. Living is becoming ridiculous, but dying is not possible.

Malvina has begun to stare at a man sitting on the bench opposite, a forty-year-old with a beard and a pipe, who is reading the paper. That man there, she whispers, isn't that man there the professor...?

No, we don't know that man there, I tell her, but I am not really sure because I have left my distance glasses at home and I can't see more than three metres. In any case, our acquaintances are 99 per cent dead or no longer able to get about. And meanwhile I am thinking that maybe I can transform Nora's studio into another bedroom, so that a carer can sleep in, but the idea daunts me. Where will I put Nora's things? The dust, the noise, strangers in the house moving the furniture about...

What's the matter? Aren't you well? Malvina asks. I wouldn't mind a *cannoli*, how about you?

Arm in arm we go towards the Sicilian *pasticceria* on the corner. I don't have anything because my stomach is clamped in a vice. While I clean the crumbs from her chin with the paper napkin, Malvina implores me: But don't tell Ana, because then she'll shout at me for eating between meals.

Look, you've spilt ricotta on your coat, you're a disaster! The mark is still there, can you see it?

The waiter turns to look at us and I realise I must keep my voice down, not let myself fly into a rage. I'd like to slap Malvina. Ruining her coat like that!

And instead I take her hand and brush away the coating of sugar from her fingers. Malvina's hands are smooth as a young girl's, but colder, softer, too soft. As if they have squeezed nothing and no one for too long.

But how solid she still is, I think, arranging her collar and scarf before we go. What a lot of life there still is in her, her ample shoulders, her plump arms. How long since you last embraced anyone, Malvina?

I at least have Venom? But she?

While we are going home I decide I will ask Gabriela if she can stop over and sleep in our apartment once Malvina has moved in. Even if the idea of such a young girl spending all her time in the company of two elderly women — her breath mingling with ours in the nocturnal air of the flat — is not only absurd, but also a bit repulsive.

Perhaps she knows someone else willing to do it.

What is an embrace?

Not the formal ones, the quick pressing of forearms, the brushing of cheeks that you have no desire to kiss, accompanied by a clashing of spectacle frames. No, a real embrace, between two people who love each other, which lasts long enough to feel a person's heat, the scent of their hair. To imprint her shape on your arms.

There are lesser embraces, though not less intense, hands for example when we take another hand in ours, or a shoulder, or a foot.

There was a time when the old woman used to massage Nora's feet every day, her own sense of touch a thing she could see and feel, travelling from the arch of the foot or from the fleshy softness at the base of the fingers up to the nape of Nora's neck, a slow bittersweet shudder that passed right through her, so that she could almost sense the response in her vertebrae as they subsided towards sleep, Nora would emit little groans of pleasurable pain, abandon herself to the pleasure, fall asleep without knowing it and she, conscientious musician, would continue to massage pianissimo, until the almost imperceptible final note.

And when she desires her even more, when she reflects

more closely and deeply on what she has lost and will never have again, it is always an embrace that she thinks of. Of Nora in her arms, the solid and warm mass of her body gathered to her in a single gesture, and her arms like walls, like the banks of a river, like land when it welcomes in the sea. The half-closed eyes, the soft and hazy vision of skin and hair, the warm fragrance that rises from her neck, the dull beating of a heart which could be yours or hers, you can't tell which, it could belong to both. An embrace like a world complete in itself, an instant of absolute victory over all separation.

An instant. Anything more is not possible, for a human being.

Perhaps for animals it is different.

Venom is a great embracer. When they are both reclining in the armchair, he inches his head up under the old woman's chin, his front paws spread out and stretching up to her shoulders, and he will lie like this for a long quarter of an hour. Glued to her, immobile, apart from the snoring that bubbles up from inside him like water gently simmering in a saucepan forgotten on the stove.

In that position she finds it difficult to read, cannot concentrate and does not dare move her arm to turn the page. So she lets the book drop and at times the purrs send her to sleep.

Now Venom is old, as old as she is, or even more so. He who was still young only a few years ago.

II

Love in the time of Isis

When she cannot get to sleep from anxiety, or is afraid and doesn't even know what she is afraid of, Gabriela watches videos on her mobile, preferably of cats. There are so many of them, each cuter than the last. Tonight she is very tired, she can feel sleep pressing on her hunched little shoulders but every muscle in her body is tense, she ought to take long slow breaths and concentrate on every muscle one at a time, feel it become heavy as if it wanted to sink into the mattress, that's what the soft-exercise lessons that she watches every so often say, but it doesn't work. Sleep bears down on her but her thoughts will not let it in, her thoughts are phantasms that frolic at the tops of castle towers, pale girls with bruised arms and dilated pupils, dishevelled curtains of hair, mouths distorted by soundless screams.

A few hours ago she received some photos on WhatsApp, she walked in circles round the phone wringing her hands, she decided to delete them without looking at them but her fingers did not obey her, the photos seemed to open by themselves. In the first there was a man with a gun pointed at another man, tied up. In the second, something was going up in flames, she scrolled past that one very fast, but the third was a corpse thrown on a green blanket with big black stains, a woman's body, a body without legs, its arms cut off, four stumps on a green blanket, on big black stains. Above a white neck into which a blade had sliced a large bleeding mouth a semi-detached head could be glimpsed.

She cried out, she covered her face, the phone fell to the floor.

Backing away, arms held out behind her, the wall, another cry. A noise, was it the door opening? Or just her heart hammering against her ribs, a bird gone mad in its cage?

Spine pressed against the wall, cheeks running with tears, she screamed without hearing herself, stopped screaming, became aware she had bitten her tongue. Taste of blood. Terror rose like water around her, soon it would be up to her lips, her eyes, it would choke her and blind her. She was saved by the calendar hanging in the kitchen, showing a rose bush in autumn gently swaying its brown leaves and plump red hips under the lacy covering of the first snow. It is last year's calendar, the *signora* was throwing it out, she asked if she could have it and she got it, it is too beautiful to throw away, and what does it matter anyway if it is last year's? Roses are always roses, snow is snow every year. She reaches for the rose bush's branches, pricks her fingers on them, feels the snow caressing her eyelids. It is the page for November, her favourite, which allows her to calm her breathing, remove her hands from the wall, advance cautiously towards the phone, which has not broken, as luck would have it.

She stabs at the keys, fingers convulsed, forcing herself so hard to picture the red hips that she cannot see anything else.

She disconnects the WhatsApp chat, keeping her eyelids half lowered, her teeth clenched, holding her breath.

She does not ask herself where he has found those 'things'. She knows that Dorin spends his time disinterring corpses on the internet. He collects hangings, executions by firing squad, victims of explosions and torture, images of men with their faces hidden under black balaclavas killing other men or women, showing off severed heads and other souvenirs. He is mad. He is sick in the head and no one takes any notice, no one except her.

The time she complained to Petra, her half-sister started to laugh. They're only photos, she told her. And you get in a panic! You're always acting the self-contained, independent woman and you start shrieking over a photo!

He's mad! He's not right in the head! He wants to go to Syria! But he doesn't even know where Syria is! Don't you hear the things he says?

To you, he says them. He only does it to impress you, Petra replied, turning the sausages over in the pan.

And then: All men are mad, I don't listen to them any more, and here Petra jumped back, swore and put a hand to her face, where spitting oil had nearly caught her in the eye. Fuck off, you and your stories, she concluded, turning down the gas.

It was her, undoubtedly, who gave Dorin her number. Or one of the girls.

She needs her mobile, so she is compelled to pick it up again, even though it feels to her she is handling one of those bombs full of nails and bolts. It's not enough to turn off the chat line, she needs to block it.

Tomorrow she'll change phone cards. Again.

She has switched on all the lights in the apartment, a quick job because there are only two rooms. She has checked the lock, pushed the bolt across, closed and latched the shutters. She has looked everywhere, under the bed and in the cupboards. Diligent and sensible as always, she has put the half-eaten meal back in the fridge.

She has made herself a camomile tea. She has washed the floor and vigorously rubbed down the bathroom tiles. Thinking of the autumnal rose bush and the red rosehips that the early snow is bringing to ripeness. Turning round every few seconds to look behind her, to decipher imaginary noises.

Now she is looking at cat videos on YouTube. Cats doing acrobatic jumps, sleeping in funny attitudes, breaking crockery, dancing on their owners' heads, licking their paws or doing the bidet thing and cleaning their bottoms. She knows them all from memory, they are one of her standard medicines, she would like to bury her fingers in their fur, look at them for hours, messengers from another world, more beautiful, non-human. If she runs out of cats before she has fallen asleep, she will move on to dogs, beginning with her favourite video, the one with the litter of basset hounds. If by chance between one cat and the next the thing on the green blanket flashes into her mind, she grasps at the branches of the rose bush. She has become very good at this type of operation, for a few moments she can smell the scent of damp autumn earth under the early snow.

But sleep does not come. In fact she is afraid even to let herself fall asleep, what might happen to her while she is lying defenceless, stretched out in bed, offered up to the night? Sleep, primitive people knew this and people who are in danger know it, the persecuted, sleep is the moment of maximum weakness, the moment when murderers reach for their knives, shadowy figures slip from the darkness to set fire to your house. Armed police come to arrest you.

Tomorrow is her free day, she thinks with anguish. She will not be able to take refuge in the large and peaceful apartment and work to the uninterrupted murmuring of the radio, as soothing as the sound of running water. She sits up in bed, pulls the blankets round her, eyes peeled in the gloom of the night light. She hates with all her strength the enemy who is preventing her from feeling safe in her own home. But hating does no good, you need to focus. Think. Act. Escape. Or your heart will explode.

It is nearly one in the morning when she gets up, dresses, prepares her bag as if for a journey: a change of clothes, a blanket, cheese, biscuits, an apple. Before leaving the building she pauses at the door, closes her eyes, presses her lips tightly together, imagines being invisible, weightless. Already dead. If she is already dead no one will be able to harm her. She knows that outside the streets are deserted, the windows dark, there is nothing but the sound of the river and its cold and rotting smell, at most a rustle underneath the dry leaves, a mouse passing slowly by, stopping to look at her, like the last time. If she is lucky she will not meet anyone else.

Courage is born out of fear. The *signora* told her that during the war her mother had not wanted to go down into the shelter, in the *cantina* below the house. She would go outside, into the street. She was so afraid of dying that she preferred to meet death head on, look it in the face, in the open air.

She goes out, closing the door noiselessly behind her back.

A few days afterwards Gabriela announces she is prepared to sleep at the old woman's apartment. She will look after the two *signore* together, she can do that, they will be fine.

Her employer tries to dissuade her.

What about your relatives, your friends? Do you want to shut yourself away with two old women?

Oh, my friends! Gabriela says with contempt. They hardly count...

But she suddenly breaks off, her big eyes go bright. But I expect I'll be free to go out in the evenings, or at the weekends. I'd be very quiet, I never come home late, I don't like to...

The old woman tries to imagine Gabriela in a chattering group of girls who laugh loudly in the noisy bustle of a pizzeria and swap photos jabbing at their mobiles with pointy little fingernails painted in blues and greens. No, this is no place for her, she would be forever withdrawn behind her forced smile, simultaneously placid and anxious, her foreignness wrapped round her like the shabby raincoat of a character in old French films, or the deerskin coat of a Mongolian princess, a mute princess whose tongue was cut out at birth by the forces of the night...

The old woman is wandering, her thoughts scattered by long nights lying awake, while Gabriela — the child inside her playing at houses — toys with the details of her new vision and falls in love with them. The studio is so sweet! I would leave it as it is, we could just put in a small bed by the window. No, why repaint it? It's clean, it's pretty! I love that little Indian picture over the writing table!

In any case, the old woman says, if you have to get up in

the night because Malvina goes potty, you'll be too tired to work the next day. And I'll be too tired to do anything as well.

Gabriela's enthusiasm sadly subsides. She even realises that she loves her flat, she would miss the view of the muddy river, the ducks, the trees, even the rodents which after a while don't seem to be brown rats after all but rabbits, from their way of nibbling, their twitching whiskers, she would miss all of it. Except the nights spent alone and afraid.

United by an unsolvable dilemma, they lose themselves in improbable solutions over the kitchen table. Meanwhile the radio announces bad weather, a stormy spell that will bring prolonged rainfall and possibly floods in consequence. Another attack in a European city, the third since the start of the month, the fifth if minor episodes are also included, of the stabbings at bus-stops variety. Walls at the borders between European States to prevent refugees from getting through. A case of corruption involving politicians, the military, industrialists and the Camorra, the biggest this week, but not as big as the one last week. The presenter of the culture programme announces the latest book by a writer specialising in the mafia, the old woman retunes to classical music.

Then Gabriela suddenly stands up and without asking, goes behind the old woman's chair and massages her shoulders. The old woman closes her eyes and feels her little fingers through the barriers of clothing, of language, of age, which separate them, other walls and other borders, equally impassable but temporarily open.

In a brief rush of happiness, the old woman thinks that she could die now, better to die whilst still alive than already half dead. But she can't, of course. And not only because one cannot die to order, but also because she still has things to take care of, Malvina, Venom.

And this strange girl, who on the other hand might manage perfectly well without her too. Or maybe she won't manage at all, but at least she will never know.

One day Gabriela stops outside the window of one of those second-hand shops that call themselves modern antique shops and is instantly transformed into the Little Match Girl. Her hands clasped to her heart, she exhales an ardent sigh: Oh, look at the beautiful rocking chair! I'd like to buy it straightaway!

No, not for herself, she explains to the old woman, but for her grandmother. The one who lives in the simple house of dried clay, with its kitchen garden of corncobs and tomatoes, and the courtyard where she used to run barefoot in her perilous childhood. And the hens and baby chicks which in winter the grandmother brings into the house, in a large basket next to the stove, because outside the temperature drops to minus twenty. One day her grandmother will come here, once she has put aside enough money for the journey.

The old woman watches her, or rather her image in the window. Gabriela is looking at herself in the reflecting window pane of her dreams, there are two of her, or she is rediscovering her true double nature at last, she contemplates herself, she is pleased and talks with herself, tells herself her fables and they become true.

And what will your grandmother do here, in the city, without her tomatoes and her chicks? the old woman asks.

She'll live with her granddaughter! Gabriela will look for a bigger flat, with an extra bedroom and above all a little terrace where there's room for a few pots of basil, her grandmother would die without something green growing.

Look, this is her, she says, bringing up on her mobile a picture of an ancient woman bulging in her shapeless skirt, with a kerchief tied round her head and a toothless smile. She is wearing plimsolls stained with earth and soil and in another shot is laughing as she raises an apron full of fluffy yellow balls, the famous chicks. Here she is again with a dog of implausible thinness, a scrawny cat, a jar of plums in alcohol, a rag rug made by herself.

Yes, the girl adds, face darkening, it is true, on the telephone her grandmother always says: I am too old to change my life, leave me here. Poor grandmother, she is already sixty-five.

Half way through the afternoon the phone rings. For a few seconds the old woman listens to the silence, it is a male silence, she couldn't say why but it is, and it is not a call centre because there are no background noises to be heard, she is about to put the phone down when a man's voice, one she doesn't know, asks to speak to Gabriela Zlatec.

When the old woman hesitates it insists: Zlatec, she works there.

Gabriela never receives telephone calls. What disturbs the old woman is not the fact that someone thinks it all right to interrupt her employee during her working hours but that decisive voice, rough and inarticulate, a shoulder barging open her door without asking permission.

Who wants her? she asks.

Another silence. Then: Gabriela Zlatec. She works there. Less peremptory, less sure of itself, but with an undertow of menace.

Who are you?

Noises, a brief, agitated conversation, then a woman's voice takes over, a put-on voice, honeyed and business-like: Excuse me, *signora*, I'd like to speak to Gabriela... could you kindly put her on?

The woman doesn't say who she is either. The old woman is tempted to hang up. But what if it was something important for the girl? How do they speak, amongst themselves, in that wild world that Gabriela lives in, the world beyond this house?

Gabriela, the old woman calls, irritated. It's for you!

I'll take it in there, says the girl. What is that on her face? Alarm, surprise, resignation?

The old woman is putting the phone down when she thinks better of it. She brings it to her ear again and hears the female voice speaking rapidly, in tones of urgent entreaty, only interrupting herself every now and then to direct an angry shout at the male voice, which is rumbling in the distance. Gabriela responds with silence at first, then with a slow and measured coldness and finally with a long tirade of impassioned accusation, it is clear that the girl is resisting but will give in, that her refusal will be brushed aside by more powerful arguments, or by the arguments of the more powerful.

Slowly, the old woman takes the phone away from her ear and closes her eyes.

Half an hour later. The old woman raises her head from the book she is reading, or trying to read (even if her mind were not elsewhere, dark spots have recently been dancing around the words, now slow like confused insects circling over water, now whirling like dervishes), and stares at the shadow which has been hovering in the doorway for some minutes. It is Gabriela.

What is it? What do you want?

Nothing! The girl turns on her heels and rushes towards the washing machine which is churning angrily in the bathroom. In the silence that follows the end of the spinning cycle, the old woman thinks she hears a sob.

It is another of those dark and heavy days of false spring, the rivers are overflowing, the earthquake victims camped out in tents are being washed down into the valley by waves of muddy water, the flowers are rotting on trees which will produce no fruit, and she is still here, beside the radio, with the tablet on her knees, taking in the dismal news without reacting, like a dead sponge on an abandoned beach. Her joints are hurting, a cold, metallic pain, its assault quite impersonal, it will sweep her away as if she had never existed, and perhaps she never had.

The old woman drags herself to the bathroom door and looks at the girl, on her knees, her head against the round door of the washing machine.

Well? she asks.

It's such a damp day, do you want me to hang these things up outside or inside? Gabriela asks breathlessly, as if she has been for a long run. Her small reddened hands are rummaging in the steel belly of the machine to pull out entrails of twisted underwear.

The old woman does not speak, does not move.

With a nervous gesture the girl shakes her hair off her forehead. Then after filling the blue plastic bowl she turns bravely round to face her.

It was my half-sister Petra, she says.

And what did she want from you? The old woman feels herself authorised to ask, the girl's whole attitude is an urgent request to be heard.

Problems, Gabriela says. They are always having problems, those people.

And how do you come into it? Said a little too brusquely perhaps.

I don't, not at all! she says, springing to her feet, with that instant change of mood that leaves the old woman lost in wonder and admiration. I told them it's nothing to do with me. I told them to leave me in peace. I'll hang these things inside, it would be better.

The old woman observes her draping the clothes on the drying rack, her movements rapid and precise as usual. Gabriela, our little daily mystery.

Who is the man with that domineering voice? she asks.

That's Gogu, the husband of Petra, who is only my half-sister, the elder daughter of my father's first marriage, Gabriela says, in the tones of a knowing little gossip, and she launches into family relationships and genealogies which immediately bore the old woman.

But before she goes she asks for an advance. If it can be managed. If it's no trouble. Leaning in the doorway, with an air of indifference that is too perfect not to be simulated, red fleece zipped tight over jeans that are faded but spotlessly clean and not torn, white shoes with blue laces, woolly hat already pulled down over her forehead. An advance, I'd be really grateful. If you say no I'll die, but it doesn't matter.

Is this for your relatives? the old woman asks. Did they ask you for money?

Nooo! the girl says in horrified denial. It's for me!

How much do you need?

Three or four hundred euros. But only if you can…

The old woman goes into the bedroom and shuts the door, searches in the secret hiding place which is frequently changed — but in recent times less frequently because she is afraid she will forget — and takes out everything there is, five hundred euros. She puts them in the girl's hands without looking at her.

Gabriela grips the money in her strong and chapped little fingers, and passionately sighs: Thank you! I have never asked you before and I will never ask you again! Thank you!

In the night, the old woman wakes suddenly after a brief but heavy sleep. It is one of those awakenings which you know means that's it, you will not get back to sleep, you are conscious of the sadness of the room around you, and around the room the city, its frenzy concentrated into the yelling of a drunkard, and you imagine you can hear the waters rising in the bed of the Po, you feel your bones becoming more hollow and filling with stagnant chill by the minute.

She thinks of Gabriela. What kind of trouble has the girl got herself caught up in?

Why have the brother-in-law and sister called her here, in her home? Assuming they are really sister and brother-in-law. She should not have given them the number, that was taking liberties too far. Or was it someone else (Ana) who gave it to them? What do those people want from Gabriela? Could they even come here, knock at her door? Are those five hundred euros for them?

A host of scenarios springs to mind, but only as flashes, short clips abruptly terminated. Gabriela is running home, the frightened sound of her footsteps on the dark stairway, a male hand grabs her by the arm, a choked cry. Gabriela in fishnet stockings, her mouth a scarlet slash, prowling the Po embankment.

The old woman is not yet so muddled, nor so saturated by her own sour solitude as not to acknowledge that Gabriela owes her nothing, when it comes to sharing personal truths. Especially because she has never asked her anything, on the contrary: she made it clear that distance and reserve are the bases of their agreement.

I don't ask and you don't say. And vice-versa. But that is not a reason for lying! she nevertheless thinks, turning over again.

And then, meanly: considering I have given you money, I have the right to know.

But know what? Another round of confusion, of pain, of errors beyond remedy, suffering and stupidity inextricably interlinked, and nothing to be done, nothing except stand and look on... no, thank you. Gabriela is sticking to her story. She has helped her, she has done what she could, she can't go any further and doesn't want to.

She goes back to sleep for a time, time being ever more curved and relative. She wakes after a few hours or seconds.

She thinks about money. Now she hasn't a cent in the house, apart from some small change in her purse, and tomorrow is Saturday, the banks are shut. She has a bank card, but she's old-fashioned, not having a single banknote in her wallet makes her feel poor. How much is there in her account? Enough, she tells herself. But enough for what? For how many years? Will she run out first or will her money?

She needs a new pair of reading glasses, she can't see anything with those old ones. Can she really allow herself to go out to the restaurant every week with Malvina? Her friend is the one who minds about these expeditions, Malvina is a gourmet and a spendthrift, the old woman indulges her passions, tries to decipher long, abstruse and pretentious menus until she loses patience and ends up ordering the same things all the time, Malvina on the other hand wants to try everything, engages the waiters and chef in irritating conversations about the cooking, whether the vegetables are served as a *julienne* or a *brunoise*. And then she pushes the food around on her plate, and then they argue, why did you order it if you didn't want to eat it? What does it matter to you, I'm paying for it, if I don't feel like eating it I'll leave it!

She turns over in bed again and thinks about taxes, the condominium's service charges, boring things that cost money, she thinks about her bank account which is dwindling, and about her expenses, which are rising. She wonders if she has paid the urban solid-waste disposal bill that she received a while ago (how long?) and where she has put the receipt. She gets entangled in the hypothetical mathematics of survival, if I live for so-and-so many years and cost such-and-such a year, one carer, two carers, three carers, no good reassuring oneself, at the back of this torment lies a single reality: I no longer serve any useful purpose, I don't earn any more, my money — the only method we have created to measure our value, the value of anything at all — has accumulated in my pockets, or rather in the vaults of the bank, which we have to hope won't go bust, my money has reached its maximum level at some point and then begun to decrease, and it has been decreasing now for so many, too many years, slowly it is true but steadily, it is draining away without producing any fruits, like a little stream that continues to water an ever drier plant.

Was it a mistake not to set up a pension? But in her profession there are no pensions, should she have chosen something else, a totally different life?

As if people with pensions were safe! Nonsense.

She puts another pillow behind her head and curses herself for allowing her thoughts to wander in this direction. There are people in this world who are really in difficulties, who sleep on the streets, who patrol the rubbish bins to retrieve what others have thrown away. She thinks of the girl with two front teeth missing who is always there kneeling at the corner of the street with a card saying *I have two children we are hungry.* (How has she come to be there? How has she lost her teeth?) She gave her two euros and Gabriela showed her disapproval: If we give them money the only thing we're feeding is the whole racket, charity has to be directed. Directed how? Who tells you these things? The priest said so, in church. Oh yes? And I imagine it was god who told him that in person.

(Since when has the girl been going to church? What church?)

But the thought of the poor and wretched of this earth, as was to be expected, gives her no comfort at all, in fact it depresses her even more.

She is frightened: frightened of not being able to see any more, frightened that new glasses might cost too much, that she might lose her last remaining molar, the one kept in place by the bridgework, that the taxman might investigate that time, forty years ago, when she evaded payment on a small sum, that a cyclist might knock her down under the arcades and cause a fracture of the pelvis, as happened to Max, or of some other equally vital bone, frightened that thieves might get into the apartment and turn all the drawers upside down, throw her pictures on the floor and tear the pages out of her books, as she heard a customer at the shop describe, frightened that Gabriela is taking her for a ride and might rob her, that her work will be lost and forgotten (and it is, that's for sure, except that most days she doesn't think about it), that the soup will be cold, that the sheets smell. Frightened that the moment might soon be coming when she has to put a thick protective sheet underneath. She sniffs them, she thinks she can smell the odour of old woman, tomorrow she will change them.

Then she remembers the afternoon, and another fear looms at her, the fear of finding Gabriela's family on her doorstep. Could they be watching her? Perhaps the phone call is a trick, worked out between them. She thinks back to the horror stories which she has always wanted to disregard but has been unable to prevent herself from hearing, stories of ultra-faithful home helps who turn out to have black souls, plotters of robbery and theft.

The fears swirl round her, like hordes of mice, nibble at the hem of her pyjamas, soon they will get through to the flesh, and she is strapped to her bed of old age, solitude and impotence like a character out of Edgar Allan Poe.

Life has no value, she thinks, we are shadows who fret away their days surrounded by the virtual images of youth and success, we are slaves and we don't even know whose, we live in terror and nothing belongs to us, neither dreams nor money.

She remembers the rush of pleasure she experienced at one time when she began a new work, she loved earning money by pursuing her own profession, it was never all that much but it was the fair reward — fair or unfair, the point was it was hers — and the money was not dirty money, it was clean and crisp and smelled sweet because she had earned it herself, it was steeped in pleasurable effort and fragrant with satisfaction, it was like warm bread that smelled of the dreams of the proud baker, she thinks, without fear of seeming ridiculous because she is so very alone in her room, no one hears her thoughts and no one cares about them, and yet that money is not there any more, perhaps it has never existed, it was only an illusion.

And then she begs the night for mercy, begs it to help her free herself from the siege, enough of taxes the dentist, swindlers, murderers, enough of cruelty and violence, of fear and the death of hopes, enough, especially, of the fearful pity for her aged body. Wasn't life meant to be something different? The fresh thrill of mornings, the long journeys through the pages of a book, the light on summer afternoons, they have disappeared, and what has happened to that sudden lump in her throat, the hot joy that would take her by surprise, when she least expected it, for the simple fact of being alive?

But all that happened when there was Nora at her side, and both of them had good strong legs and steady arms, and their hands, clasped one in the other, vibrated with power...

And finally — whether night has heard her and answered her request, or it is the evoking of Nora — a bird sings outside the window in the half-light before morning. It sings once, twice, then after a brief pause tense with waiting, it sings again, at length, with joy and patience and concentration, to deliver from evil every creature who listens.

The old woman does not know what bird it is, some unknown airborne creature of the city which lives among the chimney pots and gutters, which pecks at the rubbish bins and has smog-grey plumage — but its trilling song is a masterpiece, it wells, bubbling, to a high point, falls away and rises again, complex and at the same time simple and absolute, it sweeps from the eyelids of insomniacs all sources of anguish and transforms into feather-light wings the leaden wings of the night. It calms her heart. Heart in the sense of muscle, swollen and enlarged and frayed, which dilates and contracts ever faster, ever more strongly in the desperate effort to break out of the restricting cage of the ribs, sending its big bell's booming straight to the brain, which will soon be driven mad.

But the morning bird is an enchanter of hearts, its modulated trills soothe their exhausted prisoners' rage. It escorts them gently towards sleep.

Here it is, yes, this is life, thinks the old woman with gratitude.

Her head falls back on the pillow, tears run slowly down her wrinkled cheeks, and continue to trickle from her eyes for a while even after she has fallen asleep.

For some time the rolling shutter of the shop beneath the apartment has been raised again, and a small supermarket has appeared, spick and span, well-organised, where for twenty years up until a few weeks ago there was the grocer's. Gabriela has expressed her satisfaction: That's nice, now we'll be able to do the shopping here, it will be much more convenient.

Gabriela is being more thoughtful than usual, if possible, more tireless.

In her eyes there is no trace of fault or remorse. If she has been lying to her, she has forgotten about it, or considers herself justified.

In the shop is the same man as before, a thin and nervous fifty-year-old. Alongside him, a young shop assistant, a clumsy beanpole of a girl, and from time to time a man in a jacket who sits in a kind of cubby hole at the computer. It is clear that the grocer is no longer the proprietor, but merely an employee of the chain of small supermarkets.

He ought to be pleased he's kept his job, remarks Gabriela.

Who in the meantime has taken up again the fantastical project of communal living. She has let slip perhaps involuntarily (but is there anything involuntary about this armour-plated and wary little animal?) that this way she would work more and also earn more. While the two *signore* would save money, because the costs would certainly not amount to two salaries.

The old woman makes no comment. Gabriela is chatty, she appears to be carefree. But the little creases on her forehead have deepened recently.

The ex-grocer, now a minimarket sales assistant, also has a deep furrow above his long nose. In slack moments he can often be seen outside the place, smoking, leaning against the wall. His sadness, the old woman reflects as she passes by, is not the fine sadness of the Moroccan beggar (who has lately absconded from his post, can he be in Morocco with his child bride?) but a living torment. That furrow is like a leper's sore, you can see it from the way his hands twitch with nerves when he rubs his face, rolls a cigarette, brings it to his lips and eventually grinds it out under his shoe, it is evident that he needs to pick at his unhappiness, like a boil, to squeeze out the blood.

The old woman, who briefly and a very long time ago experienced slave labour for herself, looks at him with commiseration. Out of solidarity, she decides to follow Gabriela's advice and do the shopping here. Gabriela stops in front of the oranges, all shiny and of exactly the same size, and says: That's nice, they cost less than before! Of course, says the man, giving her a look, because the ones before were real oranges, these ones here are plastic.

Plastic? The girl's eyes open wide. And she feels one, to make sure.

The old woman observes the shop assistant with interest. His expression does not change.

In the end they don't buy the oranges, but every time she passes that way and finds him smoking outside, the old woman says hallo. He responds with a nod.

And then everything suddenly takes a turn for the worse, as happens at an age in life when, although we might still be mentally in control, we have long since ceased to believe that fortune is soon going to come knocking at our door.

The person who comes knocking is only Ana, bringing gifts of calamity. Setting a bulging bag on the floor of the entrance hall, Ana announces that these are the *signora*'s belongings which are to go to the *signora*, they need to be cleared out, the *signore* said.

Signore who? Why, Osvaldo of course, Malvina's nephew, who came this morning to collect his aunt and take her away.

Take her where? Ana doesn't know, a place outside the city, she hasn't been told where. It will be a nice place, *signore* Osvaldo does things properly, the *signora* will have a bedroom with a view of the garden, there's physiotherapy available too. The *signore* came to talk to her, Ana, yesterday, he told her to prepare a suitcase, just one because a lot of her stuff won't be of any use once she's settled in, the people there think of everything.

The old woman totters, grips a chair for support.

Gabriela puts her hands to her mouth and gives a little oh, a stifled gasp of scandal and stupefaction.

Ana presses on, informing them that the *signore* is a real gentleman, he has given her a fortnight's paid notice and within a month or two her severance pay, she trusts him, he has always been punctual and correct, even if Ana actually says 'co-rect' (a pronunciation for which Gabriela heartily despises her) because in her native language double consonants don't exist. For sure, it is a shame to lose such a good position, she won't easily find a *signora* as good as *signora* Malvina, but what can you do, that's life.

The old woman stares at her hands, stares at the floor, turns her head away. She takes a breath.

Unexpectedly, she asks Ana if she would like a coffee.

With her accustomed quickness, Gabriela grasps that the extraordinary situation justifies exceptional measures, and promptly puts the coffee pot on the hob. Ana is almost moved, or maybe she is merely allowing herself to give vent to the bitterness of dismissed employees, her eyes go damp and dark streaks begin to appear on her cheeks. I'll miss the *signora*, she says, and the old woman interprets her as meaning I'll miss the wages, the comfortable bed, the compliancy of Malvina who always agrees to anything, but she is also just a little moved and offers her a tissue because Ana can't find hers in her handbag. Perhaps she was wrong to pass judgement on her, this fat and graceless woman is after all a better human being than some others, indeed probably better than herself.

The *signore*, Ana goes on, did not in fact tell her to bring these things to the *signora*, he told her to leave everything, he would deal with it himself, but she, Ana, said that certain things belonged to the *signora*, books she had lent, a cardigan, that blue blanket, remember? And he said all right take them back then if you really want to. Inside — she nods towards the bag — there's also a big yellow envelope that the *signora* (Malvina) has always told her 'If I die or they take me away, make sure you give it to the *signora* (the old woman)' and so that is what Ana is doing now.

Slowly, while the coffee clears a bitter yellowish passage of fire down her throat, the old woman realises that this ruination — the ruination of Malvina, of Ana, and in the end her own as well — is something she herself brought about, with her own hands. Or rather, with her telephone call to the monster Osvaldo.

But he can't! she cries, while inside she understands perfectly well that he can, he definitely can.

It's not for him to decide! What about me, who does he think I am? she cries, choking with rage. The impotent rage of the righteous overwhelms her, as in the dream where, for all her good intentions, she failed to kill Osvaldo.

And what did she say? What did Malvina say?

Nothing. The *signora* didn't speak. She was pleased her nephew was taking her on an outing. She put on her best coat, the grey one.

The old woman is conscious that women have always got everything wrong. That children are to be killed, suffocated at birth, the males first of all, without making them suffer, out of mercy — but straightaway. Malvina has never had children, but her sister has, this nephew has already put his mother away, could a mere aunt expect a better fate?

And there is no remedy now, because from where Malvina has gone — even if with a view of the garden and physiotherapy available — there is no coming back.

I ring Max. He is the only one of the old friends still living who is lucid. Or more or less. Certainly with what happened to him two years ago, before the fractured pelvis and then his savings disappearing in an instant when a bank collapsed, he is no longer the Max he once was, the man who would invite us to his studio for evenings of canapés, wine and beautiful people, who really annoyed me but I went all the same to please Nora — or was it she who came to please me? Anyway, it was amusing to talk about them, afterwards, especially when Nora mimicked all those artists, critics and *contessas*. Now Max lives with a niece in a provincial hole, in the middle of the mountains round Cuneo, without a car, not that a car would be any use anyway, he has never driven.

He tells me that the snow hasn't completely melted in the fields there, in Piangelato, but the country roads are under water from the thaw, that the air is horribly damp and the ground slippery and in consequence he doesn't go out, he is under house arrest. In spite of being vaccinated he has had flu three times, with a fever every time. The house is freezing, the niece a bit mean with the heating, she prefers to spend her banker's pension on little trips abroad, for example at this moment she's on a cruise.

I let him talk on, who knows when he last spoke to anyone, he is alone like an elderly parish priest, with a despotic housekeeper who comes every morning to rearrange all his things and fling the windows wide to let in the lethal mountain air.

Max, I say at a certain point, I have to tell you something important.

But while I am telling him I realise that this call isn't going to help me at all. Max is not in the least surprised at the disaster that has overtaken Malvina

Poor Malvina, he sighs. Poor girl.

Poor my foot! She was absolutely fine in her flat, she had everything she wanted, we saw each other every day, Ana may have been a cretin but she washed her and dressed her as she was meant to, I was wrong to take against Ana, if I could go back...

But she was losing her memory, I know, I've noticed it a few times in recent months, she was very absent-minded, poor child. And then there was that episode of the theft...

That's all right, a theft isn't the end of the world. And I'm losing my memory too.

But you're still capable of understanding, of making telephone calls, if you had to call the emergency medical services in the night for example...

There was Ana, I told you!

Did she sleep there all the time?

Not all the time, two or three nights a week, she asked for it that way, she wanted some free evenings.

There you are then, you see.

Max, can't we find another solution, take on another woman for the shifts that aren't covered by Ana...

Ah, but it costs. And you're never sure who it is you're introducing into your home. Believe me, it may be better this way. There's trained staff in those institutions, nurses, a doctor comes in every day...

To hell with the doctor, Max! I want Malvina!

But perhaps I have not said this aloud, because Max just carries on, a droning sound coming down the line, is that his voice these days, this worn-out drone? Is this the same man who on those evenings of long ago, in another age, used to circulate among his drawings and his canvases with smooth mastery? Who knows if anyone remembers him, if there is any eager student who would make the effort to get up there and interview him. I don't believe so. For every venerable and famous old artist there are a thousand, ten thousand, who outlive themselves, with pendulous lips and arthritis, nobodies again, and the telephone never rings. All artists should have the good sense to die young, like Keats and Byron. At the height of their fame and their love affairs. Or alternatively completely unknown, like Emily Dickinson, taking their dreams into the tomb with them intact. Poor Max.

Poor Max has a coughing fit, I can hear him unwrapping a sweet and putting it in his mouth, he is still talking about Malvina and how everything is for the best in the best of all possible worlds, in the state she is in, he says, you don't know where you are, it's enough that there's someone there to take care of you, keep you clean, feed you and see that you swallow your pills, and believe me they know how to do it better than Ana in these places, they're used to it, you may as well resign yourself to it, we all have to pass that way some day. It will happen to us too. My niece…

Fuck off, Max.

You're shocked, I understand.

No you don't understand. You're up there in Piangelato with your housekeeper, you don't understand anything any more, you're a living corpse.

And I hang up.

Naturally I rang him back afterwards to apologise. He forgave me.

Ana didn't keep proper accounts, says Gabriela unexpectedly. Perhaps I shouldn't tell you. But it's true. When Ana went shopping for *signora* Malvina she always bought something for herself as well.

The old woman looks up from her soup, she has no appetite today.

Perhaps Malvina said she could.

Yes, cigarettes, rolls for lunch, *signora* Malvina said she could buy those sort of things for herself, but she used to buy other things as well. A blouse once. Woollen socks to send home. Lipstick. I said to her one day, Why do you put your things on the *signora*'s bill? and she answered: Well, it's not as though she's going to miss it, she's got plenty. And she never checks the receipts.

The old woman swallows with difficulty. She puts her spoon down.

And you, she says slowly, how did you react to this claim? Gabriela looks at her, unsure whether to go on or retreat.

Nothing, what could I say? It was nothing to do with me.

And she puts the fruit on the table. Do you want me to peel you an orange? They're the nice ones, from Sicily.

No. The old woman gets to her feet, making the chair squeak on the floor.

Why didn't you say so before? Eh? To Ana, first of all. Why didn't you tell her she shouldn't? You kept quiet, you didn't even try.

Gabriela's eyes become huge, her eyelashes flutter like frightened birds in a snow storm. I tried to tell her, but she wouldn't listen, she stammers.

And why are you telling me now? If you didn't speak out before, you should hold your tongue now. It was nothing to do with you but it gave you pleasure to feel superior to Ana! Don't imagine you're being honest with this belated candour. You're just a tell-tale, that's what you are. A little tell-tale.

Gabriela begins to weep silently, biting her lips.

What do you suppose it matters to Malvina, the old woman says, no longer angry but weary. Socks. Lipstick. Do you think we don't know about it, all this? Do you think these are the things that matter?

And she is thinking of Ana who helps Malvina with her showers, works her fingers into the foaming shampoo'd hair, probably singing one of those dreadful songs she listens to non-stop through her ear-buds. She is kind, Malvina used to tell her. She is considerate.

In the doorway she turns round and stares at her, she feels pity for the girl, and pity seems an unjust burden, especially today. With a last spurt of wrath she points a finger at her: Too easy, wanting to look good when there's no longer any risk to yourself.

The old woman is a reader of romantic novels. She likes — used to like — romantic fiction where sex, desire, charm and sentiment come together to set you dreaming. Unfortunately, constant reading of them makes one become more demanding, one's expectations grow, and with them irritation with the predictable, the banal. Even romantic novels are boring sooner or later, they taste false, like cardboard, with nothing nutritious and nothing pleasurable in them.

Her tastes have become more sophisticated. She is becoming fed up, and not just with literary confections, which can still have their enjoyable side, like honest trollops. She is becoming fed up above all with beginnings. With first meetings, first kisses, first times. None of them achieves the heights of the unwritten novel which has as its protagonists Nora and herself — and of which, from time to time, with delicacy, in the long wakeful nights, she sketches out a chapter with the tips of her fingers.

It is too easy to talk of how love affairs begin. Always in the same manner: a happy madness, one's life a banquet, insatiable. It is like pressing a switch, one gets a predetermined response. *Click!* And The Sleeping Beauty falls in love with the first person she sees on waking. She was programmed to do exactly this. There are people who become dependent on the adrenaline of beginnings, and never go beyond this phase, their whole lives long, having affairs that are always different whereas in reality it's the same affair, with an unknown person who is always different and always the same because one will never get to know them.

But it is *after* this invariable beginning that everything happens. It is at this point, where the majority of romantic novels end — it is precisely at this point and only here — that love begins. If it begins.

When you come to the end of a book that has kept you company for so many nights, and set it down on the bedside table with a sigh, with a few of its pages dog-eared, a few coffee stains and probably its cover torn — you experience a little wave of sadness, a feeling of emptiness, you are saying farewell to a life and a world that have held you enthralled for a while in a happy adventure.

It is only then, however, when you reach the last chapter and read more slowly, rereading a sentence two or three times to delay the moment when you will have to close the book for good, it is only then that the process starts where that life, that world, truly enter us and begin their profound work.

Endings are more real than beginnings.

Perhaps that is the reason they are hardly ever mentioned.

The ending began three or four years after the rescue of Venom. It announced itself in the most banal of ways, in the guise of some mild indisposition, and as Nora had always been strong, and habitually shown an impatient disregard for the body's minor failings, she had no interest in responding to the signals. She, the old woman, watched her suspiciously, anxiously, she studied her secretly with slowly increasing concern as time went by, but Nora ruthlessly pursued her course of life, shaking her head, gasping a little.

Refusing to take the warnings seriously and to undergo the tests that the doctor, consulted just once, had recommended. As an entirely precautionary measure.

The old woman then had to learn another of the lessons of love, which was not the first, but which turned her in a blink into a complete novice again.

The lessons of love have no effect at all on life in practice, and are ignored by common sense. They bear no relation to the teachings of the philosophers, who have only ever taught how to make do without, where love is concerned, or how to contain it within tolerable limits, and thus, effectively, do without it. The mystics are very much committed to the study of love, but only the divine sort, not the mortal. Mortal love is different from divine love because, as is obvious, it operates in the realm of the finite and in human solitude, and without the insurance cover provided by faith.

How to love someone who is destined to die, that was the course of study. Difficult to learn, like starting to speak Chinese all of a sudden.

It is obvious that if we love, we always love someone who is destined to die. But it is one thing to know this in the abstract, another thing to see the shadow of death pass over the face of a loved one.

Of no practical help at all, the thing the old woman learned in the first lesson was respect for Nora's wishes, which in the end meant respect for Nora herself, even in things that seemed senseless and foolish. As well as cruel in her dealings with someone who loved her. She did not wish to undergo this or that test? She refused to make an appointment with this or that expert? The old woman suggested, pleaded, cajoled, flew into a rage, gave up insisting, kept quiet. There was a point beyond which she could not go without deeply offending Nora, forcing her, fracturing the trust between them. A point at which she had to make the great leap between understanding and knowing her, between speaking and staying silent.

And of course what the old woman felt were not certainties but only fears. Of which she felt ashamed. Which she exorcised, as if her suspicions amounted to a summons to evil, as if she were herself calling it up, invoking it. Remaining awake at night thinking. Perhaps Nora was right, her symptoms were nothing serious. Who could know better than she, after all? She mustn't show herself to be too upset, or worried, or suffering too much. She had to trust her. Because Nora was not stupid, nor naïve, she was a strong and confident woman. She was not a little girl to be guided by a firm hand, but a beloved mystery, the mystery of love.

The old woman could have created scenes, asserted herself. Resorted to blackmail: look, you're making me ill from worry.

Could she have done?

No.

In their most routine moments, at coffee time, love was a cut-throat razor lurking in ambush between the broom cupboard and the larder. Caressing her carotid artery with its blade even as she bent over the gas ring, her hair courting disaster in the flame, love stared her out with its assassin's eyes.

Love is not a piece of trade nor a commodity. Love is not

a life insurance policy.

No one has ever given you a guarantee that she would be with you for ever. No one gives you guarantees that she will see a new day every morning. Don't trust anyone who tells you otherwise.

There are no roads marked out. There are no roads, full stop. Even the one your hesitant feet are tracing now will disappear in a few seconds, if you turn round you will not see it.

The only truth is uncertainty, and the breath of death always on your collar. Life is not a path traversing a more or less easy or arduous stretch of terrain, it's a border. With every breath you take you are at its highest point, at the watershed, on the barbed wire. Where it exists is inside you. The border runs through you.

This is what love tells her.

Months later, when Nora acknowledged her illness, it was too late. It would have been too late even before, the consultant told her. And so she had been right all along, Nora. The old woman had tried to hurry time along, as was her wont, she had run towards the bomb before it fell, like her mother during the war.

But what if the consultant was mistaken? Or was lying out of pity?

Who really knows? Who can go back and take the other road, the one that was ignored when they stood at the crossroads?

So all the old woman could do now was torment herself for not having done what she failed to do and was not able to do, and to fantasise that if she had done it everything would have been different. These kinds of guilt are the worst. There is no redemption from the guilt of not having accomplished the impossible.

For not having loved still more, enough to have defeated even love, not having loved Nora beyond Nora herself, not having achieved the unachievable.

The old woman consequently began to play her game with death several years ago.

And being astute, and made of very tough material, she kept her head for a long time.

A crucial battle took place in a city they did not know, one windy day in spring. They had gone to consult a specialist — there is no point in dwelling on the purely tactical moves in this war, those to do with doctors and therapies, even though there is much to say on that subject as well, and it is certainly not a case of underestimating the weapons that are used against the enemy, which are in fact extremely important. But even more important than the weapons is the hand that wields them, and the mind that directs the hand. And so the best doctors had been consulted, the best medicines obtained — with the usual doubts over who and which ones really are the best, and the usual lack of answers.

Nora was tranquil, even cheerful perhaps, the doctor was a calm and expert man who approached his patients as thinking beings, and this was already in itself a form of treatment.

They were returning to their hotel, unhurriedly, with the prospect of dinner ahead in a small restaurant they had spotted earlier.

They were walking through a green and flower-filled park. The sky was overcast, a gleaming metallic grey. The wind was biting. It was the end of April, and the recklessness of the plants in putting out buds and thrusting up new leaves, here in the middle of a northern city, was palpable in the air and almost offensive.

The old woman, tired, and suffering a good deal lately however hard she tried to hide it — for months she had not spent a single night without plunging into the blackest of terrors — slowed down and turned to look in the face the Thing that terrified her in the dark.

And what did she see?

She saw the grey sky filled with threatening clouds, the green of the leaves. The spray of a fountain at the centre of the park.

She became aware she was surrounded by a vast space, immeasurable, a space which held all things, yet set them apart, putting between them the distance without which nothing would exist, nothing would be what it is. And this distance that set things apart was not empty space, the void, but a constant stirring of air, a breathing that circulated among all beings. Opposing this space all round her, was she, this woman, a parcel of life entirely closed in on itself, coiled, fists clenched, teeth clenched against her own terror. She took a long breath and that distance, that stir in the air, which was not the void but had the same lightness, entered her, entered her lungs, her thoughts.

The muscles of her back, tight and painful, relaxed a little. She felt she was making the acquaintance of her enemy, they were standing face to face, looking at one another, reaching out to touch one another. It was not as dreadful as it seemed in her blacker moments.

Death was an emptiness. The great nothingness. But that stir in the air, then? What was that stir in the air which united the breathing of the budding trees with that of the clouds and with her own?

The vision, if it can be called that, only lasted a very short time, as is the way with visions. For otherwise we would be unable to bear them, our brains are not robust enough.

She was left with questions as confusing as they were illuminating: was it possible to die while continuing to feel that stir in the air to the very end, and put your faith in it after all? Was it possible to die without betraying life?

She wanted to believe, flattering herself, that death had already sent her some *billets doux*.

Certain minor physical signs which had emerged lately (a heavy feeling in the heart, breathing difficulties, spells of nausea and dizziness) suddenly seemed like precious gifts the enemy was offering her.

If Nora dies, I shall die too, she thought.

And all at once she felt filled with a joy she had not experienced for a long time, she felt light and powerful, vital and wonderful like a line of verse newly written by an amateur poet. Tomorrow the line will be rewritten and quite likely deleted altogether, but now, today, it is perfect, and this is all that counts.

She returned the smile of Nora, who was watching her with a mischievous air from behind a flowering shrub. They stood silently looking at one another for a while, as if they had only just met again after a period of separation.

That night she slept well for the first time in months.

Since death first began to circle round Nora, the slumbering jealousy in the old woman woke up and roared. The torments of jealousy are nothing new to her, Nora is a sensual and desirable woman, one of those creatures it is impossible to think of keeping just for oneself. There have been other loves, in that now almost prehistoric past when Nora could dance all night and recite poetry that would split your heart in two like a peach and gobble it up.

Now those spurts of jealousy seem commonplace, harmless little tests like air raid practice in times of peace. She watches closely over her beloved's every gesture, tears herself apart whenever, briefly, Nora is distracted or prefers her own company. She feels a dull rancour, an angry incomprehension at the idea that Nora is giving in to her illness.

She seeks out the warning signs of betrayal not so much in Nora's insouciant, almost affectionate, attitude to her disease, as in her entire past. Nora's bursts of laughter and her sudden bouts of sadness, her rare but violent rages, her all-consuming way of reacting to injustices, her gluttony for life. If she had been more sparing of herself, more cautious and diffident. Less generous, less reckless, less ready to believe and to give, with everyone, even with her. Especially with her. Perhaps she would not be ill now.

She is even jealous of Nora's suffering, because she does not share it with her, she keeps it for herself and sometimes withdraws with it. What doors is she closing in her face, what is she keeping hidden from her? Where does she mean to go, without her?

And leave her here, in this world without meaning or beauty? When the journey is not yet done?

But that April day in the park of a strange city, beneath those clouds embossed on the sky, her trump card brings her relief. She begins to breathe again, free from jealousy.

It is not a victory, in reality. It is only a pact, attached to the hope that the Rival will show itself sufficiently honest to respect its word. But did it really do that, give its word? Or is the old woman deluding herself?

In any case, it is a complete alteration of perspective, affecting not so much the dark lady as her way of seeing her. If death wishes to take Nora, it will take me as well, the old woman thinks. We shall see. As with a lover, it is a game that three can play.

From that day passion returns to fill her mouth with its pungent savour, her limbs and joints are restored to a new agility, desire fills mundane moments with colours so intense they hurt her eyes.

And it is not just a chocolate-box romance — however sweet that may be: the heart that misses a beat when Nora appears on the threshold of the room next door, as if returning from America — it is more the bite of the famished person, reviving her whole organism and her thoughts as well.

Stroking Nora's hand, listening to her voice, sitting at table with her, everything surprises her and fills her to overflowing the way it did in the very first weeks, when love made her clairvoyant and revealed to her, without need for words, that she was in everything and everything was in her. And in the gaps, when she was waiting for her, her heart used to leap from instant to instant like an athlete suspended over the abyss.

But these are not the very first weeks. This is now, a time that includes present and past and future, and no clock has ever measured so complex and wonderful an entity.

We never stop being young, even when we are old, she thinks, fretting over minor things, conscious that her life is a fresco that death has restored, returning it to its original brilliance; more than that, to a splendour never known before.

The institution where Malvina is detained is situated on a small and remote hill on the outskirts of an abandoned village where there are no longer even any hens scratching in the dirt. There are cats, yes, thin and diseased-looking cats who wander about outside the institute's kitchen, from which drift smells of soup and cooking oil.

And she doesn't have her own room! The warden says there are none free at the moment, but even if one became free they would not transfer her. In the meantime Malvina's bed is a single mattress made up on a narrow iron bedstead and this is where she sleeps, alongside an old woman in such a sorry state that she no longer gets up, and indeed is lying there, with her face to the wall, her breath laboured and wheezing. All I can see of her is a broad and stolid back and a crocheted shawl which makes me feel depressed and helpless.

Malvina is on the veranda, which you reach by following a labyrinth of corridors, going up and down ramps ridged with bars cemented into the floor so that the inmates in wheelchairs won't hurtle to the bottom. The lifts only operate with a key, and the key is jealously guarded by the warders. In theory the patients can go everywhere, in practice nowhere.

When I make it to the veranda, I am exhausted and furious. It is rage that brings tears to my eyes, falling on Malvina and hugging her with a strength I did not know I possessed. It is her, my Malvina, looking surprised and confused. I kiss her on the cheeks, I grasp her hands and try to pull her to her feet. But she is heavy, I can't do it.

I've come to collect you, I tell her. Let's go away, now. Where's your coat?

I don't know, she says. I haven't got a coat.

Of course you have. That lovely grey one. I didn't come before because I had to find out where you were, and it wasn't easy, believe me. That genius Ana didn't know, he didn't tell her, or if he did tell her she's forgotten. I had to call the treacherous rat in person to find out. Your nephew Osvaldo. It was always his wife who answered, she must be even more of a rat than he is, she pretended she didn't know. I only succeeded in getting the address out of them yesterday.

Malvina is looking at me. I get the impression, probably correctly, that she doesn't understand a word of this. Then she puts a finger to my cheek: Why are you crying?

Because I'm agitated and pissed off. I'm crying with rage. I wish I had a gun licence, Malvina, and a revolver in this handbag, but I haven't got either. That's why I'm crying.

Have you had your tea?

Listen, please don't go off the point. Tell me where your coat is and get up out of that chair. We're going to sidle slowly towards the door and then we're getting out of here. I came by taxi, it's waiting for us outside the gates. They can't keep you here by force, do you understand?

Malvina sighs, fidgets in her chair. I don't know… she says.

What don't you know?

I don't know.

The rat, your nephew, doesn't have the right to keep you here. You can leave when you want, understand?

She nods, yes, and smiles at me. It is her, it is Malvina, my Malvina. My friend. The only thing I have left of myself, apart from this old body that has lost its strength.

Why did you sign all those proxy forms and powers of attorney? You've always been totally lacking in common sense. An infant anyone can twist round their little finger. A born victim.

Malvina smiles at me. Probably when I insult her she recognises me, she is on familiar ground.

You're coming to stay with me, we'll find some woman who can sleep in, I'm still capable of getting things organised, you know? Either Gabriela or someone else. I'll put an advertisement in the paper. We'll manage.

Malvina is no longer listening. A warder has appeared, pushing a trolley, she wheels it to the table in the middle of the veranda. Only now do I notice that there are half a dozen doddering elders around us, in various stages of physical and mental decay, and all of them, either on foot or in wheelchairs, are hauling themselves towards the table. The warder is doling out tea and biscuits.

Malvina turns towards the centre of attraction, stands up.

This is the perfect moment, I say. As soon as she goes out of the room and the others are eating, we're going. Never mind the coat. We can do without it.

And what does she say in reply?

Afternoon tea!

Stop it! I urge. You must come with me. Look at me! Look at me! Do you know who I am?

Malvina looks at me, her mouth is half open, her lip is quivering slightly. Is it my own defective vision, or are her eyes out of focus?

Do you know who I am?

Yes, she says, her face clearing for a fraction of a second. You're Nora.

Then, as if this act of recognition has drained her completely, she turns her back on me and makes her way towards the table where the old people are sipping tea from plastic beakers, dunking biscuits.

Since when has she been dragging her feet like that?

Her rounded back is as impassive as that of the woman in the other bed.

I suddenly feel so tired my desire to do anything evaporates, all I want to do is sleep.

She does not even realise when I go away without saying goodbye.

It is true that the old woman resembles Nora in some ways. After Nora went away for good, her lover devoured everything that remained of her, gobbled up from the dusty remains of physical objects and retrieved from the ether — things she found at the tips of her fingers, on her tongue, in her ears, in the glottis where words hide. She metabolised Nora, absorbing her into her own organism, and adopted strategies of mimicry to transform herself, outside and inside, into the thing she had lost.

Like the carelessly dressed Charles Bovary, who after the death of Emma took to wearing only patent leather boots and well-cut, elegant clothes out of love for his wife, so the old woman, who had always been demanding and correct in her manner of dress, has become more casual, wrapping herself in an old sweater that belonged to Nora, or even putting on her shoes, always a little down at heel.

She has bought some plants, to replace the ones Nora used to look after, which had perished in the drought of mourning. She has replanted the honeysuckle on the balcony, and pruned it every year, with mixed results. And the notebook where Nora jotted down recipes, when she remembered to, the old woman now leafs through, on the rare occasions when she feels like celebrating the rites of the kitchen.

She has even absorbed some of the patterns of speech of the woman who is no longer here. She uses certain words, certain phrases that have lodged in her head, and in saying them she seems to hear the voice of Nora speaking again from inside her, and this gives her a secret comfort, at times a piquant pleasure.

And indeed Nora comes into everything. It is impossible to live for several decades in a dialogue with someone, and then break off simply because that someone has gone away. So, if Nora is silent, it is up to the old woman to keep her part of the conversation going as well. If Nora was impulsive and generous while she was prudent and diffident, it is very much a function of that dialogue, as happens in music when different notes form harmonies or dissonances.

That part of Nora which has disappeared into the great nothingness, is inside her. And they are not disembodied memories, but memories made flesh, made concrete in the elderly body which, by remembering, has transformed itself, has rendered present what is absent in whatever way it could. It is not simply the memory of Nora, it is Nora in person who in certain instants gazes from the old woman's eyes over the glasses she pushes down to the end of her nose.

The same thing would have happened if she had been the one to die: Nora would have carried the old woman inside herself, in the form of gestures, intonations, characteristic phrases. She would have worn her clothes, used her perfume. Called up from inside herself her particular notes to let them ring, loud and clear, through the silence.

In either case the result would have been what it is now: a fusing of presence and absence, a metamorphosis.

On a small scale, of course. Invisible to most people. But Malvina, who knew both of them well, has seen it. You cannot lie to dementia, thinks the old woman. Or Nora does, inside her.

Petra is a spiky woman, with thin and lifeless hair which hangs in lank curtains round a worried face, narrow and slightly mad eyes, hands concealed in gloves or behind her back so as not to reveal the eczema marks. She works in a canteen and has her hands in water for several hours a day. When she opens the doors of the big dishwashers, in a hurry so as not to waste time, because Petra is made that way and has to demonstrate that she is the best worker even if to do so she has to kill herself, the steam turns her face red, the water spills over her exposed skin which then is dried off by the brutal heat of the ovens and hot-plates. She always carries about her person an assortment of cooking odours, fried foods, stews, ragouts and meatballs in tomato sauce. She has lost her appetite, everything disgusts her. She has lost weight recently, she has stomach pains, the doctor suspects an ulcer, she hasn't had tests because the state health service takes for ever and private costs too much.

Gabriela is sitting opposite her, hands on her thighs, bolt upright and away from the chair back, and is forcing herself to breathe calmly. Petra sprays anxiety all round her like a burst water main. Gabriela does not wish to be contaminated. She has refused to go to their house, better to see each other in a bar where there are strangers present, in a neutral location where she can get up and walk out at any point without fear of being held back by Gogu's shouting, or the little girl clinging to her, Carolina, the youngest of the nieces and her favourite. Until last year Carolina was her treasure, when she said 'my niece' her voice cracked with emotion on that 'my', and it is for Carolina that last Christmas when she got her bonus, she spent it all on presents, because she could not, out of decency, shower Christmas cheer on the little girl and no one else, except that everyone was expecting this prodigality of hers, it is a family tradition which it will be very hard to break. But Carolina has changed lately, she is becoming prissy and smug like her older sisters, the look in her eyes is no longer clear and limpid, her mischievousness no longer innocent, and it is clear that at home they prompt her: ask your aunt who loves you so much for this, ask her for that. Before long she too will start to treat her as if she were stupid, like all the others. But Gabriela is stepping back, closing the little door which only a very small creature could get through, and sometimes in the evenings when she is in bed, or on her long tram rides, especially when it is foggy or raining, she sheds a few tears for that other lost little girl, but not too much because deep down she knew already that Carolina would be lost and that she was not hers at all.

Petra drinks her cappuccino in little sips, she is pensive, distracted, has two frothy moustaches around her mouth. Gabriela feels slightly guilty at feeling such aversion for her; they are half-sisters, they are united by the one father, shouldn't they love each other, support each other? She thinks of the *signora* and her friend Malvina, it is only since Malvina has been in the old people's home that Gabriela has appreciated how much the *signora* loves her, she used not to show it the way she does now, but now she has no qualms, she wanders round the house with sadness written all over her face and when she goes to visit Malvina, she is crying, she tries not to show it, but her eyes are damp and shiny, and she gives her a hug which feels as though it will go on for ever.

For the first time in her life Gabriela is able to articulate clearly to herself that this woman sitting opposite her, her half-sister, is a person she has never liked. For years she has tried to love her, has suffered from her inability to feel that love, has blamed in turn herself and the other woman.

Petra has always considered her to be stupid. Gabriela was doing well at school and she was stupid, she didn't like dancing and she was stupid, she didn't have a boyfriend and she was stupid, she absorbed blows with that closed and inscrutable look of hers and she was stupid. Only when she wanted something from her did her half-sister lavish any scrap of affection on her. For some years she has stopped doing even that, delegating the task to her youngest. How she used to thrust her into her arms when she was a tiny girl! As if she were giving Gabriela an undeserved present, far beyond her own worth and for which she ought to be moved and grateful in a tangible manner, but it was not a gift, it was merely a loan, something hired, and to be paid for at a hefty price.

Am I really stupid? Is she right? Gabriela wonders, while her glance switches from her own hands, a little reddened but smooth and undamaged, to Petra's ravaged ones. Maybe the more stupid of the two of us is her, she thinks. And she experiences an odd sort of compassion mingled with contempt for the woman, whom she knows all too well and doesn't remotely understand, for her ulcer, for her eczema, for her oldest daughter, pregnant, who has left school to marry an unemployed Brazilian (a great wedding, naturally, with at least eighty guests, and the immediate cause of the family's latest financial emergency), for the little girls doomed to resemble her, and even for that fist-wielding husband of hers, Gogu.

Petra is twelve years older than she is, just thirty-eight, but when she is without her make-up and her hair is a mess — and at the moment she is both, it wasn't worth the bother of dolling herself up just to meet Gabriela — she looks more like fifty. Her first daughter, the one who died because the hospital got her treatment wrong, she had at eighteen, back in her own country, then in Italy another three arrived, all girls, her husband Gogu is furious that she is only able to produce females, unless the two or three that were aborted between births were males, impossible to know. Petra seems unaware that her life illustrates the strongest possible argument against marriage, and every time they meet she taunts her: how come she has never got engaged, she should be starting a family, what is she waiting for, time goes by for everyone, she'll soon be thirty.

Her half-sister knows that Dorin is after her, she has seen it, as Ana has seen it, being fancied by a man is the first thing those two women notice, the main thing they think about, perhaps the only thing. They are both convinced that his appalling style of courtship, which is more like a bombardment with surface-to-air missiles than a declaration of love, is something she secretly enjoys.

Petra, who was relieved when she decided to go off and live on her own (Gogu was beginning to show her too much attention), finds it unforgiveable that she chooses to keep her address secret. (Who do you think you are, a princess, trying to go around incognito? You even put on dark glasses! Do you think they're all running after you? That where you park your arse is holy ground?)

With her cappuccino finished, Petra remains staring thoughtfully into the cup, as if she wanted to read her future in the dregs, or probably the present would do just as well, seeing that even this is very confused.

Then she suddenly lifts her head and stares at her. Gabriela is momentarily startled, as she was when Petra first walked into the bar, by the sight of the discoloured and swollen right cheekbone and the split eyebrow. But this time Petra does not raise a hand to cover the eye, she couldn't give a shit about the black eye, in fact she is smiling, an ironic and proud smile, dismissing it.

Any news of your grandmother? she asks Gabriela. Is she still alive?

She's in hospital again, Gabriela says. I sent her a bit of

money to pay for medicines, otherwise they wouldn't give her anything.

A waste of money, says Petra, shrugging her shoulders. She'll just drink it all, never mind medicines. She's pretty much drunk in the mornings already.

Don't talk like that about my grandmother!

Petra mimics her: Oh don't talk like that about my dear little granny! And then: All right, she asks, when are you going to marry him, Dorin?

Never! Gabriela says.

The half-sister laughs. With the air of one who knows better. Then: Do you see him? Do you know where he is? Because he hasn't been back to the house for a while. He's disappeared. I thought he was with you.

I don't know anything about it and I don't want to know!

Petra is enjoying herself, or she wants to make her think so. Sooner or later you'll have to get married, she says lighting a cigarette.

Gabriela tries not to let her see she is shaking. Petra would be pleased to see her shackled to Dorin the terrorist. Certainly it would suit her to get rid of that step-son of sorts, who only brings trouble, pisses off the father and gives the teenage sister a smack because she walks around semi-naked. They want her to have the worst person in the house, take him away and shut up. Except that even if Dorin was the best person in the world she wouldn't marry him for one very good reason, she has no intention of getting herself any more related to her relatives than she already is.

I shall get married when I decide, Gabriela says. And in any case, not to Dorin!

Who to then, are we allowed to know?

To the man I live with, she says, facing her down.

The sister reacts as if she has received an electric shock, her head twitches, the ash drops off her cigarette, missing the ashtray. She stares at her with her mad eyes. Gabriela returns her look. She has scored a point, a little smile of triumph appears on her lips. Petra shrugs her shoulders, passes a scaly hand over her dry lips, and then says: So that's why you don't want anyone to see your love nest. How long has this been going on?

Three months, Gabriela fires back, fast.

Italian?

Of course! I wouldn't be seen dead with one of our people.

She would like to add: someone like Gogu. But that would be going too far.

Petra continues to stare at her with those probing eyes of hers. She considers. She is wondering whether or not she should believe her, what her game is. Who this new Gabriela sitting opposite is and how she should take her. She hasn't realised she still has a moustache of cappuccino froth, and Gabriela doesn't tell her.

Petra once told her that beatings are part of marriage, that she is not bothered by them and that afterwards he is more generous and more vigorous. Since then Gabriela has avoided the subject. The thought of a more vigorous Gogu brings on nausea. For a long time now she has known she is different from Petra, and maybe from the majority of women. It is a difference she can't talk about, no one would understand, she would be laughed at. They would tell her — they already have — that she doesn't know what she's missing. That she's a bigot, a little virgin, a hopeless case. That she's scared, old-fashioned, that she's too full of herself, that she's not normal. That she's no good, she's ridiculous. That she'll be all alone. Et cetera. The kinder ones would maintain that it is a matter of time, that sooner or later she will meet the man who is right for her. A woman friend, whom she met in the days when she used to attend more regularly the small Orthodox church in the historic city centre, reassured her: each of us has her or his ideal other half whom we are destined sooner or later to meet, in this life. True beauty, she added, is not that of the body but of the soul, and a worried Gabriela, coming out of church, looked at herself in the shop windows and detected a thousand different defects. The next time, the friend introduced her to a forty-year-old cousin of hers, with a misshapen body and bad breath.

Occasionally even Gabriela puts to herself, in vague terms, the 'matter of time' theory: sooner or later she will meet a kind and handsome man, who was waiting just for her. When she pictures him she sees him with the features of a photograph in the hallway of the *signora*'s apartment, one of the many reminders of the past: a magnificent man, tall and elegant, with a face that embodies her idea of 'aristocratic' and a smile which sometimes exemplifies the definition of 'spiritual' and sometimes appears instead more 'artistic'. At the bottom dashed off with a splendid flourish, even if illegible, is penned a dedication; over time, by dint of casting sidelong looks at it while she is doing the cleaning, Gabriela has succeeded in at least deciphering the signature: Max.

When Petra asks her what her boyfriend is called, she will already have the name on the tip of her tongue: he's called

Max and he's extremely handsome.

But Petra has decided not to admit defeat: I don't believe you. You're having me on. You're not engaged to anyone. Living with someone? You?

Gabriela shrugs her shoulders, who cares if you believe me or not, it's my life, she says, part of her thoughts pinned to the image of the handsome Max. He is a friend of the *signora*, she has heard them speaking on the phone, which means he is very old by now, but no matter, in fact perhaps it is even better. She is not interested in the real Max, but the one in the photograph.

Meanwhile her brain is rapidly reviewing the faces of the women she knows, Petra, her three daughters: Vasilica, pregnant by the Brazilian, Simona, who is thirteen and according to the terrorist Dorin walks around half naked, and Carolina, who already wants to wear eye make-up, at seven. Ana, who laughs loudly and talks of men as if they were things you eat. The friends of her own age, none of whom has ever been a 'true' friend, all married or engaged — except the one from the Orthodox church, which she has stopped going to, however, since the woman introduced her to the cousin.

And it seems to her that, as a unit, they are sending her a single great message, common to the entire female half of humanity, but one she is unable to decipher. (She can't or she won't? The difference they accuse her of, is it involuntary, like her light brown eyes and the mole on the neck, or is it a choice, a disability or a perverse intransigence?)

She stares at her sister's black eye, as if she could find the key to the mystery there. She knows what happens between a woman and a man, how could anyone not know? It can't be that

that's all there is. There must be something else. What is there behind Petra's half-closed and swollen eye? Are there obscure depths of pleasure and pain, ecstasy and shame, sensations so marvellous and powerful they make you forget sixteen hours of work, the shouting every day, the kitchen smells, the ulcer, the breath of drunks, the scabby hands? Perhaps at the centre of every woman there is a black hole, from which rises a heavy and musky odour like Petra's sweat, and every woman is drawn to it, to fall into that hole inside herself, continually, like Alice in the book the *signora* lent her, but at the bottom there are no rabbits with watches and other humorous characters — there is something horrible. She does not want to fall into that hole! She is afraid of what she might find there, for example the woman chopped in pieces like in that photo, with a smile of dreadful happiness imprinted on her face.

What is it? Petra asks. Have you been stung by a wasp?

Nothing, she says, bending to hide her face. My shoe's come loose.

While she undoes and re-ties the laces with her head down she thinks very rapidly: I am not like you, it's no good trying to make me feel all wrong, I've only got myself and I won't give myself up, I'm going now, I've stayed here too long already.

She takes out the two fifty euro notes she had ready in her pocket: Here. I can't manage any more, you've already cleared me out this month.

And listen, they're the last you're getting from me, she adds on impulse, standing up. I have to think of my future, now.

Without troubling to thank her, Petra takes the notes with a disappointed look (only a hundred for a wedding, how mean), pokes a hand under the tight black jumper and pushes them inside her bra.

The last time Gabriela reluctantly accepted an invitation to dinner at their house — she hardly ate a thing — she had the pair of them sitting opposite her across the table, Vasi and the Brazilian. They were all over each other, arms sliding over shoulders, hands cupping breasts, tongues stuck together, saliva, sweat, it was hot in the too-small kitchen, there were the smells of sausages and frying oil and pickles, kisses greasy with food, she could hardly keep herself from retching. Once she was home she undressed and washed everything she had been wearing, including her underclothes.

At table, Vasi caught her for a moment when her mask slipped and sent her a scornful smile with that bruised mouth, all red and chafed because he had not shaved and his chin and cheeks were as black as the boars that come down from the hillsides and frighten motorists, and it is for this, to reduce her mouth to this state, that her seventeen-year-old niece left school and the teachers telephoned her home to speak to the parents and Petra was furious because she had to ask for time off to go and explain to them that her daughter didn't want to continue her studies, she had neither the desire nor the motivation to think or make an effort now that she had latched on to the Brazilian, and it isn't just her mouth that has gone slack but everything, legs, belly, brain, you can see with the naked eye she has filled out and put on weight, pregnancy has made her explode like a ripe fig.

Gabriela feels sick.

She is well aware that Vasi believes she is jealous. Ana

once told her, laughing in her face: But you don't even know what a man is like. She told her that some old men she had worked for were constantly putting their hands everywhere, worse than octopuses, and the things they thought fit to say! But Ana is not scared of dirty old men, no, she couldn't care less, she laughs, and if need be she hands out hefty slaps, those old men, they no longer have the strength to do the things they've got in their heads.

Gabriela is confused, lost. She knows she is not like other women, but not what she is like, nor what she wants.

She wants happiness, like everyone. She thinks she has glimpsed it out of the corner of her eye, and at particular moments she feels it descend on her, as if happiness had bent down to embrace her — but then it vanishes again. Where? Not where other women seek it.

Happiness comes for stupid reasons, little things, for example when she has finished ironing a pile of blouses and runs her hand over them and feels them still warm, and in the room there's music in the background, and the scent of flowers from the balcony. When she secretly opens a book and hurriedly reads a sentence and without even understanding it clearly she is certain it is talking about her and the words have a resonance as if a voice in tune with her were whispering for her alone, but it only lasts for a second.

And it comes at night, on certain nights, while she is having a trivial dream, like going shopping, and suddenly this thing happens. A warm and glowing seed, like the kernel of some fruit, forms deep inside her, a fruit coming luminously to life in the pit of her stomach; and in those moments it is as if she can visualise her body from within, in that amber light, and it is perfect. The fruit grows inside her, becomes ever more powerful and soft and pulsating, an incandescent sun rising in the sky of her flesh, burning like a golden flame, rising and dilating in successive waves of colour and pleasure, climbing to its zenith then slowly going red and violet and returning to merge into the night, until it vanishes.

Sometimes, afterwards, she sleeps on and has strange and beautiful dreams. At other times she wakes up, languid and at peace like a beach after the orgy of sunset.

She smiles in the dark and is happy because sweetness of this sort seems to be the herald of a wonderful life awaiting her. Everything will be all right, she will be loved and protected, blouses will be ironed to perfection, books will be talking about her. Perhaps she will have a baby, a little girl. Even if she has not worked out how to manage it without leaving her job, without having her mouth bruised by the bristly kisses of a boar or her eyes blackened by fists, without having abortions, or living in squalor. But manage it she will. She will do it all by herself. She is certain of it. She has faith.

Then she goes back to sleep.

After the old woman spoke to her roughly, calling her a tell-tale — Gabriela gathered at once that it was a harsh word and had it confirmed on Google — she sulked for a day or two. On the third day she returned smiling and renewed, turned the whole apartment upside down in a fit of enthusiastic cleaning and bleaching, and convinced the old woman that it is madness to go to Malvina's by taxi. Such a big expense for a thing like that, impossible!

Especially since she, Gabriela, has a car of her own, which

she never uses, not having anywhere to go in it.

So a new routine has been established. Once a week the old woman climbs into Gabriela's little second-hand car and together they thread their way through the ever narrowing and twisting roads that lead to the hillside where the old people's home is located.

How beautiful! Gabriela sighed the first time, and sighs each time as she gets out of the car parked in front of a lilac bush covered in pastel green foliage and already showing the heads of the flowers to come.

Behind the cars of the visiting relatives the hillside slopes gently towards lines of hazelnut trees and woods, and then rises up the other side, higher and more exposed, where vines, still bare, cling to their supports. There is a smell of coming spring, of rain, of grass pushing its way through the grey winter earth.

It's beautiful, the old woman thinks, irritated. So what?

Malvina no longer sees any of this, and not just because she is immured within, but because, sitting by the window, she no longer turns her head to look out.

She has lost her memory and her sight is failing too, the profundities of time and space are mysteries that no longer interest her. Give her the choice of open hills teeming with life and the greyish walls of her room, and it would be all the same to her — in fact, she prefers the room. Like people walled up alive in the dark ages, Malvina lives shut away inside herself, in her terrified body, only calm on the surface.

The home, backing on to a small brick church, is a former rectory which has been restored and extended through the shrewd foresight of some religious institution or other. The old woman walks through the bright public spaces with a grimace and casts a hostile and contemptuous eye over the furnishings that go with them, which shamelessly declare their provenance in the cellars and outhouses of donors glad to get rid of them, not to mention the decorations of artificial flowers, faded posters and images of blue-cloaked Virgins in garishly painted frames.

When she spots Malvina, however, the old woman cannot escape the sudden collision of feelings. What does she see in the bland and absent face of her friend that stops her breath every time? She sees Malvina as she was, and as she is now, two different people locked in battle inside the same person. She sees her past, herself, and Nora too, because their stories were intertwined, and memory constantly plays new tricks on her, for a fraction of a second, like an electric shock, she is assailed by visions or sensations which flash by too fast to be identified, a long-ago discussion in the rain, a late-evening arrival in a city they didn't know, a birthday celebrated in a certain restaurant...

Malvina — whose mind has gone but not completely, some part of it remains, she can mimic her for example, the same phenomenon by which it is said that a new-born baby smiles at the mother who smiles at it — Malvina comes to life when she sees her, maybe she is anxious too, or maybe she is simply reflecting the anxiety and agitation of the old woman, the fact is she seems to come back to life.

But it is an illusion, and lasts only a few moments.

The old woman sits facing Malvina, looks at her closely, leans forward to rearrange her hair, talks to her. Malvina follows her movements with interest. The old woman is not deceived. Malvina's gaze focuses ever more insistently on the bag leaning at her friend's feet.

How are you? the old woman asks.

Sometimes Malvina makes an effort to understand what she is being asked and reply appropriately, but hardly ever succeeds. She gets lost on the way, in the middle of a word, and comes to a halt, disappointed, bewildered. Usually though she says, without differentiation, 'yes' or else 'no', they are two words she still remembers very well, although she can no longer distinguish one from the other and attributes to them the power, somewhat excessive in truth, of summarising the whole range of possible responses.

Are they treating you well? the old woman asks. Why have they made you wear that sweatshirt? Is it yours? I've never seen you wearing it. It can't be yours, it's too small for you, see? She tugs underneath the armpits, but the arms are too stiff even to move. Who cut your hair? An incompetent goose, that's obvious. What are you doing in a wheelchair again? I told them to make sure you kept walking! And this seat is too narrow for you, it's a rusty wreck, be careful, it'll break in a moment and you'll fall on the floor!

Malvina smiles absent-mindedly, leans towards the bag.

The old woman intercepts her gesture, takes her hand. And suddenly the earthworks crumble: Why? she shouts in a passionate whisper, bringing her head close to her ear, constrained by feelings of modesty and privacy in the presence of all these elderly people, who are entirely without modesty themselves. Why did you have to do this? Why so fast? A few weeks ago you were still chattering away. Do you remember you were talking about Germana? All right, you were a bit forgetful, you always have been, forgetful and absent-minded, even as a young woman. But you still remembered Germana, you knew who she was... how have you managed to get senile like this? It's that vile nephew of yours who's to blame, it's all his fault...

The old woman breaks off to blow her nose. Malvina takes advantage to attempt another slow manoeuvre towards the bag.

And in the end the old woman gives in, takes out the box with the cakes, opens it, as Malvina gazes on impatiently, and offers them to her one by one, wrapped in a paper napkin.

With her old eyes full of tears she watches her eat, taking care she doesn't eat the paper napkin as well, and understands what a vicious beast love is. It is invincible. Love is really the vile one, Osvaldo is an amateur by comparison. The love she feels for her old and lost friend is made of tenderness and compassion, nostalgia, anguish, it includes her regrets and feelings of remorse (she has always treated her badly, Malvina, life has dealt with her harshly, and here she is now, no way of remedying things however willing, no longer possible to treat her badly, which might bring her some relief even now). Love is made up of many things, and they are all disappearing leaving another large empty space, an emptiness in which her own self disappears. And she is frightened to be reduced like this, and she is afraid of dying, and would like to be dead already. Vast, multi-layered, immeasurable, this love for the lost friend, for the lover long dead, for the unrepeatable joys and precious sorrows of the time that will not come again, love all the more vile since its victim is her, a woman in a sorry state, decrepit and an infinitely weaker adversary.

Malvina eats fast. The cakes, not many of them because

she doesn't want her to be ill, are suddenly all gone, despite the old woman's attempts to ration them out.

On the arthritic fingers, sugar and residues of cream. Malvina looks at them, perplexed, lifts them to her mouth, tastes, is disappointed. Her hand in the air, empty and sticky, the thread between action and thought severed, the walls of the mind collapsing and the winds of nothingness blowing in from every direction and creating swirls of desolation on the empty desert of her face.

And rage, love is also made of rage. The old woman froths, boils, overflows with rage. She is furious with the priests who fill everything with saints and jesus-christs, with the over-hasty attendants and their over-familiar way of talking to the patients, she is critical of the furnishings, she detests the hospital colours, the baths with their little seats and even the awful practical handrail, obligatory accompaniment to any journey and making clear that those who enter here cannot stand on their own two feet. She is furious with tea in little sachets, of some discount brand. Malvina would never have drunk the stuff, Malvina never used to drink tea, being an aficionado of coffee and also a gourmet and instead she now gulps down the tepid brew as if it were nectar.

And above all the wheelchair, a pile of scrap metal, an iron maiden. It will reduce her to a cripple. If it doesn't fall to pieces first.

What are you doing? she shouts on the way home with Gabriela, who has cut a corner rather too sharply in her view, perhaps to avoid a careless motorcyclist who flashed past her. Pay attention!

The girl apologises with that guilty little voice that makes the old woman shudder, makes her want to shake her. It can't be real, this little voice, like a mouse caught nibbling the cheese, it's a pretence, and if it was real, then watch out!

And you can stop acting the demure little thing! she commands.

You wouldn't have survived, she thinks looking at that high and anxious forehead, if that little voice had been the real you. They'd have gobbled you up already, bones and all.

Then, with a little spurt of good humour, she adds: After all, if you kill us it's only an improvement as far as I'm concerned, but not for you.

Gabriela remains silent. She bites her lip, keeps her eyes fixed on the road.

A few minutes later Gabriela suddenly emerges from the mysterious subsoil of her fears to the sunlit terraces of renewed cheerfulness, and in a voice slightly hesitating at the abrupt transition, asks: why does *signora* Malvina sometimes call you Nora?

The old woman scowls.

She didn't call you that before, Gabriela adds.

But as the old woman does not reply, she beats a hasty retreat: I'm sorry, I… I didn't mean, I'm sorry…

The old woman remains silent for a minute or two. Then: Nora was the woman who lived with me. Her name was Eleonora. Nora.

The one in the portrait in the bedroom.

Ah! pipes Gabriela's little voice. What a beautiful lady! I thought she was your sister.

She was not my sister.

Wasn't she? Nora was her sister, her mother and her father, her daughter, her lover, she was the alpha and omega, the setting and rising of the sun.

She was my companion, the old woman says, wearied and disheartened at the inadequacy of common human speech.

And there it is, the grotesque situation has arisen, now she is wondering what the girl is going to say and she is bored and irritated in anticipation of what she will be obliged, perhaps, to feel and say, and the necessity of explaining what is obvious, as clear as the sun rising in the sky, to a girl who knows nothing and believes she knows everything, although in the case of Gabriela perhaps the reverse is true. Couldn't she go on batting her innocent eyelids Bambi-style? Why now, after so much time, almost two years since this little innocent has had the run of the house, does it occur to her to involve herself in discussions of this kind?

But Gabriela says nothing. She is thinking, her eyes fixed on the road.

And then she asks: So Nora is the other lady in costume in that photograph?

The old woman takes a while to understand what she is talking about. She means the photograph from the early nineteen-hundreds (a reproduction, obviously), which hangs in a corner of the hallway, rather dark, and in which two young and beautiful *fin-de-siècle* girls, as different from each other as day from night, Natalie Clifford Barney and Renée Vivien, are playing at lady and pageboy. No, she says, what an idea, what put that into your head? And which of the two is she supposed to resemble, according to you?

The hair, says Gabriela, who does not dare say that it was the old woman herself who led her into error about that image, all that beautiful soft hair... I know it's an old photograph, I mean from olden days, but I thought it was from a play... because *signora* Nora was an actress... or isn't that right?

Indeed, Nora was an actress, the theatre photographs in her little study say so.

I see you notice things and make your deductions, the old woman says. Not without a certain amusement.

Gabriela blushes and goes quiet.

Even in the city the coming of spring sweeps away the dust and dirt, wind and rain wash everything clean, brush down the roofs and the spotted trunks and bare branches of the plane trees, the last to come into bud. Gabriela negotiates the side streets with care, slowly and thoughtfully. The old woman, for whom time passes by ever faster, for time is like a river which grows broader the further it flows, and the more it seems to dawdle the faster it goes in reality beneath its apparent calm, the old woman has not realised that they are nearly home already.

Drop me here, she says. There's no point getting involved in the one-way system.

No! Gabriela insists. It's raining, you haven't got an umbrella.

You were happy, Gabriela asks, or asserts. You and *signora* Nora. It is clear she has had to pluck up her courage to ask this. That she is taking a risk.

Happy! What an inadequate simplification. Or perhaps it is just that she hasn't thought about it in those terms for such a long time. The old woman sighs, patiently, submitting to an unwanted necessity. Yes, she says. I think so.

How wonderful! Gabriela breathes.

Exasperated, the old woman says sharply: She's dead! She died years ago! Understand! What's the good of our having been happy once, if she's dead?

Then: Let me out here, by the newsstand, where the arcade begins, I won't get soaked.

As she gets out: And listen, do me a favour. Stop going on about *signora* this and *signora* that. You're getting on my nerves.

Thanks for the lift, she adds.

She closes the car door with a bang and promptly repents, because there is no reason to be hard on the poor girl, to whom she will be leaving half her possessions anyway (or what is left of them after the State has helped itself to its share) on her death, at whatever time the event in question occurs.

Why does she wake up, why does she get up in the morning — instead of carrying on sleeping forever?

Once, in the good days — but once almost all the days were good — when the morning light made the outlines of objects recognisable, the things to be done which had until that moment remained crouching in the denser shadows would come sneaking up to the bed, like animals impatient to start the day, and prod the two sleepers, nuzzle them, thrust their damp noses insistently into their slumbers.

Little things, insignificant if taken one at a time. Duties, tasks, habits and small pleasures. The trifling daily emergencies: the animals want to be fed, the plants watered, the food cooked, the books read. And then there was work, of course. The subterranean river that flows and irrigates everything, like love, making life possible. You don't notice it until it has dried up.

Once, even irritants had some life-affirming element about them: calling the plumber, going to the dentist, paying the taxes, deciphering the cryptic and often malevolent messages that public administrations send to citizens. The living enjoy expending their energies on the daily business of life. Even in the absence of wide horizons and a future that stretches ahead for an appreciable period. It pleases them to go on living — or it doesn't displease them enough for them to stop — even when life a long time ago lost its more publicised attractions: beauty, vigour, sex, the hope that everything might change for the better for no apparent reason. Inside each of us there must be a kind of magnet that keeps us attached to life, and continues to exercise its effect even when our existence has lost all purpose, from the point of view of the species and society, and even from our own. But what is its nature? Is it about self-love, senseless desire, with no object in mind? Is it the capacity to project ourselves in other beings, as people who have children like to say? Or is it the sheer and simple repellent force exercised by death, making us cling to life even when life no longer loves us?

For the old woman, the magnet that held her solidly attached to life, even when the future had shrunk like a matted old cardigan, and the vision of humanity had turned irreversibly grey, was Nora.

In the mornings, awake but still reluctant to face the day, she used to summon back her retreating dreams, cover her head with the pillow, resist the assault of thoughts and animals who,

137

early risers by comparison, had been awake for some time, and eventually she would give in. But if her surrender was honourable, and even sweet, she owed it solely to the constant and uninterrupted radiance that was the presence of Nora in her home, in her thoughts, at the centre of her life.

How easy it was then, the crossing of the dark borders between sleep and wakefulness. As if the forces of attraction were some sort of remote control, the old woman — who was not yet as old as she is now — would get up, rub her eyes, shake her stiffened body, grope for her glasses and slowly, obediently metamorphose for the umpteenth time into her day-to-day self.

For months now, no, years, that Methuselah, Venom, has not been waking at dawn to demand food and attention; on the contrary, he remains nestled among the pillows even after the old woman has got up. To make the bed she has to pick him up and deposit him on the windowsill, where he remains, patient and stiff-limbed, waiting for the same hands to replace him where he had been lifted from, and where he will resume his interrupted slumbers.

Ah, to possess his capacity for sleep! To let time simply pass by, with no apparent boredom or pain!

And instead, sleep deserts her, the bed becomes a torment and she has to get up and begin a day which no longer holds any attraction for her, and carry out rituals that have lost their meaning. Sometimes it is a trial even to wash every morning, pass the sponge over her wrinkled body, she perseveres out of force of will, out of her sense of dignity, but what a bore.

But if the magnet that kept her attached to life was Nora, why does she continue to live after Nora has gone? And years ago, what's more?

The old woman asks herself the same question every morning, and has no answer.

On arrival, Gabriela finds her already dressed and with her shoes on, ready to go out. Don't take your coat off, the old woman tells her. You're coming with me for a moment, there's something we have to do.

Aren't we going down? the girl asks when she sees her press the button for the seventh floor, and the lift begins to rise.

No, we're going up, the old woman says.

The child is paler than ever, can she be eating enough? Or is she trying to lose weight, like her idiotic contemporaries?

There's a wheelchair in the attic, the old woman says, brandishing the key. As new. Much more comfortable than the one they've given Malvina. What do I want with it here? We'll give it a good clean and then take it to her.

Half way along the corridor to the attic, which smells of dust and is dark in spite of the flickering light, the old woman wobbles and Gabriela promptly holds her steady. Wait, I'll go, she says, you stay here, then you won't trip, or get dirty.

Don't be silly, you've no idea where it is.

Yes, I do know, we came up here, you don't remember. Gabriela takes the key from her hand. Leave it, I'll do it, the lock is difficult.

But the door, made of simple planks, gives way after a brief tussle, opens with much squeaking over the cement floor. The girl darts in, Wait, she says, while I turn the light on for you.

She is speaking breathlessly, can she be afraid of the dark?

Gabriela fails to find the light switch.

Open the window! the old woman commands. And since the girl hesitates, she pushes open the shutters of the tiny dormer window herself. It doesn't provide much light, she thinks impatiently, what she is looking for is over there where she knows very well she put it. At the other end of the little room is the wheelchair that she bought for Nora, the last, horrible, gift. It has been very little used. She passes a hand over the back, it doesn't even seem all that dusty. Here it is, she says, and in turning round stumbles on something soft on the floor, an item of clothing or a blanket. Gabriela catches her by the arm.

The old woman, who nowadays lives by habit and becomes disconcerted and agitated at anything out of the ordinary, does not know whether her heart is thudding because of this chair retrieved from the abyss of time or for some other reason, and very nearly allows herself to be led from the attic without seeing anything, but she has always been suspicious and quarrelsome and so resists. What is it? Let me see!

On the floor are some flattened cardboard boxes and on top of them, meticulously folded, a dark blanket and something white, pieces of material that look like sheets, it is hard to tell in the semi-dark.

A makeshift bed, like the ones the homeless people use down in the street.

What the fuck is this, the old woman blurts out, normally she restrains herself in front of Gabriela, but this time no.

Gabriela gives her stifled little intake of breath, surprised and scandalised.

Bewildered, the old woman clings to the arm holding

her steady and feels it trembling. The smell of the girl, hot — shampoo and sweat and lemon cologne — mixes with the notes of dust and worm-eaten wood, the atmosphere is saturated with it.

Someone has been sleeping here, she declares. Gabriela's agitation compels her to gather her wits, one of them at least must keep control.

Don't be afraid! she commands. There's no one here now. It'll be some vagrant who's come up here from the street, forced his way in, those people from the bed and breakfast on the fifth floor are always leaving the front door open, this house is like a seaport!

She looks around for other signs of occupation. She remembers that when the wheelchair was brought up here it was wrapped in plastic sheeting, it was Malvina's idea, she couldn't bear to touch it, at that time, not this particular object. Now the plastic covering has been removed and the chrome-work is shiny. Someone has been using it to sit in.

A vagrant, she repeats.

Gabriela's breathing has become faster. I'm scared, the girl says.

Stop it, there's clearly no one here now!

Let's get out of here, please! Gabriela begs, and the old woman is suddenly impatient, she feels sorry for the girl and cross at the same time. Feeling sorry for her prevails. Let's go down, there's nothing else here as far as I can see. But we'll need to come back and look again when we're calmer.

In the apartment, while Gabriela is squatting on the floor cleaning the rims of the wheelchair, which were gleaming anyway, the old woman says: but how did this vagrant get into the attic if the door was locked?

Gabriela polishes vigorously, head down.

Was it locked, the door?

No, the girl says, still not looking at her. It was only pulled to. I pushed it and it opened. That's why I was frightened before we'd hardly got in.

The old woman is silent.

Her mind is working furiously, her body feels firm, taut, oblivious to the aches and pains that afflict her. She removes her spectacles, cleans the lenses, puts them back on. She looks at the girl, her stubborn back, her little hands gripping the cleaning cloth. The back of her head repelling her stare, resolutely down.

You've been up there recently, in the attic. I certainly haven't, she says, conversationally.

It is true. Gabriela is kneeling, she brings her hands up to her face, as if remodelling it, then slowly reveals it. Now she is calm, has regained her self-control. You were the one who sent me, I went to look for that vase, do you remember? I couldn't get the door to close properly, so it was left pulled to.

And why didn't you tell me? I would have called the locksmith, had the lock changed.

I made a mistake. I didn't think it was important… I would never have thought… please forgive me. Tears run down her smooth little face. Oh my God, but aren't you scared? The idea that there's someone wandering about in the building, we could meet him on the stairs… when I arrive in the morning, or when we go out to do the shopping…

We meet delinquents every day, the old woman says coldly. All the same, it's one more reason you should have told me the lock wasn't working. Bring me the phone, I'll ring the locksmith.

Who lives up there, in the former presbytery at the top of the hill, the house of life after life?

Gradually the old woman is beginning to recognise them, not as people, because they have no names any more, they are scattered pieces of elderly humanity washed up on the last beach of all, but as collections of features or manias, the stiff and tufty feather-like hair on the head of a hopping sparrow-woman, or the deformed legs of a tree-trunk woman drifting, or the shambling walk of a wreck of an old man whom time has bled clean of all colour, leaving him with skin as grey as his hair, his trousers, his slippers.

In any case the majority of the guests remain strangers to her, every time it is as if she is seeing them for the first time, and perhaps it is true, from one visit to the next the earlier ones have died and been replaced by others, or perhaps it is herself who looks at them without seeing them and without remembering them.

Some of them have received in late old age the gift of tongues. One woman, who resembles the peasant women of a hundred years ago, toothless, skin burned by the sun, scarf knotted round her neck, is having a lively discussion with a visitor not much younger than herself in a language which the old woman attempts to decipher. Is it some Slavic dialect, a hotchpotch of languages or some dialect delivered, slobbering, from between toothless gums? No, it is exactly what it seems: sounds shorn of meaning, the pure act of speaking, without words or meaning. The woman evidently remembers that when you have visitors you make conversation with them, and therefore she speaks even though she no longer has any words. Her speech is a kind of free-style projection of noises. *Auuau ggeggnì falala maai! Gul*à*?* She is an artist, a performer. She gesticulates, postures, smiles, makes exclamation marks with her mouth. She seems content. Her white-haired listener sits facing her, his shoulders unmoving, his head lowered. Is he a brother, a cousin, the husband? He is so still that he has perhaps fallen asleep.

Another, a man, is speaking to someone on the phone. He is one of the rare guests who still have their wits about them, lucid, the old woman thinks on hearing him say to the other person, probably his son, that he is waiting for him, that he should come and collect him straightaway. Impatient, he shouts that he is late, he's already missed the appointed time. That he is waiting for him, here in the village square, outside the bar. He can't stand here waiting for the rest of his life! It is at this point that she turns round to look at him, discreetly. And she sees there is no telephone in the hand held up to his face. After hearing him repeat the same conversation with his son three, four times over, with rising anger, she ceases to pay him any attention.

A tiny and gnarled woman, like a gnome, is following the attendants around, muttering the whole time, and it seems she is repeating mantras or prayers, but if you go closer what she is actually saying is shit, fuck off, whore, bitch, your fanny stinks, and on and on, and if she looks you in the face with those little eyes which dispense a torrent of fiery evil as relentless as the verbal one, you had better get out of the way before she flies at you with claws unsheathed. The attendants keep her in check with threats and sweets and when that no longer works they lock her in her room, where the furious old woman attacks the bell and rings, rings, rings until an exasperated white coat marches in brandishing sedatives.

Many though have received the gift of silence.

A woman who could still be young perhaps — impossible to establish her age, with her features remodelled by the departure of reason everything is equally likely — is having exclusive conversations with her own body. It is a dialogue which mainly involves her feet, she questions them, she massages them and contemplates them, she places them, with a contortionist's twists, in her mouth. The attendants are keeping her tightly strapped to her chair, perhaps to prevent her from tying her limbs in inextricable knots, and from time to time they put her socks back on, which she promptly pulls off. Her feet are thin, deformed, or maybe just contracted by spasms. Her performance is a form of art of which she never seems to tire.

But the majority maintain their silence in the form of a dialogue with the great nothingness that awaits them, already has its hand on them, and to swallow them up entirely is only waiting for that minor formality, the funeral. Sitting in their wheelchairs, their gaze fixed on the void, their mouths slack and their eyes unfocused, some wring a handkerchief in their hands, others are forever unbuttoning their shirts or cardigans, which a white coat will wearily do up again, several however have abandoned even their hands to the nothingness: they lie motionless in their laps, or dangle, intent on that most perfect of exercises in meditation which is the absence of the self. They are all in the same room but they are not together. Each of them is alone in the nothingness, the nothingness seems vast enough to offer perfect solitude to vast numbers, thousands of millions of individuals completely isolated, no one in sight as far as the eye can see, neither family nor neighbours.

(For an instant she envies them, trapped as she still is in her own imperfect solitude, a solitude full of holes.)

Malvina indeed does not know any of them. Nor the woman who sleeps in the same bedroom as her, nor the one who tugs at her sleeve as she passes by.

Who is that? What's her name? What does she want with you? the old woman asks.

Malvina peers inside herself, bewildered, she seems to be searching for a memory whose whereabouts she can't remember (is it inside her? outside somewhere? in her pocket? in her slippers?) and then very slowly shakes her head.

Are you the sister? the attendant asks, while they wait for Malvina to emerge from the bathroom where they are changing her.

The old woman looks her squarely in the face, with an expression of hostility. She has an impulse to say: No, I am her lover. Even if it is not true, they have never been lovers, she and Malvina, but what does that matter? Today, in the desolate wastes of today, Malvina is all she has left of lovers, loves, friendships and dreams, a breath of Nora lives in her, Malvina is the sacred and the profane, the homeland and the ideal.

No, she says instead, scowling. She is a lot more than my sister.

The attendant is disconcerted for a moment, but quickly carries on. And this young lady here, she says turning to

Gabriela, is her niece? Was your sister married?

Gabriela blushes. The old woman bangs the floor with her stick, it would be a relief to explode, say no she was not married, she despised the very idea of matrimony and progeny, she loved women, she was particular about what she ate, would never have tolerated the food they give her here, or all these saints and jesus-christs on the walls, she was a woman of elegance, she would have died sooner than wear a sloppy tee shirt like the one they have dressed her in today, she was a stickler for cleanliness, you don't change her socks often enough, she was the best film editor in Italy, she was tender she was generous she was exasperating, she was she was she was…

A fit of desperate coughing doubles her up. She cannot say these things, she cannot say anything because every word she says could rebound on Malvina, how would they treat her if they knew she was a lesbian? Would they make her wear even more offensive tee shirts, to punish her for her pretensions to elegance? And what would they make her eat, her wayward, demanding Malvina, these women who probably earn a thousand euros a month for wiping old people's arses?

Gabriela comes to her aid, passing her tissues, pills. The attendant goes to fetch her a glass of water.

Cursing the whole world, herself included, the old woman realises her thoughts are all of the past, Malvina was, was, was. Because now she no longer is.

Today Malvina appears more than ever to be in good health, her cheeks pink, her hair combed if not well at least decently. One cannot expect too much of a provincial hairdresser.

She is smiling, she seems happy. She seems herself.

The old woman embraces her, hugs her for a long time, recognises her scent beneath the hospital one. She tells her she is beautiful. You are beautiful Malvina my darling, you were always a beautiful girl, she whispers in her ear.

Gabriela gets her mobile phone from her bag and takes a few pictures of them hugging, of Malvina laughing. In the garden, on a spring day, a bush of red roses blooming in the background.

The next day the old woman has her tablet on her lap and is looking at the photos Gabriela has sent her and is instantly horrified.

On Malvina's face is the great nothingness, it is a face without a look.

The old woman's eyes saw what she wanted to see: her friend still living, sentient, still herself. The lens, instead, has captured what lies behind desire and illusion, a woman left emptied of self.

The old woman feels she has been the victim of a horrible miracle.

The tablet falls to the floor. Gabriela runs in with a cry.

It hasn't broken, what a piece of luck!

You and your photos, the old woman mutters bitterly, massaging her eyelids with her hands.

The locksmith is a small and kind man who brings with him a box of tools heavier than himself; he is not registered for VAT, his charges are minimal and entirely off the books and he undertakes only little jobs that he can do on his own, ignoring any ideas about growth and success. The old woman is sympathetic to this mild rule-bending and wonders, vaguely, how he lives, whether he has relationships and ties, but in practice she doesn't want to know. She trusts him, she has known him for decades by now.

You see, *signora*, Ciro, the locksmith, tells her, this lock, well I've changed it, but that door won't hold, if someone wants to get through they'll get through, it only needs a good shove, understand?

And so?

So nothing. Changing the door is useless, you would spend a pile of money and then if they want to break it down they will break it down anyway. If you don't keep any items of value there, in the attic, in the end it's better to leave things be. There are so many of these homeless people in the city...

Who get into other people's attics?

Into the cellars too. You know, there are rats here in the city centre who come up from underground and do the same, and yet there are people who go there to sleep... in the end, from their point of view, they're not doing anything bad...

All the same, knowing there are people wandering about the building, forcing their way through doors, it's not pleasant, the old woman remarks.

Ah well, agreed, Ciro concedes. Nowadays burglar isn't a very precise category, it tends to broaden out... we're all vulnerable, they've got into my house twice already, not that there's anything worth stealing, but all the same... and how about this — the second time I ran into him face to face, a tall bloke, dark, a lot bigger than me...

And what did you do?

I said to him: Hello. Are you looking for someone?

And he said?

He stood there a while like this, you know, confused. He looked around, and he must have realised there was nothing much to pinch. You've probably got the wrong address, I suggested. Yes, he goes, yes, I've come to the wrong place. If you'd like to go, I'll show you out. I went to the door with him, by then it was a only a stride or two away, and I bolted it after him. I was sweating all over.

What if he'd attacked you?

I'd have got a hiding, Ciro smiles.

What beautiful gentle eyes, the old woman thinks, this homely-looking man has, with his drooping moustaches and his stunted little ponytail falling on his neck.

You wouldn't defend yourself?

Yes, I'd defend myself, but I'd take a beating, you know, up against someone like that. If I'd had a weapon, a pistol, it would have been different but...

You don't have one?

Me, no, weapons, no, no. My neighbours have, I live behind Porta Palazzo, they're a bit rough, the people there... I could probably have called them, but at the time I didn't think of it, and then in the end it was all right anyway...

And the people that do have weapons, what, a pistol?

Er, yes, my neighbours, yes, they've got guns, certainly...

Would they sell me one?

Ah, *signora*, I wouldn't know... they're rough types, you know... I can try asking but... I wouldn't know, to be honest.

But you would try? I'd tip you something in return.

No, no, nothing like that. Personally, I'm against weapons, other people get by in their own way... if you really want, I'll ask.

Ask.

Are you sure?

Doesn't it look like it?

I'll let you know, but don't be in a hurry.

I'm not.

She looks at the young men on the streets with inquisitive eyes. She wonders which of them can be the unknown but tidy guest in her attic.

There has been a new one under the porch for a while. He can't be more than twenty-five, round-faced and sunburnt like an Anatolian shepherd boy, with a neat little beard. So he must trim it. So he has somewhere he can go, he doesn't sleep here on the cold paving stones, where dogs have pissed and drunks have been sick. He doesn't give off the powerful stink of the vagrant who hasn't washed for months, but a faintly musky and salty smell, a male and vaguely feral odour, with grassy traces in it. Is he spending his nights under the flowering plum trees in the public gardens?

Be kind, *signora*, give me some change to buy my lunch, if you're willing. If you're not willing, never mind, god bless you all the same.

The old woman stops. Gabriela pulls at her arm, she is against begging and against any form of public poverty.

He is clever, the shepherd boy, where can he have studied marketing? His beard apart, his face is clean and alert, he might even appeal to her, to Gabriela.

The old woman takes out a five euro note. The boy eagerly holds out the plastic box he uses for donations: Thank you, *signora*! You're the first person to give me anything today.

I hope you'll use it for something to eat, the old woman says, feeling ridiculous.

I give you my word as a man! he replies, indeed laughing, now a young faun showing his white teeth in the red crack of his mouth. I'll buy myself something to eat. My word as a man!

Why as a man? Do you think I trust that, a man's word?

But Gabriela is making impatient shuffling noises behind her. Come away, please! she implores in a heated whisper.

What if that was him? the girl says when they have gone on a couple of steps.

What him?

The one who's sleeping in the attic. If you ask me, he is. Didn't you see the look on his face? As if he knew us.

He certainly doesn't know me. Perhaps he knows you, the old woman says.

Gabriela shakes her head, scandalised, denies it energetically.

The old woman is suspicious. You are not being straight with me, she thinks.

How are you? she asks him.

He opens an eye, then slowly the other one as well, sketches a cat-of-the-world's smile although a rather tired one and takes a long, gritty, rasping breath.

Venom has become semi-deaf, he doesn't see very well any more, until a little while ago he could still, even if awkwardly and unsteadily, jump on to the kitchen shelves to pilfer things, but now he no longer can.

It's to be expected, says the lady vet. His age is equivalent to at least a hundred in human terms. I hope you're in as good shape when you reach a hundred.

Would you like to be? says the old woman acidly.

Me, certainly not! the vet protests. That's why I smoke and drink. Sorry, I didn't mean to offend you.

Animals, the vet continues, are wiser than human beings, more in tune with their own biological destiny. When they grow old and can't do the things they used to do when they were young, well, they simply give them up. No one has ever heard an animal complaining about the onset of old age.

They know it's no good complaining. And anyway they don't talk, the old woman mutters.

He's not eating much, she then says.

He doesn't have as much need to eat.

He's always enjoyed stuffing himself. He's a glutton, a gourmet, a greedy guts. He's been hungry ever since he was small. He's been ravenous all his life.

The lady doctor gives the patient lying on the kitchen table a thorough examination. The patient is very accommodating, allowing himself to be poked and prodded while he emits asthmatic purrs.

One or two neurological problems. I'll see him again in a fortnight, she says, removing the stethoscope from her ears.

How long will he last? the old woman asks.

The vet gives her a reproachful look. (You still say stupid things, at your age.)

She lowers her head, writes on the prescription pad. In the meantime give him this, she says, handing her the slip of paper.

The old woman is peeling an apple, watching television.

Streets of a city that could be her own, city outskirts are the same all over the world. People rummaging in rubbish bins, some heaving the black sacks out in a fury, spilling the contents on the pavements, others sifting calmly through them: they have become expert in examining their findings with cool discrimination and rapidly distributing them between the plastic bags they carry everything round in. They wear shapeless clothes, probably layers of garments one on top of the other, and worn-out slippers, a few have small bags tied round their feet. An old woman in black, sober and old-fashioned but at one time elegant, leans over with effort, she seems stiff more out of reticence than lack of practice, she hesitates before plunging her hand into other people's rubbish.

That woman could be me, the old woman thinks, chewing the apple. In a parallel life.

And for a few minutes she drifts away, imagining the multiple existences her double might have led: she is a retired piano teacher who still plays her out-of-tune instrument. She has a stuffed cat on her chest of drawers, a daughter who died young, perhaps a grandson who has emigrated to the United States, who calls her to ask how she is, if she needs any money, and she says no, everything is fine, don't worry, above all don't come back. Perhaps she steals from bins to feed her dog, an old and crabby creature like herself, who waits for her at home and complains about the poor quality of the food that appears on the table. Perhaps she is wandering a little bit in the head, nothing could be more likely, she can't remember what day it is, she thinks she is newly married, there's a baby in its cot waiting for her at home or a new love, perhaps she's an angry woman instead, quarrels with the neighbours, plays mean tricks, believes she's being spied on by Russian agents who get into her brain at night to decode her dreams. And while she imagines her she envies her, if she too was as poor and as desperate she could allow herself to lose the plot, to go gloriously mad and fall in love again, she could die with eyes open and a beatific smile thinking she is throwing herself into the arms of Nora, she would understand the thing that presently eludes her, she would look reality in the face, because reality lives in the crevices of life, in its waste tips, in its least visited margins, where only the mad or the mystics or the truly desperate venture.

Another telephone call for Gabriela. The put-on voice, less honeyed this time.

Her hand gripping the phone, the old woman sends the girl a questioning look.

Gabriella understands at once (the old woman never ceases to be amazed at how she lives like this, constantly on her guard, each step taken as if she were walking through a minefield), and sends back a look of alarm, shakes her head. She responds curtly that *signorina* Zlatec is not with her today. No, she does not know where she is. No, she does not have her mobile number. Goodbye.

A few moments of silence.

Gabriela is bent over the ironing board, almost graceful in the act of folding a handkerchief, and a nursery rhyme floats into the old woman's head from her childhood games: The Pretty Washerwoman, who washes handkerchiefs for the poor of the town, jump up and down, jump once again...

The girl's arm slows, her smile becomes hesitant, the two little furrows appear on her brow. The thing is, she says, the advance I asked you for last month... it wasn't for me, it was for my family.

Hmm, the old woman mutters.

My half-sister Petra and her husband Gogu. They asked me for a loan, their bank won't give them one because he's already making payments on the car and her work isn't on any official books. That's why I gave them some money...

The story comes out in fragments, a jigsaw puzzle of odd pieces which make a picture that has no sense. In the eyes of the old woman.

Petra is the daughter of Gabriela's father's first marriage. Gogu, her brother-in-law, is a fine upstanding man who every now and then beats his wife. Years ago he tried it on with Gabriela, one evening when he was drunk, but the next day he didn't remember anything about it and Gabriela kept quiet, she would have felt guilty about accusing him of something he didn't even know he had done.

Three nieces, the little one is a sweetie, says Gabriela with shiny eyes, always on the lookout for baby creatures, preferably female, on whom she can lavish the full force of her dreams. She omits to add that the adorable niece is the girl of a few years ago, or even of last year, now transformed into a simpering little flirt and existing, in terms of her adoration, only in her imagination.

Gogu is a hard worker, she says carefully, but he has one vice, gambling, when he's finished at the garage where he works as a mechanic he can't help going into a *tabaccheria* or bar to play the slot-machines, with the daughters he is good, a strict father but a good one, the oldest is about to marry an unemployed Brazilian because she is expecting a baby, she left school in her last year at technical college, a shame because she was clever, and Petra's employer refuses to pay her social security contributions, and maybe she won't be able to go on working because she has an allergy affecting her hands, no wonder, she has them in water all day long washing vegetables and plates, Ana says she should join a union...

Ana?

Yes, exactly, Gabriela doesn't care for her at all but she is friendly with her sister, so they see each other every now and then, the new Italian boyfriend has left her, which could be seen coming, and when she hasn't got a boyfriend, Ana, who is there to keep her away?

But why did they ask you for money? the old woman says, trying to come to the point.

To pay the rent. And to pay for the oldest niece's wedding. And then Gogu has run up debts because of the slot-machines, it's stronger than him, it's like a drug, and they owe for the television as well, and so they hadn't paid the landlady for months, and Gogu also took a loan off someone or other, rough people who are now threatening him, and he was going to get evicted any day...

The old woman sighs. And how much have you given him?

Slowly, one small confession at a time, while the pile of handkerchiefs grows and the steam from the iron beads her face, it emerges that Gabriela has handed over to her relatives not only the entire advance from the previous month but, over time, all her savings.

But now, that's enough! the girl says. I've told them I'm not giving them a penny more.

About time, the old woman mutters. But they haven't given up, from what it seems. And they're telephoning you here in my home.

It wasn't me who gave them the number! Gabriela exclaims. It was Ana!

Let me get this right, the old woman says slowly, this big sister of yours has never given a damn about you, her husband has tried to lay hands on you, he's a slot-machine addict, the oldest girl is about to make a brilliant marriage and bring into the world another welfare dependant, and you've been subsidising them for years. That's a fine lesson for him, isn't it?

Gabriela looks at her, uncertain whether she is joking or speaking seriously. One never knows, with the old woman.

She puts down the iron and wipes some dampness (is it condensation or a tear?) from her eye. She plays for time with diversionary manoeuvres, folds and re-folds a vest.

I know, it was a mistake, she says. I should have been smarter. Been stronger. Left them sooner. But they were all I had... my family... my little niece... when I was small I had my grandmother, back home, but then we came here to Italy and it took me years to find my feet and get used to the way things work...

But recently she has moved away, for many reasons, among them that Dorin man (does she remember him? No, the old woman doesn't remember things very well, she hadn't been paying attention), who has also left the fateful family and has now become fixated on her. He sends her messages, photos… and that's why she is always changing her phone number.

The old woman does not understand. What photos, what messages?

He's the one who wants to be a terrorist, Gabriela explains. He has even converted, he's bought himself a Koran, but he got bored after a few pages and gave up. He's grown a beard, but you don't need a brain for that, and once, months ago when he still used to go to their house, she saw him praying on his knees on the floor, and pointed out that he was facing the wrong way, Mecca was definitely to the south-east in relation to Italy whereas he was praying in the direction of the billiards bar opposite the house which is to the west, and he flew into a rage. On top of that he drinks, and Muslims aren't supposed to drink, isn't that right? Ever since he's had these mad ideas in his head, since he came out of prison, that is (they always said he'd gone to stay with a friend, but everyone knew he was in prison), he's started arguing with his father even more often and hitting his sister, the middle one, not the oldest one, no, because she has this very tall and well-built boyfriend. And then he went away, after Gogu had almost smashed his head in. The story about his prison sentence she got from Ana, it appears that Dorin assaulted a police officer who had stopped him and another man on suspicion of dealing, or worse: the other man started a fight but then ran away and he, instead, just stood there like a lemon and ended up in prison, even as a criminal he's a failure. That's what Gogu says.

One day — when she was still talking to him — she asked him why he wanted to kill people, what was the sense in it. Dorin told her killing is beautiful. That a real man enjoys killing. In that case I'm glad I'm not a man, she replied. Anyway I don't believe you. He carried on, not listening to her: There are men who know how to get respect, they know what needs to be done, everyone should know their place, women should know their place, to hell with this shitty life, we're going to take what's due to us. And what is due to you? He didn't have an answer to this question. Dorin has never been brilliant, at school he had a teacher all to himself, but it didn't do much good. Gabriela has researched foreign fighters on the internet, there is a whole recruitment network, they go to do training in the Middle East, in combat zones. But recently it all seems to have become more amateur, anyone can improvise his own role, do it all by himself without any preparation, so Dorin too will have felt encouraged. He can act as a lone wolf, even though Dorin as a wolf leaves something to be desired, he is more like a stray dog lost on the motorway.

Is it true that men take pleasure in killing? the girl asks.

It certainly is, the old woman says, you only have to look around you to know that.

And women? There are some women who kill too, it says on television.

Women love murderers, the old woman answers in a murmur. Terror is seductive, I'm surprised you're immune to its charm.

Gabriela is silent for a moment, she doesn't know if she is being complimented or teased.

But he wasn't always like that, the girl resumes, passing without interruption from these dark tales to the idyll of childhood, when he was small Dorin was a delight, for a year they all lived at her grandmother's house in a village, he was four and they — she and her twin Ida — were six, and the three of them were always together, inseparable. He was a little blond angel, timid, and they loved him, protected him. He was their little brother. He would come and wait for them on the path on their way home from school, he would run to meet them. They used to go out together gathering the wild plums the grandmother made her plum brandy from. Then Ida died and she and Dorin didn't see each other for years, and when he reappeared, completely changed, he fixated on her. He wants to marry her. She rejects him, and he sends ugly things to her phone because he is furious.

Ugly things?

Yes, ugly. Gabriela shakes her head, and it is clear no further information is forthcoming.

The old woman is breathless. It is too much for her. This rackety family saga disconcerts her. A spurious Balkan version of Wuthering Heights, with a retarded Heathcliff who imagines he is a terrorist.

Is all this you're telling me true? she asks.

The girl places a hand on her heart. The old woman is not convinced.

What will Gabriela do to avoid the fate pointed at her like a Kalashnikov? Does the scatter-brained girl realise she is nearly ninety and can no longer help her (other than by dying and thereby making her a minor heiress) and therefore it would be better if she knew nothing about it?

I can't do any more mending on this one, the girl says, holding up the shirt draped on its coat-hanger. The collar is too worn, I'd have to take it off and sew on another, if you want to carry on using it. Maybe it's better to throw it out. And look here, under the arm…

Give it to me, the old woman says, snatching it from her hand. Throw out, throw out, that's all you people know how to do, she grumbles, knowing her words are wounding. Gabriela detests being talked about in the plural, there is nothing she hates more than being associated with unspecified others, other home helps, other foreigners, other women, defective beings, ignorant and vaguely contemptible.

The old woman hurries off to replace the shirt in the wardrobe, holding it carefully, away from her, so as not to crease it. It is made of silk, delicate white silk, which has now become the colour of ivory and almost transparent.

At one time it lit up the night, that white shirt.

She remembers that time — was it just the one time or is memory running many nights into a single occasion? — she waited for her into the small hours, the last tram had passed a while ago but she was still not back. The rehearsals were definitely over by now. But how difficult it was for a group to break up and go their separate ways, after being brought together by their shared enchantment with the theatre. She knew it, she had seen how they exchanged looks among themselves, how they looked at Nora, she knew the secret manoeuvrings and the sudden rushes of desire. By this time of night, she thought, they will be in some smoky bar drinking red wine, endlessly talking.

No, she thought after a while, Nora was with that other woman, the one with the soft voice and alluring eyes, the most brazen in revealing her desire and inciting it in others. The woman she did not want Nora to mention, better not to know, to pretend not to see, because to look in the face things that hurt takes courage and a self-confidence she did not possess, she was cowardly and prudent and stubborn. She closed her eyes but she did not let go.

And then with the passing of the minutes and the half hours her jealousy turned into panic, something terrible had happened, an accident, an assault, the city at night was ferocious and unknown, the horrible things you read about in the papers really do happen, they happen to someone who has no idea until a second before that they are the chosen one. A someone who is often some woman.

At intervals — at ever shorter ones — she went to the window and looked down into the narrow street where the lamppost had not been working for weeks and no one had come to repair it. She prayed to some unknown benevolent entity that Nora was in a warm and safe room with that other woman, and not lying on the ground in some dark corner, or in the cold river. She thought about going out to look for her — but where? She paced up and down, telling herself she was a fool. She began to pray again.

And then suddenly the white shirt appeared down below at the end of the street, lighting up the town in a precocious dawn. She put her hands to her face, wept with grief and happiness, wanted to hug Nora hard enough to hurt her, wanted to make her pay, wanted to suck from her lips all the life she had used up in waiting, wanted just to sleep at her side and forget.

If what Gabriela tells her about her terrorist cousin were true — but shouldn't he be a nephew, seeing that he is the stepson of her stepsister...?

The old woman is having trouble making sense of it all. However, if it were true, she thinks, shouldn't she go to the police?

And a voice inside her is saying: only a fool would get involved in other people's troubles.

But the problem, she knows, is not simply that. The problem is that Gabriela seems to be a marked target. The terrorist, allowing that he does exist, this pathetic specimen who fails to terrorise anyone except a slip of a girl, is going to find her in any case, and her rapacious family will find her as well — because her loyalties are anything but broken. She tells stories, to herself and to anyone who is there to hear them, but she doesn't believe in them enough to make them come true...

An intelligent girl. Who has studied. Who can do multiplication. A hard worker, honest.

Honest? Oh, certainly, when she has been out shopping she hands back the change correct to the last cent.

She has a pale blue notebook, secured with a dark blue elastic band, in which she records any overtime she does. She is very precise, Gabriela. There is no need to tell her anything twice, she catches on immediately, she remembers.

But sincere? Not that sincerity is always a reliable quality. Maybe her ideas are just muddled. Confused emotions and feelings. Can you be sincere when you don't know what the truth is? Can you understand yourself when your childhood experiences, your loves, your loyalties are so scrambled?

The old woman thinks about her mother, her wise, quick-witted mother who died so many years ago (the first great scar), about her father, whom she hated for years and no longer hates, and whose thought processes she now feels she knows intimately, about Nora, who even though so different from her was like her, a glance was enough for them to understand one another, they carried in them the same DNA of their headstrong native soil. They grew old together, becoming ever more detached from a present which seemed less and less their own.

Gabriela on the other hand comes from a country she does not know, and is living here, in a time that is no longer hers.

But then, fundamentally, what does any of this matter, to her? She is only the employer, she must maintain the distance between them, the coolness. Her clarity of thought.

What am I trying to do? the old woman asks herself. Transform her into something else, an Italian, a European? As if they were better than she is!

Quite apart from the fact that Europeans do not exist and I have never liked Italians.

Or would I like to make her into the girl of my imagination, the person I would like her to be, who thinks the way I would think? Why is it impossible to share a portion of our lives with anyone without foisting on them our dreams and our fears? And I am afraid for her but I am also afraid of her, because she has the keys to the apartment, she comes and goes on her silent little feet, she could kill me while I slept, rob me, let another person into my home...

Perhaps she has already done so, she thinks, seeing once more the violated attic, the cardboard boxes laid out on the floor. Perhaps she has already involved me in some improbable Balkan drama and I am just sitting here all unaware, making a laughing stock of myself... who knows what she says about me to her relatives?

And what is she thinking, while she is putting the food on the table? And when she works the shampoo into my sparse white hair with her slender fingers, I don't know whether I inspire disgust or pity, whether she hates me or tolerates me...

From now on, she asks herself, will it be better if I wash my own hair?

III

Things are not merely things

On that long ago spring afternoon, in the foreign city, the old woman made a pact with death. And at once Eros returned and blew his breath over the world and made it green again.

But how could she be so naive as to believe that death keeps pacts?

There were the usual stages, treatments, a surgical intervention.

While the doctors were slicing with their instruments the living tissues of Nora, the old woman sat in a grey room, her gaze fixed on the window. She drew some comfort from staring at a tree whose branches had been crudely pollarded as if, related by suffering, they understood each other.

What was happening to Nora at that exact moment? Had they already wheeled her into the operating theatre, or was she still waiting, her eyes open in the gloom of the corridor? What did the body feel, violated by cutting metal?

Love forced on her the lesson of humility humiliated. Of knowing that the one you love is here, not far from you, yet you do not know where she is, you are not allowed to be with her or see her, the body which you have caressed is offered naked to the obscene caresses of death, and you can do nothing about it. You sit here, the last of the last, and you are no one, because the one you love cannot see you, cannot hear you and your love counts for nothing. If she dies at this moment, you will not see her. You will not know the exact second, you will not be there at the final shudder. Your face will not be the final image in her eyes. They have made you strangers to one another. The bond which you believed all-powerful reveals its frailty, it is a thread of nothingness, dry and broken, it lies on the floor for everyone to trample on.

And even if she lives, while you are holding her in your arms in the days to come you will never be able to forget that this, and this alone, is the truth: love counts for nothing. It does not protect from pain it does not cure disease it does not keep death at bay. What you believe you know is just an illusion, you do not know anything about her, she is now in the arms of a lover far more powerful than you, the anaesthetic which courses through her blood. An infinitely more effective drug than your kisses and your willpower.

The old woman sat in the dingy room, eyes fixed on the tortured tree, abandoned to the torments of love: do you remember the moments when the pain took her away from you, do you remember when she turned her head aside to avoid seeing you, avoid responding to you, when she did not eat the food you set before her? Perhaps she has always known this, that she would abandon you. She wanted to. And certainly she wants to now. She cannot die if she does not want to die. Not her. Everyone else, yes, they mostly die involuntarily, the way they were born, but not her. She knows this, she wants it. She has made her choice.

The old woman battles the demon of love. It is an unequal contest and she knows she will lose. You cannot win, you cannot stop battling. She hates love.

And yet if she stops resisting the torture, if she surrenders to it, that is perhaps the only thing that will save her.

Death has made her a promise, has it not?

If Nora dies, she too will die.

And so why, just now, when Nora's life is stretched out on an operating table, why does she find no comfort in that promise?

Because love is torturing her with its most cruel weapon, hope.

Eros and hope are Siamese twins, you cannot invoke one without the other appearing, uninvited.

Did it bring you pleasure, the way the thought of dying made you feel so alive? Did it bring you pleasure, to feel twenty at seventy, to tremble at the touch of her fingers, to lie in wait behind the door with a rose? And what are you complaining about now?

The long vigil of the old woman in the waiting room resembles the long-distance flight of a passenger who is afraid of flying. It has the same emotional rhythm.

The terrified passenger sits there, paralysed in her economy class seat, muscles contracted, all contact with her body's sensations completely severed. Occasionally, when the terror expands to the outer limits of the bearable, the thought of death comes to comfort her. What is she afraid of? Of dying. But if she dies she will cease to be afraid, would that not be a relief? You only die once, it happens to everyone, what the hell!

Is that the worst thing that can happen to the old woman, apart from Nora dying? And in such an event she will die as well, immediately afterwards, at the most however long it takes her to complete the ritual formalities. And everything will be over. Simple, no?

Death appears to her in an entirely different light, a cool balm which soothes all anguish. The ideal counterweight to the human state of perennial necessity. For a split second, the interior scales are in perfect balance. Free from desire, with all the equanimity of a Zen Buddhist nun, the passenger on the turbulent flight relaxes in her seat, in a state of repose.

A fraction of a second later, the aircraft enters yet another pocket of turbulence, sending a violent shudder through her body. Her heart plummets. Calm and equilibrium are revealed for what they are, illusions. And here you are, the torturer has already finished his break, throws his cigarette stub away and gets back to work.

And everything begins all over again, as before. Each time worse.

A doctor entered the room, tired, his gown undone. He told her everything had gone well.

The old woman got to her feet, tottering. The doctor's information seemed to come from a distance, like a telegraphed message, inscrutable.

Can you tell me, doctor, if the woman I love will be with me for another twenty years? Shall we make that trip to Canada we wanted to make? Shall I be buying flowers for her birthday? Shall we go and live somewhere by the sea?

Naturally, no, he could not tell her. Nor could she ask.

'What is death,' says Socrates, 'if not the separation of soul from body? And is not being dead, therefore, this: the body, separated from the soul, has become an entity in itself, quite independent, and the soul, separated from the body, is one too, quite independent?'

Ah, yes, over the millennia, in the heads of thousands of learned speakers, not to mention ignorant ones who have their say nevertheless, body and soul have been two different things, temporarily locked in an unequal union, in which the body is like the female in human marriage: weak, voluble, impure, desirable in its youthful radiance and despised in its old age, necessary, abominable, pitiable...

And the soul in contrast, solid, rigorous, sober, coherent — imprisoned in the body like the poor male in carnal union and bound to the family with its accompanying annoyances... both of them, soul and male, constantly yearning to loosen the knot and escape to freedom in the lofty heavens of abstractions, where bodies do not exist, but ideas...

But things do not quite work like that, in this story...

The old woman is not some sort of soul and body construct, reason and sentiment, light and dark. Nor is she some sort of man and woman combination, let alone all the rest...

With her, dichotomies and oppositions collapse like blocks of flats built on slopes eroded by deforestation, tumbling down in a landslip and heaping contaminating debris on land unfit for building, even by the most determined of unlicensed builders, so that one might as well turn one's back on this ruined landscape and move elsewhere, to less worked-over places.

With her we are obliged to look at things from the peculiar point of view of someone who does not believe that body and soul are two separate entities, like the entities of Italian bureaucracy, which do not talk to one another and if they do, do not understand each other. For her, they are a single thing. If the old woman were ever to be questioned on what the soul is, and after an initial shudder of boredom she consented to give it some thought, she would perhaps say that if there is a soul inside the body, it is to do with being sentient, with her five or even more senses, with emotions and perceptions, her capacity to think and to dream. Her life, in short.

We can look for the old woman's soul in her fingertips and in all the surfaces of her body that are clothed in sensitive tissues, which bring her lover's caresses to her in her dreams; her ears which still allow her to hear passably well music and voices and unfortunately also tittle-tattle and noises; her tongue which accurately distinguishes flavours, can compose harmonies of taste and reject discords; her nose, that mad archivist of memory which records everything but catalogues nothing, the nose which just by sniffing the air can transport you vividly elsewhere, to other times and places, without telling you where, who with, what you were doing, and leaves the mind prey to subtle confusion... and even the eyes, myopic, long-sighted, astigmatic, veiled over with cataracts and undermined by macular degeneration and glaucoma, the fragile human eyes tormented by greed and longing for useless riches, the exhausted capitalists of the senses, subjected to thousands of images, wearied by cruelties and by pleasures that no longer please, like ageing despots who have seen everything, and are bored by it all...

172

And so, since her soul is inside the body the way red corpuscles are inside the blood, and if you take them out blood is no longer blood, when the old woman dies she will be dead and that is the end of it, body and soul.

None of those Socratic pronouncements on the desirability of death — that place where the good men have gone, so why not go there ourselves? It'll be fine, we'll be in the best of company — affects her thinking. Never mind that they come from the mouths of venerable philosophers and famous or glamorous personalities, to her it makes no difference, she is not falling for it.

(And consider this: she in particular would have a very strong incentive, for belief in some form of afterlife: to see Nora again. To hold her hands again. To hear the beloved voice for all eternity, to converse with her. But what eternity? She would need to forge a personal one, because the one projected by the catholic church does not envisage the glorious reunion of two women who love each other. Perhaps, when she is scatty, like Malvina, if she ever becomes like that, she will be able to concoct for herself some harebrained private version of paradise, and will derive some fleeting moments of happiness. But for now nothing yet, on that front.)

The old woman, when she dies, will be dead, full stop. No life equals no soul. No anything, finis. The great nothingness.

If something of her is left behind, in the stir of living air, it will be entrusted to other beings. In the same way that something of Nora has remained in the air of their home and in all the people who knew her, in the old woman herself first of all, in Venom the cat, in Malvina, and in so many others who have maybe forgotten her name, but who met her one day and

173

still carry inside them, unconsciously, an echo or a trace of her, even if minimal, a single frame among the millions of frames, and which nevertheless forms a part of their lives...

What will certainly be left behind is the dead body, the sad encumbrance which someone else will have to deal with, and for which on the other hand — in this respect very much like the conscientious majority of old people in this part of the world — she has already set aside in her bank account the necessary funds.

Gabriela emerges from under the portico, walks rapidly, as always, towards the corner of the street and the tram stop. The old woman, who is more worried than ever today, has gone out on to the bedroom balcony immediately after the girl's departure to spray pesticide over her geraniums, which are enjoying their brief flush of spring splendour before succumbing to the slow massacre of parasites, increasingly prolific and ferocious in the dense and toxic air of the city.

She sees her crossing the narrow road. She sees her slow down, come almost to a standstill, while from the pavement outside the window of the maternity shop a woman detaches herself and comes slowly in her direction, appears in front of her. She is holding a little girl by the hand.

She can't hear what they are saying, nor can she read the words on their lips or the emotions on their faces. She just sees the ballet of their bodies, Gabriela a step to the left, her opposite number and her small appendage a step to the right, and they are facing each other again. Another step, another counter-move.

Gabriela looks around, but the street is barred. From the

174

corner a third figure has emerged, a teenage girl in shorts whose long hair flutters like a battle standard. Gabriela is surrounded.

The stretch of pavement becomes the theatre for a menacing dance, every attempt at flight is blocked by a new encirclement. The old woman watches, fascinated. The young girls are silent, the woman is speaking, hands on hips, chest thrust forward, her unintelligible words reaching the balcony only as scraps of sound amid the noise of roadworks further down the street, an ever more insistent hammering of drums.

And Gabriela, who has now become the chosen one, the woman selected for sacrifice this windy spring, after vainly looking for an escape route behind the tub in which a thirsty shrub struggles to grow, exposed to public mockery, Gabriela in the end surrenders, her body gently coming apart, her knees going slack, her head lolling on her chest, and at that precise moment there emerges from the maternity shop a couple arm in arm, the woman triumphantly preceded by her swollen belly, the man exuding indolent conquest from every pore of his young male's body. The circle of fertility is complete, Gabriela disappears from view, swallowed up by the wall of flesh behind which the sacrifice is to be consummated.

The old woman leans over the railing, calls her, her voice lost in the ominous rumbling of evening, between the hammerings of workmen and a peal of thunder rolling in from the west which blots out all human voices. But it is not a roll of thunder, it is the number 15 tram, and with an unexpected spurt Gabriela bursts through the wall of relations ready to tear her to shreds and runs, with wind in her heels, runs so hard that the red plastic butterfly which holds her hair in place becomes detached, flutters briefly in the air and falls on the cobbles, where the first passing car will reduce it to fragments.

The circle of relations breaks up, rushes in pursuit, but Gabriela is already aboard the vehicle, the doors close, the driver is in a hurry, the number 15 moves off again screeching, the old woman draws in a long breath of relief.

She has made an appointment with Ciro on Gabriela's day off. She does not want the girl to witness their conversation and above all she does not want her to see what he has come to deliver.

With his usual mild and disarming smile, Ciro unwraps on the kitchen table the parcel he has brought with him. On the green wax cloth with its floral pattern, the black object looks like one of the tools of his trade.

Probably, he suggests, it would be a good idea to close the shutters for a moment. The neighbours, you know…

There's only a senile old man opposite, who spends all day staring at the wall and insults his daughter when she returns from work, says the old woman, but she closes them all the same, you never know.

What make is it? she then asks, weighing the thing in the palm of her hand. It is cold, heavy and slippery.

It's a Beretta 34, an old model. I got it from a friend who collects vintage weapons. He had two of these.

If it's an old model, that suits me very well. Does it work?

Certainly. I'll show you. You grip it like this, see? Firmly. You raise it level with your eyes, arm tensed but not rigid.

Where did you learn this? the old woman asks.

Partly by watching TV films. But my brother was a thief and there were weapons around the house too.

Oh yes? And where is he now?

Not with us any more. They shot him during a chase across the rooftops, only a scratch but he lost his balance. He fell from the eighth floor.

I'm sorry.

Me too. He was a criminal but he wasn't an evil person. I was little when it happened, but it has been a big lesson.

Ciro points the gun at a picture representing an undulating mountain landscape, takes aim, squeezes the trigger. Click.

That's more or less what you do. I'm not much of an expert at this sort of thing.

He lowers his arm again, hands her the weapon. You have a go too. Be decisive, firm grip. Straight in front of your nose, you're pulling it to the right a bit, see? Is it too heavy for you?

No, it's light.

The old woman pays. It costs less than she had thought. Ciro is always honest.

About that Persian blind that needs adjusting, I'll come another time. I'm in a bit of a hurry today, he says, standing in the doorway.

No, wait. Aren't there any, what do you call the things, bullets? Where are they?

Cartridges? Well, no, I didn't bring any. You're surely not intending to use it?

The old woman stares at him dumbfounded, the pistol dangling from her arthritic hand.

You don't actually want to shoot anyone, do you? You don't have to. It's for scaring off thieves, right? If you should happen to find someone had broken in, you show him that and the boot's on the other foot. In ninety per cent of cases they aren't armed.

The old woman continues to stare at him.

You grip it firmly, he repeats patiently. With your arm tensed but not rigid. That way they'll think you know what you're doing, they'll take you seriously… and if by chance they get the gun off you, they can't shoot you.

The old woman stands motionless, lips pressed tightly together.

You didn't actually want to kill anyone, did you? Ciro laughs nervously, uneasy. He stammers: It… it was j… just a deterrent…

The old woman stares at him, disappointed. Resentful.

He hurriedly takes his leave, murmuring that he'll call her about the blind, he's short on time, and then he escapes down the stairs, she follows and stands watching him, she can see his ponytail bouncing on his shoulders, and then Ciro has gone and the useless object is dangling from her hand, in full view of any neighbours on her landing who might come out at that precise moment, but they don't come out.

She doesn't want to kill anyone?

The old woman sits in the armchair, the pistol on her knees, her fists clenched.

Curse Ciro's simple-mindedness, his good soul.

It is her fault, she got the wrong person.

But why is it automatically supposed that a woman of her age, who hasn't been part of society for thousands of years, who no longer has in her life anything like love or friendship, can't possibly want to kill anyone? On the contrary, it would be exactly the right moment. What a laugh, if they gave me thirty years.

She tries to breathe slowly. To calm down. She thinks of all the people she has wanted to kill in the course of her life.

Nothing comes to mind. No one.

Come on, think harder. You are the quick-tempered sort, you have chewed on your rage for years, rage used to wake you up at night, your legs twitching with spasms of anger, as if you were kicking against chains of lead in your sleep.

Nora used to shake you, speak to you. Hey, she would say, stop that! Wake up! Dream about something else! She would stroke you to calm you. You would open your eyes, your seized limbs would loosen, you would sigh with relief.

And even now the old woman does not remember — or only distantly, the way minor things of little importance can flicker into view again long after the event — that over the course of the years she has felt murderous furies against her father, her brother, a hateful journalist, a thieving colleague, a concierge, a neighbour… and who else? Dozens, but forgotten furies count for nothing now, they can't be revived, they were no more than reflections of her impotence.

Maybe, she thinks, stroking the gun, if she had had this little toy when she was young, sold to her by someone who provided the bullets for it as well, maybe she would have used it, because she mistily recalls moments of blind rage, of lights flashing in her head, when if she had been an animal she would have bared her teeth… but would she really have done it then? Or was her rage an indication of irremediable softness?

Fury, guilt, fear — all part of life's vital substance. One cannot do without them. The same goes for desire, for curiosity and pleasure and greed. The prime material of her work. Which took her into other dimensions, gave her life rhythm and measure and an alternative tempo. In her work, these conflicts became the white-hot material of her creativity. They detonated without killing.

But the thing that brought into harmony the jarring noises of this life, what gave them meaning and even beauty, was love.

She sees Nora again, pretending to conduct the orchestra while listening to the radio. She hears her voice again: Hey, come on, life is a game.

The old woman takes hold of the pistol on her knees, raises it with arm tensed but not rigid.

Who first?

Her father, obviously. The old shit, whom she resembles. Same personality, even if the head, happily, is a different one. How hard it was to break free from him, when she was young! Has she ever really succeeded?

She squeezes the trigger. It is harder than she had thought, but it finally gives. *Click!* That's one!

Who to go after next? A lifetime's enemies are lined up before her, like suspects in an identity parade, backs to the wall. They have grown old as well, they have lost their vigour, their edge, they have osteoporosis, bunions on their feet, they walk with a stoop. She doesn't know who they are any more, who is the guilty party, and guilty of what. She moves her arm, takes aim at one man, another, a woman, but the faces fade out, even the face of the woman who stole a story, robbing her of a bestseller, years ago, what a crisis that was! And how she suffered for that piece of stupidity, she thinks, while the face of the hated rival shades off into the nothingness, she wouldn't recognise her if she saw her, other people's faces are no more than our own gaze reflected back at us.

Her arm is tired already, she lowers it slowly, puts the pistol on her knees, strokes it as if it were a dead creature. Poor little murdering beast, she thinks. You are no use to me at all.

Only then does she realise there has been this piece of metal on her knees all this time instead of the warm though now arthritic and smelly body of the elderly Venom. Until a few days ago he never failed to jump on her lap as soon as she sat in the armchair, even if it took him two or three goes, falling back each time on his stiff legs.

But today Venom has not come.

At four in the afternoon the old woman sends Gabriela up to the attic to check that there have been no intrusions. The emissary returns after a few minutes and hands the key back with a reassuring message: everything in order, no sign of alien presences.

At five, as soon as the girl has gone, the old woman slips on a cardigan, hides the pistol in its pocket and goes up to the seventh floor. The corridor is dark, as always, the air stale. She walks lightly, trying to make as little noise as possible. She stops at the attic door, listens. The sound of her own breathing makes it hard to hear anything, curse the heavy breathing of the elderly. She turns the key in the keyhole and the door swings open without effort or squeaking, Ciro has made a good job of it.

Gripping the pistol in her pocket, the old woman advances cautiously into the room.

This time she finds the light switch straightaway and in

the light of the thirty watt bulb sees that the blue blanket is still there, neatly folded. There is a smell of recent cleaning. The cardboard boxes are stacked against the wall. No other sign.

Malvina, I say to her, I know you understand nothing, but try to listen to me. Pretend! Look at me!

She looks at me. She smiles at me, her head slightly to one side, as if to say: You poor thing!

I would like to strangle her for the grief she gives me. That I give myself.

Look at me, sitting here, don't I fill you with pity? Reduced to talking to a woman in her second childhood because I don't have anyone else. I'm like that old cretin who lives opposite, with his trousers always unfastened and falling down.

Malvina lowers her gaze to the crotch of my trousers.

Ah, so you do understand what I'm saying?

Malvina gives me one of those coquettish looks of hers, coy and flirtatious, the sort that used to make me jealous fifty years ago when she turned it on Nora, I know all she wants is what I've brought in the bag, two cream slices two small rum babas and a *cannoli* filled with zabaglione, but it could also be that she is actually listening to me, is telling me something with her eyes…

Are you pleased with your new chair? Is it more comfortable?

Perhaps she doesn't even realise that the chair she is sitting in is not the earlier pile of junk.

She leans forwards towards my bag, impatient. I take the box of pastries. I tuck a paper napkin into the neck of the ugly top they have dressed her in today, this one definitely not one of her own either, I have never seen her in it. My hands are shaking. I have not slept for two nights.

It's that girl, I say. She's the one who's making me nervous. I don't know what she's up to, she's a professional liar.

Malvina bites into the rum baba, the rum trickles down her chin. I shouldn't have brought the baba, but she does like them so much. I wonder if they give her anything to drink. Or does a foggy-minded old woman not have any right to a shot of alcohol? Next time I'm bringing her some vodka. We are in the glazed veranda which looks out on the garden, the windows are open, the roses in flower. There are four other ruins in here, apart from us two: three are wrapped in their personal bubble, but the fourth is staring at us with hatred. Perhaps he would like to kill Malvina. Or me. Perhaps he would like a rum baba. I move my chair so that it has its back to him and conceals Malvina's little feast.

Gabriela is an enigma. You know, one of those women who remain suspects all the way through a crime novel. I know lying is sometimes useful and necessary, but it annoys me that she does it with me. She told me she had thrown away blankets and sheets, and instead, it's not true, they're still up there, in the attic. Someone goes there to sleep, in my attic, you understand. And she knows it and is aiding and abetting.

Malvina stirs in her chair, she appears to be looking out of the window.

Don't worry, she can't hear us.

Gabriela is outside in the garden, among the roses. She is sitting on a bench reading a book she asked if she could borrow. *Portrait of a Lady*. You'll find it boring, I told her. I like the title, was her answer.

Malvina squirms in her chair, looks at me with lifeless eyes. Two sinkholes. I immediately abandon my plan of feeding her the pastries one at a time, slowly, to keep her attention. I pass her the container, she helps herself with both hands, the second dripping rum baba in one and the two cream slices in the other.

Vina, darling, don't do that! You're getting yourself all dirty! Go slowly, no one's going to take them away!

I would like to hit her, I would like to hug her, it is a good thing I brought the wet wipes to clean her hands and face. In that instant she is Nora, she is my mother, she is me, I can't bear it.

I am tired, I don't want to fly into a rage here, start crying.

Malvina takes the *cannoli*, the last thing left, pushes it into her mouth all in one go.

Bollocks to this, I tell her. I can't take any more. I'm on the brink. Why don't I fall over the edge? Why do I get in a fury over that girl? What is she to me? I was calm, I preserved the distances. It was a poor life, but it jogged along. And then you abandoned me, you came here. You reduced yourself to this.

An attendant arrives and looks at us disapprovingly. I seize one of Malvina's hands and scrub it with the perfumed wipe. Perhaps I am hurting her. She complains just a little, humble, but does not pull away, as always she accepts any mistreatment I subject her to.

Malvina's apartment is already for sale, Ana has told Gabriela. I could kill Osvaldo.

If only I had the things. The bullets.

But that wouldn't change anything for Malvina.

And then Osvaldo is not alone.

Besides him I would have to kill the wife, the children. Exterminate the whole family. And it still wouldn't change a thing inside Malvina's head.

The pistol is here beside me. I put my arm out and touch the cold metal.

Venom is sleeping on his cushion, on the sitting room divan. He purred when I stroked him, but only opened one eye. He did not move, he remained curled up in an almost perfect circle, his tail on his nose.

The doctors said nothing, except that everything had gone well.

They did not say that Nora would live for another seven years, that we would make the Canadian trip, that there would be other birthdays.

And so these things did happen, but not as they happen when life is in full flow, things that come along, sure-footed and solid, even weighty, clad in reality like an item of clothing that at the end of the day is only on loan but which seems made to measure, and everyone credits it, there, we have achieved another year, crossed Canada from Montreal to Vancouver. As if you were owed it, and no one can take it from you, this year, this trip, it is only a moment in a long series of moments, which leads boldly into a future without limits.

And instead for the old woman every day was eaten into by fear, corrupted by the acid of insecurity. What would happen tomorrow, next month? Would there be a next month? Smile, Nora used to tell her, be happy, we're here, we're together. It's been a beautiful day, no? The old woman forces herself to do what Nora asks, and sometimes succeeds.

She had even attended a Buddhist centre, in search of inner peace. In the mornings she recited mantras, and set a little offering before a miniature statue of the Buddha, who is not god, in whom she does not believe, but only an image of illumination.

But illumination never came.

The only thing whose existence was never in doubt was love, with its burden, for now love seemed to have become the street companion of those other ragamuffins: anger, fear, fury and similar rabble. Instead of rising above them, controlling them, sorting them out. It was a soiled kind of love, tattered and torn, impure. Contaminated by all sorts of anxieties, as if by bedbugs and lice, always there making her pick at the scabs of her misery. An outcast.

The old woman felt ashamed. Of her powerlessness, of her grief. Of the panic which clamped her chest in a band of iron, and there was no breathing exercise that did any good.

Nora was much calmer than she was. Happy, even.

Happiness is a talent, either you have it or you don't. Nora had it, could laugh at things that were scarcely amusing, like her tottering steps when she rose from her bed after a crisis, or the absurd, well-intentioned circumlocutions of some of the friends who visited.

As on those earlier occasions when she had felt emotional or sexual jealousy, the old woman was jealous of the familiarity of Nora's dealings with their live-in guest, mortality.

Of the warning signs, in herself, of an illness similar to Nora's, or even different though still mortal, no trace remained.

The old woman was healthy, though afflicted with stiffened limbs and other prosaic aches and pains.

But it would be wrong to think those seven years were nothing but torment.

They were also full of joy.

Momentary, sneaking up on her, joy would ambush her, overtake her by surprise. And perhaps because of the many mantras she recited, or because the defence mechanisms of anxiety and anger had become worn out, she eventually abandoned herself to those good times. She went along with them. She even provided the conditions for them. Whilst knowing that joy cannot be produced to order, since it does not respond to summons but comes when it wants.

Things by which it was probable, or at least possible, that joy could be attracted, as a cat is attracted by the smell of fish: hearing Nora's voice. Watching her and listening to her declaim lines, sing songs. Now that she did it for her alone, a select audience, catching her by surprise, for a few minutes or seconds, lighting up the stage while peeling an apple or helping her make the bed.

Talking, on whatever subject, at odd moments during the day when all the rest was forgotten, and being fully in the presence of one another.

Praising Nora and her work and hearing her praised by others (like herself, Nora no longer worked, but an artist never really retires — and the old woman discovered that joy does not exclude vanity).

Walking over grass, on a sunny day.

Looking at Nora when she is lost in some pleasurable

thought, when she is unaware of being observed and her face is relaxed.

Touching her skin and smelling her fragrance.

The apartment cleaned and spotless after a blitz of housework — because joy can at times reward our manias.

A really well written romantic novel with its scenes of passion and sex at just the right moments.

Looking at the sea, when it is beginning to grow dark, before dinner, from the balcony of the small hotel in Sardinia where they go every year for a few days.

Listening to Nora's voice. Smelling her fragrance. The warmth of her hands.

Talking, fully present to one another, at odd moments of the day…

But it was sufficient merely to be open to it, and joy could arrive unexpectedly in the most improbable situations, for example while she was buying vegetables for dinner, or when she discovered at the back of the wardrobe an old pair of exceptionally pretty shoes, forgotten but still perfectly wearable, or when the morning air carried the scents of earth and leaves. Then it would happen, that instant which the old woman — a person with her feet always firmly on the ground — compared to an orgasm. Not any old orgasm, but the one when you make love with love, without thinking too much, because you are young and certain of yourself and very excited, and the mind is free and light, and pleasure arrives in a rush, unstoppable, almost inconveniently because it signals the end of that state of beatitude, and at the very moment when pleasure opens you wide you feel you are as vast as the universe, and as light and as powerful as a goddess.

Joy is by definition something even more rare and radiant than happiness, it is a measure of the divine that exists in human life, even for an atheist. It is as transparent and luminous as a flame, a fire that passes through you without pain, and reveals to you all the world's secrets — in a language you do not know.

This was joy for her, similar to that exact moment when the most wonderful orgasm begins, with the difference that it radiates not from inside you, from the deep well at your centre, but from every part of you at the same time, and it does not leave you languid, with a throbbing body, but simply filled with gratitude and with a melancholy so light that it could almost be described as a form of contemplation.

And then with the years, after the first, second, third, fourth, the anguish began to come and go, have pauses. Life stood on firm ground again. Death retreated — or maybe it was the old woman's defences that made it do so. Her self-confidence returned. Sometimes she forgot to be afraid for hours at a time, for whole days.

Nora was well, she had put on a bit of weight, enough to complain that her clothes were tight and had begun to talk about dieting. Venom was no longer a boisterous and inquisitive youth, he was by now a mature cat, at home everywhere, master of every situation. They had made that trip to Canada, long car journeys across the endless plains, where the sky was a landscape of its own, the mountain lakes were as green as malachite and the rainforest was a vast rustling creature in constant watery dialogue between the clouds and the ocean.

In the sixth year, without admitting it to herself, the old

woman dropped her guard. At moments she allowed herself to be invaded by the euphoria of victory. She felt a weight had been lifted. Everything seemed to confirm it, the words of the master at the Buddhist centre, the quotations each day in her book of maxims, the most commonplace coincidences, like the chance encounter with an old friend who had been ill, and was now cured.

It was then that death launched its final assault.

One day Nora tells her about an inconsequential episode. Something, she tells her, that didn't really happen except in her head.

On the return flight from Canada there was a crowd at the check-in, and when it was their turn there were no seats left next to each other. Before the aeroplane left, Nora, sitting in her allotted seat, had turned round to look to see where the old woman was. She was sitting several rows away, on the other side of the aircraft. And then Nora had thought, if the plane were to crash, they would die apart. In the final moments, she would not be able to cling to her, perhaps not even to see her.

Terror had gripped her, and — she tells her this years afterwards, laughing, in the hospital bed — it was not the terror of dying, no, but of dying without her there beside her.

So unbearable had been Nora's panic that she had succeeded, shamelessly inconveniencing the other passengers, in changing places and sitting next to her.

And shortly afterwards she had fallen asleep, at peace, forgetting any thought of disaster.

What a stupid woman! Isn't it comical?

Listen, Osvaldo, I say. It bothers me already, just to pronounce his name. I explain to him that Malvina has got worse since she went into the nursing home, that the place does not suit her, that she could come and stay with me, even though in reality I don't know myself how far I believe what I am saying. What I am proposing seems impossible, a mad solution which would turn our lives upside down.

But aren't they all upside down already? So we might as well.

I am trying to sound convincing, to be diplomatic. Doubts almost make the words stick in my throat. Would Malvina really be better off here? Would I find her too much to bear? Could we manage, the two of us and Gabriela? Do I have enough money for a second carer?

Is this how I want to live the years that are left to me? Living on top of each other, with a woman who doesn't know my name any more?

Years, months, days, what difference does it make? If Malvina were here, maybe we could die together with dignity. If only Ciro had not played that trick on me.

No, not with the pistol. Something else is needed, and there is only one person I can ask.

What did I say to Osvaldo? I don't know, but I sense he is listening in patient silence, I hate his patience, Osvaldo is nearly sixty, he thinks he is still young. He lives in another world, he despises us.

Perhaps it is because he is beginning to feel scared, detecting the odour of old age, that he despises us.

He tells me, and I knew perfectly well that he would say

this, that Malvina is fine where she is, that the staff of the nursing home are qualified, the treatment is decent and humane.

I realise that I cannot say what I would like to say: What about me? What do qualifications and decency matter to me? I want my friend Malvina, can you understand that or not? Cretin!

Now I can't remember exactly what we said to each other, or in what order. What I replied in answer to what. But it was when Osvaldo said it was nothing to do with me. That I mustn't trouble myself over it, some things are strictly family matters.

That was when I started to go off the rails. What crappy family is that? I said. Malvina's family is me, you piece of shit. Do you know who your aunt used to speak with every day? Who she used to eat *cannoli* in the *pasticceria* with? Have you any idea what her favourite cakes are, what her fears are, her ailments? Who's the one who knows everything about her? Do you know? Who's the one she can talk to about the people who are no longer with us? You haven't the slightest idea who Malvina used to see, who her friends were!

And I even gave him names, to make some impression on him I frantically tried to recall the cinema people Malvina has known over the years, the names I didn't remember I invented, I exaggerated, I must have named Rossellini, Bertolucci, maybe even Fellini. How would he know anyway? And I don't either, actually. I can't remember now if she did know them, it was so long ago. And they certainly weren't her friends. Her friends were cultivated and intelligent and strange and amusing people, and sometimes depressed as well, but not famous. And they are all dead, more or less.

And I couldn't restrain myself, I must also have told

him that Malvina hated her sister, but that's wrong, in reality it was the sister who hated Malvina, because Malvina was beautiful and had talent and was not greedy and malevolent like the sister. I told him that all Malvina got from her family were kicks in the teeth, starting from when her parents sent her to a psychiatrist to cure her! Because she had had a thing with a woman friend at university! And the sister claimed she was no woman, called her a frustrated male! She was rotten with envy because of her gifts! And her brother had helped himself and emptied the house without even saying thank you! They had robbed her of her share of the inheritance, and he was now the one enjoying the benefits, the vile Osvaldo. Thief! Thief!

I am out of breath, I have lost my voice from all that enraged shouting. My heart is pounding, perhaps it's the right time, but I succeeded in saying everything, just about everything, and I feel a powerful sense of satisfaction, as if I had avenged the wrongs of a lifetime. I see Nora before me in the kitchen, laughing and clapping her hands and saying: Yes, that's the way, go on, bravo!

Osvaldo is still speaking. I believe he is telling me that I ought to get myself into that nursing home as well, if it weren't for my age he'd take me to court, and blah and blah and blah.

Nora is no more, but she was so vividly here that her absence still has the scent of her presence — like newly mown grass.

I end the call. I go into the dining room. Into the sitting room. Into Nora's bedroom. I look around me, I open the wardrobe, go through her clothes hanging there.

Years ago the old woman decided to give them away, Nora's clothes.

Because things are only things, and the essence of Nora lives nowhere if it doesn't live inside the woman who survives her, in her head, in her blood, in her five senses.

She even made one of Gabriela's precursors help get them out, they laid them on the bed, each item on its hanger, and her legs gave way. Any attempt to move, to do anything, seemed suddenly deprived of all meaning, her limbs became infinitely weary and heavy, as when one has a fever, and she had to retreat to the armchair for the rest of the day. The clothes remained on the bed in Nora's room for days, until she recovered from the idiotic notion that she should get rid of them and understood what she should really do: treat them as treasures to be preserved with care.

In the weeks that followed, the clothes were all washed and ironed and re-hung in the correct order, silk with silk, wool with wool, each section graduated according to colour.

Since then the ritual has come to be an annual one. Nora would laugh that her clothes have never been looked after with such fanatical attention.

Things are not only things.

Not the ones, anyway, that have caressed Nora's skin, which have retained some part of her fragrance, her sweat, her body's heat.

And now she speaks to Nora's clothes without shame. Not so much in words, although at times she uses those as well, but above all with her hands. She will spend minutes caressing them, delicately stroking the material between her fingertips.

She immerses herself in their colour until it leaches into her. It is a way of looking at things, which is not so much an action as a surrendering, an opening up of oneself which allows the thing to enter us through our eyes, and this happens particularly with colours. In this way, the old woman, by nature impatient, even succeeds in forgetting the here and now, and comes close to the rarefied virtues of meditation.

The old woman was sitting beside the hospital bed and thinking of the two of them on the flight from Montreal to Paris. Anonymous, among unknown people, up amongst the clouds at an altitude of ten thousand metres. Beneath them the sea.

She was thinking about Nora's fear. Not of dying but of dying away from her.

The old woman had always been a pragmatic person. To have a job to do suited her. A task to perform, meticulously, right to its end.

Checking that the nurses were doing their duty scrupulously. Waiting to catch the doctors, for hours if necessary. With a tenacity beyond patience, in reality with a suppressed, ceaseless fury.

And then when Nora was discharged there were exhaustive readings of her prescriptions, dosages measured out to the minutest drop. Timings observed to the second.

Ooph! Nora would say, woken from her sleep to take a pill. She would swallow, and turn over on to her other side.

The old woman's love was inflexible. She had put on the miner's overalls, descended into time's subterranean depths, into the tortuous tunnels where one cannot see the light of day ahead, but only the getting there, step by step.

The final phase had lasted seven months. Seven months which brought to completion the seven years. A black number, seven, the number which brings the old woman bad luck.

And when Nora had died, the old woman was asleep. It was a particularly quiet night, with no pain or breathing difficulties. Nora's sleep was so light and precarious she did not want to risk disturbing it by lying down next to her. She had remained in the armchair, the side lamp on, yielding to an unaccustomed laziness. She was thinking neither about yesterday nor about tomorrow but only about her back, which ached, and the book she was reading. At some point, she did not consult the clock, she had given in to weariness and gone into the other room to stretch out on her own bed. Ten minutes, she had told herself.

She had woken suddenly at dawn, as if someone had taken hold of her by the throat. She could hear only the thudding of her own heart. Deafening. Wearing the clothes she had fallen asleep in, not even pushing her feet into her slippers, she had run to the room next door. What had happened, what noise or silence had brought her to wakefulness in this agitated state?

Breath suspended, eyes staring, as bemused as if suddenly swept away by a river in flood. As if detached from her own body, she looked without seeing. Nora was on the bed, motionless, her eyes half closed. She had approached, cautiously, obliquely, she was afraid to touch her.

She was breathing.

She was not breathing.

She did not seem to be suffering. It was Nora, apparently unchanged, yet some terrible metamorphosis had taken place in her.

Death had just passed by, the old woman was already a survivor.

Death — evoked every day, addressed in curses, blandishments, bargained with — had feathered her with its touch, had been here, its wake still lingering in the rooms of their life. And she, who had been preparing herself for years, what did she feel? Nothing, except a vast astonishment, which demolished her, lifted her clean out of herself. She watched herself move, heard the panting of her breath, the roar of blood in her ears, she saw herself performing dislocated actions: leaning over Nora's face seeking with her ears, her lips, signs of breathing she was unable to find, crumpling a handkerchief into a ball, seizing the telephone, letting it drop. Forcing herself to take one of Nora's hands between her own. It was tepid, inert.

For an instant time split asunder. Death had unroofed the world.

The floor beneath her feet had ceased to exist, the ceiling had disintegrated in a spider's web of cracks. Lost in a superabundance of space, the old woman moved round the room in tiny steps, looking at the objects in it, at herself, her past, fragmented into meaningless atoms and floating in infinite, thunderous, sulphur-filled skies. The walls opened up to reveal abysses as old as time, black cascades of lava.

She was no more than an atom whirling in the vaults of chaos. Massacres had been enacted on an infinite scale and were happening still amid this scenery, blood had turned into cloud, blood had become the horizon. The land was a white carpet of bones. The horizon was in flames. The universe exploded.

She looked at Nora's face. The half-open lips revealed a glimpse of teeth. The cheeks curved in, hollow, as never seen before.

She thought of the aeroplane flight, of Nora's fantasy about dying clasped in an embrace, the two of them pressing their bodies into one, turning their backs on death.

And instead Nora presented her uncovered face, the tender lips, she gazed before her from her half-closed eyes, the eyelids too delicate to protect their fragility.

And she was not there. She was sleeping, without knowing or seeing, far away, unhearing.

In the storm of sound, the old woman was emitting little gasps, from deep in her chest rose a subterranean growl, as if a small creature imprisoned down there were roaring in vain.

And then suddenly the nurse was beside her, the one who came every morning. The old woman wanted to send her away, hit her with her fist, returned to her senses, apologised.

The nurse put an arm round her shoulders, the old woman tottered.

Slowly the walls closed in on the familiar room, the heavens ceased to thunder. Time started to flow again.

Implacable, the afterwards began.

For a long time she asked herself — she still asks herself every day, even now — if, during her last night, Nora called her, if she felt abandoned, helpless because her voice could not make itself heard.

If she suffered. If she was afraid.

But she was not alone, Malvina used to tell her. You were

there, you have always been there. She knew nothing about it, she passed away in her sleep.

The old woman, who found it essential to feel guilty — her personal wickedness kept her alive and allowed her to tolerate the outrage that the world should go on turning — ignored her, turned on her looks of contempt. Malvina absorbed every punishment.

She kept her friend at arm's length, all the friends who offered her consolation. They only wanted to dilute her mourning with banalities.

Nora's was not an ordinary death, a death like all the others, past and future.

It was not the inevitable destiny of everything that has life. It was unique, special. This was a death beyond comparisons, without dimensions.

The death of Nora did not belong only to Nora, it was hers as well, the old woman's, it festered inside her, it scoured the chambers of her heart, it dried up her veins.

They said: don't dwell on it, be brave, keep living. They said: you were good together, you were happy. You are a strong person. She wants you to carry on.

The old woman retreated behind the armour of her fixed stare, responding only with nods or shakes of the head. The others were already distancing themselves from it, speaking about trivial things, one man's arthritis, another woman's little grandson, and where did you buy that jacket, it suits you so well.

The old woman kept up appearances, as she had throughout her life, held herself erect, greeted people, even smiled. Only with Malvina was there enough intimacy, and one can say love, for her to be her true self, scathing, unbearable. Hateful.

All the wrongs, or lack of recognition, that Nora had suffered, flooded back into her mind when confronted by the solemn, regretful faces of those grieving for the departed. Her career as an artist, never really acclaimed as it deserved to be. She assiduously cultivated her rancour against the doctors who had not taken her case sufficiently to heart, against a nurse who had snapped at her one day.

A cold, poisonous anger was for some time what kept her going. A hospital drip, which fed her an acid contempt for the world and for herself.

While in the meantime Malvina — humble, red-eyed — prepared her meals which she did not eat.

Then the anger left her. One morning she stayed in bed for a long time, awake, staring at the ceiling.

It was the cat who forced her to get up, coming to rub his nose on her face.

She gave Venom something to eat, washed, dressed, checked that everything was in order in the apartment. She opened the box in which she had placed the will, rewritten a few days before. It was still there, in the sealed envelope. She put it on the kitchen table, under a vase so that the cat could not knock it to the floor.

She locked the front door, put the keys in her pocket and took the lift to the top floor.

There, at the end of the corridor giving access to the attics, was a full-length window that looked out over the condominium's inner courtyard. She opened it — the wood, swollen by rains and dried out by the sun, grated and resisted but eventually gave way — and gazed at the rooftops of the city centre, some dark red and crumbling, spotted with brown mould, and others bright red, recently restored, the gables, a bell-tower to the right and another to the left, a cupola in the distance, the mountains over there, as grey as knife blades and still snow-capped. At her feet, beyond a low and rusty railing, a leap of seven storeys into the funnel of the courtyard, dark and tempting.

The old woman stood there, with the sun on her face, her arms dangling, not moving. Her head resting against the window frame, her eyes closed.

She opened them at intervals, and the light, or the sight of the tangible world, caused them to brim with a stinging liquid, which was not tears, but the secretion of life itself.

She was thinking of nothing. She was waiting.

Her breathing was calm. Her mind empty.

Then slowly she pushed herself away from the wall, hardly wavering. The railing was no higher than her knees. She felt extraordinarily light, calm.

At that moment the voice of Nora called her. It really was the voice of Nora, not a mistake, but a genuine and specific sound, as happens sometimes when one is about to fall asleep and sentences, scraps of dialogue, odd words play in your head.

It was Nora, one day in a now forgotten year, walking along a beach, the day they had found the jellyfish, Nora with her trousers rolled up to her bronzed calves, coming up behind a little boy and speaking to him. The boy, ten or eleven, was gathering the dead creatures with a stick, some of them lying there like streaks of spittle, looking disgusting, some beautiful and glistening like iridescent glass, and shovelling them into a red plastic bucket. But don't they sting? Nora asked. Then the child proudly bared his arm to show a fiery red burn. Straightaway Nora had rushed down into the water, on that cold day, into that cold sea, full of jellyfish. And powerless to stop her she had remained on the shore shouting at her and collecting the clothes left strewn on the wet sand. A few minutes later Nora returned to dry land, teeth chattering, unharmed and triumphant. To the old woman, who was roundly cursing her and trying to dry her off, she had said, laughing: Stop being so scared! I'm here! Nothing happened!

This is what the old woman heard that morning, those exact words spoken by the voice of Nora, which came from some place in her mind or maybe from the far end of the attic corridor.

She turned round to look, knowing that there was no one behind her.

She remained for a while where she was. Then she felt hungry. She had come up without even making a cup of coffee, it seemed ridiculous to have breakfast when one intends to kill oneself.

So she closed the window again and returned to the apartment.

She had gone back, to that window at the end of the corridor on the seventh floor. With no precise intentions, but each time readying herself for what, perhaps, might happen.

In reality motivated, at least the first few times, by the desire to hear that small miracle of the voice repeated. Which it was not. Not up there. Nora's voice did come back and let itself be heard again, but on other occasions, at unpredictable moments, and as was natural, especially when she was halfway between sleeping and waking. But not up there any more, among the rooftops.

Her excursions to the seventh floor became less frequent and stopped altogether. One day she found that the window had been blocked up. Perhaps someone had noticed that it had been opened, had been worried that a burglar might get in from over the rooftops.

And one day Malvina said to her: Stop all this business about you not being there at the crucial moment. That's the way she wanted it to be, haven't you understood? If she hadn't, she would have waited for you.

The old woman knew perfectly well that everything we say about death is nonsense, because we know nothing about death, and maybe in truth there is nothing to know. The only lessons death teaches us are about life. About itself, it reveals not a thing.

And hence in the end it is only life that speaks to us, and only about itself, seeking to muffle the roar of the nothingness that surrounds it.

In any event she chose to believe what her friend said. She felt sympathy for the gentle Malvina, who had been looking after her with ill-rewarded affection for weeks, and ate whatever she put on her plate. She was compliant and grateful, so much so that Malvina became slightly alarmed. Was she hatching some plan? Could she be ill? Did she want to die as well, and leave her completely alone?

Now the old woman felt pity. Not just for Malvina, but also for herself and above all for Nora. Yes, for Nora, who had gone away, who could no longer talk or laugh or sing or be what she had been, the woman she loved. Nora was now in a state of being — yes, being — but of the most fragile and defenceless kind, she existed henceforth only in the memory of the old woman and those things — creatures, places — that had known and loved her, and therefore she could not abandon or betray her. She felt her, the woman who had been the most dear of dear people, to be in her own trust, wherever she still was, in dreams, in objects around the house, in certain lights, pieces of music, sounds, in a glance exchanged with someone, a shared memory. She understood that she was the custodian of Nora, that to her, above all other human beings, was entrusted the mission of not allowing Nora to die altogether, to prolong her life for as long as possible.

She started seeing friends again. She recalled the gestures of affection, the words of praise they had had for Nora. She telephoned the nurse who used to come every morning, to thank her. In time, Nora's name entered her conversation again, with studied casualness and restrained passion, and each time her name was heard, Nora returned to live again for a fraction of a second, passing in a flash through the room, glimpsed out of the corner of the old woman's eye, or sensed in a stirring of the air, or even flickering in the resemblance or way of moving of an unknown passer-by on the street, each time something came to life, a secret presence became almost detectable, a fleeting touch.

After a few years, she could even weep. She did so in private, as if practising a secret vice.

Even now, walking down the road on Gabriela's arm, stick in the other hand, being careful not to trip on uneven paving stones or slip in the puddles or on patches of frost, she can happen to catch sight up ahead of the figure of a woman no longer young, but elegant and angular, hair still dark, striding rapidly with a certain military briskness, and the air around her suddenly turns lighter, her heart becomes an adolescent's, the streets of time open before her giving glimpses of infinite futures, in which she will be able to run up to Nora and walk beside her with that same self-confident stride.

It lasts a fraction of a second, just enough to believe in magic.

Then the woman becomes a middle-aged stranger again, and Gabriela asks her: What is it? Aren't you feeling well?

The old woman cannot get into her flat. She does not have the keys. Yet she was certain she picked them up, at least she remembers putting them on the table before going out, but they are not in her pocket, or in her bag either. And even the mobile phone is not there. Confused, ashamed as she stands in the porch, the old woman rummages furiously, coins and handkerchiefs fall to the ground, spectacles, someone stops to stare, a man picks something up and hands it to her, her trembling hand instantly drops it again.

The old woman walks away, wishing she could make her steps calm, tries to think. She returns to the shop where she has just been, asks if by any chance they have found a bunch of keys. The assistant — the fifty-year-old ex-grocer, now reduced to the abject condition of employee of the mini-market chain — offers her a stool to sit on. He tells her that her keys are not here, that she needs to calm down, get her breath back. He brings her a glass of water. He suggests she think back to what she has been doing, where she has gone. She has been to the chemist's and the newspaper kiosk, before going into the minimarket to buy lemons. He telephones the chemist and the paper man, but without success, the keys are not there either. It occurs to her that maybe they fell out of her bag on the way round the shops, or someone has stolen them from her bag, that the thieves are probably in her apartment already, she will find the drawers turned upside down, the sheets ripped, excrement on the divan, Venom dead of a heart attack or hanging from the ceiling light.

I must go, she says. Her glasses have fogged up, the black specks and threads lurking in the gelatinous substance of her eyes, once limpid and colourless, have taken to dancing a dervish dance, she stumbles amongst the boxes of fruit. Stay here another minute or two, he says, taking her arm. Where do you have to rush off to? There's bound to be someone who has a spare set of keys, what about the girl who usually goes out with you?

Yes, indeed, Gabriela has keys to the building, a phone call is all it needs, it's a pity her number is kept in the phone's contacts, and the phone has disappeared as well. Perhaps you wrote it down somewhere, the ex-grocer says again, with the patience of a mother, take a peek in your bag. She shakes her head, it's no good, Gabriela's number is locked in the phone, she hasn't committed it to memory, she can't remember it because the damned girl keeps on changing it, if this ridiculous incident had happened a few months ago she would have gone to Malvina to get her spare keys, or her friend would have sent Ana to bring them, this is what it means to have no points of anchorage any more, she is completely on her own in this part of town, in the whole city the only person she can turn to is an inscrutable girl she only half knows and who maybe isn't as supportive as she thought and lives in a street whose name she doesn't remember, along the river, kilometres away from here. It's no use looking in here, she declares irritably, pulling from the bag packets of medicines, old envelopes, sweets, tattered bits of paper, and amongst the latter, behold, a slip of blue-squared paper on which, written in the girl's looping handwriting, is Gabriela's number.

While her rescuer makes this phone call for her as well, the old woman throws herself voluptuously into the arms of other terrors; Gabriela will have switched off her phone, as she often does. Or she won't answer. How many times has she seen her shrug her shoulders and toss her head with playful, childlike triumph or with frowning contempt: I'm not answering, they can ring as much as they like.

Maybe the thief who has stolen her keys is someone Gabriela knows, maybe it was the girl herself who gave him the information: an old woman who lives alone, you only have to blow on her to knock her down. She keeps the money in her bedroom.

Her mind is a storm-tossed ship, the deck swept by hurricane force gales, the sails split, rent by the wind, the sailors fall in the sea, the mice run from the hold and rush squeaking along the cables and ropes.

Only one thing is missing to make her shame complete, and no sooner evoked than yes, it promptly happens: her bladder strains and presses, demands to be emptied of its liquids, immediately, or it will burst like a balloon. The old woman clenches her fists, grits her teeth, but she knows her resistance will be in vain. A moistness is creeping into her knickers.

The ex-grocer turned shop assistant comes back smiling, tells her Gabriela will be arriving soon. The old woman asks if she can avail herself of his kindness again, he understands without need for further explanations and shows her the way to the bathroom.

Sitting amongst the strawberries and bananas, grateful and relieved of immediate need, she attempts to breathe deeply and evenly. To think positively, for given that disasters are bound to happen there is no point anticipating them. Now that she no longer has Malvina, she must find someone else who lives nearby to whom she can entrust a spare set of keys. But it would always and only be a makeshift solution, some kind stranger who is suitable, probably him in fact, the ex-grocer, who is now pushing a trolley loaded with cans of peas and arranging them on a shelf, and the bitter grimace has reappeared at the corner of his mouth.

Suddenly she remembers an occasion when her friend was waiting for her on that bench outside, at the road intersection where the pavement has become a meeting place for pigeons and pensioners, because it was Malvina who had lost or forgotten her keys, and the old woman, who had had to break off from whatever she was doing to come and rescue her, had given her a sound talking-to.

So we are equal, she thinks, and pictures herself alongside her friend in the nursing home, one beside the other, their wheelchairs almost touching but their eyes never meeting, each of them unaware of the other. Alone together at the centre of an empty world, parallel universes of astonishment and desolation.

She watches the ex-grocer, he is precise, efficient and quick, even if there is something robotic in his movements, a lack of liveliness, as if only by becoming an automaton were it possible for him to do the work that earns his daily bread. (Before, the shop was his own, admittedly not as abundantly stocked, in fact rather sparsely, the boxes spread out on two units only, with smells of citrus fruits and herbs, the tang of olives in brine coming from a small wooden cask. And he used to move around with zest, perhaps a little brusque and irreverent, but certainly not like a robot.) She looks at his long thin nicotine-stained hands which are now sliding a customer's purchases over the scanner at the till, even the hands, indeed the hands more than anything, seem resigned, move mechanically, and only when he is smoking outside in the street, leaning against the door frame, do they become living things again and fiddle nervously with the cigarette.

And finally Gabriela arrives, fresh and smiling like a sunny morning after the thunderstorm.

In the apartment everything is as it should be, Venom is asleep on the divan and the keys are on the table, where she put them before going out, next to the mobile phone.

The old woman apologises for having disturbed Gabriela on her day off and gives her fifty euros. Gabriela demurs, then quickly allows herself to be persuaded.

While she is taking her shoes off she remembers she has forgotten the lemons she went to the shop to buy. Never mind. She asks herself how it is she hasn't noticed that the physical space in which she moves, this part of the city and its people, the world where she is able to walk and think without being overtaken by panic, has been getting increasingly narrow, is now reduced to a few streets, a few blocks around her home.

Next time she will forget her keys in the bar where she goes for coffee, along with her wallet. A thief will find them both and burgle the flat. Maybe he will be waiting for her to return to force her to confess where she keeps her money by scorching her feet with a red hot iron.

Next time she will forget the saucepan on the stove, the water will boil over and put the gas out but the gas will continue to flow all afternoon, it will rise in silent spirals filling the whole kitchen, the dining room, her bedroom, and when, staggering and feeling sick she drags herself to the bathroom and tries to switch on the light, the entire house will blow up.

The next time she leaks a drop of pee no one will come to her rescue, she will feel her underwear getting wet but it won't be only a drop, it will be an unstoppable torrent, her muscles powerless to hold it back, no force of will that has any effect, no control, only her disbelieving eyes and the warm liquid running down into her shoes, everyone will turn round to stare at her, everyone will look away, and no matter how she wishes and pleads for it to be, it will not be, it will not be, the final moment of her life.

The next time.

The decline of the body is visible to all, it is the first thing we see, and all our efforts not to see it only make it more evident.

The old woman has never greatly cared about the lines on her face and her skin going slack, starting to sag under her arms, under her chin and on the inside of her thighs. The body changes shape, her grandmother used to tell her when she went to visit her in the country as a girl. But she didn't believe it, she could not imagine that the angular lines of her body would go flabby like shrunken old marrows, or swollen and wrinkled like wood exposed too long to water. And yet, naturally, this was exactly what had happened. Her slender waist became increasingly less slender, her small, firm breasts drooped like weary flowers. Her hair became thinner and finer, and revealed scraps of pink scalp.

But decline had laid its hands on her body like a tender and all-consuming lover, persuasive and hypnotic, and she had allowed it to enfold her without offering resistance, because she had before her eyes the mirror of Nora. Although each of them aged in her own way, slightly differently, it was plain that both of them were going through the same process of mutation, and since the old woman loved Nora, she also loved her ageing, and thus her own.

The skin of Nora's face may have loosened a little, and shown more lines, but beneath it, the old woman knew, was Nora at twenty, thirty, forty, the eternally young Nora whom she knew so well, and it wasn't just a way of speaking or an illusion, it was a real and literal fact. Gradually as the years passed, Nora acquired the layers of her various ages, which a stranger may have seen as a single solid surface, but to the more attentive eyes of the old woman revealed themselves for what they were, the gauzy accretions that the spider, time, had woven round her and which with every gesture and expression shimmered like so many gossamer veils, revealing her in her various ages, the sumptuous fifties, the alluring thirties, the adolescent never seen but imagined in her dreams, until she sometimes saw through to the green and precious bud of Nora as a little girl.

Yes, decline had been kind to her, for as long as she was two people.

Then, after the death of Nora, the old woman never really looked at herself in the mirror again.

Once upon a time they used to hang coverings over the mirrors during mourning, as if closing the eyes of the deceased, and one can understand why: the real mirrors are the human eyes, the others are only substitutes, reference points, you seem to see yourself in those reflective surfaces, but all you see are the weak and lingering traces of a look which is no longer there. You see your solitude, the empty room, the white wall behind your back.

So forget mirrors, they are only objects, useful for combing your hair, taming rebellious wisps, straightening collars. They have nothing else to say.

And anyway, to talk about old age you need to consider what your body is like on the inside: pains, persistent aches, disappearing teeth, sight growing dim like frosted glass which will never again enjoy the transparency of youth. Your body, that faithful servant, that beast of burden — which you have put to work for years, have asked to stand up and sit down, eat sleep and wake, dance and stay up late and smoke on command, and only very rarely allowed to indulge in laziness or excess for its own pleasure, to loll about in the bed of its desires when it wanted to — the body no longer obeys the orders of its mistress, the will. What is this supreme human quality, free will, when your calves no longer support you? Lame horses are put down, but you instead switch roles and reluctantly become the servant of your body. Fuming, you take care of it, ten drops in the morning, three pills at lunchtime, and don't forget the cold compress. Go for walks, do gymnastic exercises. You lie on the floor, lift your legs, stretch the recalcitrant back muscles. From down there you soon realise how the balance of power has changed: you are at floor level, to get back on your feet you will have to wobble about on all fours. Your home, over which you thought you exercised absolute dominion, now enjoys its own turn, it tyrannises you, becomes ever more strange and hostile, the shelves, up there, too high to be reached, the furniture too heavy to be moved, the rim of the bath has grown higher overnight, or your legs have grown shorter. Not to mention the vast tracts of land under the bed, where the armies of dust have set up camp and get bigger day by day, readying themselves for the final offensive of the degradation which will overwhelm you.

At least if there is no Gabriela armed with broom, bucket and rubber gloves.

Blessed Gabriela.

The radio announces the news that in Mosul nineteen girls have been burned alive in the square because they refused to give in to the jihadi fighters.

The old woman closes her eyes. She passes a hand over her face.

She sees the fire crackling towards the sky, nineteen black birds with their wings in flames between the plants on the windowsill and the balcony of the building opposite, their cries become a piercing song that splits the vault of heaven.

She seems to glimpse the face of Gabriela among those faces white with terror and pointed like gaping beaks. She is afraid for her. All at once, like a curtain opening, the vulnerability of the girl is blindingly clear. Young and alone, easy prey, and that family she would be better off without, exposed to every danger, just as the doors to her home are fragile, her fists small, her breath short.

I saw you from the window, the other day, she says.

Me? When? Gabriela wants to know, with an exaggerated start of alarm.

Last week, or the one before, I don't remember which day it was. You were leaving the building, there were people waiting for you, your sister, I imagine, with the girls and some young man.

Gabriela smiles, is that a flash of relief in her eyes? Ah, yes, my half-sister with my nieces and Vasi's fiancé. They wanted me to go to the wedding but I'm not going, I have to tell him, but how?

And she launches into a tirade against the half-witted seventeen-year-old who has got herself pregnant and abandoned her studies to marry a man with no job. And who looks down on everyone because she, for one, has found a man! What a man, Gabriela remarks, he has no work, he eats their food every day and spends his time on the streets with his friends.

And the other one, the old woman says, the man who is not quite your cousin. The terrorist.

Oh him, says Gabriela. (Too off-handedly?) He hasn't been seen for a while. He's quarrelled with his father again and hasn't been sleeping at home for weeks. He's disappeared. All the better, that way he leaves me in peace.

Dorin, what an idiot! she says as she rinses the vegetables.

And to think he was so sweet when he was little, sometimes my sister and I used to play families, and he was our little boy…

Suddenly the clouds of senility part and the old woman stands in breathless contemplation of what she knew and did not wish to see.

She follows the girl's movements. With her back turned her compact little body reveals nothing. Her feet, in the simple nurse's clogs that she uses at work, are innocent and industrious. Demure, her elbows stay close to her sides like two obedient schoolchildren.

Is he the one who's sleeping in the attic? the old woman asks her point blank. Is it your cousin the terrorist?

Gabriela visibly shrinks at this thrust.

The old woman thinks she has made a mistake by putting the question when her back is turned. But perhaps her shoulders are more eloquent than her scrubbed little face, she thinks, looking at the hunched muscles of her shoulder blades, warriors armed and ready to defend.

No! says Gabriela. How could you think such a thing?

And look at me when I'm talking to you! the old woman commands. I can think such a thing because there are still sheets and blankets up there in the attic, and I told you to remove them. Someone goes there to sleep, can you deny it?

Gabriela slowly turns round. She takes a step back. Not by much, because the kitchen sink is behind her, with the washed vegetables which are waiting to be finished off in the saucepan. Again that innocent victim's look, or frightened animal's, which makes the old woman fly into a temper. Which encourages her to take it as an admission of guilt.

Is it true? Someone is sleeping up there, and you know all about it because you're the one who sent him there!

The girl gives a sharp cry, the knife falls from her hand, a metallic clatter on the floor, she thrusts her thumb in her mouth and sucks it. Blood on her lips, mingled with tears.

Who gave you permission to let him into my attic, the old woman continues, caught up in the irresistible thrill of anger. And you've even given him the key to the street door, haven't you? And the key to the apartment? Eh? Tell me, have you given him that one too? Do you realise how serious this is? I have trusted you at all times, and of course I was mistaken, what do I know about who you are, what you think, what you want? You tell me a load of balls in that sweet little voice and I'm supposed to swallow it, all too easy, I'm an old fool with one foot in the grave, you can do what you want, and in my home! I'm of no account, I'm nobody, just an old cretin with a decrepit cat and a friend with senile dementia!

The old woman stops in time before the tide of recrimination carries her too far. Her head is spinning. An excess of vitality. At her age, fury is like sex, it can kill.

You can't treat me like that! Gabriela cries, crossing her arms over her chest, over the pale blue apron she always wears, the uniform she has chosen and imposed on herself, without anyone asking her to, and which she takes care to keep impeccably washed and ironed.

You can't say those things to me! I work! I have never had a day off sick! I always arrive on time! I have never cheated you, I have never robbed you! I have my dignity, you can't treat me like that!

And ripping the apron off: I resign! I'm not standing

for this!

In a flash she is out of the door, with the speed of youth, the apron bundled under her arm. There is nothing left of her but a disturbance in the air and a cut-price scarf which falls from the coat rack and floats to the floor.

The old woman is sitting at the kitchen table in front of a bowl of cold soup. The spoon sinks sadly into the still half-full dish. From the apartment opposite comes the election-campaign voice of a politician bemoaning the waste of public funds on retrieving corpses of drowned refugees from the Mediterranean. For a moment the old woman is distracted, she thinks of the bodies, swollen and nibbled at by fish, of women men and children with whom death has been playing hide and seek, lurking in the very place they are attempting to escape it, and she thinks of the family tombs, the solemn funerals and the mausoleums of the rich and powerful, and wonders whether it would in fact be better to end like this, anonymous and with the fishes, the whole of humanity, politicians leading the way, recycled directly into life's refuse-disposal system, and without wasting private and public resources. But suddenly she is distracted from her distraction and falls once more into the anguish which is eating away at her like an acid.

Gabriela has resigned.

What will she do now? Where will she find a replacement? She has no desire to look for a replacement, she does not want to get to know anyone new, she has had enough of everything.

Venom lifts his head from the cushion where he is dozing, levers himself with difficulty to his feet and emits a series of thick catarrhal coughs. He seems to be gasping for air, his eyes dilated and staring at nothing. The old woman watches him, silently begging him not to die, not like this. Not now that she is alone, not when there isn't even Gabriela.

The world has turned very cold despite it being an unusually warm spring. From the apartment opposite come bursts of gunfire and shouts in a female voice, there seems to be a war going on in the house, then suddenly the gunfire falls silent and all that remains is the woman's voice shouting: Enough! It is the old man's daughter, who has burst into the room and turned the television off.

Those two, the old woman thinks, quarrel but don't break up. The ties of blood bind them indissolubly together in a comfortable day-to-day hatred. That is what families are for.

If Gabriela were her daughter, she would not be able to get out of it by resigning.

The following morning, at the usual time, the key turns slowly, cautiously, in the door.

The old woman's heart, which has turned into a clock, one of those old-style alarm clocks that goes tick-tock louder and louder every second as the hands get towards eight, suddenly drops through the trapdoor of her chest. She gets up, shaky, holding on to the table.

The steps in the corridor hesitate, lighter than ever, a shuffle of leaves stirred by the wind.

And finally she appears, the same Gabriela as always, her face a little pinched (has she too not been eating?), her eyes dark-ringed. They look at each other. They look away. Their eyes meet again, looking past each other.

Then Gabriela says: I bought the bread, on my way here.

The baker's was already open.

And she puts the little bag on the table, an offer of reconciliation.

The old woman thanks her.

Something touches her gently, maybe a puff of wind, or Venom wanting to jump on her lap. No, it is the girl gently shaking her, wake up, she says, it's ready. Time to eat.

She has fallen asleep in the armchair, she has slept through most of the morning. She is starving.

Gabriela seasons the salad, head bowed, then raises it suddenly as if she has made a decision, and apologises. The old woman waves a hand to say that it is not necessary.

But the girl goes on, she didn't sleep last night, she has been thinking, she is someone who thinks about her work, cares about it. She also cares about her employer's opinion of her. She understands that she has made a mistake by not telling her certain things, by not asking her permission. It is true, she took the key to the attic, had a copy made. Twice, before the handyman came to change the lock and after. But she has been keeping it for herself! She has slept up there, in the attic, only two or three times, she quickly adds, no more than that.

The mouthful of food catches in the old woman's throat.

She was scared to be at home on her own, Gabriela explains.

And before the old woman has time to ask (scared of what? Of being attacked, of being stalked, of ghosts, the werewolves of the river banks?) she admits that it is stupid of her to be scared, but every now and then it happens.

The thing is that Dorin sends her, used to send her, horrible things on her mobile, she says. Now he doesn't send them any more because he doesn't know her number, no one knows it except the *signora*, that way she doesn't receive telephone calls from anyone, fortunately. That is why her half-sister came to wait for her here, outside the building, because she could not reach her any other way. They know the address because Ana knows it and blurted it out. They have done everything they can, Petra and Ana as well, to discover where Gabriela lives, but she has never told them. On the contrary, she is especially careful to ensure they don't follow her. Sometimes she takes the wrong tram on purpose, just in case there is someone down in the street spying on her. When she wants to see them she knows where to find them, but they must never set foot in her own home.

Speechless, the old woman studies the girl who is now giving the serving dish a wipe, dipping pieces of bread in the sauce for the meatballs she has been cooking while her employer was asleep. Alone in her bubble of solitude like a nut in its shell.

Did you never think of sleeping here, she says, in the apartment? Where there are plenty of comfortable beds? Instead of in the attic among all the cobwebs?

Oh, but I cleaned it!

And then: I didn't want to disturb anyone. I was ashamed. It's nice, the attic, have you ever thought of renting it out?

You're mad, it isn't habitable, there's no bathroom! What did you do for a bathroom?

There's a squat toilet at the end of the corridor, didn't you know?

I didn't think it was still working. And you so fussy.

Weren't you afraid, with only that simple plank door, didn't you hear what the locksmith said? It would only need a good shove.

In this house I have never felt afraid, Gabriela says.

Then, smiling: Listen, you remember that little window up there in the attic? High up, in the roof. I used to open the shutter in the evenings and look at the sky. There were stars over my head! So many stars!

She gets up and begins to clear the table.

Crouched on her heels, Gabriela is cleaning the oven. The old woman watches her from behind, in her chair by the window, she looks at her little feet, her spotless white socks. The orthopaedic clogs neatly side by side on the floor. Her buttocks and bosom sliding forward and backward to the rhythm of the hand that works on the inside of the oven with a scourer. From time to time an arm lifts to push the hair from her forehead.

She looks at her and thinks that the stars, in this city, haven't been seen for decades. Not even on what seem to be clear nights. If you look up, all you see is sky, now black, now grey, now electric blue, and at times a ferruginous pink, especially in winter when the lights are on for longer and their murky pallor is refracted in the air.

And the lights of an aircraft leaving or landing, every now and then.

But stars, never.

The brain, a complicated command post which controls the hardware and software of our lives and makes them function in tolerable concord. Which makes the connection between the word 'ice-cream' and that desire for something soft and sweet that makes you salivate, which guides your hand to scratch where the skin itches. Which sends your body instructions to quiver with painful pleasure when you unexpectedly hear a song you haven't heard since you were fifteen.

This complicated command post is, in Malvina, irreparably damaged and almost extinguished. Out of use and completely useless, except for the dull and monotonous blinking of the basic vital functions, heart lungs digestion and a few others. At the most a fanciful glow flickers briefly, then as swiftly as it has appeared, disappears.

But from time to time, as if by miracle and with no warning, the dying machine begins to function again for an instant, tiny lights flicker on here and there in sequence, producing outbreaks of amazing normality, full of sense and elegance.

Thus one day Malvina greets the old woman, enunciating, gravely and ceremoniously: I am delighted that you should have come to see me.

The old woman is alarmed. She sits down with a bump. She blows her nose to buy time.

I too am delighted, she replies. And then, in a whisper so that no one else can hear: Do you want to come away with me?

Overtaken by darkness again and completely unaware of what she has just said, Malvina stares at the bag which today contains a tub of different-flavoured ice-creams, vanilla, pistachio and hazelnut chocolate, her favourites.

While her friend eats, the old woman falls back on the only kind of prayer she knows and practises, the invocation to love, in all its wonderful and terrible manifestations.

If it were possible to translate it into common speech, then prayer in this case would sound more or less like this: All praise, Malvina, to the heavenly grace of your subjunctives!

Shortly afterwards, turning round with aristocratic dignity to the attendant who handles her with brisk efficiency, Malvina announces: It would be good to defecate. In which the conditional is not a doubtful or hypothetical statement, dependent on confirmation by other events (It would be good to defecate, if you were so kind as to take me to the bathroom), but rather a cold form of courtesy, in reality an order dressed up as a wish.

The old woman translates the word 'defecate' for the dumbfounded attendant. Who remains appropriately impressed and perhaps — but probably this is an illusion — pushes the wheelchair towards the bathroom with swifter steps and a spine more deferentially straight.

The old woman watches her proceed on her way.

Her demented friend, a queen in exile.

What beautiful pillowcases! Gabriela exclaims, smoothing her hand reverently over an embroidered monogram. Are they very old? You can tell they're embroidered by hand, why don't you use them? They're still in good condition.

Put them down, the old woman commands, leave them alone, we're here to change the lavender bags, that's all, and then close the wardrobe again.

But instead of closing it she stays there, looking inside, with that stare of fierce concentration that goes beyond present reality and induces the girl to walk more lightly and even more silently than usual to avoid drawing attention to herself and attracting her wrath.

Nora's home. The apartment she was living in when she met her. A magic place, an enchanted forest where everything is possible, where there is always music in the background and something ready to eat, plants in pots and a cat who enters and leaves by the bathroom window, which is kept half-open to allow him his freedom. The cat is not the only one to come and go. Young people are continually turning up, girls and boys attracted to one another and often to Nora, who is a magnet, a pulsating focus for the desires and words that saturate the air. The old woman, who is then thirty but feels much older than the rest of them, mingles with the little crowd, admires them and fears them, is simultaneously seduced and distrustful, is warmed and enraged and cares for them — in short, a whole rebellious orchestra is playing discordant and impassioned music in her breast. And she continues to marvel at the fact that she is the chosen one who stays on to spend the night, after the others have gone away.

Between those sheets, those pillowcases embroidered in cross-stitch and chain-stitch, those mother-of-pearl buttons that get tangled in their hair, while she melts in the profanest of pleasures, she feels she is attaining something sacred with the tip of her tongue, with her sex, with her whole skin. And at the same time she feels human as never before, capable of acknowledging and loving others, of being loved and acknowledged by them.

In her memory it is always winter in those early years. Snow outside the windows, warmth under the blankets. Lying beside her, welded to her skin by the dewy perspiration of love, Nora's body, young and whole, a bare leg poking from the sheet, their breath a white vapour in the freezing room, or perhaps it is the smoke rising from their cigarettes. Nora's smile, the smell of her skin. Their fingers, bold explorers of the body's surfaces and depths, of its curves and slopes, its fullnesses and its hollows, its soft places, the hardness of its quivering muscles.

It is on those pillowcases that she understood that Nora was for ever. No, cautious and down-to-earth as she is she did not think, not even in the rush of passion, that Nora would never leave her — a thing which has always seemed to her, on the contrary, as terrible as it was likely. Simply, she realised that Nora had entered her life for good, and that even if she were to go away, she would still be here. For ever, the mortal and ridiculously limited for ever of her life.

And so it has been, she thinks, closing the wardrobe again, and the pillowcases are still here as well. Which she is careful not to use, so as not to spoil them, but amongst which she places a fresh bag of lavender every year.

Her pains keep her awake. In the yellowish glow that creeps into the room — city darkness is sullied by a thousand lights — the old woman stares at her hands, hands that feel stabbed by invisible spikes. The skin of her forearms whose weary and sagging muscles are scored by hundreds of tiny creases.

She thinks about her bones, which have become lighter and more fragile, almost hollow, yet still attached to the flesh by bundles of sinews, creaking wads of cartilage, networks of veins and tiny blood vessels, infinite in number and through which her blood runs ever more dark and sluggish. But for how much longer?

Is there a time marked out for each of us? the old woman wonders.

Death is chance and chaos. Bodies made to live a hundred years killed in an instant by the murderous will of a stranger who has never even seen their faces. Others with brains already spent and their blood congealed, kept alive for years by a machine.

To die at the right time and right moment, is that a privilege?

But when is the right time, and what is the right moment? — that is the question.

To wait for nature to run its course, or until chance takes the situation in hand for us? To waste away slowly, to sink day by day into the darkness like Ophelia in the pool, first singing, then struggling with the weeds that drag you down, then letting yourself go, trustingly, into the unknown...

But what trust, the old woman thinks, turning over painfully under the sheet made heavy by the heat of the summer night. Death is not the gradual running down of life's battery. It is a beast that eats you. When it is hungry it gobbles you up in a couple of mouthfuls, when it is feeling more indolent it gnaws you away bit by bit. Macular degeneration sets in and you can barely see, or see nothing at all: this is death having a little taste of you. Your lungs fill with catarrh, you can't get your breath any more, it is death nibbling at you. It takes its time. Your skin becomes covered in spots and moles. Your hands shake, you spill your coffee on them. Everything in you becomes misshapen, corroded. You dribble when you eat. You say the same things a hundred times over, then you'll start repeating what other people have said to you, supposing that anyone still talks to you, you'll become an old echo in the crypt of your old bones.

(And here she throws away the cushion which tumbles down the bed and hits Venom and suddenly wakes him from his deep sleep.) You will fall and break your femur, you'll be left for days on a stretcher in A & E, unknown nurses will wipe your arse for you with bad grace, they will put you in a bed with metal sides, they will call you granny.

If anyone calls me granny, the old woman thinks, I'll hit them with my stick.

If I don't have my stick I'll slap them.

If I'm too weak to slap them I'll spit in their face.

And with these proud assertions she kicks off the sheet as vigorously as she can. Venom, disturbed for the second time, drags himself with feline amiability to his creaking feet and comes to purr in her face.

Push off, stinky, she tells him. He purrs more loudly, then is seized with a fit of coughing. Crouching low, his muscles straining, his ears back, Venom tries to expel the fluids clogging his chest, a viscous gurgling, prolonged, endless.

The old woman looks at him, he is skin and bones, his fur standing on end, all spiky. How many days since he last emptied his food bowl? Today, Gabriela cooked him some fresh fish, yesterday a tiny piece of veal ground up small. But nothing doing, a couple of mouthfuls and that's all, and it seems as if he only eats those out of politeness, so as not to disappoint them.

The old woman turns on the lamp on the bedside table, looks at the time: three o'clock, too late or too early, even for an old woman with no shame, to ring the vet.

227

A few years ago, following the controversies in the newspapers, the old woman made an extensive internet search on the subject of easy death.

In the YouTube videos, the people who have chosen to die are pale and suffering. With dull or listless voices they say they no longer wish to live. Sometimes they launch appeals in favour of euthanasia. They hope their case will help make their fellow citizens and the authorities more open to this humane practice, which puts an end to senseless suffering. The right to death, they say, is one with the right to life. And it is clear that these people are not in control of their own lives any more: they cannot even blow their noses unaided.

They are usually harnessed to machines, they have needles in their veins, plastic tubes, bandages. Some of them have not been able to move of their own accord for years, sometimes the capacity for speech is all they have left, and even that is laboured, coming at the cost of immense effort. Occasionally they may ask those left behind to forgive them, usually they thank the person accompanying them.

Assisted death takes place in thoroughly ordinary rooms, with light-coloured furnishings, nothing luxurious, they are places of passage where no individual detail is designed to be remembered. The people who accompany them are for the most part mute, they struggle against tears or sit there dismayed, conscious of being witnesses to a spectacle for which there is — as yet — no code of behaviour, applause at the appropriate moment. Perhaps they wonder what they will remember of this day, if this day will change them. Even if they have prepared themselves, have possibly known about it, thought about it for years, they remain unprepared all the same.

There is a waiting room for those wishing to die, but it is a lengthy affair: visits, medical advice, waiting, documents, more waiting.

What a lot of bureaucracy, what a performance, the old woman thinks. It wouldn't do for me.

Better to throw oneself from the window on the attic corridor. (They have bricked it up.) Or slit one's veins. Or shoot oneself with a pistol. (Better, too, to have those things, the bullets.)

Those other people are no longer capable of such action, but she is, she would be.

So why hasn't she done it?

But on the other hand what harm is there in it if people prefer to die in a civilised manner, sitting quiet and composed in an armchair or lying on a comfortable bed, with just a few friends around? With no mess and the minimum disturbance. In a protected environment. Investing the money they have put aside in a sensible way. No blood to clean up, no delays for passengers on the chosen train. No fire to blacken things, no red-stained water. No crunch of bones shattering on the pavement below. All you have to do is drink a bitter-tasting poison, which acts within a few minutes, or have yourself injected with a drug that sends you to sleep, followed by another that kills you.

The old woman ponders, examines the pros and cons, now favouring taking death by the horns, and dying with those horns as a trophy like a bullfighter in the ring, now favouring the easeful blandishments of a procured oblivion.

But among these videos which are all much the same, one is different.

The subject is still young, as they say now of anyone who is not actually falling to pieces, she must be only just turned seventy. Attractive, silvery hair cut short and fresh from the hairdresser, she has chosen to die in a white dinner jacket. In the buttonhole, exploding against this brilliant whiteness, an orchid, brazenly pink. As mistress of ceremonies, a woman of similar age, dressed like a housewife who has slipped out of the kitchen for a moment to buy some milk, but in whose eyes and gestures is the chilly compassion of the maître d' of Hades.

Lying on her final bed, the woman about to die takes leave, with a hint of impatience, of a woman friend in tears (please, no emotionalism, this is nothing like a wedding!) and exchanges with the invisible cameraman her final coquetries, declaring herself single, with no sentimental attachments, and therefore available to flirt with Thanatos in person. She drinks the poison from a flask with an amused grimace, pulling down the corners of her mouth, it's bitter, is given a chocolate, asks for another, a third is denied her to avoid an indecorous regurgitation spoiling the spotless whiteness of her jacket. But how long does it take from when I drank it? she asks, one minute, two, replies the maître d', her eyes widen, as little as that? Maybe in that instant she regrets the decision she has made, has second thoughts, thinks she has been foolish, wants to live another twenty years — what a luxury, to be surprised by the eager prodding of life on one's deathbed, what emotions! — or maybe she is only thinking that she would prefer to die more slowly, take longer over it, and that she will not see how it came out on the video, what a shame! But the smile does not leave her, she is an aesthete and maintains her elegance right to the end, until the final curtain falls.

After a few moments the final sleep wraps her in its net, her hands fall back on the sheets, the muscles of her neck relax, her eyes fill with astonishment. On her no longer sentient face there flashes for an instant the sulky pout of a little girl disappointed with the gifts of miserly daylight, then all expression vanishes. The conductress of souls to the other world closes her eyelids over her eyes.

The old woman watches the video twice, three times, ten times. The woman's reason for dying remains unknown, an infirmity vaguely hinted at, perhaps boredom more than anything — but does one necessarily have to have a reason? Life is without reason, why should there be one for death? Yes, certainly there is one, she suspects: life no longer matched her expectations of it, a more than adequate reason for taking one's leave of a lover and hence why not also of oneself?

She is fascinated by the impudent charm of her performance. The deliberate frivolity with which she undertakes the great step.

She suspects, in fact she is certain, that she has falsified her medical records, exaggerated the seriousness of her condition. She has hoodwinked the examination board, who after failing her a few times gave in to her tenacity and passed her by the skin of her teeth. She got away with it.

Lazy, spoilt, a scoffing exhibitionist, this woman restores to death its quality of lightness. Why make so much effort and die squalidly alone, when I can lie here, draped elegantly before you, unknown onlookers, eating chocolates?

What cheek, what nonchalance, the old woman thinks with envy.

Death for frivolous reasons. The performance of an artist. Nora would have loved it.

A few days later, the old woman made contact with that Swiss organisation, the same one as the woman in the dinner jacket, its headquarters are in Zurich and they replied that she could register any time she wanted, just as a precautionary measure. That she could book an appointment. Certain medical protocols were necessary, interviews, various formalities.

She sent in the forms, a certificate compiled by an old friend of Max, a doctor who obligingly exaggerated her infirmities thinking he was thereby helping her obtain some form of pension, but she never did request any appointment. The matter remained shelved, dormant, not really forgotten but put aside for the winter, like a supply of wood for the stove.

IV

No waiting room for Venom

The vet has come to see Venom, she is probing his abdomen with deep fingers, she draws back his eyelids to examine his pupils, massages the ends of his paws, squeezes them to make the claws emerge. He not only submits to the examination, he is enjoying it, his muscles are loose in total acquiescence, his body is stretched out, offered up for as long as it takes, he accepts every prod as a caress, a tribute to the age-old alliance between humans and cats.

The visit goes on longer than expected. The vet, who does not like to speak or be spoken to while she is working, is distant, her face closed off in a grimace of concentration. Venom receives a thorough X-ray from her fingers. The old woman begins to become agitated.

She repeats — she has already told her not long ago — that he has had no appetite for the last few days, but this morning he ate a slice of ham. She is lying, it was not a slice but only a half, in fact less than that. In truth it was a piece no bigger than a postage stamp.

The vet freezes her with a glance. She turns her back on her. She continues to caress Venom, who responds with feeble purrs.

She asks how he is, when he moves around the house. A little slow, the old woman says. Then she corrects herself: he doesn't move, sometimes he stumbles. He tries to jump on the chair but he doesn't always succeed. He sleeps a great deal. He doesn't see well.

He's deaf, she adds. He doesn't respond any more when he's called.

The vet nods. She massages his cheeks as if she were applying a beauty mask. He's not eating, she says, because the muscles of his jaw have seized up.

Seized up? the old woman repeats, stupidly.

I think there is a mass pressing on his brain, the vet says, without taking her hands off the cat.

A mass? the old woman echoes for the second time.

A tumour, says the doctor, becoming specific.

Behind the old woman's back, Gabriela starts. The old woman turns round, quickly cuffs her on the arm.

Are you sure? the old woman asks.

Death is the only thing that's sure, the vet says. To be certain I'd need to give him a CT scan. But he'd have to be asleep before we can scan him, and the anaesthetic would kill him. Apart from which, when we do know exactly what's wrong, we won't be able to do anything about it.

The old woman is silent. The vet too.

The only thing to be heard is Mozart on the radio, *The Marriage of Figaro*, and the tick-tock of the alarm clock high up on the shelf above the table.

How long, the old woman asks.

I don't know, the vet says, shrugging her shoulders at the

stupidity of the question.

Then touched by a little compassion, she adds: A few days. A week, maybe even less. There's hardly any flesh on these bones.

She leans over the patient, who licks the hand still resting on him, and whispers to him: What are you doing, you silly?

They are silent for a while again.

Then the old woman says: A great cat.

So then the vet asks if she wants to do it straightaway, the old woman replies yes. No waiting room for Venom.

Is he suffering? There'll be moments, it's hard to tell, they're more stoical than we are. How old is he? Between them they work it out, counting on their fingers, coming to an agreement: he has reached the age of twenty-one.

The vet asks for a clean towel, Gabriela presses her fingers hard against her mouth and runs from the room, the old woman has a flash of anger and marches to the bathroom to find the towel herself, and on the way bumps into a piece of furniture which has always stood where it is now, the pain blurs her vision.

Gabriela peeps round the angle of the door while the vet slips the needle into the vein of the cat, who is now in the old woman's arms and seems to be purring, or perhaps he is only having difficulty breathing. The asthmatic purring fades away gently, Venom falls asleep. The vet bends over him to listen to his heart and informs her that he has gone already, the sleeping drug was enough, but all the same she will administer the second injection to be sure.

Gabriela suppresses a sob while on the radio the bass sings '*Non più andrai farfallone amoroso*', an aria which at that moment the old woman finds extraordinarily appropriate to the departure of Venom the cat.

He was very sociable, she says. A gentle soul. A bit of a womaniser, but that was his charm.

Her voice, nevertheless, is unsteady. Her side hurts where she banged it on the furniture. It hurts enough to distract her.

Gabriela's cheeks are running with tears. In the hallway, beside the front door where they have been sitting for more than an hour, motionless though not tied up, the vet's three mongrels, who have seen nothing but whose ears have stiffened on sensing the presence of death, whine anxiously. Quiet, you, hush, their mistress commands softly. Not content with curing paying animals, she has acquired the habit of rescuing and looking after abandoned ones. Obedient to the pack leader, the dogs fall silent. Only their tails continue to quiver.

Do you want me to see to the body? the doctor offers.

The old woman nods. Venom is wrapped in his favourite blanket and then placed in a canvas bag. She does not ask where he will be taken, what will happen to him, she does not want to know.

She opens her wallet to pay, but the woman refuses. She never takes money for this sort of thing.

While the vet is putting her instruments away, the old woman asks her if there are any leftovers she doesn't need... of that stuff.

Without looking up, the woman answers: Don't even think of it. I'd be in the shit up to the neck.

There, you see how simple it is with animals, the old woman says to Gabriela.

It seems to her that her voice echoes in the noticeably empty apartment. The cushion on the armchair, the blanket full of hairs on the divan, the bowl by the refrigerator, everything seems to proclaim a gospel of unbearable gloom.

Her side hurts. She sits heavily on the nearest chair.

He was only a cat, only a cat, but she knows very well that it is not true, there is no such thing as only a cat. They are the known and loved beings, the ones we share our daily lives with, and that is what Venom was for her. He was the only remaining witness to her past with Nora. The only one still with his faculties about him.

Do you want some tea? Gabriela asks, her voice tearful.

The old woman shakes her head. Gabriela puts the water on to boil.

What will you do now? the girl says, gazing at her with her big tear-filled Bambi eyes. What shall we do? she corrects herself.

What shall we do, what shall we do? Daddy doesn't like it, Mummy doesn't either, what shall we do if we want to make love? the old woman sings, it is a song even older than she is, she got it from her grandmother, it comes from a world that exists no longer, Gabriela does not know it and pulls a funny face.

Why should this little girl wonder what she'll do now, she thinks, staring at the tea whose steam rises towards her face and stings her eyes.

The real question for you is, she says, have you asked your relatives to repay the money you lent them?

Yes, I've phoned them twice.

And…?

And nothing, they don't have it. They told me: what do you need money for? You live alone and you have no family. We have children to bring up and now we're going to have a grandchild as well.

Do you realise the kind of life you're leading, you're letting yourself be swindled and tyrannised and you mustn't live like that any longer? Do you realise that or don't you?

And she shuts herself in the bedroom, banging the door to stave off the flood of tears that threatens to overwhelm her. But the tears do not come. Sitting on the bed, the old woman passes her hand over the place where Venom slept, among the cushions, and does not weep.

Gabriela knocks gingerly at the door, tip-toes into the room without waiting for a reply, and sets the cup down on the bedside table.

The old woman looks up, her eyes meet the girl's.

Thank you, she says. Then she makes a gesture no one was expecting, she raises an arm and squeezes the hot and rather rough little hand of her carer for an instant.

And at the same time she is thinking what a cretin she is: when the vet went to the bathroom, the vials for the injection were there, within hand's reach, in the open bag on the table! Why didn't she grab the chance?

Today Malvina does not smile at her. The absence in her expression is like fright, she has the dumbfounded face of the severely traumatised. Her flattened cheeks tremble, the dark rings round her eyes are craters, the eyes have receded deep into their sockets as if by shrinking to dots they won't have to see.

Vina, darling, the old woman whispers, wiping the corner

of her mouth with a handkerchief. Did you know my Venom has gone?

Malvina turns her head aside.

The old woman has nothing to talk about. The papers bore her, not even the case of the murderous nurse who is said to have seen off twenty of her patients (the woman with the syringe, the angel of death, a storyline already overworked, she remembers having read it in more than one crime novel) can capture her interest.

As to the rest, the usual terrorist attacks and nuclear tests. All manner of species becoming extinct, except the really harmful one, whose numbers instead continue to grow. Unseasonably high temperatures, with forecasts of a new wave of droughts. Who knows, maybe the Apocalypse will arrive in time to relieve her of her problems.

They are in the garden, in the shade of a lime tree. Gabriela, over there, is in conversation with a thin white cat which is arching its back to be stroked. A nun passes with a bunch of lilies, their scent like some sweet opiate, reminding the old woman of evenings long ago in the countryside. She turns to Malvina to read the same impression on her face, can they just for an instant go back in time together to when they were little girls in short socks, on a path through the orchards? But her friend gives no sign, stolid, unresponsive flesh, with eyes that see nothing, a nose that no longer smells anything.

She has retreated deep inside herself, not even seeming to feel the cold or the heat, she does not complain, she does not ask for the blanket for her knees if the wind blows, nor to be moved into the shade if the sun is fierce.

Why do I come here, the old woman thinks. What do I

come here for.

She looks at Malvina's hands, once they were plump and graceful but not any longer, how quickly they have become knotted and misshapen, the top joints are discoloured, one nail has turned a dull blue.

The old woman looks away. She leans back in her chair, closes her eyes. The garden is warm and scented, full of buzzing insects. Annoying flies settle on the exposed skin, the old people twitch to chase them away, Malvina does not react, lets them land on her.

Let's go, the old woman says, getting up.

While they are making their way through the long corridors towards the exit they encounter a gnome-like figure whom the old woman recognises as the foul-mouthed artist in invective, it is a while since she has seen her. She is shrivelled up, her hair stands on end and she is coming towards them with one hand on her walking frame and the other on the handrail.

The gnome plants herself in front of Gabriela, glares at her malevolently.

Rot! she spits. Your fanny's full of rot! Would you like mine instead, eh?

Gabriela covers her ears. She takes a step back. She looks around in search of help.

Her aggressor opens her toothless mouth in a laugh of triumph.

What's the matter? Why are you stopping? says the old woman, who has heard but paid no attention. And she pushes the girl forward.

Syphilitic! the gnome shouts after them, her little voice shrill and joyous.

At the traffic lights, while they are waiting to join the main road, Gabriela gives vent to her resentment: That woman. She oughtn't to say certain words. At her age. They oughtn't to let her say them.

Just listen to yourself! the old woman says, turning to the girl who is still pink with indignation. And why oughtn't she? What are they supposed to do, cut her tongue out so that she can't scandalise sanctimonious goody-two-shoes like you?

And then, more mildly: Don't imagine it had anything at all to do with you. She's just out of her head.

Like your terrorist, she then adds.

In her own way, she's a terrorist too.

Gabriela does not answer, her hands are gripping the wheel, her teeth biting her lower lip, her eyes are fixed on the rear-view mirror. With an effort, the old woman twists the upper half of her body round, her movement cramped by the seat belt, but only sees the green meadows and a motorcyclist who has stopped behind them, on the bend, and is growing ever smaller at the side of the road.

What is it? she asks.

Nothing, Gabriela replies.

Look! Gabriela says, padding up to her chair on stealthy feet, one hand hidden behind her back, her eyes shining.

And she thrusts under her nose her mobile phone. It shows two kittens a few days old, their eyes open but unfocused, offering the lens their tiny faces as yet devoid of expression. One is white with a black mark on its nose, the other black with white paws.

Aren't they sweet? Gabriela says.

Hmm, the old woman mumbles.

They were born two weeks ago, the mother belongs to a friend of my half-sister, they're a male and a female! she announces as if it were one of the marvels of the world.

I've already reserved them! Both of them! They'll be ready in six weeks!

I hope your relatives didn't take advantage of the situation to ask you for money, the old woman remarks.

No, don't worry, I'm not falling for that any more! Gabriela says, her enthusiasm undimmed. The male is the white one, the female is this black one with the socks, I thought I'd keep that one but... you choose first! Which one do you want?

The old woman pushes the phone away with some force. Not a chance, she says. I'm not even considering it.

Gabriela tries to overcome her disappointment: Of course, it's too soon. It takes time, the mistake's mine. Wait and see, maybe, in a while, you'll change your mind...

The old woman shuts herself in her bedroom muttering to herself that no, the mistake was hers in taking on a pushy young girl full of good ideas, she should have found a cantankerous, mean-spirited fifty-year-old, that would have been the right woman for her.

It is evening, one of those fine summer evenings when the scent of jasmine drifts in through the open window. The old woman is sitting in the armchair, the ghost of Venom on her lap, listening to the radio and the general din and hubbub of other people's lives.

In the room opposite, a few metres from hers, the light goes on. The daughter of the old man, who is sitting on the divan as motionless as a mummy, enters with a tray, sets it down on a small table next to the father, turns the television volume down. The old man, who is not watching the television however, indeed he has turned away from it, protests in an angry grumble.

The daughter ties a napkin at his neck, sits beside him and feeds him.

She is a woman of about sixty, grey of skin and hair, her contours shapeless, like an item of underwear that has been through the washing machine too many times. She works in some municipal office and returned, many years ago now, to live with her widowed father, an invalid; the old woman remembers that in the early days a man used to come and visit her from time to time, brought her sweets on Sundays and ate with her or else they would go out together, in the evenings there were long telephone conversations with her women friends. She had a life, in other words, but she must have lost sight of it a good while back now, the man has vanished and the friends hardly ever call any more. She is left with the television, sudoku and crossword puzzles, which she pores over at night, the old woman sees her during her periods of insomnia and when she makes nocturnal visits to the bathroom, that grey, rumpled woman, bent over the table by the light of a low-wattage lamp, with a pencil in her hand. On TV, similar in this to her father, she prefers violent action films, and sometimes the old woman is woken from her sleep by gunshots, shouts and screeching tyres.

On this particular evening the woman is feeding her father in more hurry than usual, soup, vegetable puree, stewed fruit (the old man has not had his own teeth since time immemorial), then instead of taking the things away she sits down again opposite him, looks at him.

I'm going away, she tells him. Tomorrow. Have you understood I'm going away tomorrow?

More, says the old man.

There isn't any more, you've eaten it all. At your age you shouldn't be eating so much.

He mumbles something incomprehensible, which sounds like a curse.

Have you understood or not? she insists. I'm going to hospital. I'll be there for some days. Or for ever, if I die under the knife.

What about me? the old man demands, in his rusty voice which is nevertheless very comprehensible now.

You are staying here. Assunta is coming to look in on you twice a day. She can't come at night, so in the evenings she will put you to bed and go away. If you really need to get about, there's the walking frame. Try not to fall down and fracture your femur, or you'll have to wait until morning before the ambulance arrives. Better you do it in your incontinence pad.

No, no, no, the old man says, waving his arms. The glass falls on its side and spills its contents over his trousers.

What do you mean, no? the daughter says, raising her voice. She comes up close, she stands in front of him with her hands on her hips. No what? You don't want me to have the operation? I've got cancer, get it!

The old woman turns down the volume on the radio a little more — it is playing music (Verdi's *Otello*, it's opera hour) — and leans towards the windowsill as much as the armchair will allow. Her hands tighten on the fur of the ectoplasmic Venom.

…and I can't get out of my head the reason why I've got cancer in the first place is you, the daughter continues. Apart from ambient pollution and dust particles, you are the number one carcinogenic factor and you know it perfectly well. You might even for once pretend to feel a minimum of interest in me, given I'm the one who feeds you, dresses you, wipes your arse, instead of only thinking about yourself all the time.

…I don't want Assunta, the old man mutters stubbornly, head down, groping round for his stick.

You're getting her anyway, she's the only person I could find willing to come here twice a day, you know very well I can't afford a nurse. If you had a decent pension, but let's drop that particular subject or I'll develop another cancer overnight.

At this point the woman looks up, sees the old woman watching her from her romantically jasmine-surrounded window and throws her a malevolent glare. With a decisive gesture she shuts the window, but not before turning back into the room and announcing to the old man: And note this, if I die I'm leaving you only what's required by law, the rest is going… but who the rest is going to the old woman does not hear, the window panes are fastened, the voices sound muffled and distant.

The father, in a rage, waves his stick at the daughter. She laughs, dodges the blow, makes a theatrical exit from the room, slamming the door. The empty dishes wobble on the little table.

The climbing shoots of jasmine sway in the evening breeze. Their subtle perfume soothes the old woman, who gives a little sigh, turns up the radio and gets ready to listen to the aria of the umpteenth operatic female despatched to her grave, the fair Desdemona.

The old woman is compiling a list of things that make life worth the bother of living.

Her home. It is big, comfortable, tidy, it is hers. No one can throw her out. It is not in an earthquake zone, it is unlikely to collapse on her head. And it is situated far enough away from the river to run no risk of being flooded. A place of safety, from all points of view.

Her morning coffee. When she doesn't have a bitter taste in her mouth. The scent of the jasmine. June mornings, if they are clear, which seldom happens. The taste of cherries. When they taste of anything. Music. When she feels like listening to it. Books. When they don't annoy her, when her eyes allow her to read.

Visits to Malvina. No, what brought that to mind? Those visits are at best a necessary torment, a quest without result. She tells herself she goes from a sense of duty but in reality it is to appease a hunger, and she returns hungrier than before. She expects a miracle every time, she hopes that time has done a somersault and turned back on itself, that Malvina's mind might clear like the clouds over the mountains on windy days. But it never happens.

She deletes visits to Malvina from the list.

Come on, surely there must be something else.

The well-organised clothes cupboards, scented with lavender after Gabriela has done the springcleaning. The neatly ironed cotton handkerchiefs. The snow-white sheets. The clothes lined up on their hangers, ready to use, as if she had a reserve life to wear them in.

All these are things that have always given her pleasure, a sense of intimate satisfaction. But are they reasons for living?

You don't live for a reason, the old woman mutters. You make a treasure out of what you have.

At one time she enjoyed going to the cinema, the theatre. She would always keep a bag of sweets in her pocket, for Malvina. Her friend's outbreaks of coughing at vital moments used to infuriate her and she would thrust a mint rudely into her hand, or even kick her in the ankle. Golden days.

The poets. Ah, yes, poetry. One thing it is worth living for. She promises herself she will read more of it, more often, every day. The advantage of poetry is that you only need to read a few verses at a time, without overtiring your eyes, and you feel yourself expanding like a sail in the wind.

But sometimes she feels too tired even to open a book. And the tiredness is not in her arms, but far deeper down.

The radio. When they don't blather nonsense.

Sleep, when it brings back Nora, the past, herself...

Gabriela. She has left her until last.

Gabriela is a mystery which fills her with fear. She is afraid of what she might discover.

Whether she lies or tells the truth, Gabriela is vital to her, her life depends on her.

But how can things be so out of balance between us? the old woman suddenly thinks. She gives me her energy, the mindless splendour of her youth, she polishes, cleans, irons, cooks, flatters me, puts up with me, remembers the things I forget, knows every centimetre of this apartment, goes along with my tastes and whims, is careful not to make a noise when

I'm sleeping, wears out her own young hands for the benefit of my ancient skin instead of dancing and singing and making love and laughing in the face of old age and death, the whole thing is incomprehensible, and what do I give her in return? A few cents in salary, that's it, it doesn't make sense.

Such a vast imbalance can't depend only on herself, the old woman thinks. There is something about the world that is not working properly, if two separate versions of solitude, each of them flawed but in constant communication, like hers and Gabriela's, cannot mutually lighten each other.

She is the only one who benefits from their contract, an elderly body which daily profits from transfusions of young blood to prolong her ancient life by another day. For the cost of a union-rate monthly salary plus social security contributions.

Goodness knows whether she has been sleeping in the attic again. Or whether the terrorist still frightens her, in the evenings, when she is alone in her flat with its view over the muddy river. Goodness knows whether she will extricate herself from the clutches of her relatives, from the meanness and arrogance of people, from the violence of a world in which her life counts for nothing, like that of millions of others…

Since when did she begin to fear for Gabriela?

It's a beautiful day today, don't you feel like going out? the girl says.

No, the old woman mumbles, not now.

You haven't been out for a long time, you know. Before, with *signora* Malvina, you used to go out quite often…

I wait until you're not here, to go out. In the evenings, on your day off, I get up to all sorts of things.

Gabriela falls silent.

The old woman watches her peeling the potatoes. She rinses the parsley, dries it, chops it up small on the wooden chopping board. She seems to take pleasure in doing everything exactly the way she has been taught.

But don't you, the girl says without looking at her, don't you have any other friends, besides *signora* Malvina?

They're dead, the old woman says. Or senile. Or they've moved to remote places.

What about relatives? That *signora* who always sends greetings, at Christmas...

My cousin lives in Argentina, the old woman says. She is ninety-two, she has a son with a heart condition and a grandson who lives in the United States. We've seen each other just once, around forty years ago. We send each other emails, when anyone is born or dies, in other words not very often.

Perhaps grateful for the unusually amiable response, for information given rather than withheld, and for the almost gentle tone, Gabriela smiles at her, lights up with youthful happiness. Listen, she says, I can go to the cinema with you, or the theatre, if you like.

In my free time, she hurriedly adds. Outside working hours.

The old woman looks at her over the top of her spectacles.

But I don't mean... Gabriela blushes, falters. At my own expense, I mean, I'd pay for my own ticket... if it's not too expensive... and here she stops, at a loss.

Thank you for the offer, the old woman says. There hasn't been anything I've wanted to see recently, you'll have to be patient, it's old age.

The old woman is sleeping, sunk deep into her soft bed and lying very still, in the city night that is never really night but a kind of twilight that blurs the outlines of things without obliterating them. Beside her a small dark mass, perhaps it is only the blanket partly thrown off, or the spectre of Venom who has returned to watch over her from the world of shadows.

In her dream it is war, as often happens. The old woman is walking on rough cobbles, but she is not old, she is a girl, with a young and vibrant body, bright, clear eyes. She is moving through the ruins of a large and stately city which here and there reveals dizzying views of neverending countryside, limitless skies. Life and terror have her heart in a vice, hope snaps at her calves, there is a destination awaiting her, perhaps over there amid the fires and explosions that are tearing the horizon apart. From a gap in the tumbled stones two kittens come forward, they are the ones in the photo on Gabriela's mobile, the white male, the black female with the snowy paws, they call to her, she bends down as they meow and discovers with horror that one of them, the black one, has a broken or perhaps crippled foot and an eye sealed shut by blood. A well of pity and hopelessness yawns beneath her feet, she clutches the creatures to her chest, the ground explodes a few paces away, she flees with her burden, crosses fields of stone, chasms open unexpectedly in front of her, and rivers and quagmires, a long anguished march.

The old woman stirs, she wishes she could change dreams.

And indeed, the dream mutates, all at once, with no logical transition, as happens in dreams. Nora is in her room, in stage costume, scripts, books, an open case on the bed. Are you going? the old woman asks in a voice choking with anxiety.

Nora smiles at her, her wavy hair, dark and gleaming, caressing her shoulders. The face, calm and unmoving, is exceptionally beautiful and cruel in its indifference. An icy dagger in the old woman's heart. Don't go! she begs, in a strangulated voice.

But Nora confines herself to a smile, it is her, the beloved, the being she best and least knows in all the world, and yet it is not her. The features are hers, but her gaze is something else, limpid and indifferent, turned elsewhere. If she goes, the old woman thinks, how will I manage now, how will I live. Just for a moment she has a powerful desire to beg and scream the way little children do, but she knows it would be futile.

The suitcase has disappeared from the bed. The old woman understands that Nora has no use for it, where she is now she has everything she needs. The bedroom is tidy. Nora turns her back, goes away.

The old woman remains alone, in the dream that comes between sleeping and waking. She tries to hold on to the image of the person who has gone. Even if Nora was cruel and indifferent, she is happy she dreamed about her. She would willingly spend whole nights knocking on the door of dreams, like a persistent beggar, just to see her appear for a single instant.

Nowadays she is more alive when she is not awake than when she is, she thinks cloudily, before falling back into the final sleep.

When they speak to each other, that is the moment they seem most foreign. When the syllables of a language you don't know, spoken by excited or happy or angry voices, make chains of sounds whose rings are soldered together and can't be separated into individual words, broken into units of meaning, and that is when they are most foreign because in reality at those moments the foreigner is you.

It is what happens when Gabriela and Ana are talking in the entrance hall, their whispers become explosions of noise, and then the old woman, annoyed and offended, gets up and crosses the corridor to go into the sitting room, caught between the urge to hurry so as not to feel guilty of eavesdropping and the desire to linger out of curiosity.

But Ana takes advantage of her appearing to switch tactics: They're your family, she tells Gabriela, switching abruptly to a shrill Italian, albeit an Italian shorn of double consonants. There's nothing more important than families. That's what you tell her too, *signora*: they've invited her to be godmother to her little great-niece, the daughter of her niece Vasilica, and she's saying no! Isn't that just plain wickedness?

I don't have money to give the child presents, that's all they want, they're not a bit interested in me. I'm not going! says Gabriela. Tell them to leave me alone.

Look how hard you've become! To think you were once such a sweet girl, says Ana with a fake sigh, pushing back her hair, newly washed and styled but already sticking to her forehead with perspiration. Today summer has launched a surprise assault and Ana, with two large haloes under the arms of her low-cut blouse, is its first victim.

Stop! Gabriela commands. There follows a flood of incomprehensible words, then the girl does an about-turn and takes refuge in the bathroom.

How about that! Ana says confidentially to the old woman, coming up close and bringing with her a powerful odour of overweight and overheated womanhood. The christening is important, a big celebration, everyone gathers together, they eat, they dance. But her family never see her, they're worried. I don't believe she spends every evening at home all by herself. I say there's a boyfriend somewhere...

Gabriela re-emerges at the double from the bathroom, fists clenched and ready to lash out: Enough! This is my place of work! You don't come and say stupid things about my private life here, understood? It's not right! Don't ever do it again!

And at this, after a final futile look in the old woman's direction, Ana, offended, beats a retreat.

If the old woman's rages are cold and sudden, like icebergs breaking off into the sea, churning it into tidal waves and drowning ships, those of Gabriela are long-lasting and subdued like saucepans on a light so low that the water hardly seems to be moving, but in fact boils dry until the flame is crackling under white-hot metal.

You want me to be godmother, well of course you do! she berates the spectres that haunt her, neatly threading a needle. I'm surprised you didn't think of it before! A godmother gives money, she doesn't just turn up with a happy smile and that's it, she brings a nice fat bag of money and then other presents, clothes, stuff for the house... but I don't have any money left! I am absolutely not a bottomless well, I'm not the national mint!

The old woman watches the girl, who is sewing, the brass thimble on her deft little finger, the thread moving rapidly and accurately in and out. Who uses a thimble, nowadays? Who sews? The Chinese, certainly, in their tiny backshops, their dark eyes obsequious and alert, eyes from another continent, shining heads bent over other people's cheap-price clothes, mouths full of pins. Gabriela is both everyday and ancient, she is a figure from a late nineteenth century painting, and not just because the thimble dates from the eighteen-hundreds and has been worn on the fingertips of the old woman's grandmothers, Gabriela is ancient because she is eternal, or so she seems just now at least, a woman seated quietly at her work, an image of calm and gentleness, and inside her that silent but ever-present cry which if it were one day to find its voice would sweep away the entire world.

And that woman, she dares to come here and shame me in front of you! the girl says, biting the thread off with her teeth. This house, for me it's a refuge, a — a sanctuary! Everything here is meant to be perfect, nothing ugly is supposed to get in from outside!

The old woman watches her so intently she almost forgets to breathe. Then she whispers, or maybe only thinks: It's a losing game, my girl.

Silence for some minutes. The thread slides in and out of the material, the radio murmurs quietly, on the balcony the pigeons quarrel over the rice the old woman puts out at night.

I presume they haven't repaid you anything yet, the old woman says.

It would be something if they didn't always try to pull the wool over my eyes when I ask. But it's my fault. I've always given them money. Whenever they asked, I gave them some. You wouldn't believe how many times… who bought all the children's clothes? Ten years, I've been working!

The old woman sighs.

Gabriela apologises for boring her.

But as she is folding the sewing and getting up from the table a final impassioned outburst escapes her: I'd do it so willingly, I'd love to be godmother to my great-niece, you should see her! She's so beautiful! I could steal her for myself!

What do you say, I ask Malvina, do I give her this money? I don't even know how much she needs, two or three thousand I imagine. You'd give her that, I know. You've always been annoyingly generous, kind to the point of stupidity, on the other hand good works are stupid: if you stop to think about it, goodbye, the moment's gone in a flash, and sensible grounds for good works hardly ever come up, I wish I could be like you, just give because someone's asking, without getting in a state about it.

But why should I give her it? It would end up in the gaping mouths of her ravenous relations. And afterwards, in her capacity as the little mite's godmother, she'd have to carry on doling it out for years, decades. Like taking on a mortgage.

Malvina doesn't reply, naturally, because she is not here, I am alone in the kitchen and it is still not quite dark, how long these early summer evenings are. In any case, even if she were here, or I had gone to see her up there in the hills amongst the verdant pastures of amnesia, she would not answer me, so I might as well save myself the journey.

Malvina is sitting here in a halo of tender grey, the last rays of daylight are filtering through her sparse and disordered hair, the geraniums are leaning their red petals and their plump and already pest-afflicted leaves towards her, the window opposite is dark and deserted, the mummified old man has been put to bed by mercenary hands and is certainly complaining and cursing in his place of restraint.

And if it were really her, that darker shadow amongst the shadows? Malvina! I call in an undertone. She slowly vanishes and I remain alone with my suspicions of going mad.

But at least I would be, mad! If I were to go mad all of a sudden, I would have lots of distractions, people to keep me company, like those types who wander the streets foaming at the mouth waving a fist at their mortal enemies and insulting passers-by, there may be a touch of confusion inside their heads but they have a vivid social life.

Nothing happens to old people any more, only death.

Have the neighbours all gone out this evening? No one listening to music, or arguing, no one calling the cat.

The radio I have turned off and can't turn back on for a while, curse Schönberg and his twelve tones.

I could have accepted Gabriela's offer, and gone to the cinema with her. To see what, animated Japanese cartoons? Where there are girls with heart-shaped faces and starry eyes like the ones batting their eyelashes on her mobile phone?

Instead I am here, alone, in the dark. Alone with myself, and probably with that other, the mythical terrorist cousin, who is perhaps here at this very moment, planning carnage, three floors above my head, in the attic where Gabriela, perjuring herself, says no one has ever set foot except herself... and he could decide to come down and cut the old woman's throat with the aim of burgling her home or even just for training purposes, and me with my unloaded pistol, damn that pacifist Ciro, why put up a fight anyway, it would be as good a way of dying as any other, probably better than a lot of others...

Supposing that he really exists, this terrorist.

I hardly know anything about her, I tell Malvina, who is over there by the gas rings now where the darkness thickens into a shimmering mass, I know what I imagine and what little she tells me, she is a perpetual enigma, but what human being isn't, she lies or tells the truth, probably she doesn't know herself most of the time, but one thing I do know, she is a misfit like us, like you, Malvina, and her picturesque little family is fleecing her as yours fleeced you, and no doubt a man will show up next and mistreat her, as you were mistreated by women, and it will be even worse because she will be poorer than you and without a profession and probably burdened with children, even if I don't believe it but you never know, and she will be alone, the more she is surrounded by people the more alone she will be, and the best thing that could happen would be that the Romanian mafia exterminated her relatives, or failing that happy ending she could at least win the lottery and escape to some distant place where no one can find her any more...

What good would my pittance do? To change a human being's life and their destiny you would need lots, lots more...

But that sort of money is what you have, Malvina says, it's in the bag.

And she promptly disappears, and leaves me here, interrogating myself on the infinite mystery that is the well-past-eighty human brain. The brain which makes you see your demented friend and even your dead cat here, where they are not, which makes you forget the keys and the mobile phone, makes you turn the gas switch in the wrong direction, makes you unable to remember what you ate yesterday and suddenly remember something that has been buried at the bottom of your memory for months: the bag.

Where has she put it, where has she put it.

The old woman turns on every light in the apartment, walks through every room, her heart pumping madly, its throbbing echoed in her throat, her head, in every cavity of her body, her hands move of their own volition, opening a drawer, leaving it open and scattering a box of shoes, her brain the flight deck of a spaceship caught in a storm of meteorites.

And here it is at last, the yellow bag, exactly where it ought to be, in the second drawer of the little chest in the study, along with the will, pension documents, and Nora's scarves, which still hold a trace of her perfume. But tonight the old woman does not stop to unfold them and swiftly bury her nose in them, to breathe in what few precious molecules remain before they disperse. What matters tonight is the yellow bag. And the black holes of her decrepit brain.

Having turned off the unwanted lights, tidied away the traces of her wild agitation, she sits at the dining-room table beneath the lamp that Nora used to pull over to read by in the evenings.

It is the middle of the night. The photographs come out first, heavy and slippery, Malvina as a girl, my God. The ghosts convene round the table, faces forgotten for decades smile from faded colour photos, here are Giovanna, Nico, Rosi, Paola, Luciano, Lella, Ivana, Giampiero, and who is this? Here is Max with the woman he was with at the time, who on earth was she? Here is Nora, and Nora again, and of course she is here too, the old woman before she was old, in a photograph surely taken by Malvina they are arm in arm, Nora and herself, and looking at each other in a way hard to read, in playful menace, at any moment one of them will bite the other's ear, or lick her face, or pull her hair, they are in the middle of a semi-serious argument, which will probably end in laughter and kisses but could also degenerate into real dispute, one can't yet tell.

The old woman looks at the photo while measureless minutes pass, falls in love with those two smooth, thirty-year-olds' faces, runs a trembling eye over the firm lines of neck and jaw, feels the caress of those dense tresses of hair, living, breathing animals. How unbearably beautiful her lover once was, and herself as well. And, almost ninety, for a time beyond reckoning she lights up with love for that long-ago couple, here she is, a fifteen-year-old again in a dark room, longing for the kiss on the screen, languor flooding her body, her mind a whirlpool drawing her down, the air she sucks into her lungs burning with desire like the buds that open in the woods in spring, without number and without shame.

Enough of this, it is too much. Unbearable. She hastily puts them back, pushes Malvina's wild curls, Nora's inviting, half-closed lips out of sight. Switches on the chandelier, floods the room with light, chases the ghosts from the dark corners.

Letters, greetings cards, a notebook stuffed with forgotten names. Malvina has always been disorganised. An old school report. An old exercise book with squared pages covered in her friend's anarchic handwriting: an attempt at a diary, perhaps the only one actually completed, worthy of being preserved for its uniqueness. The old woman puts on her reading glasses, deciphers with some effort a couple of troublesome love affairs, expressions of self-doubt, tortuous political questions in forms of language now fallen out of use... slowly the stream of consciousness declines into sparse jottings, notes and telephone numbers and recipes, and in these latter the writer seems to discover her only firm ground and clings to it, eventually collecting no fewer than three different methods for zabaglione and a good four for chocolate mousse.

The will. Malvina is leaving everything to her. The old woman is overcome with hilarity: Malvina, Malvina! she exclaims, and her voice echoes in the silence of the small hours, full of tenderness and rage and impatience, because how can she be so simple-minded as to leave everything to her, when the nephew has power of attorney and proxies over her accounts and has already taken care to transform this everything into nothing?

In any case, what would she do with it, Malvina's money? she thinks, opening the last remaining item, a white envelope with her name on it, and inside there is a life insurance policy made out in her name, and an assured capital sum: one hundred thousand euros plus interest, maturing on the date of the event.

What event? the old woman wonders stupidly, turning the policy over and over in her hands.

She has been unjust towards her friend: she was not as woolly-minded as she thought.

Why did she never mention it, this life insurance policy? Was she so sure she would be the one to die first? And, yes, Malvina is even the younger by a few years! If the old woman were the first to die instead, what would happen to this hundred thousand?

The old woman stands up, impatient: let it be daylight, and soon! Tomorrow morning she needs to go up to that place on the hill, the home of life after life, and do something, speak with Malvina, however absurd that may seem. She sits down again. No, think first. She needs to think.

Gabriela is alarmed. She shakes her. She has fallen asleep sitting at the table, in her clothes, slippers on her feet. She is stiff, numb with cold, her head is spinning. Her ankles are swollen.

Quick, she says, make me some coffee and then we can go, we're going to see Malvina.

Just like that, all of a sudden? Has something happened? Is *signora* Malvina unwell? If you'd phoned me and said, I'd have come in the car, I'll make you a coffee and then I'll go back and fetch it...

No, there isn't time, don't bother, we'll call a taxi.

Gabriela starts to protest, but the old woman is deaf to reason, they will find a taxi, or rather, better to book one, they'll be ready in half an hour. But before she can dial the number for the taxi the phone rings and in reply to her irritable Hello! comes a voice speaking Italian with a foreign accent, the old woman is about to hang up but it is not a call centre, it is an attendant from the nursing home who wishes to speak to *signora* Malvina's friend.

Her heart gives a leap of exultation: there, I knew it, the whole dementia thing was not real, a passing phase let's say, and it has passed, thank god, Malvina has come out of it and wants to speak to me! That's why I saw her last night, here, in the kitchen, that's what the envelope, the life policy, was about, that was it! At last!

But instead of putting Malvina on, the voice is asking for the address of the *signora*'s nephew, signor Osvaldo.

I don't have any address, she says curtly. What has that prick got to do with it?

A short pause. Whispering in the background. Good morning, says another voice, Italian and tired but authoritative, I am the doctor, we need to speak to the family of *signora* Pesenti, unfortunately they are not contactable at the moment… are you able to say whether she has any other relatives, besides her nephew?

What is all this about? Why do you have to speak to the nephew?

I'm sorry, *signora*, we need to speak to him, specifically. Or to a member of the family.

I am her family! I am her mother her sister her daughter and her sister-in-law. Speak to me!

Signora, I…

Whispering, more agitated noises. (Have you tried all the numbers? Yes, yes! And? I spoke to the home help, she said they were in Brazil, they're not answering their mobile! In Brazil? And they didn't leave any other contacts?)

What's happened? How is Malvina? the old woman croaks, highly agitated.

A silence. Then the doctor, icy and resigned: *Signora*, I am only supposed, officially, to give this news to members of the family but since they are not available I will give it to you, *signora* Malvina Pesenti passed away this morning at four fifty-four. It was unexpected, the nurse saw that she was having difficulty breathing, we called an ambulance but before it could arrive the patient had already gone. A pulmonary embolism.

The old woman stares at the bookshelf in front of her, mechanically reads the titles on the spines: *The Idiot. The Master and Margherita.* Szymborska, poems. *La chasse à l'amour. Life and Fate.* Dorothy Parker, Jane Austen, Proust, Dickinson. Lolita. Flannery O'Connor, all the short stories. What a mess, she thinks, Russian, American, French, English, prose and poetry, all together. Something needs to be done, they need to be put in order. It can't go on like this.

And then: at four fifty-four! lands in her brain like a piece of shrapnel, like a stray bullet. It cannot be by chance, surely, that this was the exact time she fell asleep, after staying up the whole night in Malvina's company, reliving Malvina's life and their shared past?

Signora! Gabriela exclaims, running over to her.

She only just catches her in time before she sinks to the floor.

She has dropped to her knees like an empty sack, a thing that has never happened to her before. It was as if she had slid into a pit of dark water and felt it close over her head without a sound.

So this is it, this is what it's like, she thought, in that millisecond of illumination before the light was extinguished.

But she was mistaken. It was only a faint.

After the early burst of hot weather, violent rain. It is cold again, the buses send columns of spray over defenceless passers-by, yesterday it hailed on the pre-alpine meadows, the small green fists of the growing fruits have fallen into the soaking grass.

But then, Gabriela reflects as the taxi slithers on the slippery road surface, if *signor* Osvaldo and his wife had not been in Brazil, they wouldn't have phoned you. They wouldn't even have told you!

The old woman does not reply, it is not a question.

The driver turns on the radio which is broadcasting a report on yesterday's massacre in Marseille and says these damned people should all be shot, he for one would know where to start, he adds, nodding towards the Moroccan who is sitting in the thin drizzle with his cigarette lighters, wrapped in layers of clothing and sadness, and the old woman turns round to look at him, yes, it is him, that's why he hasn't been seen for a while in the streets of the centre, his new place of work is here, on this deserted avenue.

Because the new and more aggressive beggars have driven him away?

For a second she thinks of getting the driver to stop and inviting the Moroccan to Malvina's funeral, he will certainly remember her and perhaps is wondering why he doesn't see her any more, for years they have trodden, ever more slowly, ever more bent, the same few streets, they have contemplated the same Liberty-style stuccoes along the smog-blackened walls, the window of the dairy with its piles of soft cheeses, *stracchino* and camembert, and the green bench at the corner, periodically vandalised by people unknown, and they have said good day to each other when they met, it can be said without fear of lying that this foreigner in his shapeless greatcoat knows Malvina better than any of her family members do.

But the moment has already passed, they are at the gates of the cemetery.

The old woman looks around, bewildered, unsure which emotion is stronger, desire or fear, at the prospect of meeting known faces, or which is worse, to see them or not see them, the few surviving friends from the old days, her memory gives way under her cautious footsteps like soft tar, who is that over there, could it be Francesco? Impossible, Francesco is dead, she is sure of it or almost sure, could that be a son? Certainties to cling to: zero, apart from Gabriela who already has her hands full dealing with the umbrella that is refusing to open and a bunch of flowers so enormous she has to keep it aloft so as not to sweep the cobbles with the lilies.

On the forecourt the groups of mourners mingle and divide, arrange themselves in queues according to their place in the hierarchy of mourning, the close relations first, then the distant, then the friends, then the mere acquaintances and neighbours and in due course each queue separates itself clearly from the others and files in slow procession through the gates. The old woman is disorientated, she does not know which funeral she should tag on to, has she got the right time, is this the right cemetery?

Some man has planted himself in front of her and is blocking her view. A bent old man, wearing a camel overcoat too heavy for the time of year. He fixes a pair of tearful eyes on her, instinctively she steps aside and looks at him mistrustfully. The man's now almost hairless head wobbles above the silk scarf round his neck. Max! says the old woman in alarm, and the syllable comes out sounding like a sob, so she adds: How long is it since we saw each other?

But is this shrunken man really Max? Max was notably tall, what has happened to his vertebral column?

The aristocratic head is now the scrawny poll of a flightless bird — how bony his nose has become, and how sharp his cheekbones, and underneath, the skull seems almost visible, yellowish and fragile, the old woman thinks, embracing him, who knows, maybe he is thinking the same things about me.

I ought to be in one of those, he says, indicating the heavily-chromed hearses with their loads waiting to enter. You two at least had each other for company. It would have been better if this had been my show.

Say something more intelligent, Max, the old woman complains, querulous and irritable.

They talk of the final months of Malvina's life. Max has always been better at speaking than listening but today he confines himself to nodding silently, as if to say he knows it all already, beyond a certain age nothing is new any more, nothing surprises or interests one. The old woman ploughs on feverishly, stubbornly, determined to spare him no detail.

Finally their funeral arrives, men in black open the back door of the hearse, scavenger beetle ready to expel the hard rainbow-coloured excrement with its pillow of laurel, red roses and white carnations (how banal, more leaves than flowers! Gabriela observes in a murmur, glancing proudly at the extremely splendid and extremely expensive lilies lolling in her little hands).

From another dark car two people climb out, a middle-aged man, bald, and a woman with tinted hair and a number of colourful plasters on her neck and her bare forearms. Only when she sees them go through the gates behind the hearse does the old woman identify them as the infamous Osvaldo and consort.

Is that it? she says to Max, who is pushing her forward. There's no one here! Where are the others?

There is one other, and that is Ana, who rushes up breathlessly explaining that the bus never came, whilst beside the coffin a priest appears wearing an embroidered chasuble and a purple stole.

The old woman feels her strength desert her. There, beneath that hard and gleaming wood, that is Malvina, her friend, a part of her life, of her memory, almost of her body she would say, Malvina's soft and chubby fingers, sticky with cream and rum, abandoned in her own...

The priest is already about his work, he has shaken the hands of the relatives and now he is blessing the casket in some haste, with one eye on the next hearse which is waiting.

Why the priest? the old woman asks, poking the woman with the plasters in the back with her stick. Malvina was not a believer.

The woman turns round, stares at her with a mixture of revulsion, caution and fear, and says: A blessing never hurt anyone.

What an idiotic load of shi...! the old woman chokes.

Ssh! Max restrains her. It's pointless protesting now.

The meagre procession makes its way towards the chapel where the committal will take place. Bringing up the rear, Ana whispers in Gabriela's ear that the woman, the wife of Osvaldo, is covered in plasters because of all the mosquito bites she got in Brazil, and she laughs, pressing her hand to her mouth. She's got enormous pink swellings, you'd think she had the plague, that's what Ramona told her, who works for them. And how furious she was to have to interrupt her holiday for the aunt's funeral! It was an all-in package, everything paid for in advance, they had to buy new return tickets but they don't know if the insurance will reimburse them, because she was only an aunt, a relative of secondary importance.

In the circular room, painted cream, vaguely neoclassical, Gabriela does not know where to put her lilies — destined to be promptly recycled for another dead person, or very likely two, if they last — and looks anxiously around but no one comes to her aid. The old woman sits on a bench beside Max. Ana takes a seat at the end of the front pew, at a respectful distance from Osvaldo and the *signora*.

A young man with hair artistically arranged over his forehead, in the manner of a romantic poet who has worn his locks away in excesses of distress, pronounces a few words that the old woman listens to but does not hear, as she fails also to hear the music, a mish-mash of classical that fills the regulation sixty seconds of silence. The young man asks if anyone wishes to speak in memory of the dear departed, Osvaldo's wife prods her husband, who rises reluctantly, takes up his position at the little pulpit, unfolds a piece of paper from his breast pocket and reads: Malvina was a good woman, an affectionate daughter and sister, a fantastic aunt, when he was little she always used to take him to eat ice creams at Pepino's and on Sundays for walks along the Po. And here Osvaldo wipes an eye.

At the news of these aunt-like activities of Malvina, the old woman is dumbfounded.

Osvaldo presses on, offering the deceased the loving farewells of her great-nephew and great-niece, his son Matteo who for reasons of work has not been able to come over from

England where he lives, and his daughter Giada, prevented by problems of health (and here Ana casts a meaningful glance round the throng for anyone who wishes to see it, because they all know that Giada is drying out in an expensive clinic near Varese).

Good, says the young Chateaubriand, after a glance at the clock, now we can say our farewells for the last time to dear Balbina. An usher opens the door and outside another small crowd can be seen impatient to come in. The young man presses a button, the coffin begins to slide towards an opening in the wall which is ready to swallow it up.

Everyone stands.

No! The old woman says, beating the floor with her stick. Don't think you can cart her off just like that! This is not Malvina's funeral, it's an abuse of power, a joke, the ultimate offence! Malvina was not a believer, she didn't want blessings or classical music, she wanted jazz, she left instructions in her will. Of which I have an authentic copy, written in her own hand. And her family has always treated her like a doormat, no way was she their fantastic aunt! Your grandparents — and here she jabs her finger at Osvaldo — when she was twenty they sent her to a psychiatrist because she'd fallen in love with a girl! They wanted to have her locked away! Her brother and sister made off with whatever they could, and the rest you took yourself after having her put in a home! Hypocrite! Whited sepulchre! And here her finger jabs frantically, while Osvaldo fixes her with homicidal eyes, the wife shrieks, Gabriela is motionless and open-mouthed, Max implores her: Enough, ssh! and Chateaubriand rushes towards her with arms outstretched, *Signora*, he says sweating and breathless, catching hold of her firmly, calm down, *signora*!

And then the old woman explodes in tears, Max passes her a clean white handkerchief, Gabriela gives her an arm in support and readjusting his hair the crematorium's poet murmurs to the bystanders unctuous banalities on bereavement and minds disturbed by grief.

The old woman is weeping from rage and frustration, because her anger does not have the power to kill anyone, neither Osvaldo, nor the wife, nor Chateaubriand, who gets on her nerves more than anyone else. Hers is only the impotent anger of an old woman who is no longer of any consequence. Her sobs make her ribs hurt, make her heart feel painfully constricted, empty her lungs which are howling in grief and fury, and her crying sounds something like: Maahhhl!-viii-naaa!

The coffin, meanwhile, has disappeared and the opening has closed again.

They separate on the forecourt. Max folds himself with arthritic awkwardness into the car, he would like to linger and chat with her for a while but he can't, the niece who has come to fetch him is waiting with the engine running, drumming her fingers on the steering wheel.

The rain has stopped. The sun appears between the streaks of dirty cloud, behind the plane trees on the avenue. It feels muggy.

The old woman takes a long breath. She feels very weak.

Call a taxi over, she says.

And then: What a painful scene.

You were so brave! Gabriela says in a rush of breath, her

eyes shining with enthusiasm. I wish I could be as brave as you are!

The old woman shakes her head. I have nothing to lose any more, she mutters, getting into the taxi.

Were you asleep? I ask.

No, I was awake, he replies, speaking in a low voice as if he doesn't want to be overheard.

Are you not alone? Is there someone with you?

No, but my niece is a light sleeper. I hope the phone didn't wake her. Do you know what time it is?

I don't care. I wasn't asleep and nor were you. I need to talk to you.

And how is anyone supposed to get to sleep when the air's so humid? It's hot outdoors, you can't breathe, but it's damp in the bedroom in the mornings, when I get up, the windows are all speckled with moisture as if it had been raining all night, but the drops are on the inside... and if I put my feet down anywhere near the window, I get wet feet, so annoying, my socks are soaked before I've got my slippers on.

Listen to me, Max, I have to tell you something. I've made a decision. I'm going to Switzerland.

Oh yes? Lucky you, still having all that energy, I'm still exhausted after that trip to the cemetery the other day, I sincerely hope no one else dies in the next few months, that they hang on until September at least when summer's over, at least I hope it is, because summer these days seems to be invading all the other seasons...

I have no intention of waiting until September. I have already made contact with the people, I've sent an email and they have replied.

Who are you staying with? That friend of yours from Lucerne, what was her name, but is she still alive?

No, Max, I'm going to a clinic, it's called *Die Begleiter*.

Oh, well, German now, I... what are you going for? Hips and knees? Did someone recommend it? Because I've given up on my hips and knees, I'm resigned to falling apart bit by bit, and I'm not letting the local surgeons anywhere near me again, but if it was a reliable place to get my prostate seen to...

They don't do prostates, it's a clinic where you go to die.

Silence at the other end of the line.

Then: In what sense?

In the only sense, Max. Become deceased, kick the bucket, amen, the end!

Max clears his throat, I imagine I can see him, he has sat up in bed and is suddenly overtaken by a bout of catarrhal coughing, his long thin exotic bird's neck moves in jerks, his beautifully-moulded hand presses a handkerchief to his mouth, the handkerchief is then carefully folded and concealed behind the pillow.

I haven't quite understood. You're surely not talking about euthanasia?

Euthanasia is a stupid word, as are all words when they just become labels. However, yes, that is what I'm talking about, Max. I thought you were awake.

I am awake, but allow me to be a trifle disconcerted as well. What has happened to you? Have you been to see a doctor, have you got something nasty?

No, I'm very well, apart from the arthritis, the aching bones, the foggy eyesight, a mutinous heart and the usual delights of old age which I'm not going to list.

I've got all those things too! I'm going blind in my right eye, the optician told me last time... but what's the matter with you then? Are you depressed? That's the worst one of all, I know, it's a subject I'm all too familiar with. Are you taking pills? They do some good, even if they make you even more potty...

But before he can embark on the usual macabre competition about ailments and psycho-physical decline, I try to explain to Max that I am not depressed, that since I've been thinking about it, since I made up my mind, I have felt in control of my life again, because I have made a decision. I am also a little afraid, certainly, as when one falls in love. I often see Nora quite clearly, it's as if I had her beside me, and not because I'm losing my reason but because my mind is more lucid, the colours are more brilliant, thoughts more clear-cut and forceful. And when I see Nora I don't experience that anguish, that irremediable sadness, as if she were behind a wall of fog and I can't touch her, I don't feel guilty for being alive — not any more. But let's not have any misunderstandings here, it is not Nora calling me — if it were her, why now, why not years ago? — it is me calling myself, it is my voice telling me: Come! And since I've been hearing that call and been thinking of answering it, I see everything more clearly, I see others, people in general, in a different way, I almost seem to love them all.

It didn't seem to me you had much love for Malvina's relatives, Max remarks.

No, quite right, I'd have killed the lot of them, I admit fair-mindedly. When I say all you mustn't take it to mean literally everyone. I was talking about people in general. It's a bit like when you get away from a family you can't bear, and the people you're leaving behind begin to seem nice, good people, because you see a better side of them, like helpless children who could have grown into something splendid, even if they haven't done so, and you feel great compassion for them and for yourself, it's wonderful and it lasts only a moment. Well, I'm in that moment and if I don't grab it as it passes it'll be the worse for me. I have to go right to the end.

Obviously Max does not understand, and I don't know how we find ourselves talking about our lives, agreeing we have been privileged people, we have seen war as young children but we were only lightly touched by it, and then we lived cushioned by the twin benefits of peace in the West and the wave of post-war developments: the events of '68, women, all those movements, we were free to think about ourselves, to make our own lives, to choose our own loves, even to carve out a little career in what we used to call 'the arts', and to reach the age we are still enjoying privileges that younger people can't even dream about... although I am no longer so sure that living in peace and in relative comfort is a privilege, it is a patchy peace, surrounded by war, and everyone is barricaded inside his own ferocious little version of peace, but maybe harshness and dangers give life more flavour and better reflect nature as it really is, just now it seems to me it would have been a fine thing to be a Kurdish fighter shouldering her rifle with pride, but I do not say this to Max because he is no longer the Max he once was.

We have lived through a golden age, says Max, and sighs, but now everything is falling apart, people are embittered, there's no money about, medicines cost something criminal and I can't keep a dog, you know, because I wouldn't be able to take it for walks now, besides which my niece won't hear of it. And I depend on her, I am bound hand and foot... what about you, have you still got that cat of yours?

I tell him about the death of Venom, and Max sighs again and says that with animals, yes, you can do that, it's right to intervene when they are suffering, but for human beings it's different, and that I could live another ten years or more.

That is a terrifying idea, Max. Not to be able to get down the stairs or get out of bed without help. Incontinence pads. Memory going. And don't start telling me you know someone who's a hundred and five and completely independent and lucid and has an amazing social life, because the ones I know, and there are plenty of them, piss their pants and don't know their own names.

You're right, but all the same... no one wants to die. We all cling to life tooth and nail, even if we don't have teeth any more... you know I don't agree with people who say life is sacred, my niece is a great one for church and between parish priests and nuns I hear this kind of stuff every day. It's a bore you know... and you, defying everyone... it seems to me like an exaggerated gesture and almost arrogant, you know what I mean? You go off, fine and lovely for you, and we stay here like idiots...

What arrogant gesture? Think about it, Max; at most I'm ahead of the times by a little. Inside twenty years euthanasia will be available on the national health, once you've paid your ticket of course, the health service is almost broke and it's getting worse, you must have read those articles as well, about old people left on stretchers in emergency department corridors for days, in the hope they'll quietly expire without disturbing anyone. We cost too much and there's no motivation to keep us alive. We're at a ridiculous age, Max. And we're more than a quarter of the population of this country, don't you feel at all guilty for belonging to such a useless and expensive category? I'm saving them the bother.

At this point we are interrupted by noises and exclamations. His niece, woken by our nocturnal conversation, has flung open the door of Max's bedroom. I can see her, grey hair flattened by the pillow, flannelette nightdress, misshapen slippers on her feet, the efficient voice of an ex-banker asking what's going on, if he's not feeling well, if he needs something, while her tone transmits the real message: are you off your head, having telephone conversations in the middle of the night? Stop it at once!

And he, who has been transformed from a rich and generous uncle into a poor relation, obediently murmurs some confused words of apology and hurriedly, breathless and guilty, hangs up.

It's Max, he whispers. I'm in the village bar, they've still got a public telephone here, but I don't know how long I can talk because I've only got a few bits of loose change.

How timid and frail his voice has become, it is barely audible against the background noise, people chattering and calling out, the furious grinding of an ancient coffee machine.

Speak up, I say, straining to hear.

Max is asking me if I still have that girl, that Rafaela. How things are between us. Whether there has been some disagreement.

She's called Gabriela. No disagreement, why?

It's just that I thought that maybe you weren't happy with her, she was treating you badly… that that was the reason…

She doesn't treat me badly. As home helps go, Gabriela is a rare jewel. Apart from the cat people, I'm leaving everything to her, I've written it into my will. In fact, I'll send you a copy tomorrow, it's better if you have one too… it's important, you understand?

But in that case, what you were telling me yesterday… is it because you miss Malvina?

Why do you need to look for reasons, Max? Sooner or later life ends. Anything that lives has to die. I'm not a catholic, I don't hold with drinking the bitter chalice right to the end, and anyway Jesus died at thirty-three, which is a long way from ninety. He'd never have made it to that age in this world. I'm a coward, Max, I'm choosing the easy way out, a slightly stylish one as well, if you like, and I don't feel guilty about it.

Max sighs. A dog breaks into high-pitched yelps and lamentations, someone has trodden on it. Poor beast, Max says through the commotion, in a sad voice that sounds tearful, as sad as the look in the eye of the Moroccan who sells lighters and sponges on the streets.

For an instant I think I might propose we do it together, this trip to Switzerland, as a couple. He needn't worry about the money, I can pay for us both.

Max propped up beside me on an immaculate bed, and him, gentlemanly as ever, unwrapping a chocolate with his long elegant fingers and offering it to me, then holding hands and going off to sleep together side by side like two celibate, decrepit sweethearts, surrounded by the perfume of the gardenia in his buttonhole.

Affecting and grotesque, the vision lasts less than a second. Better not.

The old woman is staring at nothing while the television in the room on the other side of the narrow courtyard is blathering away euphorically over some nonsense or other. On the screen two young men with spiky hair are exchanging jokes, laughing and leaping about, while the two in the room, the old man and his daughter, are watching them without taking anything in. They are sitting side by side in armchairs, with plates on their knees. The old man is eating greedily, thrusting the spoon in his mouth with a shaky hand, drips dribble down his chin and fall on his sweater, the daughter glances at him distractedly but shows no sign of moving, carries on feeding herself slowly and listlessly, an eternity goes by between each spoonful.

One of her arms is bandaged and raised to her collar bone in a sling because during the operation they found additional malignant lumps under her armpit, they had to dig them out and now the arm is swollen and painful, they will be operating on her again soon, the old woman knows because she has heard it repeated several times when the daughter is on the phone.

Between daughter and father, two armies on their last legs, a strange sort of truce seems to have been established, made of heavy silences broken by brief explosions of words. After the news, with its massacres and bleak predictions of imminent misery, a cook comes on, a Neapolitan with crafty eyes set deep in a fleshy face, brandishing a skillet with the grace of a fencer. The old man's attention is roused, audible grunts issue from his toothless mouth.

The old woman wonders if the mummy will outlive his own daughter, as he seems to be bent on doing.

Suddenly she remembers how her father used to look at her sometimes, with a mixture of pride, amusement and complacent hostility, as if he was asking himself: but is this terrible woman really my daughter? He wouldn't actually say anything. He would look at her, and that was enough.

She wonders if the mummy in the apartment opposite has ever looked at his daughter like that.

On an impulse she gets up, goes into her bedroom, opens the drawer of the bedside table, takes out the pistol. She returns to the kitchen, smiling to herself. She walks lightly, like a girl, not using the stick and feeling no pain in her legs.

She raises the weapon and points it at the window opposite.

Slowly the old man — perhaps he has caught a movement out of the corner of his eye, a shadow in the evening gloom — turns and stares. It takes him some time to focus. Seconds pass. Surprise and alarm spread across the mummy's features. He opens his mouth, shakes his head, stutters strangulated syllables of warning, ah-ah-ah-oh-oh-oh. He waves his arms about like some flighted creature, almost as if the fat slumped sack of a body could take off under the thrust of those bony and featherless wings, but there is no way he can get airborne and he falls wretchedly back into the armchair. The daughter, floating in a *bain-marie* of nothingness, or perhaps engaged in a passionate and rancorous dialogue with the ghosts of her past life, reluctantly turns away and glances distractedly across to the window. She too has not left the house for weeks, the shopping is delivered by the concierge Assunta, the same woman who looked after the father while she was in hospital. Now the world beyond the window must seem to the pair of them as unreal as a stage set: a painted world, two-dimensional, where the only movement is the waddling passage of the hated pigeons, but where now stands the incongruous figure of the neighbour across the courtyard who is waving to them with one hand while in the other she is holding up a small black object which has all the appearance of a pistol being pointed at them.

The old woman looks at the neighbour opposite with her grey hair, grey face, grey voice, with only one breast, an arm in a sling and eyes on stalks, she looks at the old man a selfish old wreck in a stained sweater, and feels a bizarre emotion flowing towards them. It is not just compassion, no, it is a sort of sympathy, almost a scornful love, a reluctant sense of wonder, as if suddenly the unpleasantness, the silences, the boredom were torn aside, a thin layer of fog broken by a burst of sun, and beneath it gleamed something tender and suffering and precious which will soon disappear again. It is to that nameless something that the old woman sends a cheerful signal, now waving both arms together, before going *click! click!* with the trigger and saying *bang! bang!*

Then she blows the smoke from the end of the barrel and lowers the weapon with a sigh, because now the game is over, the moment has passed, that's how moments are, they reveal but they don't last, half-opening the door on another dimension but never giving you time to enter it.

With a rapid gesture the old woman turns the light out and walks from the room, leaving them alone with their vision, wondering whether what they have seen was real or a dream. A laugh comes to her lips again, but the laugh promptly fades into melancholy gloom.

Zlatec, the old woman articulates. Zlatec Gabriela, with one "l".

She's a foreigner? the bank clerk asks, clinking her jewellery.

The old woman looks at her. She is hypnotised by her extraordinarily long nails, ten hard and curved appendices sprouting from the ends of her fingers and making a metallic clatter on the keyboard. They are painted an aggressive and unreflecting white, all except the nail of the right thumb, which is pink with spangles. Bony spurs on the feet of an animal from the Pleistocene Age. How does she manage with nails like that? Her little ones must have bodies with tough scaly hides to prevent them from being torn to shreds by her caresses.

Not that it's of any importance, the bank clerk continues, you can make the policy out to anyone you like of course, I was only asking, just to…

The old woman would like to ask her if, when she eats, she removes them and lays them out beside her plate, or if she uses them to tear off scraps of bleeding meat and transfer them directly to her mouth.

Zlatec, she repeats. With the final "c". Are you sure this policy covers all kinds of death?

Yes indeed, this life policy, in the unfortunate event that the signatory were to pass away for whatever reason, becomes payable to the beneficiary to whom…

All, all? There are no exclusions?

Absolutely, it covers every eventuality, you see, where it's written here: death by natural causes, accident or homicide, or caused by terrorist attack or acts of war, suicide on the proviso that it is assisted and certified, death as a result of kidnap for purposes of ransom, as a result of robbery or being held hostage, and even death from unknown causes while under arrest, you pay a bit more but you can truly sleep easy, it is an extremely effective policy, fully updated to meet today's needs. Check I've written the name correctly. And she slides a piece of paper under the old woman's nose, the old woman nods, staring at the nail that pins the document down.

Do you know her well, this young lady?

Well enough, the old woman says, speculatively. Can we ever be certain we really know anyone?

The bank clerk runs a hand through the gilded copper of her fair hair, and the old woman follows with fascination the beak-like claw carving through its tresses, after lightly flicking at the armoured spikes of the eyelashes, all bristling and ready for war.

But she isn't a relative of yours?

Where is this woman's body? the old woman wonders. Will she still find it there in the evening, beneath the layers of blusher, lacquer and mascara, the lace trimmings, the necklaces and the talons, or, after undressing and taking off her make-up, will there be anything left of her?

Look, the question isn't meant to be indiscreet, it doesn't matter to me whether she's a relative or not, you're at liberty to assign the policy to whoever you wish. My only scruple is: are you really sure you want to invest such a large sum in this way? It's fully covered, of course, the money is in the account, in any case you have yourself banked a substantial little sum from the policy of *signora* Malvina Pesenti, and because that was taken out many years ago it has almost doubled in value in the meantime, and as you know it is tax-exempt...

Yes definitely, the old woman thinks, Malvina was scatty but she wasn't stupid, she knew exactly how the land lay, that's why she didn't rely on bequests and wills but took out a life policy. And she has set her the example to follow: remembering that she has relatives of a sort as well, distant cousins, who even though they lived in the Americas, might get to hear of her death and fly here in time to dip their snouts in the trough, the old woman went to a solicitor yesterday and had her last wishes redrafted, in her presence, word by word, last wishes which now lie securely in the solicitor's safe. And today she is arranging phase two, the new life policy.

No, because you'll understand, the bank clerk continues — I'm not saying this is true in your case — that sometimes people, often elderly ones, don't be offended because once again I'm not talking about you, they can allow themselves to be influenced, not to say tricked, by someone, a carer for instance, and you know how it is, when there's money involved. True, you can always think again and redeem the policy, but that might not suit you, with time being limited...

If you have finished, I am ready to sign, the old woman says.

By the way, she says, leaving the cubicle, I don't like the colour of your nails at all, powder pink and matt white, don't be offended but if you'd seen anyone else with nails like that you'd say they looked vulgar. You'd choose something more original, malachite green, amethyst purple, or probably a simple Prussian blue. Think about it.

V

Everything around me is real

She opens her eyes. She is in her bedroom, one summer's morning, the smell of coffee, music playing quietly on the radio. Beside her, Nora.

You're so beautiful, the old woman moans, overcome by a warm flood of love and grief, putting her hands out to stroke her face.

Nora smiles, it is her, as familiar and necessary as air to the lungs, known for ever, like the first image that stamps itself on the mind of a new-born baby, as mysterious as the beating of the heart. Now then, now then, calm down, Nora tells her, indulgent. I'm here, I'm not going away. I have never been away.

And then the old woman, borne aloft on a wave of supreme wonderment, realises that Nora is alive, is here beside the bed, beside her, greying hair, face smooth and smiling; her cool dry hand touches her forehead. Then an immense weight is lifted from her chest. She is a little girl who wakes up cured after a night of fever. This is life, real life! What she had taken for life was only a dream! How stupid she has been!

If you only knew, she says. What a horrible dream! I felt

so bad!

And already Nora's arms are around her, and the old woman abandons herself to the delights of consolation. I dreamed, she whispers in her ear, ashamed, you were dead! Dead for years! And I wanted to die as well, but I couldn't!

The telephone wakes her, barely a few minutes have passed since she closed her eyes. It is still early, ten thirty in the evening.

Did I wake you? Gabriela asks. There, I knew it, I have woken you. I shouldn't have called you. I'm sorry.

What is it? Why are you talking in that voice?

I'm so sorry! I thought that maybe you were still up…

Stop apologising and tell me what's happened.

Nothing! Nothing has happened. It's just that he's here, down in the street outside my flat…

The old woman is becoming annoyed. Has she been torn from her dream just to listen to these disconnected stammerings? Does she know, the silly girl, that a moment's grace like the one she has so brutally truncated is not just rare but practically unique?

Calm down! Who are you talking about? Who is here?

Dorin. My cousin. He's down here, in the street. He's been here for nearly an hour, he's in a truck, I could see there was someone inside but I couldn't make out his face, then five minutes ago he climbed out and walked right under the lamppost and it was him. It's him!

The old woman wonders resentfully why her crumbling life has to be in a permanent state of emergency, now that Malvina is no longer losing her mind and Venom can no longer have indigestion. Then there is this person thrusting her family sagas at her, tales beside which the epic poems of ancient Greece abound in rationality and common sense. Could it be that she has no one else to turn to?

As if she had heard her thoughts, Gabriela murmurs in apologetic tones: I didn't know who to call. I don't want to ring Ana, and Petra and Gogu... that would be worse still, they have never helped me.

Her anguish softens the old woman's tight lips, forces her into a sigh of surrender. Tell me everything, but try to explain yourself. Why does it worry you so much that it's your cousin down there in the street? Has he threatened you? What is he doing with a truck?

He's driving it. Ana told me he'd found a job with someone he knows. It says on the truck Fresh and Cured Meats and there's a pig laughing. This isn't the first time I've seen him down there, he was there two evenings ago as well, I thought: he'll be making deliveries, but it's strange all the same because there aren't any shops round here. It's a dark street, no one ever comes along it.

Take a breath, please. Are you sure it's your terrorist?

Positive! I told you, he opened his door and got out, I saw him clearly. He hasn't got a beard any more but it's him. I've known him since he was little.

And what did he do?

He went to pee against a tree. Gabriela's voice is ready to crack.

Hmm, says the old woman in disgust. And then?

Then he climbed back into the lorry. He's spying on me. I'm standing behind the curtain. I've turned out the light in

287

the kitchen. But he knows I'm here, otherwise he'd have gone away, wouldn't he? I'm scared he might try to get in at any moment.

Is he alone or is there someone with him?

I can't see anyone else. Ana says there are always meant to be two of them when they go on their trips but the boss sends them out by themselves, to save money. But how did he manage to find me? I haven't told anyone where I live! Not anyone!

The old woman asks who lives in her small block of flats beside the river, if there's a neighbour she can turn to in cases of emergency. Gabriela runs through them: a deaf old woman who barricades herself inside when it grows dark, a couple of students who always have their music on too loud, a family she has been having arguments with because they throw all their rubbish in the bin together and even outside the bin instead of separating glass and plastic and packaging, the other flats are empty, the tenants evicted for not paying the rent, one is occasionally lived in by a few illegal non-EU immigrants. The street door downstairs, she adds, doesn't shut properly, you only have to give it a push with your shoulder and it opens.

The old woman thinks. Her fingers gripping the phone, her eyes squeezed tight in concentration and filled with floating spots. Something else is working in her, over and above her troubles. Emergency is life and life is emergency, had she perhaps forgotten? If at ninety and with arthritis that sends bolts of fire through her bones she is Gabriela's sole safety anchor, then she needs to steel herself and become young again, there's nothing for it. She gets to her feet and begins to walk up and down. Listen to me carefully, she says. Call a taxi now. Tell him when he arrives he's to press the entry phone, does the entry phone work at least? Well, so long as you can see him from the window, right? While you're waiting, put some things in a bag, a change of underclothes, a pair of pyjamas, all the things you'd need if you were going away for a couple of nights, then as soon as you can see the taxi down below, but not before, understood? Not before! Go downstairs and make a run for the car.

What if he follows us?

In that case you tell the driver not to drive off until he's seen you to your destination, seen you enter the building and shut the street door. If he looks doubtful, you promise him a tip.

But where am I going? Where am I to tell him to take me?

Why here, obviously. Hurry up! the old woman commands, with the sense — once again, at last — of standing like the captain on the bridge, ready to save the situation.

Her hands are trembling as she takes off her slippers and puts on her shoes, buttons her blouse. How long will it take her to complete the operation? Certainly more than the twenty or thirty seconds that pass between one glance at the clock and the next. Turn all the lights on in the apartment, because light brings courage, brings clarity to the darkness. Peer from the little balcony, still no taxi in sight. Prepare the bed in the study, no, there'll be time for that later.

She makes a rapid decision, leaves the apartment, locking it behind her with a turn of the key. She summons the lift. She will wait for the girl in the entrance lobby, so that if by chance the terrorist — whoever that may or may not be — follows her here in spite of the one-way system and the pedestrian zone, and if the taxi man drives off again without making sure the passenger has reached her goal safe and sound, as every responsible taxi man ought to do but often doesn't, because responsibility is not part of the mental make-up of the postmodern man, Gabriela will not face the danger alone. The terrorist will have to deal with her, who does not constitute a formidable obstacle, admittedly, it would only take a shove to knock her to the ground, and then Gabriela will definitely be lost because instead of rushing for safety upstairs she will stop to help her...

The door closes again on the empty lift. The old woman does an about-turn, opens up the apartment again, goes back inside. She takes her shoes off. She slips out on to the balcony: no cars down in the street, other than the ones irregularly parked by customers of the pizzeria opposite, who come outside in groups to smoke, and catching the euphoric whiff of disorientation that comes from being a little way off their usual patch in this narrow street, take to imitating nocturnal animals and emit yells and howls to ravage and disfigure the night and the peace of other people, cowering behind the walls of their ancient apartment blocks.

A sorry thing for an arthritic lioness to have to consider, whether she is going to be more of a hindrance than a help to the person she aims to protect. The old woman pours herself a glass of port, swallows it in two gulps.

But she can't just stand there, waiting, and not sally out to face whatever is about to happen. I don't know what I'm doing, she thinks, in one of those flashes of divided consciousness which at moments of trouble stands to one side and speculates on that other self which is running in circles like a headless chicken.

Enclosed within the four metal walls of the lift, she seems to hear a squeal of brakes, voices in altercation. She imagines Gabriela dragged away by the terrorist while the pizzeria customers applaud the shouts and violence as one of the most tried-and-tested and popular games that couples play.

And even as the old woman realises that she has come out in her slippers and left the house keys on the kitchen table and is cursing old age and herself, the street door opens and here is Gabriela, alone, wrapped up tightly like a sweet in her pale blue canvas jacket, with her bunch of keys in her fist and her eyes bigger than ever.

Gabriela's footsteps in the next room. The shuffle of felt slippers on the floor. Between the excitement of the evening and the knowledge she is not alone in the apartment, the old woman is too agitated to think of sleeping. Amazing the way subtle elements — almost inaudible sounds, the girl's smell, soap and young skin — infiltrate and fill the room, the mind.

They are sitting in the kitchen, Gabriela has repeated her story, with as much detail as she is capable of — she is not a talker, Gabriela — blowing on her tisane, drinking in careful little sips. Reticence, that supposedly feminine quality, akin to modesty and other reductive virtues, is so ingrained in her that she is unaware of it, she responds to the old woman's questions with repetitions: He sent me horrible things on my phone, what horrible things? Horrible things, with a shrug of the shoulders. Deep down, he isn't bad, he was so sweet as a little boy, then he changed, changed in what way? Changed.

But he is not bad. Deep down.

And the old woman getting worked up explaining to her that one needs to stay on one's guard with people who are not bad. Deep down. Only in fairy-tales does the big bad wolf bare his long yellow fangs and frighten children, in real life the lone wolf very likely has a timid smile and runs a flower shop.

Gabriela nods. With the versatility of youth, she has moved on from fear to relief and is now beginning to enjoy the effervescent sensations of novelty and adventure: she will be sleeping here, in the home she knows so well but which has been until now a daytime place, she will get to know it at night, she will lie between the sheets she has washed and ironed but between which she has never slept, tomorrow morning she will hear the bird the *signora* talked about, which sings at dawn. Then they will be going.

Where to?

To Switzerland, the old woman says with an evasive gesture.

Switzerland!

We're going to meet a friend. And while she says it she can see once more the impertinent smile of the woman in the white dinner jacket, and wonders how she will explain her business in Switzerland to Gabriela, if she will ever have to. It doesn't matter, she will think about it tomorrow.

Then, anxious: Have you got your papers with you? Valid for travelling abroad?

Yes, of course, Gabriela is thorough and shows a degree of foresight as ever. She always has her identity card on her. How wonderful! And how will they get to Switzerland? No, not by train, and not even in a hire car, there's her own car! The thing is, she didn't come here by taxi, taxis are expensive, and you have to wait for them, sometimes taxi drivers refuse even to come to her part of town at night, but luckily immediately after they had spoken to each other on the telephone, Dorin had driven off, he and his truck, vanished! So she came in her own car, which was parked just outside the building — no, she was very careful, there was no one in the street, no one saw her! It's much nicer and cheaper to go in one's own car!

The old woman is left feeling confused by this, a little offended. Is her advice not good enough to be acted on? Only afterwards, as she is pulling off her socks and finding it an effort to reach her body's extremities, has she decided that the girl has been lying again. Probably the whole story is false, there wasn't any terrorist, any truck under her window. Only the twisted thoughts of her indecipherable little brain.

Lying stiffly in bed, as if someone were spying on her and might catch her in the usual untidy and irate twitchings of insomnia, the old woman is listening.

Footsteps again. A chair being pushed aside. One of the panels of the bookcase being opened…

May I? Gabriela asks, hesitating behind the closed door.

What?

Take a book…

Take whatever you want. But remember tomorrow morning you have to drive.

Only for a moment! Thank you! Just a few minutes. I can't possibly get to sleep straightaway, I'm too agitated.

Sounds of blankets pushed back in the room next door. Pages turned. A little burst of coughing. The old woman stares intently into the dark above her head. The silence all around her expands, swarms, crackles, the pizzeria has closed, the last customers have departed, no one goes by in the street, the convolvulus on the balcony grows, sends out its small green lance like a reconnaissance party, encounters the ironwork of the railing, begins an encircling movement which by tomorrow morning will have been completed, a page has been read and is now set aside, it passes from the world of things yet to happen to the world of things which have already happened, another page opens to the light, the old woman cannot get to sleep, she sighs, she tries to clear her throat, a hawking cough, a failed eruption, the sad effort of an exhausted Vesuvius.

A small knuckle taps at the door.

What is it? the old woman calls shrilly.

You're not asleep then? Am I disturbing you? Can I come in?

The old woman hauls herself into a sitting position, fastens the nightdress over her wrinkled chest, glares at the intruder fiercely. What do you want?

Gabriela does not answer. She is wearing cotton pyjamas, her bare feet are in the flip-flops that used to be Nora's and she is clutching to her chest a book, a finger inserted in it to mark the place. It occurs to the old woman that she might be scared. Not of this apartment, not of her, but of everything around her.

Can I read to you? she asks. I'd be glad to… if it's not a nuisance.

Hrrmm, the old woman growls.

The book that Gabriela has chosen concerns two little girls who, in the wake of certain unlikely but not impossible coincidences, find themselves together, alone, on an unknown island, where they must survive until someone comes to rescue them, if anyone ever does. In a voice that gradually grows less hesitant, Gabriela reads the adventures of the two youngsters, castaways like the Robinson children, their awkward alliance which turns into friendship, the dangers and discoveries that await them, and the old woman listens frowning, patient, staring at the ceiling. The book is part of a series for children, twenty or so volumes with hardback covers in vivid colours which live in the display case in the study.

At a certain point she has had enough. Why pick this one? she bursts out. It's a book for pre-adolescents, don't you realise?

But it's wonderful! Gabriela protests, contrite. The cover is so lovely...

Yet you pretend to read Henry James, the old woman remarks maliciously.

It takes Gabriela a moment to understand. Oh, that one! I've nearly finished it, I'll bring it back next week.

There won't be a next week, the old woman says.

What? Why?

Nothing, a bit of nonsense. I'm talking rubbish, I'm going soft, at my age it happens. You must have got used to it by now. Carry on, but only up to where they cross the rope bridge and meet the donkey, then shut the book and go back to bed.

You've read it! You remember it!

Yes, I remember it, mutters the old woman, turning on her side because her bones are torturing her and also to avoid seeing the reader's now ecstatic face, while the two little girls advance into a forest which once came out of her mind and under her fingers was transformed into the marks that summon it into existence, this evening, after all this time, on the blank page.

When she wrote it, twenty years ago, before the beginning of the end, she was a different woman. Nora was healthy, the illness had not yet wormed its way inside her, or at least it was only just beginning, in great secrecy, having deliberated and decided to allow them a few more years' stay of execution the better to catch them out; Venom was a young cat recently operated on to halt the erotic excesses which had driven him to disappear across the rooftops and get lost, with frantic searches in consequence and a great deal of pathos on the part of everyone involved; and Malvina, what was Malvina doing? She was still working, certainly, she had even received that lifetime achievement award which had so lifted her, she had finally felt recognised and appreciated, only to realise a few months afterwards that in effect it had been a consolation prize because her work was beginning to be given to other people, younger than her and more in step with the times.

Now the book lives there, the last but one in the row of volumes in the same series, which enjoyed a certain success and brought in sums of money sufficient to let them live decently and even to put something aside. Before, there were others, in varying genres: crime novels of the old-fashioned sort, going back to her youth, appreciated by a limited readership but never reaching the bestseller lists, practical guides on various subjects, written in the moments when the need for money was more urgent, and even a pair of "real" novels, the only ones to appear under her own name, and presently relegated, along with ancient diaries, letters and postcards, to a closed and locked glass cabinet.

In the early stages of Nora's illness she had continued to write, she had thrown herself into her writing with ferocity, she would have liked to wear her fingers away, make them bleed in furious hammering at the keys, by day, late at night, at every moment when fear and desolation got the better of her, writing was her drug, and like all drugs at a certain point it had ceased to have any effect. And in any case she was already old by that time, and had seen, or thought she saw, the relief on her publisher's face when she informed him there would be no further titles, that was it, it was time to retire. The publisher knew nothing about Nora. No one, in the circles she frequented for her profession, knew anything about her, and it was not so much for fear of gossip because she lived with a woman, these things become known in the end and are accepted among people of the world, people who work in professions that are defined as intellectual, it is taken for granted that human variance is of little importance — even if naturally it was important to her, immensely important — no, that was not the reason for her choosing to stop, to fall silent, but because in those places, with those people, she was a different person, or several different people, as the pen-names demonstrated too, she was the product of her own creation and only in that way could she have begun in the first place and then continued to write and to publish, in an anonymity protected by names not hers.

Only by this device could she enter bookshops and see her titles on the shelves and feel herself what she was, a person not connected to them, because the books had their life and she had hers, and this way everything was in its proper place. Her friends could not understand it, Max, for example, was constantly urging her, sometimes jokingly, sometimes seriously, to claim her own works, to value herself, to harvest the fruits of her labours etcetera, lectures which she bore although they annoyed her because she loved Max, if she hadn't she would have been furious and told him — a thing beyond his understanding — that she wasn't acting like this out of modesty or female self-doubt and still less out of reserve, but in order to be free and not to betray a personal truth, for reasons, in substance then, very different from the ones he imagined, in fact quite the opposite of them.

Had it been, ultimately, a case of pride? Or that love of anonymity which often attaches to women, who only have their own name to offer to the dubious appetites of the world, given that the family name always comes from the male side, and she had no desire to be sewn into that particular bag? Or was it simple realism, the confirmation that as a matter of nature and temperament, she could not bear the fiction of being a public persona?

It hardly matters, now. Only Nora, out of all of them, had fully understood her, and without need of words. Nora, who was an actor and hence several different persons, Nora who embodied other lives by exposing her own body to the gaze of strangers, and allowed that gaze to envelop her but not deflect her from her course, she understood very well this need of hers to remain without a name in order to remain free.

Their first encounter had been in a bookshop. There was a poetry reading and Nora was lending her voice to the verses of various local poets, before an audience of aspiring writers amongst whom was the old woman (at that time a young one).

It was a formal occasion, full of pretentions, in the presence of a number of academic personalities, everyone treated each other as the best of friends but adulation and reverence flowed like water, far more copiously than the sparkling wine which as always in these cases was rationed out with parsimony. The more she listened the more she realised that the only true poetry present in the room was the voice of the reader, and her whole youthful person. At the end of the reading, scorning the buffet, Nora had approached her and without hesitation, without hiding the obvious, that she was choosing her, specifically and solely, to the exclusion of everyone else, had murmured: Are you dying of boredom as well?

A few minutes later they left together, without saying their farewells.

But at a certain point in her career as a scribbler when it appeared inevitable that she was to be revealed, the old woman cannot even remember now how it happened that they convinced her to 'take herself seriously' as a professional, to bring together the scattered elements of her life, open the border between the public and the private, blah, blah, blah, in short to declare herself a writer. A huge error. The old woman still blushes to think about it. Her two "real" novels, much more full of effort because they had been weighed down by doubts and anxieties and therefore lacked any sense of adventurousness or authenticity, much more slender works because she had suddenly seen them through the eyes of the readers and the ambitions of the publisher and had realised she had no idea at all what might be "real" for readers and publishers and had therefore ruthlessly cut out everything that seemed too much her own and insufficiently universal, they had been neither successful nor unsuccessful, but had been for her sources of countless petty and pitiful mortifications.

She knew beforehand that she would be forcibly projected into the world of quantity, where more books would be expected from her, a world where every minor success was a failure and every slightly bigger success a humiliation in comparison to the more resounding achievements of some other writer — at her age, she thought, she could by now face all this with a sense of measure and equilibrium. The true things, the important things, lie only in personal relations, between one individual and another, and hence between the person who writes and her reader, Nora used to say, looking at her tenderly, as if she wished to console her in anticipation of what awaited her.

The episode that returns to her mind this evening, in the darkness of her room, on the eve of her departure for Switzerland, in this week which will not be followed by another, is being approached by a woman in a bookshop in a town not her own, after a presentation that felt listless and banal and left her thoroughly drained. The woman is more or less the same age, of similar height and is dressed in a style not far different from her own. There is hesitation in her eyes, though they are eager, it is clear that she desperately wants something and will not go away until she gets it. The woman tells her she recognised herself in her book. The old woman, who considers the book a failure and is already ashamed of it, smiles, faking gratitude as best she can. The woman tells her they are alike, the two of them, and in a certain sense it is true, they are of similar build, similar age, even their names are similar. The woman says she feels she knows everything about her, and the old woman thinks she must get away as soon as possible or she will miss her train. The woman insists on passing over her contact details. Hastily cramming her things, glasses, pen, diary in her handbag the old woman says that books are the outcome of the act of writing, an expression she hates as soon as she utters it, and that a book is one thing and the author another. The woman looks at her with fierce desolation. The desolation in her eyes is not from now, it is ancient, decades long, maybe centuries, probably she has inherited it from her mother, to whom it has been transmitted by a long sequence of unhappy ancestors. The old woman wants to escape from the now deserted bookshop, from the echo of the words that have been spoken, from the dregs of wine in the plastic glasses, her heart is crying: Home! Nora! bed! And instead she lingers, misses her train (she will catch the next one and arrive very late, with a headache), she drinks an aperitif, an *amaro* which she does not like, with the woman in a sad bar on the point of closing, and listens to the woman suppressing her unhappiness and speaking to her of how she completely identified with her protagonist, and the old woman now realises that this woman has read a book which is not the one she wrote, and she would try to tell her so if she did not fear it might wound her and if she had not by now understood that she and the stranger are talking two languages which use the same words but are in reality mutually untranslatable. She feels as if she is in a film by Antonioni about lack of communication, or has been transported back to the days of her first, painful amorous experiences. She feels the weight of responsibility which the stronger has for the weaker, she cannot shirk it. Not even when she begins to feel victim of the ruthlessness with which the woman denies her the right to exist and insists she should be only and specifically that thing which she is not, "the writer", exactly as she imagines her. Naturally she is waiting for the woman to tell her that she writes as well, and when it happens she welcomes the expected revelation with relief, it is the lesser evil, one to which she is accustomed (friends and acquaintances have not spared her over the years) and it is almost with gratitude that she receives her request, yes, she can certainly send her what she has been writing, she will read it, but she should know that she has no influence in the publishing world, and so on.

The woman subsequently writes her a letter, once again invoking characters and events from a book parallel to the one she has written, but totally different and in which every word has been given unacceptably altered meanings. Things that she would never say. Things that she did not say, and which slightly resemble, however, a piece written by a certain reviewer, which profoundly wounded her without her being able to work out exactly why. He did not tear her to pieces, but he transformed her book — he as well! — into something else, something approaching the opposite of what she had believed she was writing.

And she felt guilty, as we always feel guilty over a misunderstanding of which we are the victim, because it is clear that to some extent we are the ones who have exposed ourselves to this very misunderstanding.

In the last phase of Nora's illness the old woman had started to write again. It was different. Writing is usually necessary for anyone who does it, otherwise they would dedicate themselves to more sensible and profitable occupations, but in that particular period it had become for her even more necessary, so essential that she did it without thinking about it. She wrote down what was happening, what she saw and thought and feared, the questions she did not voice aloud, the hopes she did not dare cultivate, the sins, guilty feelings, weaknesses which she suddenly felt an absolute need to confess, in short writing had become a prayer, a dialogue with the only divine element conceivable within the old woman's atheism: the mystery which had the power of life and death over Nora.

What are you doing? Nora would ask. Nothing, she would reply, claiming it was notes for some future work or other, emails to send, accounts to draw up; in reality she was writing with no plot and no design in mind, from one breath to the next, and Nora was perfectly aware of it, so much so that one day she asked her to read what she was writing, and she, flushing with shame, desire and terror, told her: wait a bit until I've got it organised, it's no good as it is, I have to revise it, and the moment had passed, Nora had grown weaker to the point of being unable to read and had then died, and the old woman, left alone with her voice unheard and having failed to throw herself from the seventh floor, had continued to write for months, like a robot controlled by an external and irresistible power, until the writing had exhausted itself of its own accord and there was nothing else for her to do except go on living.

Those pages, text files, documents ordered in their disorder, constitute the old woman's real works, and they will disappear along with her, as is only right and just, when a stranger's hands throw away her computer without troubling to see what it contains, unless they are the curious hands of Gabriela, who tonight has opened one of her books because it has a pretty cover, and which might perhaps in a not too distant future, rummage among the writings as she has in the wardrobes, pulling things out one by one, pausing to touch them, dreaming over them, smoothing them with her hard-working little fingers...

The old woman dreams she is twelve years old and living in the country, in the garden of the house to which she was evacuated along with her parents to escape the bombs falling on their city. It is a poor house, an old farmhouse, nestled on the mountain slopes, dark inside and permanently smelling of stone and shadows, of damp earth and wood smoke, because you have to keep a fire burning in the fireplace until late spring to keep the dampness away. She lives there with her mother, her father returns only at weekends, he has his work to go to in town even if there is a war on, she and her mother occupy two rooms and the people whose house it is, a family of five, have squeezed themselves into the other two on the ground floor to make room for them. The staircase is made of wood, and steep, and creaks every time you go up or down, the WC is at the end of the kitchen garden, under a rowan tree that in summer trails little clusters of orange-red berries.

The farmers who are their hosts have three children, a girl much older than her and two boys only a little younger. Within a few weeks they have become her brothers, her gang, among them she enjoys the prestige of coming from the big city and secretly she admires them for the things they know about animals and plants. She goes down to the village with them, to school, in a small classroom whitewashed in chalk, with worm-eaten wooden benches covered in the graffiti of pupils from a hundred years before. In the afternoons they wander freely through the countryside and swim in the freezing pools of a river. Like them and together with them she goes about bare-foot on the warm earth of the kitchen garden, lifts her skirt to wade in the ditches, and the mother allows it, freed from the worries of life in the city, for she too is caught up in this unforeseen suspension of normal life, this unhoped-for island of peace in the middle of the war.

The old woman, who in her dream is a little girl, as one could then be at twelve, not a teenager or a pre-adolescent but a proper little girl, with bare legs under a cotton dress much snagged by wild brambles, breathes the air of her childhood which smells of the future, and is happy.

No expensive fragrance, no other perfume, only perhaps the young skin of the most beloved body, will ever be more sweet and electrifying than that one. The smell of time not yet used up, of life still to be lived, which mingles with the smell of the wild roses and the meadows under the sun.

The old woman sleeps, deeply, in the last threads of night, which yet holds off the day. The dream lasts a few seconds, but — as happens only in dreams — it is a vertical instant, a probe, a sounding which goes from the deepest well of memory to the highest heaven the dreamer can dream, and thus is outside all time and measure.

On the threshold, Gabriela looks mistrustfully at the woman who has rung the bell. She keeps the door half closed, leaving barely a crack, and is holding the coffee pot in her wet hands because she has run to open the door while she was making the coffee, before the intrusive ringing can disturb the *signora*.

The woman — a forty-odd brunette chewing a stick of gum and with a large canvas bag slung over her shoulder — introduces herself as a social worker. She has come, she says, to see the *signora*.

Two deep furrows appear on Gabriela's brow.

Are you a relative? the woman asks. The carer?

I am the housekeeper, the girl replies, her diction clear and crisp. Do you have an appointment?

The intruder is obliged to admit that no, she does not have an appointment. She peers in, the apartment is in perfect order as usual, Gabriela is torn between the desire to let her see for herself (take a look, you won't find another house as clean and tidy as this!) and hostility, the latter prevails. The crack narrows.

The *signora* is busy at the moment, Gabriela says. (The old woman is in the bathroom, she got up later than intended and she would certainly not be pleased to be discovered in her dressing gown by this unknown woman.) What do you want with her? she adds coldly.

The woman removes the chewing gum from her mouth, stares at her, annoyed, it is clear she thinks she is the one who should be asking the questions. She informs her that she has come to evaluate the situation of the *signora* regarding health and accommodation, for purposes of social welfare. Sometimes the elderly are not capable of living alone, they have problems, and then it becomes necessary to intervene, for their own good.

Gabriela is horrified. She is well aware who social workers are and what they do, because years ago they threatened to take away her niece Carolina when Petra was forced to do a lot of overtime and in consequence left her at day nursery beyond its official closing, and the teachers couldn't keep her there because they had to go home themselves and at that time of day even Gogu was working, or playing the machines, and the eldest daughter was an airhead, she couldn't be trusted to see to her. So she, Gabriela, had given up a good job she did in the afternoons to take a morning job instead which allowed her to go and fetch Carolina from nursery school. That this individual should wish to evaluate the *signora* strikes her as a personal outrage even more than a threat, but she knows she must hide her feelings. The *signora* is very well, she says with what she hopes is a convincing smile. She doesn't have any problems.

The social worker sighs, she replaces the chewing gum in her mouth (probably after abandoning the idea of disposing of it in some other way while a judgemental eye is on her) and informs her that she has received a report. From the neighbours. That the *signora* has been showing signs, yes, to put it bluntly, of not entirely balanced behaviour.

Which neighbours? Gabriela asks, scandalised.

This the social worker is unable to tell her, it is a privacy issue, but Gabriela is quick to catch on: I know, she says, it's those two opposite, the father and daughter, or rather the daughter because the father is a vegetable, but she's a wicked woman, malicious, always on about the pigeons, it's obvious she's got it in for the whole world because she lives this dog's life, and then she's ill, she's got cancer, she'll probably die before her father, which is enough to be angry about but isn't a reason to take it out on my *signora*, who is a person of the utmost propriety!

During this tirade Gabriela advances on to the landing, still holding the door half closed and obliging the social worker to take a step back. Listen, the woman says, unnerved by the resistance she finds herself faced with, they said something about threatening behaviour, even a weapon…

Weapon? What weapon?

I can't tell you. A pistol, if you really want to know.

Gabriela's laugh rings like a war cry in the echo-chamber of the stairs. A pistol! But the woman's mad! She's lost her mind! In our house! My *signora*!

The social worker takes from her bag a packet of cigarettes, makes as if to light one, changes her mind.

Why don't you people go round to her apartment? Gabriela continues pitilessly. Then you'll see what sort of woman she is! Then you'll know who you should be listening to! The last time she washed her floors must have been Christmas! And the father, always in those greasy pullovers full of holes! There'll be mice in the kitchen, in that apartment! Go round to theirs, instead of coming knocking here!

The social worker looks at her watch. Listen, fine, I dropped by seeing I had a spare half hour, but I can't waste time, with everything I have to do, if now's a bad time and the *signora* can't…

She certainly can't, she's having a bath and I can't disturb her just now.

The intruder has no option but to acknowledge her temporary defeat and promise, or threaten, that she will be back.

Not without an appointment! cries the girl to her departing back.

Who was that?

Sweet-smelling from her ablutions, her hair newly arranged, her eyes clear, her body still erect in the green and purple dressing gown from India, her feet in worn but once elegant slippers: a sweet old lady. So she appears, emerging from the bathroom, to her guardian and defender.

No one, the girl says. I'll put the coffee on straightaway.

What do you mean no one? Why were you laughing?

It was a Jehovah's Witness, Gabriela says with an innocent and happy smile. I told her her god was of no interest to us. And not to come disturbing people. And to take that chewing gum out of her mouth.

(On Jehovah's Witnesses she is well-informed, she was one herself for a month or two, a few years ago).

And she marches off to the kitchen, with her coffee pot.

The old woman gives her a hard stare as she walks away.

Let's get going, she says.

Now?

Yes. I told you last night. We're going to Switzerland.

But you haven't packed your case.

The old woman's confusion is only momentary. She has forgotten.

I don't need any luggage, she says. Even though, in fact, it is unlikely that the *Die Begleiter* people will be so prompt in ushering her where she wishes to go as to obviate the need for a travellers' basic necessities, a tooth brush, a change of underwear.

A strange weariness suddenly comes over her. The case.

What is she to put in this case? Her favourite scarf, or the foulard that belonged to Nora and on which she tipped, one day, the very last drops of the perfume she always wore? Her best-loved geranium, the red one which has stubbornly kept flowering for years?

To say goodbye to this apartment, to take responsibility for another abandonment, is a task beyond her powers.

Sit down. Have some coffee, if it hasn't gone cold. Gabriela pushes the chair aside for her, places on the table mats the jar of jam, the plates with the toasted bread and the *biscotti*. How lovely! I've never been to Switzerland! Will we see the mountains?

The old woman is seized with hilarity. Of course, there won't be any choice. That's where we have to go, up into the mountains. Will your poor old car make it?

But of course it will! Didn't I do well, coming here in my own car? Now it's already here, waiting for us! I managed to park it in the avenue on the other side of the gardens, that was a piece of luck! And then, biting energetically into a slice of toast that crunches under her teeth: Don't worry about the case, I'll do it. You won't need many things, if we're only going away for a couple of days, will you?

And then, she adds, when we get back we'll collect those two kittens. Don't say no! They're almost ready!

In the end everything she needs fits in her black bag, the one she always took with her when she went out with Malvina. It is more capacious than it appears from the outside, and contains:

identity card (valid)

passport (expired ten years ago)

driving licence (also expired)

two thousand Swiss francs fresh from the bank. In a roll with a rubber band round them

about a thousand euros in banknotes of various denominations

a wallet with 37.80 euros in coins

a plastic bag containing various blister-packs of medicines, amongst which: anti-inflammatory capsules (useful in case of arthritic pains), pills for high blood pressure, laxative tablets, indigestion tablets, cough sweets, and others no longer identifiable, some of them out of date

two clean handkerchiefs, on which a few drops of eau de cologne have been poured

credit card (just renewed)

a manicure set, scissors-nail-clippers-tweezers (rarely used but indispensable when travelling)

a pouch with needles, black thread and white thread (ditto)

a medical certificate from some years ago (attesting that the person herein referred to is afflicted by a serious form of depression)

the house keys

a gold ring with diamonds (present from Nora)

a 34 calibre Beretta (unloaded)

a hand-written copy of the will and photocopy of the life policy (in sealed envelope)

While the old woman grumbles that there must be a map of Switzerland somewhere in her apartment, Gabriela counters her with Google Maps. With those you can go anywhere.

So now she is sitting with Gabriela's phone on her lap and following their journey, a flashing blue dot tracing the network of streets and dual carriageways that are taking them out of the city. The air is cool this summer morning, clouds are racing across the sky, but soon it will be hot, as it was yesterday and the preceding days.

The radio is announcing today's attacks in European capitals, the discovery in the Mediterranean of a boat full of bodies thought to have come from Libya, the advance of xenophobic right-wing groups in five EU countries. The nuclear threats of an Asian dictator with a face as round as a Chinese lantern. Turn it off, the old woman says. Or put on some music.

Gabriela appears to be immersed in her own thoughts. Once out of the city, the old woman's feelings of unreality and anxiety disappear at the sight of the blue-tinted mountains capped in white, of the green of the hills, the fields gleaming from recent showers. She winds the window down, she seems to smell the scent of countryside, of trees, perhaps her nostalgic brain is making it up, she breathes in deeply, she lets the draught ruffle her hair. She remembers a long-ago trip in a 2CV with the roof down, sitting in the seat next to her a girl whose face she can't now bring into focus, they were twenty, their hair streamed behind them like banners.

She recalls the sense of freedom as she gripped the wheel between her hands, ahead of her endless roads leading to the great North, to the Russian steppes, to the immense valleys of Asia. She has certainly not seen it all, the world she imagined stretching before her along those roads, when did she stop wanting to see it? There came a moment, impossible to put a finger on a precise date, when desert islands and natural paradises ceased to exist, she doesn't know if that was the outer reality or just her already somewhat tired inner thoughts, and permanently retreated to exist now only in the memory of things vaguely dreamed about but never seen.

It could have been the time when, on a particular hillside on the Ligurian coast where she and Nora used to walk, the scent of woodlands disappeared to be replaced by the smell of scorched tree-trunks and car exhausts. The time when, driving through the countryside of her childhood, she lost herself in a tangle of ring roads and bypasses. When she read about the island of plastic floating somewhere in the middle of the ocean. When suitcases became too heavy to hoist on to luggage racks in trains. When she saw on television smoke rising from the bombs in the same square in Istanbul where one day during Ramadan they had lingered until sunset among thousands of people patiently waiting to begin their silent and orderly mass picnic. When the Arctic ice cap began to melt at an accelerated rate, and photographs appeared of polar bears adrift on ice floes. When floral tributes were laid on the Berlin pavement right in front of the bench where they had once sat to eat chips from paper cones. When Nora's illness changed the cartography of the planet. When a certain colony of stray cats vanished from a Sardinian island, from one year to the next. When she read that tuna fish in the Mediterranean were feeding on the corpses of people who had drowned. When… when…

But all this is highly relative, the old woman thinks, there is no reason to think that the world can't appear mysterious and magnificent to someone of Gabriela's age, for whom desert islands and stray cats will be of no significance whatever, and who will see other marvels, with other eyes. Someone who will see splendour where I see desolation, who will be curious about things that I find frightening. People different from me, as I was from the elderly of seventy years ago. Mutated creatures, perhaps, with other appetites and other fears, and why not? Blood of a different colour. Gills in place of lungs. A brain more powerful and evolved than mine. Or more simple and cunning. Who will possess abilities I have never dreamed of, and for whom good and evil, love and sorrow will be words without meaning, or a meaning I am unable to imagine.

Gabriela drives with great concentration, eyes darting from carriageway to rear-view mirror, hands tight on the wheel. She is not used to major roads and heavy traffic, so far their afternoon excursions to visit Malvina have led them almost entirely along twisting minor roads among the fields.

The old woman is wondering whether Nora's ring would suit the girl, too big for her ring finger, she would have to have it made smaller. Or wear it on the thumb, as is done nowadays. With a sense of peace and almost relief, the old woman realises that her life is moving towards its end, is in reality almost over already, there is little left to do, her existence is now extremely tenuous, a delicate thread which will not withstand the first good tug, all the people who might remember her are dead, apart from Max, who will soon remember nothing, however, not even him, all the human beings who held in themselves some part of her, like a specific colour on the palette of their lives, those who could complete a sentence she left half spoken, divine her mood from her tone of voice, all the people for whom she has existed, a figure with distinct outlines, with her particular ways of saying things, her bouts of impatience, her bursts of laughter, her pet subjects, expounded and much repeated, the things she never said, the kisses and casual encounters, the illusions, the embarrassments, the hopes betrayed, the minor triumphs of vanity or of friendship — they are all gone. And each of them has left something in her, but at the same time has taken away a piece of her. And now, from constantly losing pieces, little is left. There remains a frail shell, uncaring and tired, fed and maintained in a state of decorous decency by the girl who is holding the steering wheel of their journey.

She and Gabriela are united by a bond she cannot find a name for, they have neither common blood nor those shared memories which give the past a shape, their first words were spoken in different languages, and they think their thoughts in different languages. And not only because they come from separate countries, but because they were young in eras very distant from each other, she nearly a century ago and the girl barely yesterday. For two years they have shared their time and their daily space, but not their dreams, their reading, their experience of the world. They are two strangers who have met at a crossroads and have walked together along a road which is only in appearance the same road, but in reality each of them is following a path entirely her own, towards a destination quite different from the other's. Something of her will remain in Gabriela too, but it will be a trace as light as a dried leaf kept between the pages of a book which has never been read to the end, one day she will come across it reduced to crumbs and will no longer remember when and where it was picked up.

Remember me lightly, forget me lightly, echoes in her mind the line of Marina Cvetaeva.

And for an instant the old woman knows the most perfect calm, her ego dissolving completely into all of this, she accepts the unknown laws of life, she submits with equanimity to the murmuring breath of the universe and allows herself to be lulled, trusting, by the infinite waves of Time.

Then the moment passes. The sun emerges from behind the clouds, it is warm, a fly is monotonously, obsessively, buzzing against the car windows, the old woman tries ineffectually to swat it or to direct it towards the crack in the window and liberty, then lets her arthritic arm fall, her head feels heavy on her neck and demands to be allowed to fall back against the head-rest, and for the umpteenth time — it is happening with increasing frequency now, she is becoming lethargic, a machine for sleeping! — her old body and her old thoughts surrender to something more familiar but not far different from nirvana, sleep.

She dreams she is in a room with simple furnishings, a large bed, a window. She is waiting for someone who is due to make an important delivery, no, to take something away, where is the yellow bag she put on the table? It has disappeared. Suddenly she wonders about the view from the window, where is that uniform whiteness coming from, is it fog, or a fall of snow? She goes over to the window but cannot make anything out. On the other side of the glass there seems to exist only a whitish light, devoid of shape or movement. She steps back in alarm. But before alarm can turn to terror here is Gabriela, entering the room in her blue work-coat and telling her she

316

can rest easy, that *signora* came but she sent her away. The old woman shouts: You shouldn't have. I was expecting her! But the girl explains that it was nothing to do with the *signora* in the dinner jacket but rather an importunate Jehovah's Witness. She is lying, the old woman knows that, but there is nothing she can do about it and she is even faintly reassured. Then the girl says: Get up, see how beautiful it is outside, and she then sees that beyond the window is a green and rolling landscape, but they are not the impeccable Swiss hills with their neat caps of greenery, they look more like the thickets, ravines and rocky scrubland of her infancy. Even the room around her has changed, it is the interior of an old mountain *ciabòt*, a stone hut, there are tables and a smoke-blackened fireplace, it is an inn, it smells of *polenta concia*, cooked with cheese and butter, and wine. The old woman realises she is hungry, no, starving.

She opens her eyes to see a rising road, slate roofs on the slopes, vases in the windows, splashes of red and violet bright enough in the sharp light to hurt the eyes, she has been asleep for less than twenty minutes but the pains have vanished from her joints, her muscles are demanding she stretch her legs.

Aren't you hungry? she asks Gabriela, who looks odd behind her dark glasses. Where are we?

I don't know, I got confused at a crossroads, I think I've taken the wrong turning.

But haven't you got Google Maps?

It's not working, my phone's run out of money.

Don't look so worried, it's not a big drama. You could have used mine, or rather you could have thought of that beforehand when we were looking for that map at home...

we'll go back to the crossroads where you went wrong and look at the signposts.

But she does not give her time to do so. She suddenly has a clear memory of having already seen the village which lies a little below the road, there is a restaurant in these parts, just here, a rustic place where they make gnocchi and serve it with a white wine from this valley, a lucky coincidence to wake up just at the moment they are about to pass it, she needs to turn round at once, at the next bend. Gabriela obeys, clumsily, turning the wheel at the last minute. Here, this is where it is, a hundred metres from here, or just after the next crossroads, unless it's behind that little stone wall, memory is playing hide and seek with her, sending her false indications (there was a wall, yes, but alongside a different road, climbing the side of different mountains), but she does not give in and in the end her tenacity is rewarded, Stop! she shouts, it's here, we've arrived.

She climbs out of the car, clutching the bag to her chest, without waiting for her escort to come and open the door for her, the sharp air pricks at her skin, lightning quick visions flash through her mind, drunk on oxygen, of the possibility of spending days roaming these mountains, the mountain air is a tonic as invigorating as icy water on her wrists and their sluggish pulse, she will show the girl Lake Sils and the teeth of the Jungfrau, the medieval towers of Bern and the library of St. Gallen, they will eat trout under the pergola of some country Gasthaus. She has her credit card with her. They could even cross into France, they still have time to take another road and head towards Chamonix, France is less expensive than Switzerland, it would be wonderful to drive through

Burgundy and press on as far as Brittany and Normandy. The sea in Normandy, with the wind and the big chairs like sea shells on the beach. Gabriela has never been to Paris, how is it possible that a girl of her age doesn't know Paris? Maybe that little hotel near the Opera still exists where she and Nora stayed the last time, how silly to think of going directly to Zurich without enjoying herself a little first, it's exactly this shutting herself away as if embalmed in her tomb, instead of getting out and about, travelling, that has aged her. She should get some air. She should spend the money she has, as well as the money she doesn't, what else are credit cards for, and who gives a damn, once you're dead, who can come asking for it?

She feels well. Physically well. What a marvellous sensation of strength in her legs, the desire to walk, the muscles lively and impatient, the young woman she used to be is still alive inside her, here she is, she breathes in the air and the sun, she breathes in the scent of the mountains and the future, and a moment is all it needs, it is truer than anything else, life is still here. And it exists inside her, not the reduced life, the remaining dregs, of a woman of ninety. New as this year's leaves, as the grass gleaming in the sun, not yet turned dry by the summer.

She would like to spring forward and run, but good sense, and the treacherous gravel, restrain her.

If death is in a hurry, let it come and get me, she thinks, and there flashes into her mind a song by Vecchioni from the seventies about a soldier fleeing the death that awaits him in Samarkand, and she begins to hum it to herself.

Only when she is at the restaurant door does she realise it is closed, and probably has been for years judging by the dust. The restaurant sign dangles from the wall of the building, peeling. The bars on the windows are rusted, in the flower tubs the weeds triumph over the remains of ancient geraniums.

She does not recognise the place.

She is not even sure she has ever been here.

She turns round.

Gabriela has her back turned, the sun seems to be pinning her to the ground, there is something disjointed about the way she is standing. She is looking towards the far end of the large forecourt, where a lorry is making the gravel crunch under its wheels, amid the rumbling of its engine. It is a middle-sized articulated lorry, with rigid sides and painted white, the side bears an image of a pink pig, laughing, a napkin knotted round its neck.

From the driver's cab a young man jumps down, slowly lifts an arm to shield his eyes, stands motionless staring at the girl.

He is wearing faded jeans and a black T-shirt. His hair is cut very short. No beard. He is not especially tall, nor muscular, and seen from here, by the watery eyes of the old woman, he appears thin and lost. Nonetheless, it is at once clear to her — a gust of cold, mossy wind from the mountainside, a booming in her ribs — that it is him.

The terrorist.

A flash of clarity like a bolt of lightning. I do not know what is happening, no, I do not know why the terrorist should have suddenly appeared on this mountain road, why, deep down, I find myself so unsurprised to see him, as if I were expecting to meet him, but I know that everything is real around me. I am myself real in a way I have not been for some time. In the green of the trees — a living, trembling, moving mass — I seem to make out each and every leaf, even though I know that this cannot be true, my glasses are not as powerful as that. A river is flowing at the bottom of the valley, I can hear it as clearly as I can see the white foam on the rocks.

I hear the sound of my footsteps, each one with its own distinctive, slightly different ring on the gravel. I hear the voice of Gabriela imploring me to stop, Come away! Come away! I hear her open the car door and then, after waiting a few seconds, close it again. I hear her following me, I know without turning round that every step she takes is a battle between courage and fear, courage wins and she catches me up, takes me by the arm. Her cold little hand on the light material of my sleeve.

Ah no, I say, since he's followed us this far, now let's see each other face to face.

The boy has a narrow, childlike face. I was expecting it to be browner — foolishly, because he is not Arabian — his skin is white and rosy, he has a prominent mole on his cheek, dark eyes with notably long lashes, curling upwards, the kind of lashes that women pay money to have done at the beautician's. As to the rest, he is not good-looking, but nor is he ugly, a face like any other, expressionless, closed, it seems as if he doesn't see, for his eyes are directed elsewhere, like the lenses on mobile phones where you only have to press a button and they look at the person who is looking into them rather than at the world outside.

Hello, I say. So you exist. I admit I didn't believe in you, I had my doubts.

He avoids my gaze, fixes on a point to my right. I turn round to look, but no there is nothing there.

Let's go, says Gabriela. It's my fault, I knew he was following me, I saw him, I didn't tell you because I didn't want to alarm you, I was hoping he would go away.

There are a lot of things you don't tell me, I remark. Let's go where, if this fellow is going to keep on following us? And to him: Finally we meet, Dorin.

His name makes him start. Perhaps for an instant his eyes focus on me, but then he returns to his not-looking pose. It is not difficult for me to see in him the little boy Gabriela found so sweet twenty years ago. But he has grown up, inside that delicate, tense boy's body, behind his closed face. I feel an urge to knock, *tap tap*, if you're there show yourself!

I have heard a fair bit about you, I tell him. As I said, I was sceptical. But I am pleased to know you.

He shifts his weight from one foot to the other. I suddenly feel his anger, it hits me with the force of a kicking animal. Behind his motionless mask, the unseeing eyes, Dorin is furious. He has turned aside so as not to have the sun in his eyes, now I see him in three-quarter view and notice that a nervous tic affects his right cheek. The hand he is holding up to shield his forehead comes down and clenches in a fist. I see what I had not noticed at first: he is tired, he has two dark haloes round his eyelids, he has probably been awake all night. Maybe this boy only needs someone to talk to him, a thing that can't very often happen to him in his life.

Listen, I say, why don't the three of us go and sit somewhere, have something to eat and have a chat. This restaurant is closed, but we'll find another.

Dorin turns his head abruptly, I don't know if he is surprised or disgusted by my proposal. If his ears have heard it, if his mind has registered it. There is a brief cawing sound then a tune explodes, a Turkish or gipsy song, he grabs the phone that is protruding from the back pocket of his jeans and answers with the sulky: Yes! of a child unjustly punished. From the phone comes a rumbling male voice, a deep bass, contrasting with his and making it sound much lighter, almost feminine. The boy turns his back on us, walks away a few paces. I hear him say: Yes, yes, I'll be there very soon, half an hour and I can make the delivery, I ran into traffic, it isn't my fault, I had a puncture. Yes, a tyre.

Before he has had time to slide it back into his pocket, the phone rings again, a burst of song. I told you I had a puncture! he yells. Tell the boss!

Dorin wanders away, squeezing the phone so tightly it could break in pieces, his sweaty T-shirt sticking to his back, underneath it the muscles stand out like knotted cords.

Gabriela tugs at my arm: Let's get away! You don't know him, she says. It's impossible to speak to him. He's mad.

I am about to tell her that we are all mysterious and dangerous, all of us mad in our own way, that maybe it is worth trying, even if in reality I know very well that Dorin considers it beneath his dignity as a young male and would-be terrorist to exchange even two words with a person like me, not just a woman but an old one and with a school-mistressy manner, even if I have never been a schoolmistress, and who thinks she can teach him how to live his life while all he wants is to get me out of his way, annihilate me like an obstacle of no significance. If looks were enough I would be dead already, smashed to smithereens, like in the cartoons — but what superpowers, he can't even look me in the face.

He is still your cousin, I say to Gabriela. We could eat together, what's strange about that, or even have a coffee, and maybe in these very normal human activities a word or two would get through to him, might persuade him to let his guard down for a couple of seconds, and maybe some dim flicker of thought might force its way into his mind... I dry up, not wanting to appear pathetic. In any case Gabriela is not listening to me, she is pulling me towards the car and at the same time saying she's sorry, it's her fault, she shouldn't have come to me in her car last night, he saw her, he hadn't gone away but just parked a little further off and when she came out he followed her, and he's been doing so ever since we left and this is not the first time, it also happened on certain days when we went to visit *signora* Malvina, and she was always afraid she would see him behind us, or that he would play some trick with his motorbike, driving us off the road, that's why she was nervous...

Now he's afraid I'm going away and not coming back, he thinks you want to take me away! she says, pulling me by the sleeve.

But how can you have lived like this, I ask her. At the mercy of a mental defective.

And suddenly Gabriela is being snatched away, seized by the arm, she struggles to free herself but he is stronger, he has spent hours days and maybe months building his strength for this, she falls to her knees and he drags her bodily while she continues to kick out, the only sound is the scraping of the gravel, everything is happening in total silence and this makes it all the more frightening. Now the girl, wriggling free, draws her arms and legs tight against her chest and lets herself fall, she tries to curl in a ball, weld herself to the ground, but she is grabbed by the arms the shoulders the hair and hauled to her feet, she makes herself fall on the grit again, is forced to get up with a flurry of punches and kicks, it happens twice, three times, every time a little closer to the parked and waiting truck.

I do not know if the noise I hear is the sound of thunder beyond the mountains or my own breathing.

Time expands, as happens in those strange moments when the invisible portal that separates the possible from the impossible, normality from catastrophe, silently opens in life's backdrop, revealing its nature as mere scenery, and reality bursts through.

In my case reality is a piece of cold black metal which is lying in my bag, on top of the perfumed handkerchiefs. Ready for use.

He is about to heave her up into the cab of the truck when I tell him to stop.

He does not listen to me, he does not turn to me, I don't count. It must be Gabriela's eyes that convince him, they are staring at me, and I can perhaps see myself mirrored in them, an old woman dressed in dark clothes, with a silk scarf round her neck, holding a pistol and pointing it at head height, as instructed.

Let her go! I shout. My voice sounds different, interesting, a voice not heard before.

For a brief moment I regret a missed career as a terrorist, which I might perhaps have had the chance to follow, if it had been offered at the right moment. If I had been just a little younger in those days, or maybe, if I had followed different courses of study, sought out other company… I see once again — what a lot of things can happen in less than a second! — the images from a German film I enjoyed, in which a young woman belonging to the Baader-Meinhof gang pulls out a pistol and points it with outstretched arms, in a magnificent gesture.

And for the first time Dorin sees me. No, I am wrong: he does not see me, he sees the barrel of the Beretta looking him in the face, and accords it a respect which I do not possess. The great shooting penis. Although a handbag version.

He hesitates. He is troubled. He does not concede he is afraid before he has tried out, as though experimentally, other well-known feelings: shame, inadequacy perhaps. His hands loosen their grip on Gabriela, and I take a step towards him to encourage him to let her go altogether. I hold the muzzle of the pistol against his face.

A disgusting sensation. It feels as if I am touching him, his skin, the pallid forehead, I sense his compliance like a live thing yielding to my metal, I see the eyes shaded by their long lashes dilate, the pupils grow round and congeal. I quickly pull the weapon back. It seems important to maintain a degree of dignity in what I am doing. You kill if you have to but you don't rape.

In that very same moment I also know that I would not kill him, even if it was loaded. Why? Because I'm not in the habit of it? Maybe in order to kill you have to get used to it, that is why there are apprenticeships to train people for violence, you need to torture, slaughter your mother and father, violate your sister. Or give a bit too much importance to some idea or other, a thing which I have always found difficult.

I would not kill him because between the two of us, his life or mine, I would without a shadow of doubt prefer to lose my own. Would I have thought the same way twenty years ago? I shall never know.

But it is not just about my life, which is not important, but Gabriela's. Which is why in the end I shall perhaps have to kill him.

(If it weren't for the fact that the pistol is not loaded.)

He has put his hands up. Freed from his grip, Gabriela has slid to the ground, she retreats over the gravel on all fours, her sobbing almost soundless.

Stop it! I order her. Get up and take this! I throw her the bag, it is better she holds it, I need to have both hands free for the pistol, or what would Ciro say?

Dorin the terrorist is standing stock still, rooted to the spot: *Freeze!* as they say in American films, and continues to stare at my penis (unloaded) now a hand's breadth from his frontal bone, apart from a slight quivering of lips his face is completely without expression. What is he thinking about? About how to escape, how to get possession of the pistol? Or maybe he is simply spellbound by the weapon, he is not thinking anything at all, he is pure contemplation, as if before god, and indeed he is transfigured, an innocent child, seized with wonder.

Where is Gabriela? I try to follow her movements, for a second I fear she has tricked me, that a gesture of hers, a gleam in her eyes, will reveal that she is on his side, that between him and me she chooses him, or even that the whole thing was a conspiracy, that the slippery thread of her little lies has finally tightened round my neck, and it is made of steel. Because this possibility does exist, with women. With any human being, but between two women a little more. I risk turning my head for a second and I see her, she is on her feet. She is trembling, her light-coloured trousers are torn and stained with blood where the gravel has skinned her legs.

I order her to get in the car and follow us. She slowly recovers from her astonishment, backs away, obeys me.

We are still face to face, Dorin and I. Oddly, for a moment I think that for him, for this young man whom I do not know and do not understand, death would be a kind of liberation, even more than for me. We have arrived at this point by different routes, but now here we are. Made more alive, both of us, by the exhilarating nearness of the end. I feel almost fraternal towards him. Towards this retarded young terrorist. Who would like to inspire fear in everyone, but succeeds only in frightening a girl.

I smile at him. Come on, get in, I tell him in a friendly manner. Get up into your cab, we're going away now.

He does as he is told. Keeping the gun on him all the time, I circle the cab and climb up beside him. It is a riskier operation than it seems, because I have to open the door, and thus lose contact for a second. Fortunately Dorin is still dumbfounded in holy astonishment by his encounter with the gun, and his lorry is a small one, not one of those monsters you have to scale like a mountaineer. The step is nevertheless high for me, I stumble, I am forced to look down — but he, transfixed in adoration of my Beretta 34, does not move. He is waiting for me. We are accomplices.

I'm ready, right, go! I say with a sigh of relief, settling

into the seat. We're turning back.

He appears amazed. He wears a sulky frown. He takes his eyes off the muzzle, now fixing his gaze on a point to the side of the pistol. He must have been a hard case for his teachers. Calmly, enunciating the words clearly, I repeat that we are turning back, he must reverse and leave this forecourt area, take the road in the reverse direction, in the direction he came from.

The gear stick grinds, the wheels squeal, we set off. It is tiring to keep both arms raised in order to hold the gun as it should be held, but what has to be done has to be done. Luckily I feel no pain at all, not the arthritis in my bones or joints, nor that cursed stiffness in the shoulder, it will be the adrenaline, do we need to be in peril of our life the whole time to feel in such good shape?

I know what to do, naturally. I am not acting blindly. I bluffed for a moment, but then my ideas sprang into focus. I explain to him, we might as well speak during the journey, I still believe in words after all, that is how I have lived and how I will die, it is too late to change. In a tone which I hope sounds as conversational and reasonable as possible, I tell him that we are now returning to the tollbooths at the motorway junction, where I will get out and he instead will join the motorway in the direction from which he came. That he will not be able to leave the motorway however for a good quarter hour or twenty minutes, and to do the same stretch in the reverse direction and return to the tollbooths will consequently take him around forty minutes, and in the meantime Gabriela and I will have gone, he will not find us again. I tell him that I have no intention of taking Gabriela away, and where to anyway?

The girl will make her own life, where and how she wishes, dragging her bodily away and grabbing her by the hair is not the way to persuade her to love him, I tell him that not all desires can be realised and not everything belongs to us, you have to come to terms with it, and this happens to everyone, not just to him, but perhaps I don't tell him this, I only think it, because I don't want to sound as though I'm preaching and I know how much young people, especially the slightly backward ones, hate preaching, it is difficult just now for me to distinguish words only thought from words said aloud, and amongst other things I hope Gabriela has understood that she is meant to follow us and is doing so, and I shift a bit in the seat, just enough to glance in the little mirror and confirm that yes, she has understood, she is following us.

I should not have doubted her. It is not the first time she has risked her skin, that girl, she must be used to traumatic events by now, equipped for survival. I am proud of her.

We are coming down from the mountain, below us the hairpin bends unwind, the valley broadens, as we take one curve I see a green meadow opening out to our left, some way below, it slopes away gently before plunging towards the valley floor. A party of day-trippers has spread rugs on the grass, a few metres from the side of the road and fringing a small patch of woodland. Someone is taking the sun, someone else is sitting in the shade of the acacias and beeches, there are women bending over picnic baskets. To one side, a girl lying on her tummy with an open book in front of her, is immersed in her reading. And all the while, in the background, like the voice of a friend, the river running along the valley floor.

Into the driver's cab there gradually seeps an unpleasant

smell, sweetish, like the smell of sausages going off. I ask my terrorist — just to make conversation — how long he has been in his lorry, and whether the refrigeration unit is working or has broken down. Because in that case the goods he is carrying will all have to be thrown away.

As could be predicted, he does not respond. He is driving with concentration, his mouth half open, and I am thinking that it is a miracle we are both still alive, because the death wish emanating from him is truly potent, now. He is turned in on himself, he is mortified by his sudden humiliation, the defeat of his plan. I can feel his hate pressing up against me, crushing me, depriving me of air.

The ringtone music explodes in the cab, carrying us suddenly into some low-grade Balkan bar and the whirling dances, the facile seduction, of drunken men. He brusquely thrusts a hand into his back pocket and pulls out the mobile, throws it on the floor of the cab. The music stops and starts again, another swirling dance, it seems it will never end, until Dorin's foot, in a large black trainer, new, expensive and unlaced, stamps on the thing several times and silences it.

I am breathing with difficulty. The air is hot, tainted and thick with fury.

My arms hurt. They are trembling. How many minutes have I been holding them up, the muscles contracting with the effort? I lower them a fraction, a centimetre or two, no more.

And, as if I had made exactly the move he was waiting for, his elbow shoots out and hits me hard, the pistol falls, he bends to grab it, the lorry swerves but stays on the road.

The elbow has hurt me, but it is strange, it is as if the pain was being felt by someone else, not by me. Dorin turns towards me, points my pistol at my temple.

Watch the road, I tell him. Don't lose your concentration! Mind all these bends!

He ignores me. The barrel is pressed to my temple, I edge away from this obscene contact, which is clearly not repellent to him, to kill and to rape in a single action, it is natural that he should be excited, he follows me, he matches my move. He squeezes. He presses the trigger.

Click. Click. Click.

We look at each other. It is the first time we have really looked at each other. Progress, I am thinking. Black eyes, innocent lashes. When he is amazed he becomes a little boy again. I wonder how many women have loved their murderer in the moment he killed them. My reaction instead is to laugh. Memories of former games in the courtyard at home. Idiot! I tell him, it's not loaded! Or perhaps I just think the words.

He tries again, obstinately, *Click! Click! Click*, he is going wild, he shoots randomly, at my head, at the windscreen, my stomach, his feet, he is slow, it takes him a while for the facts to sink in, he is disappointed, he is angry with me, I have tricked him, he has let himself be tricked by an old bitch, and suddenly the situation is too funny to resist, good manners can't prevent it, I laugh out loud, a shout of triumph, a laugh I haven't laughed for ages. For an instant I think that even he must acknowledge it, that he must admit that it is a splendid joke and we can only laugh about it together.

The blow arrives as if someone had thrown a stone, the dry *crack* of something breaking, my head rebounds against the side window, a moment of darkness and then my hand flies to my cheekbone, I see blood on my fingers. He has struck me with the pistol. He hits me again twice more, with less force, in the neck and on the shoulder. He lacks all sense of the comic. An effective method, however, of silencing me.

And it is at this point that the certainty comes that this is the end. I feel no pain, not yet, only a sort of dizziness — there is something not right with my lower jaw, and the vision in my left eye, and suddenly my tongue seems to have become huge, it fills my whole mouth. The blood pulses in my head, loud enough to render me deaf — and yet I can still hear the river, down in the bottom of the valley — and I tell myself we are here, the moment has arrived. I shall not be going to Switzerland. And not to France either. A shame.

The truck is swerving out on the bends, the wheels keep grazing the edge of the road beyond which there is nothing, except a green precipice.

For a few endless moments we go on like this, in brotherhood still, I and my personal angel of death, a retarded terrorist by the name of Dorin. A rather unpleasant individual all in all, but as a four-year-old a sweetie. I am holding on to the seat, blood is dripping on to my white blouse and my trousers, I don't feel anything like pain, just this throbbing, my body is merciful. I look ahead, I wonder when the moment will come for the leap into space, after this bend or the next.

Is he going to push me out of the truck or will we go over and bite the dust together?

Does he know, what he's going to do? Difficult to tell. His hands are fused to the wheel, his fingers would have to be broken to prise them off it. He is immobile, he doesn't even seem to be breathing. If it weren't for the tic in his right eyelid, the long lashes that are fluttering like the wings of an insect in its death throes.

And then suddenly — never let your attention drift, never get distracted by details or your own trivial concerns! not even in the penultimate instant of life! — I remember the day-trippers with their rugs spread in the sun and the picnic baskets, the girl who is reading, in the meadow that broadens out at the side of the road. Are they round the next bend or the one after?

He too remembers them. They are the ones we're making for. There they are below, on the grass, they are on our right now and level with the road and within a few minutes, perhaps a few seconds, we will have reached them.

I see Dorin's hands turn the wheel and begin the swerve, they are young hands but they have a fatal hesitancy, they have never yet killed, apart from in dreams maybe, so that when my old woman's hands lay hold of him with all the strength left in them, digging the nails into his skin, they catch him by surprise. Did he perhaps think he'd finished me off? Didn't he know, old bitches like me are hard to kill? We are pointing straight at them, but we are going to miss them. He turns the wheel to the right, I turn it to the left. I hurl myself at him, I am on top of him, I clasp him, this my young and retarded brother, I embrace him with my whole elderly and easily broken body, I have him right under the one eye still open and working, I suffocate him with love like a real woman, my non-existent muscles against his hard and stiffened ones, I even sink my teeth into an ear, I feel the warm skin split under my wobbly teeth, you would not have said so when you saw me, sweetie, but I am a tigress and this is my final pounce.

He shakes his head to break free, he relaxes his grip on

the wheel. He opens his mouth but no sound emerges, only his frantic, whistling breath.

The people in the meadow, I see them sit up on their rugs, I catch their alarmed, disjointed movements, I hear their shouts, I see the surprised expression of the girl who has looked up last of all and is still in the story she is reading — but we are already beyond them, we have just missed them, the wheels are no longer touching the ground, we are flying towards the spot where the meadow dips away, into the scattered scrubland that conceals the river.

They will watch us fall, perhaps smashing into a tree, perhaps turning over and bouncing, they will tell it all to the police, and when they pull us out and find the pistol they will think it was his, the more logical explanation, so long as Gabriela keeps her mouth shut or lies, a thing which, as it happens, she does exceedingly well.

How long a second can be. And how fast thoughts. Before the end, before the impact and the shattered bones — but maybe I shall be spared that, because I feel my heart swell as if ready to rupture and an immense pain, rich with life, explode inside my ribs, and I know that the cardiac muscle will probably stop beating immediately after the crash, if not before, even — I still have time to think so many things. Of thanking someone, I don't know whom, but a thought expressing gratitude must yet be directed at someone, and so I launch it into the limpid air of this summer day, I dedicate it to whoever can catch it, gratitude for the enormous luxury being granted to me, no, not luxury, let us use the appropriate words for this exact moment, for the grace which has been granted me, to disappear in a few instants on a sunny day, and in a way which is, all in all, natural, with no waiting and no bureaucracy, I couldn't have wished for better, I hadn't felt so alive for years, thank you, my dear terrorist, and forgive me for having substituted myself for your prey, but I really couldn't leave Gabriela in your hands, it was too much for me. I understand that you are angry, it must be frustrating for an aspiring terrorist to collect only one victim and a ninety-year-old at that, but try to forgive me — do you not also feel the wonder of this moment? You still have a fraction of a second to make peace with yourself and with me, look at the trees, the mountains, don't think about anything, breathe, it is your last chance.

The sky darkens, but I know it is darkening only for me, that for the ones up there with their picnic and open book, for Gabriela and all other living people it remains blue and limpid, a perfect summer sky for all those who live and dream, and then I seem to hear the voices of Nora and Malvina and other people who are waiting for me, but perhaps it is only the noise of the river at the bottom of the valley, and then the darkness is torn apart and the leaves, so clear and sharply-defined a moment ago, vanish in an explosion of light.